Bedlam Bewitched

CHERYL SPANOS

Deadnettle
Publishing

characters, including a twitchy embezzler, a skeleton dog, and a trio of whiskery, meddlesome old sisters with magic powers. Bedlam's heroine wears scratchy sweaters and keeps a romance novel tucked into her apron pocket, but behind her bookish appearance, Cory is a romantic with a zest for adventure and a stubborn streak. *Bedlam Bewitched* is a breathless ride through a magical world that readers will not want to leave.

—Melanie Denman, Author of *Visiting the Sins*

If you enjoyed the magic of Harry Potter but with a twist of romance and intrigue, then *Bedlam Bewitched* is for you. As a teenager, Cory inherits her father's portion of an enchanted bookstore, full of snarky talky tomes and illicit romantic yarns. Cory just wants to enjoy her "tea and a cozy" but ends up being sucked into a vortex of magic, intrigue and ultimately love. Spanos' book is awash in slapdash comedy and dripping in attitude. I couldn't put it down until its satisfying end.

—David George, Author and Past-President, California Writers Club

Romance, mystery, and witchcraft blend with clever humor to make *Bedlam Bewitched* a book with something for everyone. You'll root for the heroine of this wonderfully entertaining story. It's YA, but suitable for all ages.

—B. Lynn Goodwin, author of *Disrupted, Talent, Never Too Late: From Wannabe to Wife at 62* and owner/editor at writeradvice.com

For John and Mary

Chapter One

Tempest Brewing

This was the second worst day of my life. My worst day? That happened one month ago, when my father walked out on Mother and me. And today, my favorite uncle abandoned me too. The unfairness of it burned white behind my eyelids and collected in pools at the corners of my eyes. If only there was a spell to fix this. But no charm that I knew would bring my father back or raise my uncle from the dead. At least, not one that was legal. I swiped away my tears and willed myself not to cry.

My uncle's coffin rested on a pedestal here at the front of the mortuary. I steadied myself against the half-open casket, my fingers digging into its silky lining. Over the casket, an engraved placard read "Horace Knightly, beloved brother and uncle." Horace's massive frame nestled in scarlet satin. His hair was sparser on top than I remembered and ringed with graying fringe. His eyebrows were bushy and wild. I'd never seen a mouth on a dead person that looked right. Beneath his walrus mustache, Uncle Horace's mouth was quirked into an odd, tight-lipped, closed-mouthed grin. Almost as if he'd been laughing at some inside joke.

He couldn't be gone. But I knew the body in front of me was an empty shell. Not the vivacious uncle I knew and still loved. Uncle Horace wouldn't be caught dead in this dull gray suit and pale blue tie. Maybe that was the joke?

Despite the smile that momentarily creased my lips, my tears welled up again. I sniffed and blotted my eyes. Mother sidled beside me and touched my arm. Her eyes glistened too. I hugged her and buried my face in her graying curls.

"Oh, Cory," she said. "Horace would have been so pleased that we both came back to say goodbye. He does look good, doesn't he?"

I nodded, unable to utter a syllable.

She patted my back, then pulled away and stared into the casket at her older brother. Her fingers fiddled with the pearl buttons on her linen suit jacket.

"Your Aunt Gertrude made all the arrangements." Mother dabbed her eyes with a tissue.

Heels clattered on the linoleum behind me. I expected to see my stout, formidable Aunt Gertrude, my mother's older sister. Instead, Aunt Elspeth, Mother's younger sister, sauntered up in a stylish dress of violet silk that made Mother's tailored suit appear dowdy. Aunt Elspeth's slim figure took twenty-years off her age. My own dress felt snug. I plucked at the simple black sheath, aware that I was my mother's daughter.

"So good to see you, Cory." Aunt Elspeth smiled at me. "Don't I get a kiss?"

Aunt Elspeth leaned forward until her cheek grazed mine. We kissed the air, then repeated on the other side.

"Gertie always makes the arrangements." Aunt Elspeth's tone hinted of dissatisfaction.

"Now, Elspeth." Mother pursed her lips. "You know she means well."

"Yes, but look at this place." Aunt Elspeth sighed. "So gloomy and, well, traditional."

She had a point. Electric lights in the guise of candles flickered from brass holders on the walls. The lights emitted a weak, tea-stained aura on faded wallpaper above dark paneling, a poor substitute for the brilliant California sunshine outside. Decaying flowers and musty age permeated the stagnant air. My nose wrinkled. Evergreen Mortuary, a sign by the entrance read. Ever-Dark-And-Gloomy was more accurate.

"Horace wouldn't have chosen this." Aunt Elspeth flapped her hand as if to dismiss our surroundings.

At her gesture, the flowers spilling from bouquets and wreaths rimming his casket seemed to come alive. Anemones waved their tentacle-like petals. A Creeping Charlie inched its leafy tendrils down the side of a vase. Fresh lilies and sweet-scented roses exuded their aromas. Ah, yes, this display suited my uncle. Not that gloom and doom.

"And he certainly wouldn't have chosen that tie." Aunt Elspeth leaned over Uncle Horace's coffin and whispered something in his ear. A tiny spark flared, then extinguished with a pop. My uncle's tie changed color from pale blue to a sunny, golden yellow.

"There." Aunt Elspeth smiled. Her eyes sparkled with mischief the way Uncle Horace's had. "That's much better."

Mother just shook her head slightly.

The yellow tie did look much better—cheerful like the uncle I remembered. Uncle Horace would have liked that, but I wasn't so sure about Aunt Gertrude.

I glanced behind me looking for her, but she had not yet arrived for this private family viewing. Aside from the mortuary staff setting up folding chairs for the service to follow, we were the only ones here. Other mourners and friends of the family were expected shortly.

"Now, Cory." Aunt Elspeth looped her arm through mine. "Tell me, dear, how have you been?"

"Fine," I lied. I buried all thoughts of boarding school, my father, and my messed-up life. "School's fine." But an uneasy feeling crawled over my skin as if the Creeping Charlie had me wrapped in its sticky tendrils.

"Dear, you don't have to pretend with me." Aunt Elspeth leaned in. Her voice lowered. Her ruby lips turned down in her most sympathetic pout. "Your mother told me how hard it's been on you, you poor thing. Losing the bookstore must have been awful."

Losing the bookstore. Even I knew that was code for losing Daddy. My arm stiffened in Elspeth's grasp. I didn't want to even think about the foreclosure of my father's business. Or what came after.

"But I have a secret that will make you feel better." Her teasing smile widened, and I knew she was dying for me to take the bait. Despite growing apprehension, I couldn't help myself.

"What secret?"

"Horace left you his share of his business," Elspeth said, her voice trilling in a sing-song.

"Bedlam Books?" I stared at her wide-eyed. "Here in Berkeley? Left to me?"

"Well, not entirely to you," Mother added. "Since you're underage, your holdings will be held in trust until your eighteenth birthday. But yes."

My vision blurred. Images from my father's former business loomed in my memory. The shingle outside his London shop had read "Dawkins and Smyth Booksellers."

And then in smaller lettering: "Paul Dawkins and Ulysses Smyth, Proprietors." Banners had covered that store front: Going Out of Business. Final Clearance. Everything Must Go.

And everything went. Including Daddy.

I gulped. "Me in Uncle Horace's will?"

"Of course, silly. You always were his favorite." Aunt Elspeth smiled like a black cat that had just eaten a juicy bird. "I was Horace's witness. There's not much that happens around here that gets past me."

Aunt Elspeth spoke truth on both counts. Although the youngest of the Knightly siblings, she knew all the family secrets. My bachelor uncle had no heirs. Had I thought about it, I should have expected to inherit something. But I hadn't thought about that at all.

"So what do you think?" Aunt Elspeth's shapely eyebrows waggled in a suggestive dance. "Will you move back here and help Jack Wickham run the store?"

Jack Wickham? I hadn't seen Jack in ten years. Not since I was seven.

"Well, I . . ." I sputtered.

Jack and I were both kids then, back when his father, Old Man Wickham, had been Uncle Horace's business partner. Mother told me that Jack had taken over for his father two years ago when the elder Wickham had died. What was Jack like now?

"Oh, silly me," Aunt Elspeth prattled on. Her voice sounded distant. "Why would you want to move to California? You have school and friends and a life of your own in London. And there's that charming young man." She tapped her ruby lips. "What is his name? Something fishy. Finn?"

"Gil," I said. "But that's over now."

I avoided Aunt Elspeth's curious stare, while visions of a handsome soccer player with chiseled features intruded on my thoughts. Then I recalled the nymph-like co-ed hanging off his arm. The remembrance of that rejection added to others and pricked hot under my lids. I squeezed my eyes shut to cast out the memory.

"I'm so sorry, dear." Aunt Elspeth laid a manicured hand over mine.

"I'm fine," I said, more to convince myself than her, and plastered on my bravest face. "Only three months and exams until graduation."

Inside, I warmed to the idea of leaving the austere buildings of the boarding school and my old life far behind. My time at MAGI, Millhouse Academy for Gifted Individuals, was coming to a close. Given our current financial situation, Mother and I had been thinking about a gap year after high school, so I could earn money for college. This new opportunity couldn't have come at a better time.

"You're better off without him." Aunt Elspeth patted my hand. "That's always been my motto. It's carried me through three marriages."

"Four marriages," Aunt Gertrude said, as she bustled up to the casket beside us. She eyed Aunt Elspeth, her voice laced with disapproval.

A matronly black dress resembling a clergyman's cassock covered her from floor to stiff-necked collar. She patted down her silver hair, checking that every strand was in place. An unnecessary precaution. Her hair had been lacquered and pulled back in a tight bun, rather more like a helmet than a hairstyle.

"Oh, look what the cat dragged in," Aunt Elspeth whispered in my ear. Then she addressed my eldest aunt. "You're looking stunning today, Gertie. That dress is you."

"Thank you," Aunt Gertrude said with a prim nod.

Then she frowned, as if deciding whether or not she had just been insulted. The ample flesh on her neck rippled over her upright collar. Four great whiskers quivered on her double chin.

Aunt Elspeth's lips twitched, hitching up in a smirk. Gertrude's mouth pursed in a tense line. Mother looked away, her fingers fidgeting with her buttons. My eyes darted from aunt to aunt. The hairs on my arm tingled with static.

"Gertrude," Mother said, her voice artificially bright. "We were discussing Horace's will. What do you think?"

"What's to think?" Aunt Gertrude harrumphed. "She's too young and inexperienced to go into the book business. I've told Jack as much. One failed bookstore in the family is enough."

My mouth tumbled open, too stunned to reply. Aunt Elspeth jumped in before I could recover my voice.

"Just what are you insinuating, Gertie?" Aunt Elspeth said. "That Cory had something to do with the foreclosure? She's just a girl."

"My point exactly. She's just a girl—"

"I am not just a girl. I'm seventeen." I glared at Aunt Elspeth, indignant that they've both just dismissed me as if I was still a baby.

"Now, Gertrude . . ." My mother's feeble protest also fell on deaf ears. Aunt Gertrude ranted on as if she hadn't heard.

"Ulysses was far too indulgent. Irresponsible. Imagine leaving her alone to run that shop for him—"

"Now just a minute," Mother said. "You had no business telling Jack Wickham that."

"I thought he had a right to know." Aunt Gertrude

thrust up her chins and regarded her sisters with a self-righteous air. "As co-owner of Bedlam Books, it is his business, too."

"Gertrude, what exactly did you tell Jack?" Aunt Elspeth said.

"Only the truth." Aunt Gertrude straightened. "That I counseled Horace against this arrangement, but he refused to listen. She's much too young and inexperienced. And Ulysses hasn't exactly set a good example—"

"Stop!" My raised voice startled even her and finally silenced her.

"Temper. Temper." Aunt Gertrude huffed and looked straight at me. "Like father, like daughter."

"I am nothing like my father." I stared into Aunt Gertrude's watery eyes, my face growing hotter by the minute. "Nothing like him at all."

What if there was some truth to her accusations? What if I was just like my father? What if I was the reason that Daddy's business failed? Why else would he leave Mother and me? Now that Jack knew, he would never want to share a business with me. My aunt's betrayal jolted me as if I'd been struck by a hex. Buzzing filled my ears. I braced myself against the casket and stared from Aunt Elspeth to Gertrude. Blindsided by my own relatives. Oh, Uncle Horace, how could they?

"Did you ever think about how I would feel?" I shook my head.

"Now, Cory, don't." Mother reached for my arm, but I brushed her away.

My stomach clenched. I was going to be sick. I had to get out of here.

"She's just overwrought," Mother said. "The shock of Horace's passing. She was so fond of him."

"Why did you tell Jack?" Aunt Elspeth's voice was shrill.

"He had a right to know." Aunt Gertrude's insistent drone drilled in my ears.

I turned to flee. Only then did I notice other mourners who had come to pay their respects. Men and women dressed in drab colors milled among rows of folding chairs. I avoided their inquisitive, or was it pitying, glances. When had they arrived? How much of our conversation had they overheard?

My face flamed. Losing my father and then my uncle was bad enough. Why did my own family have to humiliate me on top of everything else? My eyes stung. Objects blended in a watercolor blur. I couldn't see the door, but I rushed to get away.

Halfway across the room, my leg slammed against the side of a chair and sent it screeching across the linoleum. I careened into someone solid. Forceful hands gripped my shoulders and steadied me. A man's hands.

"Excuse me," I said, not looking up lest he see my tears. I stared down at pressed trousers and a pair of polished wingtips. "Sorry."

"Cory?" The man's voice inflected with surprise.

My head jerked up. Inquisitive, blue-gray eyes stared back at me through my blurry haze. I blinked.

"Are you okay?" he said.

I nodded.

"My condolences." He released me and looked away, appearing to stare toward the casket.

"Thank you." I dabbed my eyes on my sleeve, grateful that he'd given me a moment to collect myself. I smoothed the front of my black satin dress.

Then I surveyed the tall, broad-shouldered man standing

before me. A young man. Maybe twenty. His hair was dark, cut close and neatly combed, except for one rebellious curl over his forehead.

"Do you remember me?" A wistful hope lit his eyes. He held out his hand.

Jack Wickham. Oh, toadstools. I should have guessed.

"Jack?"

I could only imagine what vicious things Aunt Gertrude had told him about me. Chagrin seared my cheeks. I would've give anything to trade places with Uncle Horace now. Yet I forced my lips to smile.

He smiled in return, obviously pleased that I'd remembered him.

"Nice to see you again." I took his hand. His fingers felt pleasantly warm. Mine were burning.

"I wish the circumstances were better." Jack inclined his head. His fingers closed over mine the way people wrap their hands around steaming cups of cocoa. "I am sorry for your loss."

"Thank you." I blinked and withdrew my hand.

He seemed kind. Perhaps he had not heeded Aunt Gertrude's warnings. Perhaps her gossipy tales had not tarnished his opinion of me.

"Please, Elspeth," Mother said from somewhere behind me, her voice cracking with emotion. "That's enough, Gertrude."

"Stay out of this, Millicent," Aunt Gertrude bellowed.

I turned to look back toward Uncle Horace's coffin. Aunts Elspeth and Gertrude squared off, glaring at each other, while Mother stood beside them wringing her hands.

"Why, you ungrateful hussy." Aunt Gertrude's chins trembled. "*Myosotis.*"

Uncle Horace's necktie changed from yellow to forget-me-not blue.

"You batty old cow," Elspeth screeched. "*Narcissus.*"

The necktie turned a daffodil yellow. Blue. Yellow. Blue. Sparks flew. Then *POOF!* Uncle Horace's tie incinerated in a flash of heat and flame.

A black puff billowed over the coffin. I gaped, dumbstruck. The roses on the casket wilted. The lilies shut their petals into tight buds. The Creeping Charlie skittered back into its vase, trembling.

My two aunts stared into the coffin at the smoking remains of the tie, their mouths open and wordless. The buzz of whispered conversation in the room ceased. Silence, except for Mother's sobs. Eyes around the room turned to gawk.

I stole a glance at Jack's face. I read shock and dismay in his wide eyes, disapproval on his compressed lips and clenched jaw. He jerked his head away as if he couldn't stomach my aunts' disgraceful behavior. He turned back, now regarding me. His eyes, once so blue, now appeared gray. Confusion clouded his gaze.

"Please convey my regrets to your family," he mumbled. Then he pivoted and strode out an exit.

First, Aunt Gertrude told him unflattering tales and now an embarrassing fight. What will he think of us? Of me? My fingers groped for the back of a chair. I sank into the padded seat, listening to the hiss of expelled air. Deflated. Humiliated. Mortified.

After my aunts' feud over Uncle Horace's casket and the strained memorial service that followed, my relatives scattered like leaves before a hurricane. No family luncheon. No comforting food. No fond stories in remembrance of my uncle. I should have gone straight back to Aunt Gertrude's where Mother and I were staying, but after what she'd said about me, Aunt Gertrude was the very last person I wanted to see. Perhaps visiting my uncle's bookshop was yet another mistake, but it seemed like the logical thing to do . . . especially since he'd left me his share of it.

I stared down Telegraph Avenue trying to get my bearings. After all the summers I'd visited, you'd think I could find my way. But I was just a kid then, and Berkeley looked different with the university in session. Hordes of college students crowded the sidewalks, backpacks slung over their shoulders, earbuds in their ears. I heard the *deedle* of a smart phone. Nothing looked or sounded familiar.

I squinted at the nearest street sign. Someone jostled me

in passing—a tall man in a dark suit. I turned. Among the sea of jeans and sweatshirts, his suit was easy to pick out. I shot him a glare that would've withered frog spawn. Oh, no. Jack Wickham. Again.

"Cory?" He mumbled an apology, as flustered to see me as I was to see him.

"Oh, hello, Jack." I averted my gaze, hoping he hadn't noticed that I'd just given him the stink eye.

He cleared his throat. "What are you doing here? I thought you would still be at the, um, memorial."

Of course, he had no idea how the ceremony had ended. He'd stormed out before the start of the service. After my aunts' shocking quarrel, could I blame him? But my uncle's funeral was the last topic I wanted to discuss.

"That's over now," I said, feeling my cheeks pink. I diverted the conversation. "Actually, I was on my way to Bedlam Books."

"You were?" His eyes widened, eyes the color of the clear skies overhead. "The shop is closed today. For the funeral."

Closed? I should have expected that. Nonetheless, I was determined to see my uncle's bookstore.

"Oh?" I sniffled. "I only wanted to see the place again for Uncle Horace's sake. Do you have a key?"

"Yes, of course. I, um, was going there myself. Why don't you come along?"

"Thank you." I flashed a wan smile.

He led me up a street with no sign. My feet hurt in these stupid high heels, but I tottered along beside him. One intersection over, he turned left down a narrow lane. Ah, Chanting Way.

At casual glance, Chanting Way appeared like many other Berkeley streets off the beaten path. It had an air of dereliction as if it belonged to another time. Mom-and-Pop establishments lined both sides of the narrow lane with even an old head shop among them. I passed a homeless man huddled in the doorway of a boarded-up store front. But Chanting Way's otherness was more than a whiff of patchouli and a splash of tie-dye. A magical tingle hung in the air like the ocean mists that crept in at twilight.

Hide in plain sight. That had been Uncle Horace's motto, a philosophy shared by many in the magical community. And Berkeley provided the perfect venue. With a reputation for the eccentric, no one here batted an eye at the strange shops that took up residence along this street. My uncle and his store fit right in.

Jack halted in front of a quaint bookstore wedged between Madam Voyant's Psychic Boutique and a shop selling healing crystals. It was a balmy March afternoon, but the bookstore's windows were frosted with snow, though it never snowed in Berkeley. I touched the miraculous flakes, feeling their icy wetness melt in my fingers. I peered inside at the titles on display. I resisted the urge to press my face against the panes as I had at the start of every summer vacation. Bedlam Books, my Uncle Horace's bookstore.

Keys jingled as Jack unlocked the deadbolt. When he'd finished, I reached for the brass doorknob in the shape of a dragon's snout and pushed the door open. Bells tolled a welcome as Jack ushered me inside.

A labyrinth of wooden bookcases stretched from floor to ceiling, shelves sagging with the weight of their contents. Smells of leather and paper greeted my nostrils. So familiar. So inviting. I inhaled again. Was that the sweet odor of Uncle Horace's pipe tobacco? My uncle wasn't the sort to hang about after death moaning and groaning, but I felt his presence here as if he were playing hide and seek with me among the books as he had when I was little.

Jack hovered nearby, fiddling with the keys in his hand. His eyes followed me. I remembered that look, the same one he'd had as a boy watching Horace and me play. The look of someone who longed to join in the fun, but didn't dare.

I ventured in further and peered among the stacks. I tugged the high heels from my aching feet and let my dress shoes dangle from my fingertips. My bare feet felt warm on the worn, wooden floorboards. The skirt of my best dress rustled.

"May I interest you in our Best Spellers?" a carved figurehead on the end of a bookcase whispered.

Fangs for the Memories, a title in blood-red lettering blinked to entice me. The memoir of a vampire? The carved visage winked at me. A jovial, round face framed in leafy hair and beard. So like Uncle Horace.

"No, thank you," I whispered in reply and bypassed the section of popular books.

"I can feel Uncle Horace in every nook and cranny." I glanced at Jack and gestured toward the leafy replica of my uncle. I breathed in the comforting aroma of old paper and exhaled a sigh. "It's like coming home."

Jack's hand jerked. The keys in his grip jangled with the cacophony of chimes caught in a stiff breeze. Was it something I said?

"This doesn't seem the best time." He strode toward me. "But since you brought it up."

"Brought up what?"

"The shop." He gestured at the shelves surrounding us. His insistent stare transfixed me. His eyes now appeared gray. Overcast. "That is why you're here, isn't it? Greeley must have contacted you as he did me with the terms of Horace's will. He left his share of Bedlam Books to you."

For the second time today, I was ambushed with this news. But no lawyer had told me. My aunts and mother had beat him to it. Once again I was reminded of my Aunt Gertrude's insinuations at the funeral parlor. *Like father, like daughter. Irresponsible. She's too young and inexperienced. One failed bookstore in the family is enough.* My teeth clenched. Just what had Aunt Gertrude told Jack about me?

A prickly silence stretched between us. My gaze dropped to the floor. I shifted my weight from foot to foot.

"So I heard," was all the reply I could muster.

"I'm afraid that makes us business partners," Jack said. "At least, temporarily."

"What do you mean, 'temporarily'?" My head whipped up to face him.

"Well..." He fingered a small scar above his lip on his clean-shaven face. "I intend to buy out your share of Bedlam Books. I've just come from Greeley's office. He's drawn up the papers. You'll find my offer generous."

He didn't even know me and already he'd decided that I wasn't fit to be his partner. I bristled. Who does he think he is?

"What if I'm not interested in your offer?"

Jack took a step backward, creating a little more space between us. He straightened his striped, conservative tie. He shrugged his shoulders beneath the dark suit jacket and pressed his palm to his breast pocket. With every passing minute, he reminded me more and more of his strident, dour father.

"Please, Cory," he said, but his patronizing tone didn't

help his case. He cleared his throat. "I know about the fore-closure of your father's business."

Of course, he knew. Thanks to Aunt Gertrude's big mouth. I could only guess what other tales she had told him.

"That was my father." I hissed through gritted teeth and closed the gap between us. "It had nothing to do with me."

I straightened to my full height. Even on tiptoe, the top of my head reached only to his nose. I jutted my chin up. I would not be intimidated.

"Please, I mean no offense." He shuffled backward another half-step. "This is business. I wouldn't be a very good businessman if I didn't do my homework. Bookselling is a hard trade even in the best of times. And these aren't the best of times."

"You're afraid," I said, "that I'm going to drive this bookstore into bankruptcy. Is that it?"

Jack's father, Old Man Wickham, always did like his dragons in a row. A place for everything and everything in its place. He had been the antithesis of Uncle Horace. I never understood how they got along. Now it seemed that Jack had turned out just like his father.

"Look, I can see I've upset you." Wickham raised his hands in a gesture of surrender. "Clearly, I've chosen the wrong time to discuss this. All I ask is that you consider my offer." He withdrew a packet from the inner breast pocket of his suit jacket and pressed it into my palm. "Here."

He smiled with the strained civility of a shopkeeper faced with a difficult customer. So calm, so polite, so infuri-atingly self-controlled.

The crisp document crinkled in my clenched fist. I wanted to wad up his papers and throw them back in his condescending face. Oh, and add a hex for good measure. Instead, I forced my lips to smile.

"I'll leave you to think it over." He nodded a curt farewell and strode down the aisle out of sight.

I stared down at the crumpled paper in my hand. I still couldn't believe Uncle Horace had left his bookstore to me.

"Uncle Horace," I whispered into the ether. "What should I do?"

I looked to Horace's wooden likeness for guidance, as if it was the real thing. But the leafy carving on the end of the aisle snored, eyes closed in oblivious slumber.

I glanced down at the document in my palm and sighed. It wouldn't hurt to look at Jack's offer. I opened the packet and smoothed out the creases. My eyes widened at the amount. He'd offered a generous sum. Mother and I needed this money. Between the bankruptcy and my father's desertion, we had little left to live on. With this, we could make a clean start.

Did I really want to be involved with another bookstore? Mother didn't know the first thing about the book business. I was the one who helped Daddy in his shop. Daddy. I stifled a sob and choked back the word. My high heels slipped from my fingers and clattered to the floor. I stuffed my toes into the uncomfortable shoes, grinding my heels against the floorboards. The dust had barely settled on the ruins of my father's shop, the memory of it, of him and his abandonment, still painful and fresh.

Of course, we'd take the money. That settled, I refolded the offer and tucked it inside my purse.

A shower of purple fairy dust drifted down from the bookshelf beside me. I glanced up to see a stooped crone beckoning from the cover of *Mother Grime's Nasty*

Rhymes, a childhood favorite. I pulled the book from the shelf and flipped it open.

"O thou, fair maiden, my destiny be." I heard Uncle Horace's voice, his rich, chuckling bass. "Wilt thou stay a spell with me?"

A smoke ring puffed from the open book. I pressed my nose to the page. Aromas of tweed, shaving soap, and, yes, Uncle Horace's pipe tobacco wafted up.

Twelve years erased. I was five years old once more, a little girl with brunette ringlets nestled on Uncle Horace's roomy lap.

O thou, fair maiden, my destiny be.
Wilt thou stay a spell with me?
Bibbity bobbity peppery pea.

Uncle Horace's voice boomed as he read to me. On the pages of the book, a tiny princess dressed in a gown of shimmering tulle waltzed with a troll. My little girl feet couldn't keep still, tapping to the rhyme. I recited along with him.

Yes, dear troll, with you I'll spool.
Then beautiful maiden turned into a ghoul.
Bibbity bobbity flippery fool.

Before my eyes, the lovely maiden twirled, transforming into a pimply beast, then grinned and kissed her troll. My five-year-old self squealed with delight, although I'd heard the tale countless times before.

"Uncle Horse." I took his face in my five-year-old hands

and turned it until our noses touched and we were staring eye-to-eye. "I want to be like you when I grow up."

"Of course you will, Pumpkin." He smiled, and I knew that the thought pleased him. "And would you like a bristly, walrus mustache, too?"

His whiskers tickled as his peck warmed my cheek. My little-girl-self giggled. I fingered my upper lip to make sure he hadn't actually made a mustache grow there.

"I mean I'm going to have a bookstore just like yours."

A bookstore just like his. That was supposed to be my father's bookstore, the one he and I would run together. Warmth flushed my face. Tears blazed trails down my cheeks. That dream had drowned when my father left us. Left me.

I wiped my cheek with the back of my hand and inhaled again. Pipe tobacco. Not my imagination. It was a sign. An omen. Uncle Horace had spoken. At last, I knew what he intended. Uncle Horace hadn't deserted me. He hadn't abandoned me like my father had. In giving me his bookstore, he was giving me back my dream. This was his way of providing for Mother and me.

A plan materialized in my head as clearly as the apparition of the troll dancing above the pages of my open picture book. I'd finish up my last few months of high school at Millhouse Academy, then Mother and I would move back here and I'd work at Bedlam Books.

A giddy giggle escaped my throat. I kissed the page, imagining Uncle Horace's prickly whiskers brushing my lips. Then I slipped the book back onto the shelf. What I was about to do was nothing less than insane. But if there's one thing I did know, it was books. I could make this work.

"Yes, dear troll, with you I'll spool," I recited. I extracted Jack's offer from my purse and ripped it into shreds. "Bibbity bobbity flippery fool."

Chapter Three

Dust Up

After the funeral, Aunt Gertrude refused to speak to either of her sisters. So that afternoon, Mother and I moved out of Aunt Gertrude's house and in with Aunt Elspeth. I thought Mother would be angry when I told her I'd torn up Jack's offer, but she wasn't. Turns out, she had a surprise of her own. She had been contacted by my boarding school. My father had neglected to pay my tuition at Millhouse Academy, so with less than three months until high school graduation, I was being booted out. I was livid. How could my own father do that to me? Even if we accepted Jack's offer, the money wouldn't come soon enough to help, and it was too late in the school year to transfer somewhere else.

Until she could get things sorted out, Mother thought it best that I go to work at Bedlam Books. She sent a note thanking Jack for his generous offer and informing him of our decision, but I had not spoken to Jack myself. I had no idea how he had taken the news.

So three days after Uncle Horace's funeral, I marched

down Chanting Way en route to my uncle's bookstore. My first working day at Bedlam Books. Nerves wriggled like tadpoles in my gut.

Ahead in the distance, I glimpsed a stout, silver-haired form in a black dress exiting the shop. Aunt Gertrude. My footsteps slowed. I hung back and watched, while she sped off in the opposite direction like a bullet train in search of a collision. What was she doing at the bookstore today? Whatever it was, it couldn't be good.

At the front door, I hesitated, my fingers inches from the dragon-snout handle. My cardigan prickled against my arm. I tugged on the sleeve of the itchy sweater and fidgeted in the knee-length pencil skirt, clothes borrowed from my mother. *You want to make a good impression on your first day*, she'd said. *Look professional.* I checked my reflection in the window. I didn't feel professional in these clothes, I felt out of place. I winced, then forced a smile and reached for the doorknob. Here I come, ready or not.

Bells tinkled a welcome as I walked through the door of the magical shop. Comic books chuckled as I passed. Jack Wickham glanced up from his post at the register behind an oak counter. His face fell.

"Ah, Miss Smyth," he said.

Miss Smyth? What happened to Cory? I glanced back over my shoulder out toward the street. Was my Aunt Gertrude behind this sudden formality? Or was it something I had done?

The small tan book he'd been perusing snapped shut. Before it closed, I glimpsed pages filled with tiny writing. An address book or professional contacts perhaps. He stashed it under the counter before I could get a proper look.

"Good morning, Jack," I said, attempting a cheery tone.

"What can I do for you today?" he said.

"I've come to work." I swept away a mousy brown curl that had fallen into my eyes and tucked it behind my ear. "You did get Mother's message, didn't you?"

Jack studied me the way one might regard an opponent in chess. Contemplating his next move?

"Well, about that—"

"I could take over the register for you," I said, seizing on the first idea that popped into my head. "I'm sure you have other things to do."

I had loved to help Uncle Horace ring up customers' purchases. I glanced at the cash register, the old-fashioned kind with typewriter keys and a bell that dinged when the drawer popped open. The same one Uncle Horace had used when I was little.

"Oh, no." Jack shook his head.

"Okay, then restock shelves?"

"No." He squeezed his eyes shut, rubbing them with thumb and forefinger.

"What then?" I crossed my arms. "I'm here to work. We're partners now whether you like it or not. Uncle Horace decreed it in his will."

A grimace tightened his jaw. Vertical creases spiked between his eyebrows. It didn't take a psychic to see that he didn't like the idea one bit.

"All right." He cleared his throat, his Adam's apple bobbing over the collar of a crisp button-down shirt. "If you insist, you can start by dusting the shelves."

"Dusting?" I blinked.

"Yes, I believe in keeping a clean establishment."

What did that mean? I bristled. Was that an insult aimed at my dearly departed uncle? Or maybe even a dig at my father?

Cool and calm, Jack leaned against the counter in a

long-sleeved dress shirt and tie. A bright white shirt without as much as a smudge on it, and so neatly pressed that I could still see sharp creases up the length of each arm. Even on a workday, he hadn't rolled up his sleeves. Of course, he believed in keeping a clean shop. What else would I expect from Mr. Everything-in-its-Place?

Fine then. If that's what he wanted. I bit my tongue.

"Okay," I said.

I turned to face the nearest shelf and raised both arms as if conducting an orchestra. As I muttered an incantation, dust motes lifted and spiraled into the air in miniature tornados.

"Not that way," Jack said, shattering my concentration.

The spell shriveled on my lips. The twisters dissolved, arrested in mid-spin, and dust particles settled back on the shelves. I turned to confront him.

"And why not?"

"There's too much magic in the shop already." He waved a hand toward bookcases brimming with magical merchandise. "One wayward spell and the whole place could go up in smoke."

Fairy dust shot like miniature fireworks from the shelf next to me and sprinkled my sleeve. The comic books burst into guffaws from their stand at the front of the store. True, magic could be unpredictable. But a dusting charm?

"That's ridiculous." I flicked fairy dust from my cardigan. "There's nothing harmful in a little cleaning spell."

"Nor is there in a simple color charm." Jack's brooding gaze locked on mine. "Yet what destruction your aunts created with that one."

I gasped. My retort had gone up in smoke faster than my uncle's necktie. Jack's quarrel was not about cleaning at all. This was about my bickering aunts and their behavior at the funeral. He had lumped me in the same cauldron with them.

"Dust by hand." He whipped a feather duster from under the counter. "You can become familiar with our current stock at the same time." He gestured behind him. "Please start at the back of the shop."

Of all the dirty, rotten . . .

He was deliberately trying to ruffle me, trying to force me to leave. Well, he wouldn't get rid of me that easily. I would not be a pawn in his little power game. I shot him a scorching look that would have reduced any other man to a pile of bat poo.

If dusting was what he wanted, that's just what I'd give him. I snatched the feather duster from his hand, pivoted in my flats, and marched into the labyrinth of shelves. Bookcases slid sideways as if on rails, rearranging around me, clearing out of my way. I turned down a wide aisle that formed a corridor straight to the rear of the shop. I attacked the shelves at the very end of the aisle, the farthest from Jack Wickham. The duster in my clenched fist flicked across book spines with such vigor that feathers flew loose.

These shelves contained dictionaries, encyclopedias, and references on every type of magic. Perhaps I could find a good hex for Wickham in one of these. My eyes skimmed the titles. *Curses, Foiled Again: A Beginner's Guide to Counter-Spells*. That was no good. I wanted a curse, not an antidote.

Tainted Trinkets and Talismans. I didn't have any of those.

Aha! My fingers closed on a copy of *Hilarious Hexes and Practical Jokes*. That was more like it. Something harmless, but uncomfortable, like a pinch of itching powder in his shorts.

I tugged on the spine, but the volume wouldn't budge. My choice remained wedged between the side of the bookcase and *Miss Mumbles' Guide to Exasperatingly Proper Conduct*, a book on wizard etiquette. Was this one of those "hilarious hexes" or had the bookcase warped?

I pulled harder. The book of tricks popped from the shelf. *Miss Mumbles* toppled from the bookcase as well and fell open on the floor. A Victorian lady in a lacy shawl spiraled up from the leaves and hovered ghostlike above the pages. She pursed thin lips in a disapproving pout.

"Above all, a magus must never use their powers for harm," Miss Mumbles said, lecturing like a prim schoolmarm. "We must employ our talents only for good. And one must never ever hex the general populace . . ."

I jumped as footsteps approached. Miss Mumbles gasped and disappeared in a puff of magic dust. Her guide on etiquette banged closed. Despite her admonition, I stuffed the manners manual back on the shelf and reached for the book on pranks. Yet a tinge of misgiving tightened my chest.

A young woman in heavy boots clomped up the aisle toward me, clad in black from head to toe. A large crucifix dangled from her neck. Eyes circled in dark eyeliner focused on me and the book in my hand. She quickened her pace, a question poised on black-painted lips.

"May I help you?" I said, before she could ask.

"Do you have Shelley's *Frankenstein*?"

"Have you tried the non-fiction section?" I shelved the book on pranks, then waved the feather duster to point her in the right direction.

"Non-fiction?" Confusion fogged her raccoon eyes. "Mary Shelley's *Frankenstein*?"

"Yes." I nodded. "Where else would you expect to find the transcribed memoir of Victor Frankenstein?"

She stared at me as if I'd asked her to kiss a toad. Really?! It looked like I would have to locate the book for her myself.

"Come with me." I motioned for her to follow.

It took only a minute to find the title. Victor Frankenstein's likeness waved at me from the cover and patted the monster beside him. But when he saw my customer, he struck a dignified pose and stood motionless. All around us, the animated figures on the covers of the books froze, concealing their magic. Ah, of course, why hadn't I realized it before? The girl was a plebeian, not magically gifted. Not a magus like me. No wonder she didn't know where to look.

"Here you are." I handed her the paperback.

"Thanks."

The minute she touched the charmed book, a wisp of magic escaped from it like a genie let out of a bottle. It now appeared like any ordinary book.

Behind her back, the Count on the cover of *Fangs for the Memories* eyed her jugular with a lascivious stare. In her Goth garb and black makeup, she looked as if she belonged with him on the cover of that book. Even I had mistaken her for a magus.

"Interesting books," she said, skimming the other titles on the shelves. Then her gaze turned on me, scanning me from head to toe, sizing me up. Me in my mother's clothes. My cheeks grew warm.

"Anything else I can help you with?" I said.

"Um, no," she said, then walked off.

As she left to pay for her purchase, I glanced back over

my shoulder toward the reference aisle and the book on practical jokes. I bit my lip, thinking of *Miss Mumbles*. I needed a different strategy if I wished to convince Jack that I was nothing like my aunts. Maybe a hex wasn't such a good idea after all.

I resumed cleaning, absently whisking my feather duster across the shelf and tickling the Count. He displayed his fangs in a toothy grin. Was he flirting with me? I returned a teasing wink. I always did love a good romance.

A good romance, how brilliant. I'd dust the romance section and browse the titles at the same time. With a grin of anticipation, I traipsed across the bookstore toward the place where Uncle Horace had shelved the romances. I stopped in front of a large oak bookcase and searched the shelves. *Betty's Book of Bitter Batters*. *Crock and Cauldron*. Cookbooks?

Perhaps Uncle Horace had moved the romance novels. My eyes scanned the neighboring shelves. No buxom heroines swooned on their covers. No dashing rogues winked back at me.

Had Jack moved them? I thought of his father, the elder Wickham. Old Man Wickham used to wag a scolding finger and glare down at me over the top of a pince-nez, those little wire glasses balanced on the end of his nose. Old Man Wickham had never changed a thing. Like father, like son. So where had all the romance novels gone?

My footsteps beat a path toward the front of the store. I found Jack where I had left him, leaning against the front counter, bent over a large black book. The pages were filled with book titles, a massive list in miniscule print. A small wand the size of a pencil and a stack of new hardcover books sat on the counter beside him.

"Jack?"

"Yes?" he said, not looking up.

He retrieved a book from the pile and passed the wand over the cover. The pages of the black log fluttered, flipping open to a new entry. Writing appeared on the page in a crabbed scrawl. I read the name of the new book along with its identifying information. Ah, this black book contained the store's inventory. Jack was logging new acquisitions. Apparently, his admonition against using magic in the shop applied only to me.

"Updating inventory, I see."

"Yes." Jack placed the book he'd just scanned back on the counter. His gaze flicked up. "Did you want something?"

"I can't find the romance section." I waved the feather duster toward the back of the shop.

"That's because there is no romance section."

"No romance?" My jaw dropped.

"I've made a few changes." He plucked another new title off the pile and swept the wand over the cover. A corresponding entry appeared in the log. "I have no room on my shelves for drivel."

My shelves? Drivel? How dare he? Besides, I'd done my homework. This was bad for business. I slapped the feather duster on the counter.

"You can't do that." My index finger tapped the pages of the inventory. "Romances account for fifty-five percent of all paperbacks sold and thirty-nine percent of fiction overall."

Jack yanked his hand from the inventory, leaving the wand on the open logbook. He surveyed me more warily now. Clearly, my comment had caught him off guard.

"And where did you find those statistics?"

"*Wicked-pedia*," I said, unable to suppress a grin. My

chest puffed beneath the prickly cardigan. I crossed my arms and waited. His move.

He stacked the book on the finished pile. Instead of conceding ground, he chuckled.

"You can't believe everything you read in *Wicked-pedia*. Any magus can enter anything he likes. No Spell Checkers to verify the facts."

He waved his hand to dismiss me and reached for another book. But I would not be dismissed. I dropped my arms and straightened. My fingers clenched into fists.

"I do have some experience with books, you know," I said. "I helped my father in his shop."

"A fact that I'm trying to forget, Miss Smyth."

An oblique reference to my father's failed enterprise. He glowered at me with a look that would cow a troll.

"Well, I . . ." I stammered.

"I grew up here learning the business from my father and your uncle. I have been full partner since my father's death. And you're not a partner yet."

Everything he said was true. Jack was the senior partner now. I wouldn't even fully inherit my part until my eighteenth birthday. But Uncle Horace had left his share to me, and I had experience too.

"The Charing Cross district in London is world famous for its books," I said. "My father's shop was one of many bookstores there. New books, second-hand books, specialty books, anything you wanted could be found. I helped him in that shop for years, since I turned fourteen."

"Before it was liquidated." He paused, allowing the words to hang in the silence between us. "London is not Berkeley. You know nothing of the market here."

Defensive words swam in my brain. True, I didn't know

the market here. No place, even one as cosmopolitan as London, was quite like eccentric Berkeley.

"The failure of my father's bookstore wasn't my fault," I said. "That wasn't my doing. He—"

"Did you help your father run his bookstore or not?"

"Of course, I helped him."

"Then you helped him fail. You can't have it both ways." Wickham dismissed me with a wave of his hand.

Had I really expected him to believe me? Especially when I wasn't even sure that I believed myself. My shoulders drooped. My excuses drowned in a pool of red ink.

"In order to survive, Bedlam Books must change." Wickham's gray eyes bored into mine. "We cannot compete in every market. Bedlam Books will become a specialty boutique. From now on, we will sell only classics and literature of the highest caliber. If you must have your romance, you can buy one in any discount store."

Wickham's knuckles whitened on the book in his hand. He seized the wand and whisked it across the cover. Then he plopped the book on the pile with more force than necessary.

"And what did you do with all the romances?" my voice squeaked.

"Returned them."

"Returned?" I gasped. How could he?

Returned paperbacks would never be sold or read. Instead, their covers would be torn off and sent back to Pentacle Publishing and the books themselves reduced to pulp. All of my favorite romances. Gone. All gone. And all because of him.

Chapter Four

Less Than Half

I headed straight for the back of the shop, the feather duster clutched in my fist. No more romance novels? How could Jack have returned my favorite books? What else would he come up with to vex me? At the back wall, I made three left turns around tall bookcases, and then one more.

A small enclave of shelves surrounded me on three sides like a dead end in a maze. This had been my favorite hiding place as a child. Even Uncle Horace had not been able to find me when I was hiding here. People seldom visited this area of the shop. Leather-bound tomes filled these shelves—rare, old volumes no longer wanted—and the arrangement of the bookcases created a cozy retreat, far from the front of the store and the exasperating Jack Wickham.

I took a deep breath to calm myself and looked around. Thick dust caked the books on these shelves as if no one had been back here for years. This corner was filthy, unlike the rest of the store. How could Jack, with his ironed shirts and polished shoes, have allowed this corner to become so dirty?

Starting with the bottommost shelf nearest the corner, I swept accumulated dust from the books. My finger drew across a binding, exposing the rich, brown leather underneath. I blew, sending plumes of particles skittering from the cover. If only I could get rid of Jack so easily.

Beneath the dirt, a beautiful old tome with gilt-edged pages was revealed. No title on the spine. I opened the book. My fingers caressed onionskin pages so thin they were almost transparent. No words on the pages. Only pictures that looked like stained glass.

I turned a page and stared at a portrait of two lovers dressed in medieval garb and locked in an embrace. The fair lady had curly, brown hair, not unlike my own. Her partner was tall and dark, the proverbial fairy tale prince. He reminded me of one of those hunky heroes on the cover of a tawdry romance. I sighed. There would be no romance novels for me today.

Closing the book, I returned it to the shelf. Two scraps of paper fluttered to the floor. Not book pages. A photograph torn in two. I picked up the pieces, fitting them back together.

I gasped. The handsome teen on one half of the photo was unmistakably Jack. He looked younger, but just by a year or maybe two. He was dressed in a dark suit, like the one he'd worn to Uncle Horace's funeral, but his face held none of the hardness. Instead he smiled in this photograph, gazing at the young girl with a look of absolute adoration. My chest tightened. Taken with his expression, an unbidden thought popped into my head. How different things would be between us if he ever looked at me that way.

The object of his affection in the photo smiled, a teenage

girl with dimples and golden curls. A pale blue gown draped her slim figure and flowers graced her hair. From the way she was dressed, the photo must have been taken at a high school dance.

Jack had a girlfriend. Who was she? I flipped the photo over and read her hand-written note penned in pink on the back. *To Jack. All my love, Becca.* A dozen sickening hearts punctuated her loopy handwriting. I cringed at the sight of them.

Had Jack torn the photo? Perhaps they had broken up and he'd ripped up the picture in a fit of rage. That's just what I'd done to my father's picture when he abandoned me. But how had this recent picture come to be in a dust-covered book?

I studied the torn photograph in my hand, the neglected shelves, and the ancient book with no name. It was as if time had forgotten this place. Apparently, Jack had forgotten about it too. Given the dust and cobwebs, maybe he didn't even know this corner was here?

"Cory?" My mother's voice called to me from elsewhere in the shop. "Cory, dear."

My mother here in the shop? What was she doing in the store today?

"Over here," I said, stowing the photograph in my skirt pocket. I snatched up the feather duster and navigated the bookshelves, winding back in the direction of my mother's voice.

I turned the corner and found her in the cookbook section. A smocked apron covered her oversized blouse, her too-long trousers rolled up at the ankles.

"There you are, dear." Mother bustled up, carrying a large silver tray. A steaming china teapot, three teacups, and matching saucers balanced on top.

"I didn't expect you here today," I said. "Is everything all right?"

"I was upstairs working in Horace's flat and thought you could use a break. I've brought you some tea."

Ah, of course. I remembered her plan to clean out Uncle Horace's apartment. I cast a glance at the ceiling, envisioning the rooms overhead. Bedlam Books occupied the ground floor of this building, old Mrs. Hastings lived in the apartment on the second floor, and Horace's flat was on the third.

"Thanks," I said, taking the tray from her hands. I eyeballed the three teacups then looked past Mother for a third person. It dawned on me then. Jack. Oh, no. She was planning on inviting him to join us.

I cast about for a place to set down the tray. Mother summoned a four-legged stepstool. It hobbled across the wooden floor until it reached her, then mushroomed into a small café table. A ladder resting on the nearest bookshelf glided toward us on rails. Its rungs stretched and widened, forming a bench the perfect size to accommodate Mother and me. I placed the tray on the table and settled onto the bench seat. Mother poured out two cups of steaming brew.

Something rustled on the far side of an adjacent bookshelf. I caught a glimpse of white in the narrow gap between two books. Mother took her place on the bench next to me, then turned toward the sound.

"Jack dear," she said. "Would you like some tea?"

Mother, No! My hand jerked. Scalding tea sloshed from my cup into the saucer underneath, barely missing my fingers.

Jack stepped around the bookshelf with a small stack of hardcovers in his arms. Shelving new books? Then why the ruddy tinge that colored his face? Just like when he was a boy and used to spy.

"No, thank you, Mrs. Smyth," he said to my mother. "This is a bookstore. Not a café."

"Nonsense." Mother added a dollop of milk to her tea. "Horace always had an afternoon cuppa. All the book-stores have cafés now. You should think about it. Would be good for business."

He swallowed. I could see the muscles in his jaw tighten. I knew firsthand how much he disliked having others tell him how to run this store. Yet he managed a smile.

"I'll take that under consideration, ma'am." He nodded and strolled off, scanning the shelves as if looking for space for the books in his hands. Clearly, he had no intention of considering her suggestion.

"So?" Mother turned to me. "How is your first day?"

"Fine." I glanced in Jack's direction. The last thing I wanted Mother to know was how badly things were going between me and Jack. I changed the subject. "How are things upstairs?"

I lifted my teacup to my lips. Mother sighed. She took a long, slow sip of tea. The tired circles under her eyes appeared to darken.

"Elspeth and I have been upstairs all morning sifting through Horace's things. A dreary business. You would not believe the stuff that man saved."

"Aunt Elspeth is upstairs?"

Imagine my stylish aunt in an apron and rubber gloves cleaning out Uncle Horace's apartment. Impossible. That she was not down here partaking of tea and gossip? Inconceivable.

"Why didn't she come down then?"

"After what happened at the funeral?" Mother shook her head and took another sip. "No, she feels just awful."

After the fight she'd had with Aunt Gertrude, I couldn't blame her. I would be too embarrassed to show my face anywhere. Imagine having to apologize to all those relatives. No wonder she was upstairs cleaning out closets. Doing penance.

"What about Aunt Gertrude?" I said.

"She's not speaking to either of us." Mother sighed again. She appeared to stare at something distant, her eyes glassy. "If only Horace were here. I could always count on him to patch things up. That man could charm tears from a crocodile."

The image of my crusty Aunt Gertrude popped into my head, supplanted by one of a crocodile in a prim black dress and bonnet. A reptile in drag. Just the sort of ridiculous thing my uncle would have conjured. I lifted my cup to cover my grin.

"You miss him, don't you?" I whispered.

"Terribly." Her china cup chattered against the saucer.

"Me, too." I squeezed Mother's hand.

"Cory?" Mother paused. "Elspeth and I were talking."

She turned to face me now, not even bothering to blot her watery eyes. She gripped my hand, and I knew something was up. She hadn't come down here just to gossip.

"Elspeth and I, we both agree that you and I should move into Horace's vacant apartment. It would be perfect for us. Especially for you."

I couldn't believe my ears. I envisioned rolling out of bed and tumbling down the stairs to work. Of course, it would be perfect. There was only one catch. Uncle Horace had left the building to my mother and aunts. All three had to agree.

"Won't Aunt Gertrude object?"

"If she's not talking to us," Mother said, "she can't very well object, can she?" Mother's eyes sparkled as a glimpse of mischief peeked through her tears.

"Are you sure?"

"Well, we can't stay with relatives forever. We've worn out our welcome with Gertrude. I don't want to do the same with Elspeth. And we can't afford to rent anywhere else."

"It would be nice to have a place of our own." I smiled and nodded. "I would love to stay in Uncle Horace's place."

"Good." A wan smile brightened Mother's countenance. She patted my hand. "It'll be so good to have you back with me where you belong. No more boarding schools."

Leave it to Mother to find a silver lining in my getting kicked out of school. Still, I frowned. How could my father have been so irresponsible as to let my tuition lapse? And with only three months left? That just proved it. He didn't care a newt about me.

My grip tightened on my china cup. Well, I didn't care about him either. Mother and I would be just fine without him. I didn't need him or that stupid Millhouse Academy.

Millhouse. Things had been in such upheaval lately that I'd forgotten all about high school. Since I couldn't go back there, I suppose I could finish my education somewhere here. There wasn't much of my former life left at Millhouse anyhow. With Mother relocating here to Berkeley and Daddy gone, who was left for me there? Gil? The boy who dumped me? No, thank you. But I'd packed only a couple of suitcases for the week, expecting to come for the funeral and little more. I hadn't anticipated that I would come here to stay.

"I'll need a couple days here at the bookstore to get

used to it, but then I'll have to go back to London for my things."

"Of course, dear." Mother nodded. "Perhaps Elspeth could go with you to help with the packing. In the meantime, I'll get Horace's apartment ready for us here."

"Would you like some help upstairs?" I said.

"Oh no, dear." She squeezed my hand and smiled like a giddy schoolgirl with a secret. "You're needed down here in your new business."

Oh, if she only knew. I didn't have the heart to tell her that things were not going well between Jack and me. I took a large gulp of tea, emptying my cup.

Why was Wickham so difficult? He acted as if he and he alone owned the place. He wouldn't even listen to me. Treated me like a know-nothing kid. I was only a couple of years younger than he was . . .

Suddenly, a thought struck me. Perhaps this was what it had been like for him as the junior partner under Uncle Horace. And now, he was the senior partner. Oh!

"Mother, about my inheritance?" A quick glance around confirmed no sign of Jack. I lowered my voice. "Are Jack and I equal partners in the business?"

"More or less." Mother's head bobbed.

More or less? What kind of answer was that? I leaned closer.

"What do you mean?" I said. "Is my share more or less than half?"

"Well," Mother said, "when you factor in that we own the building, yes, we do own half."

"But you, Aunt Elspeth, and Aunt Gertrude own the building. I don't." My portion of the pie was shrinking by the minute. A feeling of dread sank to the pit of my stomach like stale crust. "What about the bookstore itself? You hold my share in trust for me, right?"

"Yes," Mother nodded. "Your aunts and I hold it in trust jointly, but only until you turn eighteen."

"My aunts?" I echoed. "Both aunts?"

"Don't fret, dear." Mother patted my hand. "We're all family. Bedlam is the family business, after all."

But I did fret. Aunt Gertrude had taken Wickham's side. She'd made her position clear at the funeral. Aunt Elspeth had her own agenda. Of the three, only Mother could be counted on to side with me. And all three held sway over my share. No matter which way I sliced it, I owned less than half of the business. Oh, bat poo.

"So Jack Wickham is the senior partner and he has controlling interest?" I said. My shoulders sank.

"It'll be alright," Mother said, seeing my troubled look. Her fingers delved in the pocket of her apron and extracted a paperback. "Here, this will cheer you up."

I took the book from her and gazed at the cover. A bewitching beauty in a cleavage-baring gown beckoned with a come-hither look. Her dainty fingers clutched what I surmised to be a vial of love potion. Wanda Witherspoon's *Tainted Love*. A romance by my favorite author. The second book in her acclaimed *Poisoned Passion* series.

"Where did you get this?" I said.

"There are several boxes of them down in the basement," Mother said, gesturing toward the stairs at the back of the shop. "I found them when I was moving some of Horace's things and remembered how much you loved a good romance."

Books in the basement? Had she discovered where Jack had stashed all those romances? At least something was going my way. A sly grin hitched my lips. Perhaps I was not too late.

"Thank you." I hugged her, my prize still clasped in my fingers. "You're a love."

"I've kept you from your work long enough," Mother said. She drained her teacup, then pushed the table away. "I should be getting back upstairs. I think your uncle was cultivating fungi in the shower."

With a wave of Mother's hand, the tea tray, cups, and saucers vanished. Another pop and the café table became a stepstool again. Mother rose to go.

A quick glance at the surrounding bookcases betrayed no trace of Jack. One last look over my shoulder, then I sprinted to the basement stairs, flicked on the light, and descended the precarious wooden staircase.

A single bulb dangled from a ceiling socket. No windows shed natural light on these gray cinderblock walls. Dusty jars, cobwebs, broken lamps, paint cans, and assorted debris overflowed shelves cobbled together from warped boards. Piles of newspaper and cast-off junk littered the floor. Except for a cleared space nearest the furnace. There, cardboard boxes were stacked in neat towers, conspicuous in the disarray.

I picked my way across the floor and opened the topmost box. A packing slip addressed to Pentacle Publishing rested on top. Underneath, a bevy of teary-eyed beauties and their hunky consorts waved at me from intact covers. Eureka! Paperback romances filled this carton and probably the ones beneath it.

What should I do? I glanced up toward the bright light streaming through the doorway from the bookstore above. My relationship with Jack was already strained. How would he react if I defied his wishes? Yet I could not abide the thought of all my romances relegated to paper pulp. I had to save them somehow.

I could hide them in Uncle Horace's apartment upstairs. But then I'd have to explain to my mother and aunt. Mother had troubles enough of her own and I didn't know how Aunt Elspeth would react. I couldn't risk involving them.

My fingers tightened on the copy of *Tainted Love* in my grip. Instinctively, I reached for my pocket to conceal my book. Something crinkled. Ah, the photograph. I thought of the beautiful book and my hiding place. Brilliant. What better place to conceal these romances than in my secret enclave among all those lovely old books that nobody seemed to want?

And Jack? He would never approve of what I was about to do. But what he didn't know wouldn't hurt him.

Chapter Five

Unhappy Medium

The next morning, Jack Wickham waited for me at the front of the store by the comic book display. An empty cardboard carton lay at his feet. Just the sort of box that had contained all those romance novels. My breath caught. My footsteps slowed. Had he discovered where I'd hidden them?

I wanted to flee to the back of the shop and check on my books. My fingers felt for my copy of Wanda Witherspoon's *Tainted Love* tucked in the pocket of my apron along with the torn photograph. I tapped my novel for good luck like a talisman. Then I forced my eyes forward and my lips into an innocent smile.

"Good morning, Jack." I pointed toward the back of the shop. "I have some dusting to finish up. A few shelves I didn't get done yesterday."

"Ah, no," he said. "I need your help with something else."

An odd smile hovered on his lips, a forced sort of

pleasantry. My eyes focused on the tiny scar twitching above his upper lip. Something was afoot. Another of his games?

"I'd like you to pack up the mystery section for me, please. You'll find some empty boxes next to the register."

"What?" I stared, dumbstruck. Jack was eradicating more than just romance novels. "Not the mysteries, too?"

Jack's chest swelled under his button-down shirt and striped tie. Muscles in his jaw tensed. He massaged the back of his neck. Any semblance of his former smile disappeared.

"I thought I explained this yesterday," he said. "We must specialize."

My fingers groped for the book in my pocket. First the romances and now the mysteries. I knew he had his own plans for the shop, but eliminating all the genre fiction? That would be bad for business. My stake might be less than half, but I was still an owner. Were we partners or weren't we?

"Don't I have any say in this?" I straightened to face him, thrusting my chin up.

"I will not argue this point." He stared down at me with smoldering eyes. "Now please box up the mysteries, while I take care of these comic books."

He dismissed me with a wave of his hand, then turned toward a wire stand filled with comics. Beefy superheroes flexed muscles on their comic book covers, unaware of their imminent demise. Jack snatched several from the rack and dropped them in the box at his feet. I bristled, gearing up for another fight.

"Why are you making all these changes now?" I shook a finger at him. "You don't fool me. You couldn't wait for my uncle to die, so you could take over."

Jack's jaw tightened. Bands of sinew rippled on his

neck. On the cover of a nearby book, the handsome Dr. Jekyll transformed into the hideous Mr. Hyde.

"I'll pretend that you didn't say that." Jack's voice remained even, but his white-knuckled fist wrapped around a comic book and squeezed one well-oiled Atlas in a vice grip.

Light reflected off his tie tack like a spark on the blue and gold stripes on his tie. Visions of my feuding aunts filled my head. Would my partnership with Wickham end up like that? My uncle's beloved bookstore up in smoke? All because of me?

I bit my tongue. The last thing I wanted was to jeopardize this business. Mother and I both needed this to succeed. The survival of Bedlam Books was our survival too. I needed to collect myself. I needed time to think.

I strode to the desk, scooped up a packing box, and headed for the back of the shop. Behind me, I heard the slap of a comic book landing in a box, then the creak of the wire stand and someone snickering. How odd. I couldn't picture Jack laughing nor imagine what he would find funny.

I glanced over my shoulder. Nothing appeared amiss. I refocused my gaze toward the back of the store. My feet wove a path through the bookshelves, heading for my hidden corner and the romance novels.

Had my secret been discovered? I stepped into my private enclave behind a towering shelf of books. Stacks of boxes cluttered my corner, right where I had left them yesterday afternoon. Reaching for the top carton, I lifted the lid and sighed with relief. My romances were still there, undisturbed.

Now what should I do about the mysteries? The empty cardboard box poked against my shins. I peered around the corner and glanced toward the front of the shop. How would Jack react if I refused his orders?

Mother's words echoed in my head, as I recalled her conversation with Aunt Elspeth last night. *You catch more flies with a spider than with a stink bug. Make a stink and you drive the flies away. But the spider smiles and bides her time, all the while spinning her sticky web.*

Did I want to be a spider or a stink bug? I had already made a stink. That approach wasn't working well at all. Neither did I wish to smile and comply as if I agreed with Wickham and his stupid plan. I chewed my lip. My fingers twisted my apron. If only Uncle Horace were here. He would know what to do.

I retraced my steps about halfway to the front of the shop, then turned right. The mystery section. Yesterday, I had dusted all these shelves, filled to capacity with books. Today, the bookcase was empty.

"What the devil?" I said. The carton in my grip slipped to the floor. What had happened to all the paperback mysteries? Had Jack boxed them up already? Was this some sort of joke?

"Welcome to the department of mysteries," a ghostly voice moaned.

A wet squelching noise sounded from the front of the shop, then the clatter of something metallic hitting the floor. Muffled curses followed, growled in a man's baritone. Tittering laughter erupted, a cascade of high-pitched hilarity.

What now? I raced toward the front of the shop, then skidded to an abrupt stop. Jack stood facing the rack of comics, while mounds of shiny meringue covered his face and dripped onto his tie. My eyes traced lemon-colored spatters down his pressed trousers to an overturned pie tin on the floor. Rubber chickens, not comics, filled the carton at his feet. Gales of giggles erupted from the comic books.

"Jack, what happened?" I said. But I could guess. Those cheeky comic books with their practical jokes weren't going away without a fight. I clamped a hand over my mouth to cover my grin.

"Isn't it obvious?" Jack swiped the goop from his eyes, then stared at his soiled hands as if deciding where to wipe them. "Don't just stand there, get me a towel."

"Yes, of course."

My eyes flitted to the checkout counter, finding nothing to use, then down to the bib apron that covered my skirt and blouse. I fished my romance novel and the photograph from the pocket and tossed them on the counter, untied my apron, slipped it over my head, and handed it to Jack.

"Here, use this."

"Thank you," he said, more a surly rumble than a reply.

He mopped his brow with my apron, wiping goo from his red face. But meringue frosted the dark curl that dipped onto his forehead. He wiped his hands on the apron, then surveyed his soiled trousers and grunted in disgust. Smudges of lemon cream marred his once-neat clothing.

"Have you finished with the mysteries so soon?" he said, still dabbing up gunk.

"That's just it." I shrugged. "The mysteries are gone. The shelves are empty."

"Empty?" Jack's head bobbed up, his piercing gaze focused on me. "Do you mean to tell me the mysteries have disappeared?"

"Yes." I nodded.

Jack's eyes narrowed, clouded in ominous darkness. The creases on his brow deepened. He strode forward. Ffpppppt. Ffppppt. A sound filled the room as if he'd stepped on a whoopee cushion. The comic books burst into guffaws. Jack pivoted.

"Enough." He pointed at a cartoon character on the cover of one of the magazines. Red sparks flew from his fingertips. "One more prank and you're headed for the incinerator."

I gasped. My hand clamped over my mouth for real this time. The comic book laughter stifled. I assumed that his threat was intended for them and not me. But I'd never seen any Wickham, neither Jack nor his father, lose control.

His jaw clenched and unclenched. He lowered his arm and stared at the apron gripped in his other fist. He didn't look at me as he handed the meringue-smeared apron back.

"I'm going to get changed," he said. "Mind the shop until I return. And please clean up that mess."

"What should I do with the comic books?"

"I don't care," he said, tension filling each syllable. "As long as they're out of my sight by the time I get back."

Jack marched out of the room, his head held high. A ginger-haired, freckled face on a cover blew raspberries after him.

"Now you've done it." I wagged a finger at the redhead on the comic.

The carrot top responded by mooning me from the cover. Arrogant little twerp.

I folded my soiled apron to contain the sticky mess, stuffed it under the counter until I could wash it properly, and pushed up my sleeves. Time to clean up. First, I had to find a new location for the comic books. Why not the empty shelves that used to house the mysteries?

I wiggled my fingers and whispered an incantation. The magazine rack sprouted legs. I marched the insolent collection toward the back of the store near the empty shelves in the mystery aisle. I rearranged the books on the rack, burying the comic book with the freckled face behind a heftier volume. Three hundred muscled Spartans preened and strutted across this cover, trying to impress me with their prowess. I flashed my prettiest smile. They'd have no problem keeping Mr. Cheek in line.

One more thing. I waved my hand over the sign. Letters morphed and rearranged until "Comic Books" became "Graphic Novels." Perfect.

Minutes later, the mess on the floor was mopped up. I took my place behind the counter nearest the cash register and watched a few customers meander the aisles, browsing. Business was slow this morning.

My romance novel lying on the counter beckoned. Perhaps I could snatch a couple of minutes of reading. I reached for my paperback, stashed the torn photograph inside the back cover, and flipped the book open.

Ah, *Tainted Love*. Heath, our hunky hero, had dismissed the attentions of the fair heroine, the demure Catherine. Enter the femme fatale, Lady Gwendolyn Fairbanks, a worldly woman of means and machinations. Gwendolyn had set her sights on our hero and intended to reel him in using every lure at her disposal. No deceit was beneath her. No neckline too low.

"Heath," Gwendolyn breathed, slipping a dainty, gloved hand into his. "How delightful to see you again."

She sank in a graceful curtsey, aware that her décolletage and form-fitting gown displayed her endowments to best advantage. A slight rise in Heath's eyebrows and a twitch of his lip informed her that the effect was not lost on him. Indeed, no man with a pulse could fail to notice Gwendolyn Fairbanks.

I shook my head. How could Heath fall for her? Didn't he know she was the wrong one?

"Excuse me," a girlish voice said, interrupting my reading.

My gaze flicked up. A young woman with a row of studs lining her earlobes peered from other side of the counter. She eyed my romance novel. Wafts of steam drifted up from the open pages of the book.

"What's that you're reading?" She pointed at my paperback.

"Nothing." I snapped the book shut and covered the title with my hand. "Just a romance."

Undeterred, she leaned over as if to read through my fingers. "Do you have another copy? I couldn't find any romances on the shelves."

"That's because Mr. Wickham . . . er . . . Bedlam Books isn't selling romances anymore."

"You've got one." She pointed at my novel again.

"Yes, but this is a leftover." I swept my paperback from the counter and stuffed it underneath out of sight. How could I have been so careless? "Not for sale."

"Oh," she said.

Her face fell. Her slim body shrunk in her layered sweatshirt and artfully-torn jeans. She turned from the counter and ambled toward the door.

I couldn't bear to lose a customer. It wasn't as if I didn't have the books. What was I going to do with all those romances anyway? But Jack would be furious if he found out that I was selling romances behind his back. Oh, Uncle Horace, what should I do?

"The customer is always right." Uncle Horace's voice spoke from somewhere in the recesses of my brain.

I glanced around to make sure that Jack wasn't within

earshot. No sign of him yet. I bolted after her, catching her at the door.

"Wait," I said.

The girl turned.

"Maybe I can find something for you." My fingers beckoned her closer. My voice reduced to a conspiratorial whisper. "Now you can't tell anyone. We might still have a few romances out back. If you let me know what you want, I'll see what I can do."

The young woman considered me for a moment. Her face brightened. There was nothing as alluring as a shared secret.

"Do you have any Desiree Dubois?" she whispered.

"The *Black Widow* Series?"

"Yes." She nodded.

"You're in luck." I smiled. "I think we have her latest. Pentacle Publishing released it this spring."

"I'll take it." The young woman glanced toward the counter where my romance novel remained hidden. "And the one that you were reading."

"All right. Wait here."

I sprinted to the back of the shop. With a quick look over my shoulder, I slipped between the shelves and dug through the boxes for the two requested titles. Within minutes, I was back to the front of the store and my waiting customer. My fingers flew to ring up her purchases and conceal the books in a plain paper bag.

"Thank you for shopping at Bedlam Books," I said, handing over the parcel.

My first sale. A happy feeling flittered like a bat in my chest. A satisfied customer and two books sold. I much preferred selling books to returning them.

"Please come again." I grinned and waved, as my first customer exited the shop to the chime of the doorbell.

A dark-haired woman wrapped in scarves slunk from behind the bookcases and approached the desk. Her colorful skirts jingled as she walked, as if she were wearing bells under all those layers. Where had she come from? Certainly, I would have noticed her.

"Hello." She smiled, her full lips painted a garish red. She extended her hand, laden with rings on every finger. "I'm Madam Voyant. I own the shop next door. You must be Cory Smyth."

Ah, Madam Voyant of the Psychic Boutique. That explained the gypsy dress. Part of the business, I supposed. But with a title like Madam, I had expected an old woman. This one appeared to be in her early thirties.

"Yes." I shook her hand. "Pleased to meet you."

Her fingers grasped mine. She bent over the counter and turned my hand palm up. Her face lowered, her large hoop earrings drooping forward. A scarlet fingernail traced the lines on my palm. I shuddered.

How odd. But she was our neighbor and I didn't want to appear rude. I steadied my breathing, repressing the urge to yank my hand away and swat her as if she were some overgrown insect.

"Do you read the palms of everyone you meet?" I said, affecting a casual tone.

"No." Voyant glanced up from my palm long enough for me to catch a glimpse of her unpleasant smile. "Only the people I'm interested in." Her finger tapped. "Aha. As I suspected."

"What's that?"

"This broken line here." She dragged her fingernail over my palm. "Your love line. Unlucky at love."

Why would she suspect that? My palm tingled along the path she'd traced. I stared down at the faint creases on my hand. What garbage. How could the lines on my palm reveal anything about Gil or my father or any of the other broken relationships in my life?

"I am always right." Her large hypnotic eyes bored into mine. She pointed out another crease. "This line here. Tragedy in your future. You should go away. Far, far away."

"That's enough." I yanked my hand free and wiped my palm against my skirt to erase the lingering sensation of her touch. "I just got here, and I have no intention of going anywhere, no matter what some silly line on my hand tells you."

"Then I offer you a word of warning." Madam Voyant straightened, drawing herself up to her full intimidating height. Taller than my short, compact frame. Her dark eyes flashed. "Stay away from Jack Wickham."

"Jack?" I couldn't stifle my incredulous snort. "You think I'm interested in Jack? That's what this is all about?" I giggled. "I assure you I have absolutely no interest in Jack Wickham."

Madam Voyant didn't laugh. Apparently, she, like Jack, had no sense of humor.

"You don't fool me," she said, her voice like a knife slicing through silk. "I make my livelihood by reading people. You have pathetic, desperate girl written all over you."

What? My mouth gaped open. Before I could think of an intelligent retort, Jack strode forward. No more meringue or signs of his previous mishap.

"Claire," he said. No growl as before either. His calm shopkeeper's voice had returned. "How nice to see you."

Claire? Her name was Claire Voyant. Even I wouldn't come up with a stage name that ridiculous.

"Jack," she said in a breathy whisper.

She dipped her left shoulder, causing the scarves to slip aside. The peasant blouse she wore underneath bared enough cleavage to give me an eyeful, even from my vantage point on the other side of the counter. I could imagine the view she flashed Jack. I thought of Gwendolyn Fairbanks and her décolletage. But Voyant was easily ten years Jack's senior, and her actions had a creepy vibe.

"What can I do for you today?" Jack grinned and inclined his head in polite interest. I couldn't tell if he was he just being neighborly ... or did he like her?

I grimaced. Ick! Couldn't he see that she was poison?

"Cory and I were having a get-acquainted chat, weren't we?" Voyant's gaze flitted in my direction, then back to Jack. "Did you know that Cory likes romance novels?"

An uneasy feeling crawled over my skin. The romance novels. Oh, no. She had overheard my conversation with that young woman.

"Yes." Jack cleared his throat. "That subject has come up."

"We don't sell romances any longer," I interjected.

"So I understand." Madam Voyant looped her arm through Jack's and latched her talon claws onto his sleeve. A possessive move. She shot me a look that would curdle cream. Her poisoned-apple lips smiled.

I didn't have to be a mind reader to understand. She had witnessed my clandestine transaction with the young woman. She knew my secret. And if I came between her and Jack, she would personally see to it that her dire predictions about me came true.

Chapter Six

Misfortune Number Three

I leaned over a low partition and fiddled with the hard-covers on display in the front window of Bedlam Books. Gone were the delicate fractals of hoarfrost that had framed each window pane. Gone were the flakes of Uncle Horace's magical snow that had dusted the windows. Even the featured books had been replaced. Sun shone through sparkling clean glass onto literary and non-fiction titles. No more pot-boilers. More of Jack Wickham's changes.

I repositioned the books, switching *Great Hexpectations* with *East of Hedon*, hoping for a more pleasing arrangement. But no matter what I did, the display still didn't look right. Even the dust motes didn't dance in the shafts of light. They just lay there, sleeping like the snoring form on the cover of another famous literary work—one of those South American novels full of ghosts and generations of people with the same name. Magical realism, they called it. Well, magic was real, and that was just redundant.

I heard the slap of flip-flops on the wooden floor. A

young woman in a t-shirt and jeans approached. She studied me through a fringe of stringy blonde hair.

"Excuse me." She flipped the hair out of her eyes. "My friend Brittany was here yesterday and bought some books." She stole a sideways glance over her shoulder, then lowered her voice. "Are you the one with the romance novels?"

Sweet Merlin. My first customer couldn't keep her gob shut and had been sharing our little secret.

What should I do now? I stole a glance toward the wall separating our shop from the one next door. I pictured Madam Voyant and her crystal ball on the other side. Her threats of yesterday spun in my brain. I was already in a kettle of brew. Could I possibly get in any deeper?

Jack's words rang in my ears. *If you must have your romance, you can buy one in any discount store.* Well, he was wrong. Those plebeian stores may sell romances, but a non-magical shop wouldn't stock Wanda Witherspoon, any more than they would sell *Mother Grime's Nasty Rhymes* or *Crock and Cauldron.*

I surveyed the young woman before me and thought of all those lovely romances going unread. Bedlam was a magical bookstore after all. If we didn't sell magical romances, then who would?

"What can I get for you?" I said, with a quick glance over my shoulder to make sure that Jack was not within earshot.

"Do you have Nigella Plume's latest?" she said. "I've read her first two books already."

I nodded and turned to fetch the Nigella Plume, but the girl grabbed my arm and pulled me back.

"And I'd like the one Brittany got," she said. "The one with the love potion on the cover."

"*Tainted Love?*"

Her golden head bobbed.

While Jack was occupied with another customer, I scurried to the back of the shop and my secret cache of romance novels. Before he could catch me, I smuggled the books past him and sent my satisfied customer on her way. Two more romances sold. Cha-ching!

By mid-afternoon, another woman pulled me aside. So much for my secret. Word that I was trafficking in charmed romances was getting around.

So far, Jack appeared none the wiser, but he was bound to notice sooner or later. I had to smuggle the last batch past him hidden under my cardigan. Could it be more obvious? I felt like one of those seedy characters in a trench coat selling fake watches on a street corner. Psst! Want to buy a bodice-ripper?

I was jumpier than a warty toad. I needed a plan, so I slipped away to my private retreat to think. I had just reached the back corner of the shop when a giggle erupted from my hiding place. What was that? My feet stopped short. Were those cheeky comics up to more of their practical jokes?

I peered around the bookshelf into my secret corner. No comic books. No cream pies. No rubber chickens. But a movement on the shelf to my right caught my eye. Was that Jack spying on me?

My eyes skimmed the bookcase. A solid row of bindings faced me. Paperbacks packed the shelf, no space between them to afford a view into my enclave. No way even a peeping Wickham could see in here.

I pivoted to go, when a flash of light drew my gaze. My head turned to catch the culprit. Not fast enough.

I inspected the shelf more carefully this time. Nothing but paperbacks, most packed so tightly that only their spines were exposed. One book was propped facing outward. A man in a trench coat and fedora graced the cover. At least, I thought it was a man. The fedora was pulled down so low and the collar of the coat so high that all I could see of the face was a huge single eye staring through a magnifying glass. The eye blinked. I blinked back and read the title. *Cy Clops, Private Eye.*

A mystery? What was that doing here? Visions resurfaced of the empty shelves that had greeted me in the mystery section yesterday. I staggered backward, bumping the stacked boxes containing romance novels. My hand seized the cartons to keep them from toppling over.

My gaze flicked to the shelf once more, this time reading the spines. All mystery novels. They hadn't been here yesterday. These shelves had been filled with old leather-bound tomes. How did these paperbacks get here? Had Jack discovered my secret hiding place? Was this his way of telling me that he knew?

By the end of the work day, I was a jittery mess. Madam Voyant's veiled threats from yesterday and the appearance of the mystery novels in my secret hiding place were getting to me. Two misfortunes in a row. People said that thirteen was an unlucky number. Not me. My unlucky number was three. Bad things didn't happen in thirteens. Bad things happened in threes.

How did all those mystery novels wind up in my secret place? It was not as if they could walk there by themselves, could they? Then again, infuse an object with magic and one never quite knew what would happen next. Thoughts of Wickham covered in meringue popped into my head.

Still, the most logical culprit was Jack himself. Jack in my hideout? Reclaiming all my romance novels? I waved off the thought. I didn't want to even consider the possibility.

I'd been avoiding Jack all afternoon, but now it was closing time, and I needed to talk to him. I stood outside his office door and took a deep breath, bracing myself against possible misfortune number three. My knuckles rapped on wood.

"Come in," Jack said with a resigned sigh.

I opened the door and stepped inside. Jack sat behind Uncle Horace's massive hickory desk with its clawed feet. Papers and files were stacked in neat piles on the left. A cup brimmed with fountain pens on the right. Fussy, old-fashioned pens, just the sort I would expect Jack to like. In between, the polished surface of the wood gleamed. Gone were the clutter and knick-knacks that used to litter my uncle's desk. I couldn't ever remember being able to see the desktop.

Jack bent over an open ledger, intent on his writing. Columns divided the page into accounts receivable and payable. A stack of receipts lay on the table at his elbow. He did not look up from his work, but copied amounts from the receipts into his records.

"Jack," I said. "We need to talk."

"If this is about my changes to the store," he said, "there's nothing further to discuss."

"No, not that. It's just that I have to leave for London."

His hand stopped writing, paused over the ledger. The fountain pen seemed frozen in his grip. Still, he didn't look up. The effect was unnerving.

"I have to return for the rest of my things," I said. "I brought only a couple of suitcases with me for the funeral, as I wasn't expecting to stay. And well, all that's changed now ..."

Words tumbled from my mouth, tripping over themselves on the way out.

"I see," he said.

But did he? His gaze appeared to focus on the page in front of him. The pen twisted in his grip. My words evaporated into the ether.

"When are you leaving?" he said, his tone calm and measured.

"Tonight."

"And returning when?"

"In a week, or less."

"Very well. I'll do my best to cope in your absence."

Was that sarcasm? He resumed writing, his pen nib scratching across the page. *Skritch. Skritch.* He hadn't even spared a glance for me. I stood, dumbfounded. How had I imagined he would react? Another argument? A gloat of triumph at my departure? Yes. But not that he would ignore me.

I looked over his shoulder, anywhere but at him. And that's when I saw it. Sitting on the cabinet behind him mounted in a silver frame was a picture of ... Becca.

The same girl as the one in the photo in my pocket, I was sure of it. She was maybe a year older in his portrait. But I would recognize those perky blonde curls and dimples anywhere.

"Who is she?" I pointed to the girl in the silver frame. "I've been here a week and I haven't seen her around."

Jack swiveled to look where I'd pointed. When his eyes lit on the picture, a pained expression flashed across his face. By the time his gaze turned to me, his mask of indifference and self-control was back.

"No one you should be concerned about," he said.

No one? Uh huh. I didn't think so. Becca was definitely someone. So what had happened between them? Did Madam Voyant know about her? Perhaps the crazy psychic had chased her off too? But whatever it was, clearly I wouldn't find out from Jack.

"Oh." I turned to go. "Well, then, good night, Jack."

"One more thing," he said. "The paperback mysteries, have they turned up yet?"

My breath caught. He knew. My denials remained lodged in my larynx. Fortunately, my back was turned toward Jack. Otherwise, he would have read the panic on my face as plainly as the numbers on his ledger. I shook my head.

"Too bad," he said. "They'll turn up sooner or later. Have a good trip."

"Thank you." I croaked out my reply, then fled the room.

The latch clicked shut behind me. My body melted against the solid door. I wrung my hands. In my absence, what would become of all my romance novels, and now the mysteries hidden in my secret enclave?

Why hadn't I hidden those books up in Uncle Horace's apartment? If only I could relocate them all now, but there wasn't time. I couldn't move all those books with Jack in the building and no customers to distract him. I couldn't do anything.

Perhaps I should cancel my trip and stay. But the tickets had already been purchased, plans made. Aunt Elspeth was all packed and ready to accompany me. I had to go. I had no choice but to walk away and leave all my precious romances behind. And Wickham would find them. Surely, this was misfortune number three.

Chapter Seven

Becca

That evening, Aunt Elspeth and I boarded a plane bound for London. An eleven-and-a-half-hour red-eye from San Francisco to London's Heathrow. We were flying Transylvania Air, the world's finest in "Fly by Night" travel. All their flights had evening departures.

I plopped Auntie's carry-on bag on the seat, a designer carpet bag made of material that looked like embroidered tapestry. Something clunked inside. Whatever she'd packed in there, her bag weighed a ton. I had to use a levitating charm to hoist it into the overhead bin. I stowed her second bag and hat box beside it. Other passengers trudged up the aisle toward the back of the plane and the cheaper seats, dragging their luggage behind them. I slipped into the window seat and stuffed my small carry-on under the seat in front of me. My body sank into plush leather. Aunt Elspeth had upgraded my coach ticket to first-class.

"I never fly coach," Aunt Elspeth said, settling into the aisle seat beside me.

She adjusted the silken scarf that covered her hair and neck. She extracted a pair of dark sunglasses from her purse and put them on, then reclined in the seat as if she were sunning herself on a beach in Cabo San Lucifer.

At least Aunt Elspeth could get comfortable. I fidgeted. My thoughts drifted back to Bedlam Books and the romance novels I'd left behind. Would they still be there when I returned? What new havoc would Jack Wickham wreak in my absence?

Shortly after the plane took off, an air hostess glided up to us. The woman was tall, slender, and pale. Her garnet lipstick and ebony hair washed out her porcelain skin.

"Velcome to Transylvania Air," she said. "May I offer you a cocktail?" She reeled off a long list, spoken in a heavy Romanian accent. "... vite vine, red vine, and, of course, Bloody Mary."

"Anyone I know?" Aunt Elspeth tittered at her own joke.

Our hostess did not appear at all amused. She stared at Aunt Elspeth and waited in silence. My aunt's snickers faded.

"I'll have a glass of red wine, please," Aunt Elspeth said.

"And for you, Miss?" The stewardess nodded to me.

"The same," I said with a pleading glance at my aunt. Mother would have never let me order alcohol as I was underage, but maybe Aunt Elspeth would? Her firm head shake told me I was out of luck.

"The young lady will have a Virgin Bloody Mary," she said.

Our flight attendant glided away as silently as she'd come. Aunt Elspeth nudged me with her elbow.

"No sense of humor," she whispered, jerking her head toward our departing stewardess.

"Just like Jack Wickham." I scowled. "He can suck the warmth out of a bubbling cauldron."

"Our Jack?" Aunt Elspeth lowered her sunglasses and peered at me over the top. "You must be mistaken, dear." She patted my arm. "Now his father, there's another story."

I was not mistaken. I recalled Jack's tight-lipped disapproval and the cold gray of his eyes. Mr. Unflappable did not have a sense of humor.

"So how are things going between you and Jack?" Aunt Elspeth winked, then eyed me with an expectant stare. Clearly, she was waiting for me to dish.

I would not take her bait. I didn't want to talk about Jack. Didn't want to even think about him, thank you very much.

"Fine," I said.

"Just fine?" She edged closer.

"Just fine." I nodded, then changed the subject. "I think I'll read for a bit."

I fetched my bag from under the seat and pulled out my romance novel. A good love story was just the antidote I needed to distract me from my troubles.

"Wait." Aunt Elspeth tugged on my arm. "I have something for you."

She slid a pristine business card onto my novel. It showed the front display window of Uncle Horace's bookshop complete with frosted panes and Horace's magical snow. Underneath were the words "BEDLAM BOOKS, 1313 Chanting Way, Berkeley, CA 94704, Horace Knightly and Robert Wickham, proprietors."

"Where did you get this?" I held up the card and stared at my aunt.

"Your mother and I found these in Horace's apartment." She leaned over and studied the card. "But it's not quite right anymore, is it?"

Her manicured fingers wiggled. The letters on the bottom of the business card rearranged, until it read "Terpsichore Smyth and Jonathan Wickham, proprietors."

"That's better." Aunt Elspeth smiled, admiring her handiwork.

"Terpsichore?" I grimaced. "You know I hate that name. I wish you'd use Cory instead."

"Terpsichore was your great grandmother's name. You were named for her, you know. She was a marvelous dancer."

No offense to Great Grandma, but Terpsichore was a hideous name. Pronounced Terp-SICK-ory. One would have to be sick to saddle a child with a name like that. Fortunately, my parents had enough sense to substitute a nickname. I waved my hand over the card, changing the wording once again.

"Cory Smyth and Jonathan Wickham, proprietors," I read. "I do like the sound of that."

Jack's name should have come first as he was the senior partner now. But I had to admit that I liked the order better this way.

Auntie Elspeth grinned at me like a Cheshire cat with a secret. She lowered her head, eyeing me over the top of her sunglasses. What was she playing at now?

"He likes you, you know." Her words slid out in a sibilant whisper. She waggled her eyebrows.

"Who?" I said.

"Why, Jack, of course."

"Uh . . . I don't think so."

"Dear," she said in a voice that sounded just like

Mother's. "I've known Jack since he was a boy. He's been in love with you since you were children." Her eyes glazed as if looking at something far away. "Don't you remember how he used to watch you and Horace play hide and seek among the towering bookcases of his bookstore? And when you invited him to join in . . ."

Aunt Elspeth's voice babbled on, waxing nostalgic. And I was five years old again, playing my favorite game with my favorite uncle.

"One, two, three . . ." Uncle Horace's bass voice rumbled over the stacks.

My turn to hide. I'd just found my uncle crouched in the mystery section. My feet dashed for the opposite side of the store, my eyes searching for a hiding place. Then I remembered the most perfect spot, a little niche in the children's corner. I turned abruptly and smacked right into Jack, then a dark-haired boy of about eight.

Jack had been following me, spying. I'd seen him peering at me from between the books, watching our game. Now his eyes stared, wide with horror at being discovered. He turned to run away, but I seized his hand.

"Wait," I whispered. "Come hide with me."

At the invitation, Jack glanced toward the office where his father, sour Old Man Wickham, wrote in his ledgers. Jack stood stock still, knobby knees protruding from beneath the creased shorts. His hot fingers warmed my hand. He was dressed in a starched, short-sleeved shirt with a clip-on bowtie. Clothes too formal for play.

". . . nineteen, twenty." Uncle Horace's voice boomed. "Ready or not. Here I come."

"Come on." I gasped one last invitation, before I let go of his hand and ran.

He followed, no longer a spy, but part of the game. I ducked into a little cubbyhole in the children's corner, the perfect size for the two of us. Jack tumbled in after me, the smile on his face so wide that his grin alone could have filled the cubby.

"The poor boy didn't have many friends." Aunt Elspeth's voice again, summoning me back to the present. "His father kept such a tight hold on him. Afraid he would lose him." Aunt Elspeth's lips pursed. "He'd already lost his wife."

Jack's mother had died when he was a toddler. That much was true. I supposed that was why he'd become so attached to me when we were children. He needed some female attention. But it was a childhood crush and nothing more.

"That was a long time ago," I said and reached for my novel.

The pieces of the torn photograph slipped out from under the cover and fell. I scrambled to catch them before Aunt Elspeth could see. Not quickly enough. Her always manicured fingers scooped them from the space between us.

"What's this?" she said, inspecting the torn photograph.

Oh, rats. Now I would be forced to explain why I was carrying around a picture of Jack. In a romance novel, of all places. I could only imagine what my aunt would infer from that.

But then again, maybe I could use this to my advantage.

Jack wouldn't tell me about Becca, but Aunt Elspeth would. She knew all the gossip.

"I found it in the shop the other day between some old books," I said, affecting a casual tone. "Jack won't tell me about her. I was hoping that you could. So who is she?"

"That, my dear," Aunt Elspeth tapped the picture, "is Rebecca Burgin. She was Jack's fiancée."

"Jack was engaged?" I snorted a laugh. "I can't imagine Jack married to any woman."

Aunt Elspeth huffed and straightened ram-stiff in her seat. I would never tell her so, but the self-righteous indignation on her face made her look just like Aunt Gertrude. Only skinnier and without the whiskers.

"Why not?" she said. "He was absolutely devoted to her."

Something about Aunt Elspeth's resemblance to Aunt Gertrude brought out the rebel in me. I couldn't resist a cheeky comeback.

"Then where is she now?" I smirked.

"She passed away about a year ago," she said, her voice softening.

"What? Becca dead?" I muttered. "Why didn't anyone tell me?"

"Jack didn't want anyone talking about it. And we respected his wishes."

The shocking news, coupled with my own insensitive remarks, sent heat rocketing up my face. I stared down into my lap, regretting my hasty words. My tongue felt clumsy as if swollen to twice its normal size.

"How did she die?" I whispered.

"Killed in a car accident." Aunt Elspeth shook her head. "Broke his heart. He's not been the same since. When she died, he withdrew." She held out her hand with her palm flat, then closed her fingers like flower petals curling up into a tight bud. "He keeps everything bottled inside now. Just like his father."

Jack's image filled my head. His buttoned-down shirts and bottled-up emotions. For all her fanciful notions, Aunt Elspeth did have one thing right. Jack had become just like his father.

"Then you came back." Aunt Elspeth's hand unfurled. The sly twinkle lit again in her eyes. "It's destiny. You two belong together."

"What?" I huffed, jerking upright in my seat and crossing my arms. "Jack and me? You're crazy."

"Am I?" Aunt Elspeth arched a tweezed eyebrow.

She slid the sunglasses down to the very tip of her nose, all the while studying me. Whether she was stalling for effect or gathering her thoughts, I couldn't tell. But the pause was maddening.

"Why do you think he made you such a generous offer for your share of the business?"

"To get me out of the way," I said. "So he could implement his changes to the shop without my interference."

"No, silly." Aunt Elspeth tittered and shook her head. "He was rescuing you. He knew that you and your mother had financial trouble and was trying to help."

"Ha!" I blurted. "Even if he was trying to help, which I doubt, that doesn't prove he likes me. What about his girlfriend?" I practically spit the words. "Claire Voyant?"

"Jack's not interested in her."

Aunt Elspeth's response was so matter-of-fact that I almost believed her, until I recalled how Voyant had accosted me in the shop. Even Jack's behavior had changed in her presence. And what about her threats?

"Tell her that." I planted my hands on my hips, almost

spearing Auntie with an elbow. "She actually threatened me. She thought I was after *her* Jack."

"Oh?" Aunt Elspeth raised her hand to cover her mouth.

I wasn't buying her feigned surprise. A telltale splotch of pink blossomed on her pasty cheek.

"Aunt Elspeth?" I glared. "What have you done?"

"Well?" She shrugged. "I may have suggested that you and Jack were involved. I may have exaggerated things a teensy bit."

I gasped. "Why would you do that?"

"I've never liked that Voyant woman." Aunt Elspeth's lips puckered as if she were sucking a lime. She wagged her finger. "Rebecca wasn't even cold in the grave, when Voyant was all over Jack with her casseroles. That woman is a man-eater."

"She's more than a man-eater," I muttered under my breath. Voyant knew my secret and she was out to get me . . . and I had my own aunt to thank for it.

Clearly, Aunt Elspeth was determined to play matchmaker. Her altered business card suddenly made sense. Oh, toadstools. The last thing I needed was my aunt's meddling.

Our flight attendant returned with a small bottle of Bordeaux and a wine goblet for Aunt Elspeth and a glass of tomato juice with a celery swizzle stick for me. I stashed the business card and photograph in the pages of my romance, while the attendant poured out Auntie's wine. Then she slipped away.

"Cheers." Aunt Elspeth raised her goblet in a toast.

"Cheers," I said, clinking glasses.

My aunt reclined in her chair with drink in hand, resuming her I'm-on-vacation pose. Following her lead, I took a hearty guzzle from my glass. My novel beckoned to me once more. Wanda Witherspoon's *Tainted Love.*

I opened to my place and took another swig from my drink. Where was I? Oh, yes. Heath, our hunky hero, had just arrived at the Pump Room in Bath for a Regency ball. All of Bath society was abuzz with the much anticipated arrival of Lady Gwendolyn Fairbanks. All but Catherine, the demure heroine of our tale. Her attentions were directed elsewhere.

Catherine spotted Heath from across the ballroom. Who could mistake his noble, dark-haired head that rose above all others? No man in Avon was his equal. But decorum would not allow Catherine to run to his side. She would have to wait until he noticed her.

Then his eyes met hers. Her heart pranced at the grin of recognition that broke over his face. Heath wove past the dancers, heading straight for her. Catherine stood on tiptoe and craned her neck to track his progress across the crowded ballroom. Her hand, clutching her empty dance card, fluttered to her throat.

Words on the page blurred. I blinked. Perhaps it was the late hour. I swirled the remaining juice in my glass, creating a little whirlpool. I swallowed the last gulp and closed my eyes.

Engines droned outside my window. My hand loosened on the book. Faint music hummed from somewhere nearby. A lilting melody. A waltz? A hand touched mine.

Candlelight glinted off the crystal chandeliers of a sumptuous ballroom. Heath stood before me in ascot, vest, trousers, and cutaway coat. He bowed. I curtsied, now dressed in a Regency gown of blue with an empire waist. Dancers pranced around us. The Pump Room? How had I arrived here?

"May I have this dance?" another gent said, inclining his head.

Before I could refuse him, he seized my gloved hand and twirled me around. The ballroom swirled in dizzy spirals. I staggered to a stop, and searched the faces for Heath. He had disappeared among the other dancers. My feet hastened forward. I must find him.

Music swelled. Ladies and gentlemen stepped apart, forming two straight lines. A man waited at the end of the line in a blue cutaway coat. The wavy dark hair. Heath.

His clothing was Heath's, but the man was not. His eyes shone blue like a clear summer sky. He clasped my hand in both of his as he had at my uncle's funeral. Jack?

Closing in like neat rows of books packing shelves, the dancers and ballroom morphed into Bedlam Books. A shadow draped in scarves slunk from the end of an aisle. Madam Voyant. Seeing me with Jack, she arched plucked eyebrows.

"Jack," she said in a breathless voice. "I will tell you Terpsichore's little secret."

"No." I pulled away from Jack and lurched down the aisle after her.

The skirts and petticoats of my gown tangled around my legs. My feet could not move fast enough. Voyant thrust her hand toward me. Red sparks flew from her fingertips.

I shrank against the bookcase. A blast of crimson flashed before my eyes, then swished past me, narrowly missing its mark. I watched in horror as it exploded upon Jack's chest.

"Jack," I screamed.

Someone seized my shoulders and shook me. "Cory?"

My eyes fluttered. My heart beat a tattoo. What? My fingers grasped cotton clothing and leather seat. Only the hum of jet engines and the dim glow of cabin lights. I was in an airplane. A midnight flight to London.

"Are you alright?" Aunt Elspeth leaned over, fixing me with the most curious stare.

I shifted in my seat, shaking the stiffness from my limbs. My paperback romance tumbled to the floor.

"All a dream," I muttered.

"Must have been some dream." Aunt Elspeth's lip hitched up in a mischievous smirk.

"It was nothing," I said.

"Nothing?" Aunt Elspeth waggled her eyebrows in a suggestive dance. "When a girl moans in her sleep and utters a man's name, it's definitely something."

"No." I gasped and shook my head. "It's not like that at all."

"Right." The grin widened on her face. She didn't believe me one iota.

Chapter Eight

High Tea at Tattings

I stared at pewter skies out the window of my soon-to-be-vacated dorm room at the Millhouse Academy for Gifted Individuals. London rain pattered a melancholy tune against the glass. A double-decker bus navigated the roundabout. A car horn blared. Students slogged up the pavement under a sea of bobbing umbrellas. I would have been heading off to class with them if my father had bothered to pay my tuition. I huffed and turned from the window. Instead, I was packing up the remains of my boarding school life at MAGI.

Empty boxes and filled cartons were stacked beside a tower of paperback and hardcover books, which rose from the threadbare carpet like a miniature skyscraper. I reached for the pile and began filling the umpteenth box of the day.

My former roommate Daphne reclined on my bed, reading *The Diviner*, a gossip rag. Nearby, Aunt Elspeth removed an armful of winter clothes from the cupboard and plopped them on my quilted bedspread. An empty suit-case rested open against the foot of the bed.

After three days in London, I thought we'd be further along than this. We'd spent two days already packing up Mother's tiny flat, sorting through our family possessions, deciding what to discard, donate, or ship back to the states. I hadn't thought there was so much left of our former existence.

"Cory, dear." Aunt Elspeth held a cable-knit sweater at arm's length and shook her head. "You really need to update your wardrobe."

"Why? I like my clothes." I rearranged the books in my box to squeeze in a few more.

Instead of packing my cardigan in the suitcase, Aunt Elspeth dropped it back on the bed. She rummaged through the clothing pile, sized up a wool tartan skirt, then tutted with disapproval as if she'd just plucked it from the bargain rack of a discount store.

"Cardigans and plaid skirts?" She frowned. "Really."

"What's wrong with that?" I said.

"Nothing, if you're fifty. Now don't take this the wrong way, but you dress like your mother."

"She's right." Daphne looked up from her newspaper and snickered. "You do dress like your mother."

Of course, Daphne would agree. She had dyed her spiky, short hairdo pink. Her idea of dressing up was a "good" pair of jeans and a t-shirt with a skull and cross-bones on the front. That was fine, if you worked as a sales clerk at Howling Wolf Music or moonlighted as a backup singer for The Gargoyles.

"What would you have me do?" I glared at Daphne and her eyebrow ring. "Spike my hair and wear jeans? I hate jeans. They make me look fat."

"You're not fat." Aunt Elspeth tossed my skirt back on the pile. "Curvy is what you are. All the Knightly women are voluptuous."

"You're not." I surveyed my aunt's slim figure in her form-fitting blouse and skinny black trousers.

"I'm not?" Aunt Elspeth quirked a shapely eyebrow and grinned. "If you promise not to tell, I'll let you in on a little secret." She snaked her fingers down her torso. "Iron Maidenform corset."

"You use magic to enhance your figure?" The book in my hand slipped, missing the box altogether. I scrambled to pick it up. "But that's cheating."

"Every witch needs a little help to counteract the effects of gravity and time." Aunt Elspeth winked. "Everyone does it."

My Aunt Gertrude with her round, apple shape popped into my head. Imagine trying to stuff her rotund figure into an Iron Maidenform. She'd pop the rivets right off.

"Not Aunt Gertrude." I giggled.

"Well." Aunt Elspeth preened, admiring her reflection in the full-length mirror mounted on my cupboard door. "There is a reason why Gertrude remains an old maid, while I have attracted four husbands." Her index finger crooked, beckoning me forward. "Come here."

She stood me in front of the looking glass. But all traces of my reflection had vanished. Instead, I saw Mother standing in what appeared to be the living room of Uncle Horace's apartment back in Berkeley. Mother in her smocked blouse and loose-fitting trousers rolled-up at the ankles. Was this some trick?

I blinked. Wait a minute. Mother had used the large framed mirror mounted over Uncle Horace's hearth to summon me, calling us on the Prism Communication Network.

"Hello, Cory dear." Mother with her tight, graying curls waved at me from inside the mirror. "Hello, Elspeth."

"Hello, Millie." Aunt Elspeth peered over my shoulder. "How's the cleaning going on your end?"

"The apartment is almost ready." Mother glanced behind her, and I wondered who else was in the room with her. She came closer and lowered her voice. "Oh, the things that man saved. Did you know Horace had a skeleton in his closet?"

"Don't we all?" Aunt Elspeth shrugged.

"No, I mean a real skeleton," Mother said. "Any idea what he could have been using that for?"

"I cannot fathom." Aunt Elspeth snickered.

"Ah, well." Mother glanced behind her again. "I'll have to think of some way to get rid of it. It keeps popping up in the most unexpected places."

Just like all those mystery novels that turned up in my hiding place at Bedlam Books. A vision of Jack invading my secret corner popped into my head. I shoved the thought away. I'd rather have a skeleton.

"How are things down at the shop?" I said.

"I don't know." Mother shook her head. "Jack has closed it temporarily. He's posted a sign. 'Closed for renovation' or some such thing. I hear a lot of moving going on down there."

Oh no. Not more changes. My romance novels. The mysteries. Would they still be there when I returned? I chewed on my lip. Why hadn't I stayed behind?

"How is your packing going?" Mother said.

My eyes flitted to the pile of books on the floor and the

empty boxes. Not well. But I couldn't tell Mother that. I didn't want to worry her.

"Fine." I affected a cheery tone and sidled over a smidgeon to block the view of all the clothes on the bed. "We should be back in a day or two."

"Good." Mother snuck another glance over her shoulder. What was she looking for? That skeleton?

"Come home soon," she said.

Her image faded from the looking glass. I was left staring at my sorry reflection in baggy trousers and woolly sweater. Yikes. I did dress like my mother.

Ah well, I'd best get packing. I turned to go, but Aunt Elspeth seized my shoulders.

"I'm not done with you yet." She surveyed me up and down. "Let's see. A nip here. A tuck there." She cinched my roomy pullover in at the waist and muttered an incantation. "*Constrictus.*"

Threads in my sweater contracted as if I were wrapped in the coils of a boa constrictor. I sucked in a breath. The knit top shrunk, conforming to my shape in clinging curves.

"That's better," Elspeth said. "Now perhaps a more flattering neckline. *Collum.*"

The sweater's collar stretched into a more revealing scooped neck. I thought of Lady Gwendolyn and her décolletage. Daphne grinned and nodded her approval.

"Now doesn't that look better?" Aunt Elspeth stepped aside and appraised her handiwork. She smiled. "You do want to look attractive for Jack, don't you?"

"No." I shook my head. Still playing matchmaker? Why wouldn't she keep quiet about him?

"Who's Jack?" Daphne perked up. Her paper landed in a messy heap on the bed.

"Cory's dashing new business partner," Aunt Elspeth

said. "Cory claims she's not interested. She's being very closed-mouthed about him." She smirked. "Except in her sleep."

Daphne laughed and gave me a cheeky look. "Sounds a lot like Gil."

"Jack is nothing like Gil," I said, feeling a flush of heat rise over my cheeks. Gil. My cheating ex-boyfriend. I was over him and his two-timing ways. Former boyfriends, like corpses, were better off left buried.

"Gil?" Aunt Elspeth leaned toward Daphne, trolling for gossip. "Whatever happened to him?"

I glared at Daphne. Don't tell. But Aunt Elspeth already had her hooks in.

"Dumped her," Daphne blurted.

"I'll bet he wouldn't have, if you had worn that." Aunt Elspeth pointed at my altered sweater and winked. "And taken your nose out of a book once in a while."

"And deny you your fun at my expense?" I turned back to my half-packed box and tossed in a couple more books.

"Well, look at this room." Aunt Elspeth swept her arm in a grand gesture to indicate my humble bedroom. "Nothing but books and a bed. You and Horace are two halves of the same cauldron. No wonder he liked you best."

My hand reached for a paperback romance on the pile. I eyed the hunky stud on the cover. At least, a good book doesn't cheat on you.

"This one's not half bad." Daphne plucked a lacy black sweater from the clothing pile and held it up to her chest. "Oh, I almost forgot. While you were away, a man came looking for you."

"My father?" I said, before I could stop myself. Hope bubbled up in my chest. Daddy had come back for me.

"No." Daphne shook her head. "Not him." Just as quickly the bubble burst.

"An older man," she said. "Said his name was Hawkins or Dawkins or . . ."

"Paul Dawkins?" Aunt Elspeth looked up from her packing.

"Yeah, that was it."

Paul Dawkins was my father's former business partner. I pictured his balding head, bespectacled face, and watery eyes. He had some nerve calling here after what he did to my father. My fingers squeezed the book in my hand. That stinking rat.

"What did he want?" I said, although I really didn't want to know.

"Wouldn't say." Daphne pulled my sweater over her pink-haired head and tried it on. "He seemed nervous, anxious to talk to you."

"Why would he want to talk to me?" I said.

"I never liked him." Aunt Elspeth frowned, her lips puckering as if she'd just swallowed something unpleasant. "Twitchy little man. Reminds me of a ferret."

"Acted like a git, if you ask me." Daphne crossed to the mirror and checked her appearance. The lacy black top, which would have been tight on me, looked great on her. "Hey, Cory, can I borrow this one? I'm meeting Seamus at the Knight's Arms tonight."

"Go ahead," I said. "Keep it." I didn't care about sweaters anyhow. I sealed the box I'd been packing and pushed it against the wall with the others.

"Well, I'm done for the day." Aunt Elspeth brushed off her hands. "What say we all go shopping? What do you think, Daphne?"

"Yes, let's go." Daphne nodded, then looked over at me.

I glanced at the still empty suitcase and heap of clothes on the bed and sighed. When it came to packing, Aunt Elspeth was no help at all.

"You've hardly packed a thing," I said. Who was I kidding? I wanted to get out of here as much as they did. The thought of Dawkins looking for me made me nervous. And I could use a break.

"Oh, all right."

"Good." Aunt Elspeth strolled toward the door. "I'll just pop into your powder room and freshen up, then we can go. I'm in the mood for Tattings and high tea."

"Aunt Elspeth, you know I can't afford Tattings."

"Nonsense." Her sing-song voice carried from the other room. "It'll be my treat. While we're there, we can do something about your wardrobe."

"Brilliant." Daphne giggled.

The Tea Room at Tattings was located on the fourth floor of the upscale department store. Light flooded the room through tall windows dressed in floor-length brocade draperies. Unoccupied tables covered in fine linens dotted the marble floor. Golden sconces mounted on the wall added to the rich ambiance. Occupied tables and chairs floated in mid-air. This was high tea, after all.

Aunt Elspeth, Daphne, and I chose an empty table nearest a window. I looped my purse and lone shopping bag on a hook mounted on the back of my chair and settled into the comfy, tufted seat. Aunt Elspeth hung her purchases on the back of her chair too, so many that I expected the chair to topple over from the weight. But it did not. She lit on the seat with the grace of a bird on a perch. Daphne plopped into a third seat. Then all three chairs and the table levitated like a bubble aloft on a gentle zephyr.

The table rose until our heads were just shy of the carved ceilings. Through the window, I had a gorgeous aerial view of the local Knightsbridge neighborhood. Cars and lorries motored in the city street far below. I surveyed a beautiful multi-storied stone building across the street. But that building didn't compare to the palatial structure that was Tattings. This department store occupied an entire city block.

"Tea time, ladies," Aunt Elspeth said.

When I turned back, each place had been set with a luncheon plate and matching china cup and saucer. In the center of the table, a teapot steamed, wrapped in a quilted cozy to keep its contents warm. A tiered tray appeared laden with golden scones and dainty cucumber sandwiches with no crusts. Pots of rich clotted cream and jam materialized beside the tray.

Aunt Elspeth poured out three cups of amber brew. "Milk or sugar?" she said.

"No, thank you." I shook my head. I liked my tea black.

Aunt Elspeth added a drib of milk to her cup. Daphne spooned three heaps of sugar into hers and stirred. I helped myself to a scone, slathered it with strawberry jam, and added a generous dollop of cream. The sweet pastry melted in my mouth. Mmmmmm.

"Ah." Aunt Elspeth lifted her cup to her nose and inhaled the steam. "Now this is more like it."

She sipped her tea. I knew just what she was thinking. This was much better than packing.

"Cucumber sandwich?" Aunt Elspeth placed a finger

sandwich on her luncheon plate and passed the tray. "I've been thinking. As long as Jack is making changes to the shop, you ought to consider adding a café."

I snorted. I clamped my linen napkin over my mouth to prevent bits of scone from spraying the table. A gulp of tea washed down the crumbs.

"Mother already suggested that," I said. "Jack pooh-poohed the idea. He'll never go for it."

Aunt Elspeth hadn't been there that morning last week. She hadn't witnessed Jack's condescending dismissal when Mother brought me tea at the shop. The idea would never fly.

"Now, don't be so sure." Aunt Elspeth wagged her finger at me. Her lips curled in a sly smile. "There's always a way around a man. You just have to approach him properly."

Maybe it was the confidence with which Aunt Elspeth expressed her assertion. Or maybe it was her track record at getting men to do her bidding. If she and Mother helped, perhaps together we could convince Jack.

"A little café would be nice," I said. "I suppose we could sell tea."

"Of course, you could." Aunt Elspeth winked. "Any witch worth her salt can brew."

"And scones." Daphne seized one from the tray and waved it. "You must have scones."

"But the books?" I shook my head. "Imagine the spills. Jack would never go for food and drink in the shop."

"Well." Aunt Elspeth paused, her teacup lifted halfway to her lips. She took a slow deliberate sip, then lowered the cup. "Can't you set up a separate area, cordoned off from the rest?"

I thought of the former mystery section, which was now

empty except for the comic book stand. Perhaps I could set up a few tables there. The shelves would be perfect for storing cups and canisters of loose tea. It could work.

"It would be a boon for business." Aunt Elspeth eyed me over the top of her teacup. Her shapely eyebrows danced. "Everyone likes a read with their cup of tea. You'd make a little extra money. How can Jack object to that?"

Tea and a "cozy." Who didn't like a fun mystery with their morning or afternoon cup? Or a steamy romance? I could sell tea to the customers and peddle the mystery and romance novels on the side.

"It's brilliant." Daphne nudged me and nodded her encouragement.

What a wicked idea. And the best part of all was that Jack Wickham wouldn't want anything to do with a tea shop. That would be my domain. A tea shop would keep him out of my hair and make it easier to sell books on the sly. Was a tea corner the answer to my problems?

"We'll have to convince Jack," I said.

"He could hardly refuse you." Aunt Elspeth patted my hand. "Especially with your aunt AND your mother backing the plan."

Her eyes sparkled with mischief, the same glitter that must have been shining in my own. I knew then that I had a fellow conspirator. Three against one. The odds had just changed in my favor.

"Cake." Daphne's eyes brightened as a dessert trolley bobbed up next to our table. Frosted layer cakes of every flavor and description filled all three levels.

She served me a slice of the chocolate one. I took a bite, savoring the balance of sugar and fat. I didn't know which was sweeter, the cake or my ingenious little plan.

Chapter Nine

Dawkins and Smyth Booksellers

I marched down Charing Cross Road, past the dozens of bookstores lining this street, but my feet beat a familiar path to one particular shop. I never should have come. It was stupid of me. A stupid, childish hope. But these were my final hours in London. My bags were packed, and the rest of Mother's and my belongings had been shipped. Aunt Elspeth and I would depart for California later this evening. This was my last chance, and I thought that maybe he would be here.

I stopped in front of the vacant storefront. A "For Lease" sign filled the display window that once held my favorite books. I glanced up at empty hooks in the overhang, envisioning the wooden sign that had dangled there. Golden letters on the shingle had spelled out "Dawkins and Smyth Booksellers." Ulysses Smyth. My father.

I gazed through plate glass into the empty interior of his former bookshop. Bare floor-to-ceiling bookcases covered the walls, running the length of the store on both sides and along the back. On the far wall, I could see the faux book-case that concealed the basement door. How conspicuous it now looked with its fake leather bindings, a full bookcase amidst empty shelves. Once it had belonged. Now out of place. Just how I felt.

My throat tightened. I blinked back the tears stinging my eyes. Daddy should have been here, with me beside him, helping him in the store. Just like it used to be. Until every-thing had unraveled a few short months ago.

I saw myself once again at my father's old desk. My fingers were digging through a carton of new romances, fresh from Pentacle Publishing. I was searching the contents like a magpie looking for shiny treasure, pulling out each new release one by one, lining them up on Daddy's desk, and giggling with anticipation. Getting the latest novels was like Christmas. Which one should I read first?

My father approached and surveyed the growing stack of books on his desktop. He planted his hands on his waistline and pretended to frown. But above his trimmed salt-and-pepper beard, the corner of his mouth twitched, betraying him.

"Cory, you're supposed to be checking inventory," Daddy teased. The grin widened across his face and his hazel eyes twinkled.

"I am," I said, pointing to the canary yellow packing slip. "I have to make sure they shipped the right ones, don't I?"

"And I suppose you'll have to read them all, too."

"Of course, how else will I know which to recommend to our customers?"

Daddy chuckled, laugh lines shooting from the corners of his eyes. "Don't take all day. I need your help." He glanced at his wristwatch and his smile faded. "Quarter-past ten. Paul is late again today. What's keeping him?"

I glanced over at Mr. Dawkins's desk. Stacks of paperwork filled his in-tray. Ink splotches stained his blotter. But Paul Dawkins's balding head was not bent over his ledgers, and his eyes did not stare back at me, magnified through the thick lenses of his spectacles. This morning, my father's business partner was absent.

The door clicked open. Shop bells tinkled. My eyes flitted to the entrance, expecting to see the wiry little man bustle in. Instead, Mr. Pembroke, the landlord, heaved his great bulk through the doorway. He closed his umbrella and brushed the damp from his mackintosh. Droplets sprayed everywhere, flecking nearby books with damaging water.

"Please, Mr. Pembroke," I said, dashing forward. "The books."

"The books are not my problem, Miss Smyth." His bristly eyebrows knitted together over his glare. "I've come about the rent. It's overdue."

"There must be some mistake." Daddy strode to my side.

Together, we neared the doorway and the waiting Mr. Pembroke. Father wasn't much taller than I and Pembroke's imposing frame towered over us. He looked down and frowned. Flesh hanging from his jowls jiggled.

"There's no mistake." He stabbed a finger at my father, as more droplets flew from his sleeve. "You owe three months' rent, and I want my money."

"Three months?" Daddy's eyes widened. "That's impossible. Paul handles all the bills. He's always paid promptly."

"Not for some time." Pembroke craned his thick neck

to stare over my head, his eyes scanning the shop. "And where is Mr. Dawkins?"

"He's running late this morning." I grasped Pembroke's soggy sleeve and gestured toward my father's desk and chair. "Please, come in. Have a seat." I forced my lips into what I hoped was a reassuring smile and patted his arm. "I'm sure that he'll be here soon." I glanced out the shop window up the street. Where was Mr. Dawkins?

"No time for that." Pembroke shrugged off my hand as if flicking the rain from his sleeve. "Now if you'll just pay up, I'll be on my way."

"Paul keeps the checkbook," Daddy said, shrugging his shoulders under a rumpled dress shirt. "What do you expect me to do, raid the till for three months' rent?" He raised his arms in a gesture of entreaty. Perhaps it was my imagination but the sweat stains under his armpits seemed to enlarge. "Please, if you'll just talk with Paul, I'm sure we can sort this out."

"I've already waited three months," Pembroke said. "I've served notice. If you can't pay, I'll find another tenant who can."

"You'll kick us out?" I said. "Close down the store? But we've been here for years. You can't do this."

"Oh, can't I?" Pembroke's face turned scarlet. Spittle flew from his lips. "I think you'll find I bloody well can!"

"Please, Mr. Pembroke, a little more time." I reached for his sleeve once more. "Father will find Mr. Dawkins and talk with him. He'll get you your money."

"You have forty-eight hours." Pembroke jerked his arm free from my grip. His stare zeroed in on my father. "If I don't have all the money in my hands by then, you will hear from my solicitors. Good day, Mr. Smyth."

He popped open his umbrella, sending fresh showers

over the nearest books. Then he opened the door and exited into the London drizzle. I dried off books as best I could, while Daddy stood wordlessly watching Pembroke's massive frame retreat down the rain-drenched pavement.

Fortunately, there was no one else in the shop on this wet morning to witness Mr. Pembroke's tirade. I glanced back at Dawkins's empty desk, then looked at my father. He reached to secure the lock on the door, then flipped the sign in the window to "Closed." Making sure that we weren't interrupted, I supposed.

"Come, Cory," he said with an urgency that frightened me.

I followed him back to Paul Dawkins's desk. For a moment, he stood just staring at the cluttered desktop. I chewed on my lip.

"What are we going to do?" I said.

"We're going to find where Paul keeps our checkbook, that's what."

"Go through his desk?" It made me uncomfortable to go through someone else's things. But then again, our business was at stake and this was an emergency.

My gaze flicked to the door. Still no Dawkins. Daddy approached his partner's desk and rifled through the pile of papers in his in-tray.

"Business correspondence. Recent invoices. Nothing out of the ordinary." Daddy huffed and sank into the swivel chair. "Cory, go to the safe and bring me the ledger."

I ran to the back room and the large safe in the corner. I knew the combination by heart, since it was my job to lock up the daily cash register receipts at closing time. Inside, I found an oversize black book, the store's ledger.

I brought it to Daddy. He flipped to the most recent entries. Over his shoulder, I scanned pages divided into accounts payable and receivable, orderly rows and columns filled with numbers. Every penny spent or taken in by our bookstore was recorded in this book. Daddy's finger traced a path to the bottom line. It showed a modest balance.

"See, I knew we had the money." He jabbed at the bottom line. Then his finger reversed course up the payables column. "Where are the rent payments?" He flipped to the previous page and then back again. He shook his head. "Well, we'll just have to find that checkbook. Then I'll write Pembroke his check and be done with it."

He peered under the ledger and into the open desk drawer. Clearly, that's where he'd been looking while I went to fetch the ledger. But the checkbook was not in Dawkins's top drawer.

A crumpled page protruded from the bottom desk drawer. I could just make out the gas company insignia on an exposed corner.

"Look." I pointed at the paper.

Daddy grasped the handle and pulled, but the drawer wouldn't budge. His fingers were too thick and clumsy, but with my daintier hands I was able to tease the page out. The heating bill. Marked unpaid. Overdue. Oh, toadstools.

As the sight of another unpaid debt, my father's face turned ashen. His shoulders tensed. His voice became gruff and urgent.

"The key to Paul's desk must be here somewhere." He checked the bottom of Dawkins's in-tray, upended his pen canister onto the ink-stained blotter, then slid his hand under the seat cushion of his chair. "Blast it all."

"*Liberatus.*" He growled the spell and tugged on the handle again. But the drawer wouldn't open. This was no simple lock. This drawer must be where Dawkins kept the checkbook.

"*Liberatus*." He shouted the spell this time, then yanked the drawer with all his strength. "Open, damn it."

Still, the lock wouldn't yield. His arm swept the blotter, scattering pens across the desktop. With a moan of frustration, Daddy propped his elbows on the open ledger and dropped his head into his hands. His fingers kneaded his scalp through thick, graying hair.

But when he'd swept his arm over the blotter, the smudges left a key-shaped outline on the blotter paper—a picture of what lay underneath—just like the brass rubbings I'd done with paper and crayons as a little kid. I ran my fingertips over the blotter, feeling the outline of something small, flat and hard hidden under the paper.

"I found it," I said, retrieving the key. It glowed a faint coppery pink, emitting an aura of magic.

Daddy's head jerked up. His eyes fixed on the object in my hand. I fitted the key into the lock and turned. Sparks spit from the tumblers. *Click*. The drawer popped open.

Papers spewed out. More overdue bills. The electricity, the heating bill, rent notices, shut-off threats. The dates went back one, two, even three months.

Underneath, we found another large black book, a second ledger like the first. Placing the two side by side, Daddy and I compared them. While the first recorded a modest profit, the second showed page after page awash in red ink. I gasped. Dawkins, my father's trusted business partner, had cooked the books.

"How could this be?" Daddy muttered, shaking his head. "Sales have been steady. Holiday business was good. I counted the receipts myself. Where has all the money gone?"

At the very bottom of the drawer, we finally found the checkbook. Dawkins had been writing checks at regular intervals, the same amount every two weeks. His scribbled notation read "MT" followed by a string of digits. MT? We had no creditor with those initials.

"A deficit, unpaid bills, mysterious withdrawals." Daddy stared at the page. His hand fisted with building rage. "Why, Dawkins, that sleazy, stinking weasel." He slammed his fists down on the desk with such force that the ledgers jumped. "No wonder he won't show his face. All this time, he's been embezzling from our business and falsifying the records to cover his tracks."

From that moment on, Dawkins and Smyth Booksellers had spiraled into bankruptcy. Clearance banners spanned our front windows. *Going out of business. Everything must go.* Books that didn't sell were divvied up. Anything still in print was returned to the publishers. Used books and out-of-print titles were sorted into lots and sold at auction. The auctioneer's gavel still rang in my ears. *Going once. Going twice. Sold.* My father had no choice but to liquidate the business. He'd needed the money to settle our debts. Once the store was gone, he went too. Sailed away in his Beneteau sailboat and never returned.

Bile rose in my throat. I swallowed and turned away from the now-empty storefront. There were too many ghosts in this place. I wished I could send them all packing. Why had I come back here?

My hand reached into my coat pocket for a tissue and felt a small business card. I pulled out the card, the one that Aunt Elspeth had given me on the plane. *BEDLAM BOOKS, 1313 Chanting Way, Berkeley, CA 94704. Cory Smyth and Jonathan Wickham, proprietors.* I held a second chance in my hand, a new beginning for Mother and me. I wouldn't make the same mistakes my father did. I would make my bookstore profitable, and no matter what happened, I wouldn't abandon Mother.

"What's that?" a familiar nasal voice said.

The shock of recognition rattled my body as if I'd been hit by a hex. Paul Dawkins. He must have followed me here. How long had he been watching me? I stuffed the card back in my pocket and twisted to face the short, nervous man.

"What are you doing here? Shouldn't you be in jail?"

Dawkins shoved his hands in the pockets of a worn trench coat with patches on the elbows. His pocket gaped open, unstitched at the seams. He looked down at his scuffed shoes and shuffled his feet.

He muttered so low that I had to lean closer to hear.

"Out on bail. A mate posted for me." His head jerked up. "Is there somewhere we could talk? Somewhere not so public?"

Behind his thick glasses, his eyes darted up and down the street as if looking for someone. A warning tingle raced over my skin. Hairs stood on end. I wasn't going anywhere with him.

"Haven't you done enough already?" I said. "Anything you have to say to me can be said right here."

"Please, Cory." He glanced over his shoulder, then leaned in and lowered his voice. "I'm looking for Ulysses."

I laughed. A blurted blast, sarcastic and cold. "I don't know where my father is. And I wouldn't tell you even if I did."

"You've always been a good girl, Cor." Again, he snuck a glance up the street. "I need some money. A couple hundred quid. A small loan. I'll pay you back, eh?"

A loan? From me? He must have bats in his belfry if he thought I'd loan him a single penny. Not that I had anything to give him.

"What?" I straightened and fixed him with a look that would pop the bulging eyes from a toad. "No."

Dawkins shuffled backward a step. His small frame shrank in the overcoat. His thin, blonde mustache quivered on his upper lip.

"You don't understand," he said. "I was in a tough spot, and Flanagan loaned me some money. If I don't pay him back, he'll send his mates after me. You don't mess with the likes of Flanagan. No telling what he'll do." His pleading watery eyes grew larger behind the thick lenses. "Now if you'll—"

"Whatever mess you've gotten yourself into, I don't want to know."

I turned to walk away. I didn't want to hear his excuses. Wasn't it enough that he'd destroyed my father's business, my family, my life? Nothing could compel me to help him now.

"Cory, please." Dawkins seized my arm. His bony fingers pinched my flesh, his grip like icicles of cold. Shivers of revulsion raced up my sleeve.

"Let me go."

Defensive magic surged through me. A jolt of electricity leapt from my skin to his fingers. Shocked, he yanked his hand from my arm. I was free.

Run. My feet pelted down the pavement. The sound of my heartbeat pulsed in my ears. My breath puffed in fits and spurts. My thoughts focused on one thing: Fleeing from him.

I turned the corner and slowed. No footsteps pursued

me. Yet my arm throbbed where he'd grabbed me. His phantom fingers gripped me still.

I rubbed my arm, trying to erase the feel of his hold. A few short hours and I would be far, far away. An ocean and a continent would separate us. Paul Dawkins, that thieving weasel, would not find me there. I reached for the business card in my pocket. My amulet of hope. But my fingers closed on nothing. My business card was gone.

Chapter Ten

A New Deal

As soon as we returned to California, I asked Aunt Elspeth to take me directly to Bedlam Books. It didn't matter that it was mid-morning and that I hadn't had time to freshen up after our eleven-hour transatlantic flight. The fear that Jack Wickham had taken advantage of my absence to make more changes in the shop spurred me on. Had he discovered my hidden cache of romance novels?

The bell chimed its familiar welcome as I entered Bedlam Books. Home once more. But no comic books giggled a greeting. The comics had been banished to the dark recesses that once housed the mysteries. I stood surrounded by leather-bound classics dressed in tans, burgundies, and browns—a landscape of solemn hues. And something else was amiss. No bursts of pink or purple fairy dust flew like fireworks over the juvenile books. Had he removed the children's books?

I sped toward the children's corner to investigate. Jack knelt in the middle of this section, loading picture books into a carton. What the devil? I peered into the box. An old crone frowned up at me from the cover of a storybook. *Mother Grime's Nasty Rhymes*. A childhood favorite of mine. He was not getting rid of that. I snatched the book from his box.

Jack looked up from his packing. His eyebrows shot up, disappearing under the dark curl that drooped over his forehead. His eyes widened, taking in my scoop-necked blouse, the one that Aunt Elspeth had modified.

"Ah, Cory." His lip twitched. "You've returned."

"And none too soon." I hugged the book of fairy tales to my chest, blocking his view. "More changes? You're not eliminating the children's section, are you?"

"No, I'm relocating them to the back of the shop."

The back of the shop? Near my hideout for the romances? I chewed on my lip.

He looked away, appearing to focus on the few remaining picture books on the shelf. "Did you enjoy your holiday?"

A faint blush tinged his clean-shaven cheek. Embarrassment? Or was he hiding something?

"You know I didn't travel for fun, Jack," I said. "Don't change the subject. First, you eliminate the romances, then the mysteries. Why so many changes?" I waved my hand toward the front of the shop. "Even the front display."

Jack turned back to his work. He removed another handful of children's books from the shelf and packed them in the carton at his feet.

"Now that you mention it," he said. "Have you seen the romances?"

My grip tightened on the book of fairy tales in my hands. Sweat moistened my palms. I fought the urge to peer over my shoulder toward the bookcase enclosure where I'd hidden the romance novels.

"The what?" I said.

"There were several boxes of romances in the basement, which I intended to return." His gray eyes bored into mine. "They have disappeared. Just like the mystery novels."

He paused with his hand on an early reader. A gypsy woman draped in shawls gazed up from the cover. She looked like Madam Voyant with her large hoop earrings and veiled threats. The psychic next door had witnessed my clandestine sales. She must have snitched on me and told Jack about my secret hiding place. Was that why he'd relocated all the mysteries there?

Sweet Merlin, I was caught with my fingers in the potions cupboard. But why would Voyant tell? I had given her no reason to spill my secret. My gaze flitted to a distant shelf. What could I say in my defense?

"They haven't turned up yet?" I said, my voice artificially bright.

"No," he said in a baritone growl.

"No?" I refocused on Jack. Had I heard correctly?

"No," he repeated. He shook his head. His brow furrowed. "It's all very troubling. I can't afford to absorb the cost of several cartons of lost books."

I can't afford? My moment of relief evaporated. His not-so-subtle slight rankled.

"Don't you mean 'we'?"

I plopped the fairy tale book into his carton, burying the gypsy under *Mother Grime*. A puff of fairy dust shot up from the box. I planted my hands on my hips and glared at Jack.

"Pardon?" He stared back with the clueless expression of a troll.

"We, not I, can't afford to absorb the cost. We are part-ners now, or have you forgotten?"

"I've not forgotten." A slight smile curled his lips. "Curiously, several women came into the shop and asked for you while you were away."

Oh no. Had one of them blabbed? I stared down at the hag on the cover of *Mother Grime's Nasty Rhymes*. She brushed fairy dust from her skirts, wagged a gnarled finger, and fixed me with an evil eye. I swallowed and glanced back at Jack.

"Did they?" I said. "And did they say what they wanted?"

"No." Jack shook his head. But his gray eyes stared with more intensity. He was fishing, and I was on the hook again. Well, I wouldn't give him the satisfaction.

"I did make a couple of sales last week." I straight-ened and flashed a smug grin. "Perhaps they appreciated the service."

"Hmmmm. Perhaps." He frowned and went back to his packing, straightening the books in his carton.

"What did you tell them?" I said.

Jack stuffed *Mother Grime* down between the other books in his box with a little more force than necessary. Then he slapped the flaps closed.

"Only that you were gone and that I didn't know when you would return."

"What?" I bristled. "I told you why I'd gone to London and when I was returning."

"Yes, you did."

Jack rose and faced me, taller than me by half a head. Muscles in his jaw tightened. But his voice remained even and controlled.

"You're still as impulsive as I remember," he said. "Your

sudden rejection of my offer proved as much. I thought that perhaps when you went to London, you might have reconsidered and decided to stay there."

"Well, I haven't." I thrust my chin in the air. "For your information, I've packed up my London life and I'm . . . I'm here to stay."

"Glad to hear it." His tone was infuriatingly polite and devoid of emotion. Was he mocking me?

He pivoted on his heel and walked toward the office with his long-legged stride. But I was not finished with him yet. I trotted after him.

"Are you?" I said to his back. "Then perhaps you will be interested in a few changes that I would like to make?"

Jack's steps slowed. He turned to face me. One dark eyebrow arched.

"Such as?" he said.

"I want to open a tea shop on the premises. Tables, tea, and conversation about our books." I pointed behind me. "We have space in the mystery section now and I think it will be a boon for sales."

Jack chuckled. A flippant laugh. He shook his head. "That's out of the question."

"Why?"

"Food and drink in a bookstore?" He gestured at the surrounding shelves, bulging with his leather-bound treasures. "Think of the books."

"I am thinking of the books." I waved both hands toward the sagging shelves. "A café will draw people into the store. They'll spend time here browsing and buying. And the tea sales themselves will generate income."

"No." He waved me off, then turned away.

"No? Just like that?" I grabbed his arm, my fingers feeling sinewy muscle beneath his cotton dress shirt. I planted myself in his way and fixed him with a stare that would shrivel frog spawn. "You lied to me. You don't want me here. You couldn't make that any clearer, bossing me around, ordering me to dust. I'm part owner too. You can't treat me like this."

He could have flung me aside and brushed past. Oddly, he didn't shake off my hold.

"That was never my intention." Jack looked away, his eyes gray and stormy. Color rose on his cheeks. Mr. Unflappable was looking distinctly discomposed, and his hesitation fed my courage.

"I've held my tongue long enough," I said. "You still haven't offered any explanation for all your changes here. I think you owe me that much." I let go of his arm, but did not back down. My chin jutted up, my eyes level with the scar above his upper lip. "This is my uncle's bookstore. His body is barely in the grave and you alter everything. Why? Under Uncle Horace's management, Bedlam Books has been a thriving business for years."

"No, Cory." He looked into the distance and back at me. "It hasn't. Bedlam Books hasn't been profitable for years."

"What do you mean?" Visions of Paul Dawkins loomed in my brain.

Jack swallowed. I watched his Adam's apple bob over the starched collar. He stared at the shelf next to us.

"For the past two years, we've hardly been able to make ends meet."

I staggered backward a step and shook my head. This could not be. I thought of Dawkins's excuses, his crooked ledgers, his bald-faced lies.

"But your offer for my share? How can you afford . . . I don't understand."

Jack faced me once more. The distance between us appeared to have restored his composure.

"I have money from my parents' estate. I've been using my inheritance to shore up the business. These changes are an effort to return Bedlam Books to profitability."

Bedlam Books failing? No, this couldn't be true. Was he lying to me, like Dawkins had?

"I don't believe you." I shook my head. "Show me the books."

Jack's nostrils flared. He studied my face with a hardened stare.

"Very well," he said with a tight-lipped nod.

Jack led me into his office and the massive hickory desk that had belonged to my uncle. He extracted the account book from a drawer and plopped it open on the desktop, inviting me to read. Income and expenses were recorded in black ink in the left columns. The rightmost column showed the balance. The store's bottom line? Red ink.

My mouth went dry. These books weren't tampered with as Dawkins's had been. No one would falsify records to show a deficit. Oh, bat poo. Jack was telling the truth.

"Do you still want to be my partner now?" Jack's jaw stiffened. His gray eyes took on a steely cast. "You should have taken my offer while you had the chance."

He strode off, his clipped gait echoing on the wooden floor. I didn't try to stop him this time, but stared down at the ledger. Visions in red ink swirled in my brain. Bedlam Books in financial trouble? How were Mother and I going to live?

Back in my secret enclave, I paced the floor along a narrow slot between stacked cartons of books. My romances were still here, confirming my suspicion that Jack had not yet discovered this corner. If he had, the romance and mystery novels would all be gone. But even the knowledge that my secret was safe provided scant comfort. Bedlam Books was failing and Mother and I needed income.

My fingers gripped a paperback romance. Oh, why had I lied about these books? Should I confess? Tell Jack about the romances I'd hidden and the mystery novels that had turned up here?

If we didn't tear the covers off these books and return them, then we wouldn't get our money back. We could not absorb the cost of all this. I chewed my lower lip. As much as I hated to admit it, Jack was right.

On the cover of a steamy romance, a studly hero flexed his muscles, his shirt unbuttoned to expose perfect pecs. Imagine ripping the cover from that. I squeezed my eyes shut. On the black insides of my eyelids, I saw all my favorite paperback romances, covers torn off, pages reduced to pulp. I'd been through that once before. I couldn't do it again. Uncle Horace, what should I do?

I opened my eyes, spotting the mysterious book with onion-skin pages. Its cover lifted a fraction then dropped closed again, as if inviting me to browse. I sat on the floor and pulled the large tome onto my lap. It flipped itself open. I expected to see the picture of the embracing lovers. Instead, the open page depicted a floral china teacup and saucer. The tea shop, of course.

No, I wouldn't return these books. Selling them would be more profitable in the long run. I would follow through with my plan to peddle them on the sly. That was the best way to save my uncle's store.

If only I could convince Jack to let me have my tea shop. But how? Aunt Elspeth's words whispered in my head. *There's always a way around a man. You just have to approach him properly.*

What would make Jack amenable to my suggestion? A little potion in his afternoon tea would do the trick. But he never ate or drank in the shop, not even in the office. I could think of a few hexes or maybe a broomstick to the head, but neither of those seemed very sporting.

I glanced at the full carton of romances. From the cover of *Tainted Love*, a buxom beauty preened, wearing a devious smile and a low-cut gown. She puckered her pouty lips and gave me a saucy wink. Lady Gwendolyn Fairbanks. Now, there was a woman who knew her way around a man. Her feminine wiles had always worked on Heath. But would they work on Jack?

I approached the stacked boxes, affecting a sultry, hip-swaying stroll. I imagined Jack sitting at his desk with his characteristic stony expression. I thrust out my chest in my sweater with the scooped neckline and oh-so-slowly bent over the stacked boxes.

"Oh, Jack," I purred in a breathless whisper. My lower lip jutted out in a pout. "I want to open a café on the premises. Just a few tables in the corner. You'd hardly notice."

I smiled and fluttered my eyelashes, batting my lids in my best imitation of a coquette. My vision flickered as if lit by a dysfunctional strobe light. So disorienting. Then the boxes beneath me shifted. I grasped to catch them, but my fingers missed. My body listed to one side. Ouch! My hip slammed against the nearest bookcase. I righted myself and massaged my bruised leg. So much for my seductive stroll.

Who was I kidding? I was no Lady Fairbanks. I couldn't do any of that. There was only one other option.

The office door stood ajar. Through the gap, I saw Jack sitting behind the massive hickory desk, bent over his ledgers. *Skritch. Skritch.* The nib of his favorite fountain pen scratched the paper.

On the wall behind him, the pendulum of an old-fashioned Bavarian clock ticked the passing seconds. I surveyed skeletons carved on the face of the old wooden timepiece and the little door above the clock face. When the hour chimed, miniature bats would flitter out that door and back in again to the tune of "Danse Macabre". My heart fluttered in my chest like the beating of tiny wings. Courage, I whispered to myself.

I knocked on the office door.

"Yes?" he said.

I pushed the door open and approached his desk.

"Jack?" I licked my lips to moisten them. "I'm sorry."

He stopped writing, the pen poised in his fingers. His head tilted up to face me. Between knitted brows, creases marred his smooth forehead. Pale gray eyes locked on my face. He said nothing, waiting for me to continue.

"I won't stand in the way of your changes," I said. "Do whatever you think necessary to keep Bedlam Books afloat."

His mouth slackened. His rigid jaw relaxed. His granite exterior softened. He dropped his gaze, appearing to stare down at the ledger on his desk.

"Thank you," he said.

Behind him, the pendulum swung. I took a deep breath. The time had come. Now or never.

"In return," I said. "Grant me a tea shop on a trial basis. It was Mother's idea. She'll help me. Aunt Elspeth has agreed to finance the whole thing. It won't cost us a penny. We'll make a separate area, away from the books.

I'll take full responsibility. I do believe it will bring business into the shop and earn a little extra on the side. Please." I drew in another trembling breath and concentrated on the steady tick-tock of the clock.

Chapter Eleven

Something Familiar

Later that day, I trudged up the back stairs to Uncle Horace's flat, a broomstick in one hand and a bucket of cleaning supplies in the other. Bedlam Books, on street-level below, was closed for the day. Mother and I had come to finish cleaning what was to be our future home.

I passed by the door to Mrs. Hastings's second-floor apartment. I recalled her wizened face, rambling tales, and boasts that she would live to 104. The doddering old woman had never been in a hurry for anything. How did she ever end up with a name like Hastings?

I sighed and continued up one more flight of stairs. Ahead of me, Mother led the way to the third-floor landing and the entrance to Uncle Horace's apartment. She fitted an old-fashioned skeleton key into the lock.

"The apartment isn't perfect," she said, still fiddling with the key. "Horace was a bachelor, you know. But with a few feminine touches, I think it will work quite well for us."

Granted, I hadn't been here in years. But if Uncle Horace had lived here, how bad could it be? Bachelor or not.

"I'm sure it'll be fine, Mother."

She coaxed the key from the keyhole, then opened the door a crack and peeked inside. The wire handle of the loaded scrub bucket dug into my fingers. Couldn't she go any faster? What was she doing?

"Here we are," she said.

She threw the door open wide and waved her arm in a sweeping gesture like a game show hostess revealing a grand prize. I resisted the urge to roll my eyes. It wasn't as if I hadn't seen Uncle Horace's living room before. I followed her inside. Mother made a bee-line for the kitchen. I lowered my cleaning supplies to the floor and closed the door.

A familiar leather sofa, overstuffed chairs upholstered in tweed, and a large fireplace dominated the room. I crossed the carpet, my footsteps sending little puffs of dust sprouting into the air. My fingers reached for the sofa's smooth, chocolate brown leather, the texture and color of old book bindings. I envisioned Uncle Horace's hefty frame reclining on this sofa, perhaps reading a book in front of a roaring fire.

The hearth was large enough to accommodate a cauldron. Not a fireplace one would expect to find in a third floor apartment. The bricks and mortar emitted a slight glow of magic. I glanced into the large, framed mirror mounted over the mantel, half expecting to see Uncle Horace reflected in the glass. Everything in this place reminded me of him. Being here, surrounded by his things, was oddly comforting like being enveloped once again in his warm embrace. Tears brimmed behind my lids.

Cupboard doors banged. I blinked and turned toward the kitchen.

"Mother?"

Horace's kitchen consisted of a row of cabinets mounted along the far wall. A butcher block counter, solid like my uncle, separated the kitchen from the living room. The counter and a couple of barstools substituted for a table and chairs.

Mother's gray-haired head bobbed up from behind the counter. "Yes?"

She checked inside the next cabinet, working her way down the row. Obviously, she was searching for something. Either that or she had gone a bit loopy.

"What are you doing?"

"Nothing," Mother said. "I already cleaned out most of the cupboards. I tossed out the chipped dishes and bent flatware. I don't think he entertained much, your uncle." A nervous laugh punctuated Mother's comment.

I shook my head then resumed exploring the apartment. I entered Uncle Horace's former study.

The setting sun streamed through a window, shedding a rectangle of light on a massive hickory desk with an uphol-stered office chair, the kind on wheels that swiveled. The claw-footed desk was identical to the one downstairs in Jack's office. Built-in bookcases spanned two walls, their shelves warped from the weight of the books they'd held. The shelves were empty now, barren in the fading sunlight. In fact, the whole room seemed lifeless without all of my uncle's books, knick-knacks, and clutter. What had hap-pened to Uncle Horace's library?

"Mother?" I called toward the living room. "Where are Uncle Horace's books?"

Mother bustled into the study. She glanced over her

shoulder into the living room. Then she turned to me with a vague smile.

"What did you say, dear?"

"The books?" I gestured toward the empty shelves. "What happened to all of Uncle Horace's books?"

"I gave the complete collection to Jack."

"You did what?" I gaped at Mother. "Without asking me?" How could she have given away Uncle Horace's library without asking first?

"Well, he was very interested." Mother shrugged. "I thought it a nice gesture, him being your business partner and all."

"I'll bet he was interested." I huffed and crossed my arms over my chest. I glared at Mother. "All those wonderful books."

"I'm sorry, dear." Mother patted my arm. "I've upset you. I didn't know you wanted them. Besides, I thought you'd need the shelf space for your own collection."

That much was true. My own books would fill several of these bookcases. I thought of all those cartons Aunt Elspeth and I had shipped from London.

I plopped down on the office chair and scooted it forward until my forearms rested on the bare desktop. My hands clenched into fists and then relaxed. What good would it do to raise a stink? Too late anyhow. The deed was done. I couldn't very well go asking for Uncle Horace's books back, could I?

For a moment, my thoughts lingered on Jack, imagining him sitting at this desk's twin, downstairs in the office.

"How are things going with Jack?" Mother said.

"Fine." I wasn't being evasive. It was the truth. My cheeks warmed. I don't know how it happened, but Jack and I had reached an understanding.

I stared down at the desktop. Fading sunlight cut across its wooden surface, dividing it into panels of light and shadow. Divided just like Bedlam Books. Jack had given me charge of part of the shop. My domain, over which I had complete jurisdiction, included the comics display, the children's books, and the former mystery section.

"I've taken over the children's corner." My fingers traced swirls of wood grain lit in orange light. "And Jack agreed to the tea shop. I'm going to put it right where the mystery section used to be."

"How nice," Mother said. "Horace always did like his afternoon cuppa. He would be thrilled."

I nodded. I'd deliberately left out the other half of the deal. My fingers migrated to a shadowy patch of desktop. In exchange, Jack had assumed authority for the rest of the departments. And I had agreed to butt out.

"What wonderful light in this room," Mother said. "This would make a marvelous bedroom for you. Of course, we'd have to get rid of that desk. We'll add a bed and perhaps a wicker chair with padded cushions for reading."

"Yes." I nodded.

"And a plant trolley by the window." Mother glanced in that direction, now engrossed in her decorating plans. "Dead nettle and toadflax always liven up a room. And maybe a delicate filigree of spider-spun curtains."

I stared at the bare window, picturing dainty webs of lace shimmering in the light. An iron-scroll trolley would nestle underneath, brimming with plants. The silvery foliage and tiny pink flowers of dead nettle would spill from a basket. Spikes of toadflax would leap from a vase like miniature pastel snapdragons. Truly, Mother had a knack for decorating.

"What a great idea," I said. "Aunt Elspeth has offered

to finance the tea shop, but I could use your help with decorating. Say you will."

I hadn't seen Mother this excited about anything since before my father went away. I knew I was doing the right thing.

"Why, of course, dear." Mother smiled. "I'd be happy to help. It's our family business after all."

Yes, our family business. Mother's and Aunt Elspeth's and mine. But she was only half right. I glanced down at the partitioned desktop and sighed. The rest belonged to Jack Wickham.

My hand reached for the top desk drawer and slid it open. Mother jumped backward as if she was expecting something to pop out. Then she leaned forward and inspected the inside. But the drawers were empty, all of them. What was she looking for?

"What was in Uncle Horace's desk?" I said.

"The usual." Mother's tone was cheery and nonchalant, but her fingers fidgeted with her blouse buttons. "Old legal papers, photographs, letters, and such."

"What did you do with them?"

"Threw most of them away. But we saved some of his things." She pointed toward the bedroom next door. "In the old steamer trunk in his bedroom."

"Can I see?" I pushed back from the desk.

"Of course."

She followed me out of the study and into my uncle's bedroom. This room also had been stripped of Uncle Horace's usual bric-a-brac. A king-sized bed with a feather mattress and a huge steamer chest were all that remained.

I headed for the trunk. Mother bustled to the closet, peeked inside, then shut the door again. Her shoulders sank a notch. Her whole body relaxed.

"The Banishing Charms must have worked," she muttered.

I hoisted open the trunk lid, but I didn't look inside. Instead I stared at my batty mother. Had she finally gone round the twist?

"What Banishing Charms?"

"Hmmm?" She approached the chest and looked inside. Pretending not to hear me?

"What Banishing Charms, Mother?" I planted my hands on my hips.

"Oh, would you look at this?" She plucked a framed photograph from the box and held up a faded picture of Gertrude, Horace, Mother, and Elspeth as children, lined up according to age. Clearly, she was avoiding my question.

My mouth opened to protest.

The aroma of Uncle Horace's pipe tobacco wafted upward. I spied his pipe, a pouch of tobacco, old photographs, letters, and strange little gizmos that hummed and whirred when touched. This trunk contained a veritable trove of Uncle Horace's wonderful things. I dropped to my knees. My hands dove into the treasure, my fingers rummaging through years of memories.

I pulled out a stack of postcards bound together with twine. I untied the string and flipped through the pile, each one from a different city, each one addressed to Uncle Horace in childish handwriting. My own handwriting.

"Look." I showed the postcards to Mother. "My postcards. He kept them."

"That's nice, dear."

Mother glanced at the postcards, then turned her attention back to the faded photograph of her siblings. I flipped through the cards in my hands.

"This one's from the year we spent in Boston." I held up a postcard of the swan boats in Boston's Public Garden.

"Salem," Mother corrected. "We spent the year in Salem."

She was right. Before he'd opened his London bookstore, Daddy had been a traveling salesman for Wizard Widgets. Tops in sales for eleven years running, he'd boasted. We'd moved around a lot, mostly to little towns and isolated magi communities. I'd collected postcards everywhere we went.

I turned several cards to the bottom of the stack and stopped on one featuring a picturesque lighthouse on a windswept bluff. "Here's Land's End."

I flipped to the next. My index finger tapped a postcard depicting Big Ben.

"London." I sighed. "I think that was my favorite. Apart from the summers."

"Mmm." Mother nodded. "I liked the summers best."

Of course, she would. Before we moved to London, Mother and I would return here to Berkeley to visit her family every summer.

"Staying with Gertrude." Mother continued to stare at her picture, eyes growing misty.

I grimaced. "I liked it better when we stayed with Aunt Elspeth."

"Did it matter where we stayed? You spent all your time here with Horace in the bookstore anyway."

Mother was right. I grinned at the memory of my uncle and hours spent with him and all those wonderful books.

I flipped to the next card. Not a postcard, but a photograph of Daddy and his sailboat—a 25 foot Beneteau that he'd named Rhapsody. A used sailboat bought for a song, purchased when we still had money. Daddy loved that boat. But did he love me? Then why did he leave? Tears welled in my eyes.

"What's wrong?" Mother said.

"Nothing." I sniffled and looked away. I flipped the photograph to the back of the pack so she wouldn't see. But she did. I heard her gasp.

When the bookstore failed, my father left us both. Just sailed away in that stupid boat of his. No warning. No explanation. No forwarding address. My grip tightened on the cards, as if holding on could have made him stay.

"It's not your fault." Mother patted my shoulder. "You know that."

But it was my fault. He opened his London bookstore for me. For us. But the bookstore was my dream. Not his. Daddy was never the kind to remain in one place. He always seemed happiest when we were traveling.

I wiped my tears on my sleeve, bundled up the cards, and tossed them back in the trunk. I rummaged, searching for more treasures and better memories. My fingers closed on a silver frame, containing a picture of Uncle Horace holding what looked like a furry black slipper.

"What's this?" I showed Mother the picture.

"That's your uncle's dog."

A dog? I inspected the "slipper" in the photograph. I could just make out a pair of shiny, black eyes and a little nose under that mop of fur. Some kind of terrier. Imagine my huge uncle with a little lap dog.

"I didn't know Uncle Horace had a dog."

"He acquired it after we moved to London." Mother lowered her voice. "Well, it wasn't common knowledge, but it was his familiar."

"Uncle Horace had a familiar?"

My uncle had a magical companion? A guardian? Not

that it was unusual for magi to have familiars. After all, Aunt Gertrude kept a baby alligator. But familiars were so traditional, and there was nothing traditional about Uncle Horace.

"What magus keeps a dog as a familiar?" Mother shook her head. "A cat or a rat I could understand. Or even one of those pickled things he kept under the kitchen sink. But a dog? Imagine what people would say. They already thought he was a bit odd."

A canine was an unusual choice for a familiar. Dogs were so . . . well, plebeian. Man's best friend and all that. I pictured my great big uncle walking a little bitty dog. What an incongruous sight. I giggled. How utterly perfect.

"What was his name?" I said.

"Mac-something . . . something Scottish." Mother pressed her fingers to lips. "MacTeague, that was it. Oh, Horace loved that mangy mutt."

Mother stared over the lid of the trunk. Her eyes widened. Her face paled. I twisted to see what had captured her attention. Something stirred from under the down comforter on Horace's king-size bed. The lump slunk toward us under the covers.

"Hell's bells," Mother whispered, backing away from the trunk and the end of the bed. "I thought I'd gotten rid of that thing."

One by one, the pieces came together. Mother's cupboard inspection, her nervousness, the Banishing Charms. She'd been trying to eradicate some horror. My eyes fixed on the migrating lump. That horror.

A flash of white protruded from under the downy covers. A pile of bones tumbled off the bottom of the bed and clattered to the floor, a skeleton about the size of a small domestic cat, but with a stubby tail which wagged to and fro.

The framed picture slipped from my fingers back into the trunk. I slammed the lid closed and scrambled to my feet.

The creature bounded toward me. Its jaw hinged open, exposing sharp canines. I shrieked and sprinted out of the bedroom. The assembly of bones bolted past Mother and scrambled after me into the living room, its claws clicking and skidding on the floorboards.

"Stand back." Mother raised her hand and pointed at the possessed skeleton. "I'll get rid of it once and for all."

I gasped. Sparks danced on Mother's fingertips as she chanted an incantation. The bony beast skidded to a halt halfway between us. It regarded Mother with its head cocked to one side like an inquisitive hound. Its hind end shimmied, the stubby tail wagging like a metronome on steroids.

"Wait." I shouted and waved at Mother. "Don't. I think it might be friendly."

At the sound of my voice, its skull turned to face me. I could see faint traces of shiny black eyes in its empty sockets. I could imagine its panting tongue hanging over the ivory jawbone.

"MacTeague?" I said.

"Horace's dog?" Mother whispered.

I nodded. "Or what's left of him."

Mother studied the skeletal creature. Sparks extinguished. Her extended arm dropped to her side.

"Come here, MacTeague." I slapped my thigh.

The wagging assembly of bones bounded toward me. He jumped up and pawed at my knees. The vertebrae on his neck stretched as he sniffed me. I bent down to pet his skull, feeling the soft, wet lick of a phantom tongue on my hand.

"See, he knows his name." I looked up at Mother. "So this was the skeleton in Uncle Horace's closet? This is why you've been looking in all the cupboards?"

"Well." Mother's cheeks pinked. "You would too if that nuisance kept popping out of closets at you. It gave me quite a fright. You're not honestly thinking of keeping him, are you?"

"I might," I said. "I think I'll call him 'M.T.' for short." I snickered at my own joke.

"A skeleton dog as a familiar? Imagine." Mother clucked her tongue and gave me a stern look reminiscent of Aunt Gertrude. "I'm going to clean the kitchen."

"M.T. and I will tackle the bath." I scooped up the skeletal pup in one arm and grabbed for the scrub bucket with the other, then marched to the bathroom.

I sat MacTeague down on the mosaic tile floor and surveyed the bath. A claw-footed porcelain bathtub in the middle of the room gleamed. Apparently, Mother had already tackled that. But a patina of grime stained the ceramic tiles on the walls and floor. Mildew blackened the grout lines between them. I dumped bristle brushes and sponges from my scrub bucket and refilled it with warm sudsy water.

"*Ablutus.*" I whispered the incantation and beckoned to the pile of cleaning implements.

Brushes sprang to life and dove into the bucket of water. Then they leapt out again and began scouring the floor. MacTeague gamboled among them, chasing first one then another, until his bony snout was covered in soap bubbles. He shook himself from nose to tail. Bones rattled. Water droplets would have sprayed the room if he'd had any fur.

A soap bubble dislodged from his nose and hung suspended in air. I could only imagine MacTeague's playful bark, as he had no vocal chords left. The only sounds were my whispered incantation, the rhythmic swish of the brushes, and the click of his toes pattering on tile.

Then something like a moan resonated in the bathroom. My whispered words hushed. The spell broke. Brushes stopped scrubbing and leapt back into the bucket. Sudsy water sloshed over the top, pooling on the tiles.

I heard the ghostly groan again. MacTeague cocked his head to one side, listening. Then he padded to the sink and pawed at the pipes. He sat down and lifted his head as if howling.

The haunting sound traveled the pipes, carried up from somewhere below. What could make such a racket? A ghost? A ghoul?

"Mother?" I poked my head out of the bathroom into the living room.

Mother stood in the middle of the room, directing a broom while it swept the floor. The broom whisked a pile of dirt into a waiting dustpan. Mother turned to face me.

"Is there a ghoul in the bathroom?" I said.

"No." Mother stared. "What makes you think that?"

"There's a strange moaning noise coming from the pipes."

"One moment, dear." Mother glanced behind her, just as the broomstick swept something under the living room carpet. "Oh no, you don't."

Mother waved her hand. A corner of the carpet lifted, exposing a sizeable pile of dirt. The dust vanished, and the miscreant broom toppled to the floor.

Mother followed me into the bathroom. I pointed to

the pipes under the sink, the source of the strange baritone hum. Mother laughed.

"That's no ghoul," she said. "That must be Jack singing."

"That's not possible." I shook my head. "The shop is closed. Anyway, sound couldn't possibly carry up two floors."

"Two floors? Don't be silly, dear. Jack lives downstairs in the second floor apartment."

"Wha—what about Mrs. Hastings?" I sputtered.

"Mrs. Hastings? She's been dead for years."

"What? So how long has Jack...?" I couldn't even finish the sentence. I jabbed my finger toward the floor and the apartment below.

"He moved there about a year ago," Mother said.

How did I not know this? I stared down at the floor, imagining a bathroom in the apartment below. I heard the water running and recognized the off-key song of a tone-deaf baritone. Jack down there, naked, singing in the bathtub? I could feel the heat flaming my cheeks. I must have turned three shades of red.

Chapter Twelve

Bad Boys

Mother and I spent the night in Uncle Horace's apartment, despite my discomfort at living in such close proximity to Jack. After all, my mother and aunts owned the building. We had every right to be here. Given our current financial straits, Mother and I couldn't turn down free rent. Where Jack chose to live was none of my concern.

The next morning as I left the apartment, I heard Jack's footsteps descending the back stairs below me. He was bound to find out sooner or later that we'd moved into Uncle Horace's apartment. Why should I hide it? Nonetheless, I paused on the upper landing, frozen like a rabbit caught in the crosshairs of a hunter's gun. After his footsteps faded, I tiptoed down the stairs and slipped through the back door of Bedlam Books.

I glimpsed Jack marching toward the front of the store, presumably to open the shop for business. My feet beat a path in the opposite direction toward the newly-relocated children's section. My domain. I had boxes of picture books to unpack and shelve, the same ones that Jack had packed up yesterday.

In passing, I glanced at bookshelves filled with ghost stories and tales of horror for our young adult readers. Overhead, the fluorescent lights crackled with static, flickering on and off. Simulated thunder rumbled. Dangling cobwebs brushed sticky threads against my face.

One aisle over, I arrived at the new children's section for our smallest readers. Here, the bookcases created a cozy corner much like my secret hiding place. The lights in this area glowed rosy pink. Bright-colored cushions lay in a willy-nilly heap to provide seating for the children. I grabbed a cushion from the pile, knelt, plucked picture books from the open cartons, and arranged them on the lowest shelves.

A copy of *Mother Grime's Nasty Rhymes* tumbled from a cardboard box and fell open on the floor. A beanstalk sprouted from the page, its leafy stem spiraling toward the ceiling.

> *Jack Splat, the thieving brat,*
> *Had nothing but a bean,*
> *He grew a vine,*
> *Then up did climb,*
> *To rob the giant clean.*

Clinging to the vine was a miniature boy no bigger than my thumb, a tiny golden goose tucked under his arm. The handsome lad puckered up and blew me a kiss. I grinned. Bad boys were so hard to resist.

A dark shadow fell over my picture book. The lad scampered down the vine, which wilted and disappeared back into the page. Thunder rumbled from the next aisle. I looked over the top of the book to a pair of creased trousers.

My eyes followed the sharp creases upward past a starched oxford shirt to the astonished face of Jack Wickham.

"Cory?" he said. "I didn't hear you come in."

The doorbell chimed, announcing a new visitor. Jack glanced toward the front of the shop. Obviously, he had expected me to come through the front door this morning.

"I was in early today." I plucked *Mother Grime* from the floor. "Setting up the new children's section."

My eyes looked away, focusing on the task at hand. I rearranged the books on the shelf and displayed *Mother Grime,* cover facing outward. I extracted several more picture books from the carton.

"Of course," he said. "Well ... er ... carry on."

I listened for the sound of Jack's wingtips retreating across the floorboards. At the entrance to the children's corner, he paused and glanced back at me, frowning. His brow crinkled. Then he disappeared around the next bookcase.

"May I help you?" I heard him say.

"I'm looking for the young woman who works here," a female voice said.

"That would be Miss Smyth," Jack said. "She's over in the children's section. I can take you there."

"Not necessary," the unfamiliar voice replied. "I'll find her myself."

A strange woman looking for me? What could she want? I had an inkling. My fingers groped for the romance novel hidden in the pocket of my work apron.

I jumped up and peered from the children's section to see a middle-aged woman striding toward me. She toted an enormous handbag and wore a wide-brimmed hat trimmed in flowers and satin, a fancy hat one rarely sees except on

British monarchs. She carried herself with a confident, determined air, very much like Aunt Gertrude.

Jack didn't follow her, but stared with brooding eyes. He fingered the scar above his lip.

"Miss Smyth?" The stranger extended both hands to me. "Tallulah Price."

"Nice to meet you." I nodded and smiled. I offered my right hand, expecting a handshake.

She tucked me under her arm as if we were long-lost friends, instead of new acquaintances. She steered me back into the children's section, out of sight of Jack's curious stare.

I heard the door chime. Good. Another customer.

"You sell romances," she whispered. More a statement than a question. "I'm interested in buying."

She shook her huge handbag and flashed a wad of bills. A buyer for my romances. Clearly, I'd underestimated the allure of the forbidden, and the inability of a woman with a secret to keep her mouth shut. What right did I have to complain, especially when our bookstore stood to profit?

"Do you have Nigella Plume's *Dark Seductress*?" she said.

"I'll have to check my stock," I said. "Is there anything else I can get for you while I'm there?"

"What do you have by Desiree DuBois?"

"I'll see." I nodded and ducked out from under her wing. "Please wait here."

Back in my secret corner, I sandwiched four romances—the Nigella Plume and three different Desiree DuBois titles—between two large children's picture books and smuggled the lot past Jack. Thankfully, he was distracted by the new customer. Tallulah Price purchased all four romances, paid in cash, and carried the books out in her oversized handbag. I grinned and crinkled the bills in my apron pocket. Another satisfied customer.

Despite Jack's assertions that enchanted romances were a dime a dozen, ours was the only shop for miles around that sold them. Tallulah would be back. I was certain of it. A woman must have her romance.

I made my way to the front of the shop to ring up the purchase properly, update the inventory log, and deposit the cash in the till. A young man in a black leather jacket, blue jeans, and boots stood near the counter. He swiveled to face me, a mop of straight black hair framing his face. His eyes were all warmth and sparkled with humor. His mouth broke into a crooked grin over a stubble beard.

"You work here?" he said.

"Yes." My heart fluttered faster than dragon wings. I'd forgotten why I'd come to the front desk in the first place. My feet were no longer touching ground.

"I'm Rod," he said, extending his hand.

"Cory." I shook his, feeling the calluses in his palm. A real man's hands. His grip was strong.

When I let go, his gaze darted away, but his lopsided grin lingered.

He appeared to study something on a nearby shelf. All the magazines froze in his presence. Nothing moved on their covers. He wasn't a magus, I could tell. But the spell he'd cast on me made my knees go weak.

"This is quite the place ya got here," Rod said, looking around. "You really went all out with the special effects."

He strolled over to the carved figurehead mounted on the end of an aisle and inspected it. He stood eye to eye with the carving. The figure remained stock still. Then its nose twitched.

"Ha. How's this work?" Rod looked over at me,

indicating the carved visage with his thumb. "Animatronics?"

"Something like that," I mumbled.

He turned back to the shelf, eyeing the magazine covers once again. As if to betray me, something flashed on the cover of *Teen Witch* magazine. "Be Beguiling: 20 Simple Beauty Spells" blinked in iridescent purple type. His eyebrows waggled. The grin widened.

"Are you a witch or something?" Rod leaned his shoulder against the bookcase in a casual stance, arms now crossed over his broad chest. His gaze slid over me, taking in my mousey brown hair, the beige sweater, my tan work apron, and black skirt. "You sure don't look like a witch."

His eyes settled on my face again. I could feel my color rise, flushing my cheeks. Wouldn't you know it? I couldn't think of a single intelligent retort. The heat had melted my tongue.

"So?" Rod shot me a cocky grin. "You got a wand or something?"

"Oh, no," I said, as my tongue loosened. "Too much trouble. You know wizards and their wands. Always comparing. Fighting over whose is the biggest. And bragging about who knows how to use it ..."

Rod erupted in a great, barking laugh. His eyes sparkled and danced. What had I said? Realization dawned, as my brain spooled back the conversation. My innocent banter mistaken for ... Oh, toadstools.

Then I noticed Jack standing nearby. How long had he been there? How much had he overheard? Plenty, judging from the expression on his face. The look he gave me would have stopped a charging werewolf in its tracks and sent it limping away with its tail tucked between its legs.

My words shriveled on my tongue. Waves of chagrin

washed over my face. I could not look Rod in the eye, but stared down at my shoes, wishing that I could shrink into the floorboards.

"Well, gotta go," Rod said, after what seemed like an ice age. "See ya around, Cory."

My eyes flicked up. Rod ambled toward the door. I watched his retreating form, his broad-shouldered back in the smooth leather jacket. What was he doing here? He didn't seem like the bookstore type. I wanted to call out to him, but I couldn't summon a single word.

I caught sight of his wink and that cocky grin. I waved goodbye as he disappeared behind the closing door. My body melted into the closest bookcase. My sweater felt too tight, too warm. I fanned my flushed face.

Jack sidled over next to me, until our shoulders almost touched. He straightened the books on the nearest shelf, but didn't look at me.

"You can't be serious," he said, keeping his voice low. "Him?"

"Why do you care?" I said. I thought of Voyant with her low-cut blouse and her fawning looks. "You have Claire."

"What?" Jack faced the books, not me. But I still caught the momentary look of confusion that flashed across his face. Then muscles in his jaw worked. "Don't change the subject. He's a plebeian. He's not one of us."

"Why does that matter?" I faced Jack and planted my hands on my hips.

"You know why." His head snapped up. His icy stare sucked away any lingering heat from my encounter with Rod.

"Oh, come on." I shook my head. How could Jack be so old-fashioned? "This is the twenty-first century. This is Berkeley. We've lived side by side with plebeians for decades now." I jabbed my finger toward the street outside. "No one even bats an eye at the tarot card reader next door or the spiritualist down the street." I waved my hand toward the carved visage on the bookcase. "He thought Monty here was some sort of animation."

"Animatronics, yes, I know." Jack's eyes narrowed, blue clouding over into steely gray. Tension built with each word. "That's precisely my point. He didn't believe you were a witch. As long as he can come up with a logical explanation for the things he sees, he won't be bothered by them. But what happens when he sees something he can't explain?"

"Nonsense." I waved Jack away and turned to go. "People are more open-minded these days. Besides, who said he's coming back."

"Oh, he'll be back." Jack seized my wrist.

Where his strong fingers circled my arm I felt a jolt of electricity. I twisted to face him. He released me and shuffled away a half step, as if aware that he'd crossed some sort of invisible line. He cleared his throat and swallowed. His Adam's apple bobbed above the crisp collar and tie. Mr. Unflappable looked distinctly flustered.

"No, they aren't," he said, his voice tight. "Not as open-minded as you think."

He pivoted and marched down the aisle on some errand or other. Bewildered, I watched him go. My fingers migrated to the place where he'd touched me. My skin still tingled as if he'd awakened some latent magic there.

Chapter Thirteen

Credentials

The next day, I finished rearranging the children's corner and proceeded to the former mystery section. Mother and Aunt Elspeth were to meet me there at noon to discuss plans for the tea shop. I glanced at my watch. A quarter to twelve.

A quick scan of the mystery section confirmed that Mother and Aunt Elspeth had not yet arrived. A young man sheathed in a black leather jacket stood with his back to me, browsing comic books from the lone rack. Strangely, no snickering laughter sounded from the magazines. Muscled titans on the covers stood stationary. Could it be . . .?

I edged closer for a better view. Dark hair obscured his face, bent over an open comic book. He shifted. His head turned, revealing a strong jaw flecked with a stubble beard.

"Rod," I said out loud, although I hadn't meant to. Jack had been right. He did come back. What was he doing here?

Rod looked up from the comic book in his hands,

straight at me. Hell's bells. Caught staring. Warmth flooded my cheeks.

"See anything you like?" I said, hoping he would mistake my curiosity for attentive service.

A spark lit his brown eyes. His face broke into a jovial grin. He laughed, a deep chuckle. What had he found so funny? It didn't appear to be the comic book.

The words I'd spoken spooled in my brain. *See anything you like?* Oh, toadstools. Another pick-up line.

"I meant the books, of course." Heat radiated from my cheeks.

"Yeah." The lopsided grin widened on Rod's face. He glanced down at the comic in his palms, then back up at me. "This one's pretty good."

I nodded, grinning like an idiot, almost as if a hex had rendered me mute.

An awkward silence filled the space between us. My ears burned. Several aisles over in the young adult section, thunder rumbled. The shop bells chimed a prolonged ring.

I glanced toward the front door. My tongue loosened. I turned back to Rod.

"Please excuse me," I said. "That must be my mother and aunt. They're supposed to meet me here today."

I hurried toward the front of the shop, eager to escape my embarrassing encounter with Rod. Normally, Jack would be working the front desk, where he could greet any new arrivals. But I didn't hear his baritone voice. Only a single set of approaching footsteps and the soft tinkle of bells.

Pungent odors of garlic, onions, and something unidentifiable filled the shop. My nose wrinkled. Would Jack allow food among his precious books? I'd never even seen him eat in the shop. I rushed over to greet the newcomer, rounded the first bookshelf, and almost smacked right into her.

"Madam V–Voyant?" I sputtered.

She straightened when she saw me, drawing herself up to her full height. Her chin jutted out, her dark eyes flashing.

"What are you doing here?" She clutched a covered ceramic dish to her bosom. I eyed the casserole. Ah, the source of the odor.

"I work here, remember?" I said.

"I'd heard you'd left." Her poisoned-apple lips turned down in a frown. "Where's Jack?"

"I don't know." I glanced toward the front desk. No sign of Jack. "Maybe he went to get some lunch. It is almost noon."

"I know that." She tossed her head, shaking the large hoop earrings that dangled from her lobes. "That's why I've come."

I hardly had time to process her comment when Jack approached, threading his way through the stacks from the direction of his office. He sniffed. His face puckered.

"What's that—?" The moment his eyes lit on Madam Voyant, his demeanor changed. The sour expression melted into one of polite congeniality. "Ah, Claire."

"Hello, Jack." Voyant tittered and fluttered her eye-lashes. "I've made you lunch. One my special recipes."

She tipped open the lid of her dish to give him a peek. An overpowering stink wafted anew through the stacks. I wrinkled my nose again and drew back, glimpsing the contents of her dish—a mixture of pearl onions and garlic cloves floating in a viscous, stringy green glop. Like eyeballs floating in snot.

"Ah." Jack shuffled a half-step backward. "You

shouldn't have." The oddest expression, a sort of stiff-lipped smile transfixed his face.

"I insist." Voyant pushed the casserole into Jack's hands. Her scarlet lips curled. "I made it especially for you."

"Thank you," he said, the forced smile tightening his lips. "I'll enjoy this . . . um . . . savory lunch later."

"I was hoping we could enjoy the meal together." Voyant cozied up next to him. She walked her painted nails up his bicep. He inched away, restoring a little space between them.

"I'm sorry, I can't," he said in a tone that I now recognized as his polite shopkeeper's voice. "I'm working. Perhaps some other time."

His gaze darted here and there, as if looking for a place to dispose of the vile dish. Could I blame him? Her casserole in our bookshop? The stench alone would drive away business.

"I'll just put this in the office for you, Jack. Okay?" I took the covered bowl from his hands. He did not resist.

Voyant's grin soured. Before she could object, I sped away toward Jack's office. I could feel the heat of her glare boring into my back. Had my impulsive move been a mistake? Imagine what she would say to Jack next. Would she spill my secret about the romance novels?

The shop bells tinkled again.

"Good afternoon, Jack dear." Mother's voice.

"Good afternoon, Mrs. Smyth, Mrs. Kingston." Jack's reply.

"What is that terrible smell?" Aunt Elspeth said. "Has someone run over a skunk?"

Saved by my relatives. Voyant wouldn't dare tattle on me in front of them. Not when they would take my side against her. I exhaled, only now aware that I'd been holding my breath.

Alone in the office, I placed the ceramic dish on Jack's spotless desk, making sure the lid was on tight and its icky contents contained. Madam Voyant or her casserole, I didn't know which was worse. I shuddered.

A much earlier conversation with Aunt Elspeth popped into my head. *Jack's not interested in her. Rebecca wasn't even cold in the grave, when she was all over Jack with her casseroles.* My aunt's words suddenly made sense. So it was true! Hadn't I just witnessed Jack's reaction? He wasn't interested in Madam Voyant.

I glanced over at the photograph of Rebecca Burgin, Jack's deceased fiancée, sitting on the shelf behind his desk. My mind replayed the rest of that conversation with Aunt Elspeth. *Becca. Killed in car accident. Broke his heart.* That he kept her picture up was proof enough that he'd loved her. It was the only item of a personal nature in his office.

If the other things my aunt had told me that day were true, then ... *He likes you, you know.* Her words that had seemed so preposterous on the plane, now seemed plausible. Was it possible that Jack had feelings for me? My heart leapt like bubbles boiling up in a cauldron. But my eyes could not look away from the picture of Rebecca. Perhaps Jack was not ready to love again? Just as quickly, the bubbles burst.

I closed Jack's office door on my way out. Mother and Aunt Elspeth waited for me by the register, conversing with Jack. Madam Voyant hovered by his side. I caught the words "Horace" and "apartment." My steps slowed.

"What of it?" Mother said.

"Well," Jack said. "I heard you upstairs, cleaning out Horace's apartment. Your sister, Gertrude, indicated that you would be looking for a new tenant. Claire here has expressed interest."

Madam Voyant? In Uncle Horace's apartment?

"Over my dead body." I had whispered the words before I could stop myself.

"What?" Jack pivoted to face me. Oh, rats! Had he heard me? Or worse yet, had Voyant?

"I–I only said 'Oh, my . . .'" Once again warmth crept up my cheeks.

Aunt Elspeth's lips curled in an arch grin. She was closest to me, and I knew she'd heard me perfectly well. The conspiratorial glint in her eye revealed that she shared my opinion.

"She said, 'Oh, my, what a pity.'" Aunt Elspeth looped her arm about my waist and pulled me into the circle of conversation. "You see, Jack, you're too late. We've already found the perfect tenant for that apartment."

"Oh?" Jack's voice inflected with surprise.

"Cory, here." Aunt Elspeth squeezed me in a sideways hug.

"Is that so?" Jack's gaze refocused on me. His blue eyes changed to misty gray.

Voyant said nothing. Her lips puckered. Her eyes narrowed. The look she gave me would curdle cream. Oh, no. First, her casserole and now this. If I didn't say something quick, she'd rat me out to Jack for sure.

"Not just me," I said. "We . . . Mother and I have taken Uncle Horace's apartment. After all, she and my aunts own the building."

"You moved in?" Jack said.

"Yes," Mother nodded. "Just the other day."

Jack glanced from Mother to me. The scar above his

upper lip twitched. If I didn't know better, I'd think he was stifling a smile.

"I see," Madam Voyant said, her voice suddenly silky. Her eyes slotted, her sideways glances like daggers aimed in my direction. "I won't keep you any longer. Please excuse me."

Jack escorted Voyant to the door, then marched off in the direction of his office. To dispose of her snot-and-eyeball stew, no doubt. Imagine eating that disgusting concoction. My stomach flip-flopped at the thought.

"Oh, Cory." Aunt Elspeth tugged on my sleeve, bringing me back to the conversation. She motioned to the front of the shop where Jack had moved the literary classics. "This would make a lovely setting for your tea shop. Look at the light. Your tables would be visible through the front window."

"No, not there." I shook my head. Jack would never agree to that. Per our arrangement, the front of the store was his territory. "Come with me."

I led Mother and Aunt Elspeth toward the back of the store and the former mystery section. To my astonishment, Rod was still there reading comics. Attracting his attention was the last thing I wanted to do, in light of my earlier silly schoolgirl behavior. I focused on Mother and Aunt Elspeth.

"I was thinking we would set up shop here." I gestured to indicate a patch of open floor surrounded by empty bookshelves. "Perhaps three or four tables with chairs. There's room for the teas and such on those shelves over there." I pointed to a large built-in bookcase on the side wall.

Aunt Elspeth planted her hands on the hips of her slimming black trousers. One tweezed eyebrow rose. Her lips pursed.

"The light is not as good," she said. "It doesn't have the ambiance."

"Oh, Elspeth." Mother turned a scolding eye on my aunt and nudged her with an elbow. "I think it will be fine. The lighting can be improved and we can provide all the ambiance it needs. Can't you picture the canisters of fragrant tea and a row of porcelain teacups?"

"Yes." The hard look on Aunt Elspeth's face softened. "But she'll need cupboards and a sink."

Cupboards and a sink? I'd never stopped to think about renovations.

"Won't that be expensive?" I leaned in toward Aunt Elspeth and Mother, and lowered my voice to a whisper. "We don't have any mon—"

"Don't worry, Cory." Aunt Elspeth put her arm around my shoulder. "I told you I'd finance the renovations. Whatever it costs. After all, this is our tea shop."

"It'll be fine, dear." Mother smiled. "Now about these renovations..."

Rod sauntered over. His brawny presence overshadowed my short, stout mother.

"Didn't mean to eavesdrop," he said. "Renovation is my business. We've been working a job up the street." He hitched his thumb over his shoulder. "I've been checking out the area on my lunch break. Maybe I can help."

My mother and aunt turned to face him.

"Aunt Elspeth, Mother," I said. "This is Rod."

"Rod Tyler." He shook Mother's hand and offered his business card with the other.

I peered at the card he'd given her. Mahoney and Tyler Construction. He was a contractor. That would explain his burly build. My eyes skimmed his muscular physique robed in leather jacket, t-shirt, and jeans. He didn't look old enough to own his own business. In his early twenties maybe.

"Elspeth Kingston." My aunt slipped her hand into his. "Pleased to meet you, Mr. Tyler." A sly smile curled her lips. "Cory, you've been keeping secrets. Keeping him all to yourself, are you?"

"Auntie, please," I blurted. Did she have to say that? "Rod and I only just met yesterday."

She batted her eyelashes in a manner that would have rivaled Lady Gwendolyn's. Her face lit up. Clearly, his finer attributes were not lost on her. Rod grinned and laughed at the compliment.

"I see the family resemblance." He winked at me. "You three look like sisters." Rod was a charmer.

"Oh, I like him, Cory." Mother beamed at him.

Not Mother too? I had expected my aunt to respond that way, but my level-headed mother? My own face had grown so hot that I could have melted into the floorboards.

"So, Mr. Tyler, what do you recommend?" Aunt Elspeth looped her arm through his and latched on to his muscled bicep.

"It's Rod." He grinned at her, then walked her to the built-in bookcase and inspected the shelves. "Installing cupboards and a countertop would be no problem. I'll have to demolish this bookcase."

"And a sink?" Mother said, as she and I trailed after them.

"That might be more of a problem." Rod thumped his knuckles on the back wall of the bookcase. "I'll need to open up the wall and run some pipes for the plumbing. Any idea what's behind here?"

I shook my head. Mother stepped to the left a pace or two and pointed up at the ceiling.

"The kitchen in the apartment above should be somewhere around here," she said. "There would be plumbing for that, now wouldn't there?"

"Yep." Rod nodded. He stomped a booted foot on the wooden floorboards. "What's below?"

"The basement," Mother said.

"A basement?" Rod grinned. "I like that. No crawling into tight spaces. If I could have a look, then I'll know where I can run the water lines."

"What can you do about the lighting?" Aunt Elspeth said.

Rod looked up. Fluorescent fixtures stretched across the ceiling in long rows. The tubes gave off different colors, depending on department. The mystery section was bathed in pale purple light. Several of the tubes appeared to have burnt out. Funny, I hadn't noticed that before.

"Those fixtures look pretty old," Rod said, studying the ceiling. "Degroot's with a 36 inch baffle. Stopped making those in the eighties."

I couldn't fathom what a baffle or dig roots might be. But if they'd stopped making them, that didn't bode well for our plans. Our café needed lights.

"Oh, no." My fingers twisted my work apron. "Does that mean we'll have to replace all the lights too?"

"Not to worry." Rod winked again. "I have a buddy in demolition. There isn't a light fixture I can't get for you."

"But if they don't make them anymore," I said. "Won't it be expensive? We can't afford—"

"For you, I promise a real good price." He reached over and swiped his thumb across my cheek. His flirty move set my face ablaze with heat.

"When can you start?" Aunt Elspeth smiled up at Rod and batted her eyelashes.

What? Was Aunt Elspeth really going to hire him on the spot? Granted, the prospect of seeing a lot more of Rod held appeal. My fingers drifted to the place on my cheek where he'd touched me. Even so, all this was happening too fast.

I shot a sideways glance at Mother and caught her eye. The vertical creases on her brow indicated that she was concerned too. Aunt Elspeth was getting carried away.

"Elspeth," Mother said. "I'm sure that Rod is a fine contractor, but we'll need to get other bids."

"Sure. No problem." Rod's warm brown eyes focused on Mother then me. A confident grin broke over his face. "Take your time. Now if I could take a look down in the basement, I could give you a quote."

"Of course, dear." Mother beckoned him to follow her. "Come with me."

She bustled off toward the rear of the shop and the door to the basement. Rod strolled after her. I listened for the sound of his work boots tromping down the aisle. When I was certain that he'd reached the back stairs, I turned to Aunt Elspeth.

"What are you doing?" I seized my aunt's arm and shot her a look that would have scared the warts off a toad. "You're not serious about hiring him, are you?"

"Well, I might." Aunt Elspeth shrugged. Her index finger tapped her ruby lips. "He seems competent. And I am financing the renovations."

"Don't you think you're being a bit hasty?" I said. "We know nothing about him."

A rustling noise came from behind the nearest bookcase. I turned as Jack stepped around the corner into the mystery section, holding a pair of hardcover books. Spying on us?

"I couldn't help overhearing," he said. "I agree with Cory. I'm not sure it would be wise to hire him."

Really? This was a private conversation. I hadn't asked for his opinion.

"I didn't mean that she shouldn't hire him," I said. "Only that we should check his credentials first."

"You do that." The muscles in Jack's jaw tightened. He looked away from me and addressed my aunt. "I'm certain his credentials will be found lacking. In case you hadn't noticed, Mrs. Kingston, he is a plebeian."

A plebeian. Not that old argument. How could Jack be so narrow-minded? I thrust out my chest and tipped my chin up. I stared at Jack eye to eye . . . well, eye to nose.

"This is a construction job," I hissed. "I don't think his lack of magical ability has any bearing here."

"Shhh." Aunt Elspeth bumped my shoulder. She stared between me and Jack. Her tweezed eyebrows danced. "Here he comes now. And don't his credentials look marvelous?"

Rod strolled up the aisle right behind Mother. I looked back at Jack. His mouth opened to argue, then clamped shut. His lips formed a thin, tense line. His eyes grew stormy and sullen.

Standing side by side, Jack and Rod were about the same height, both tall and dark. But the contrast between them couldn't have been more obvious. Jack's body stiffened, buttoned-down and uptight, while Rod's easy air exuded devil-may-care charm.

"I've got what I need." Rod patted the breast pocket of his leather jacket. "I can work up a quote and drop it off. Say Monday?"

"Yes." I nodded. "That would be fine."

"Great." Rod flashed me a lopsided grin. "By the way, my company offers financing. Nothing down and no payments for the first sixty days. Here's my card, if you need to call me."

He pulled another business card from his pocket and handed it to me. Our fingers brushed. Electricity tingled like sparks from my fingers.

"Thanks." I could feel the blush rise over my cheeks.

"It was a pleasure meeting you, Rod." Aunt Elspeth gave his hand a playful squeeze. "I look forward to doing business with you."

"Same here." He squeezed Aunt Elspeth's hand in return, then shook Mother's. He winked at me.

I smiled. His offer of financing was appealing, especially given Mother's and my current monetary situation. With a loan, maybe we could shoulder some of the expenses ourselves. Then Aunt Elspeth wouldn't have to put up so much of her own money.

As Rod walked off, I watched his retreating bum in his perfectly-fitted jeans. I thought of all those hunky heroes on the covers of my romances. Aunt Elspeth was right. His credentials were marvelous.

Chapter Fourteen

Not as Dead as I'd Hoped

No sign of Rod this morning. Not that I really expected to see him before Monday, when he'd promised to have an estimate on the tea shop renovations. I wouldn't have minded another glimpse of his devil-may-care grin or his bum in those right-fitting jeans. Jack's jealous reaction was like frosting on a cake. What girl wouldn't be chuffed at having not one, but possibly two young men vying for her affections? I should have been giddy, except for a niggling premonition that something was about to go terribly wrong.

After the unpleasant encounter with her snot-and-eyeball casserole earlier this week, I was certain that we would receive another visit from Madam Voyant. Her tart frown and huffy departure told me all I needed to know. She was deeply disturbed by the news that I was not only still working here, but now living in close proximity to Jack. I knew that she was dying to tattle on me about the romance novels. Surely, she would corner Jack and spill my little secret.

My ears pricked up every time the shop door chimed. I listened for the swish of Voyant's many scarfs or the soft jingle of the bells on her skirts. I glanced over my shoulder at every footstep or foreign sound. But Madam Voyant never came.

At closing time, I was just about to gather up the day's receipts and empty the till when the shop bells tinkled one last time. Not Voyant. A blonde woman in a floral spring dress and heels trounced through the door.

"I'm sorry. We're closing," I said from behind the register.

"Oh, I'm not here for books," she said with a shake of her perky blonde curls. "I'm looking for Jack Wickham."

"I think he's in the office." I glanced in the direction of Jack's office then back at the vaguely familiar-looking young woman. What did she want with Jack? Like a black cat, my curiosity got the better of me. "I can take you there."

"No need." Her manicured fingers waved me off. "I know my way."

Without waiting for me, she flounced off in the direction of Jack's office. I took the next aisle over, moving faster in my flats than the clickety-clack of her high-heels, and reached his office door first.

"Jack?" I knocked on the already open door and peered inside. "Someone here to see you."

Jack looked up from his seat behind the large desk, just as the woman crossed the threshold. When he saw her, his mouth fell open and all the color leached from his face. The pen he was using dropped onto the open ledger.

"Hi, Jack," the woman said in a breathy whisper.

"Becca?" Jack's hoarse reply.

Becca? Rebecca Burgin? His dead ex-fiancée? I felt for the door frame behind me and listed against it.

"Yes, it's me. Your Becca." She stepped into the office and spun in place, giving him a 360 degree view. Like a model on a runway, she showed off her slim figure in the floral, knee-length dress. She stopped, now facing him again and raised her arms in a ta-da pose. "I'm back."

I gaped at the girl, comparing her to the one in the photograph behind Jack's desk. The woman in front of me was a dead-ringer for the blue-eyed blonde in the picture. And she was very much alive.

"But that's impossible." Jack swallowed hard, his Adam's apple bobbing over the collar of his crisp dress shirt.

"You're supposed to be dead, aren't you?" I blurted at doppelganger Rebecca.

"Obviously not." She turned and flashed me a dimpled smile. "Or I wouldn't be here right now."

"How?" Jack's brow crumpled, but his stormy eyes never left her.

"After the accident, the doctors told Mom and Dad that I wouldn't make it, but my Aunt Claire found someone else. A specialist. It was an experimental procedure. Very experimental."

I shook my head. None of this made sense. Aunt Elspeth told me that Rebecca Burgin had died. From Jack's wan pallor, I knew he believed that too.

"So you faked your own death?" I said, struggling to comprehend.

"No, I did die. Kinda. It's complicated. You wouldn't understand." She waved me off as if my question was inconsequential.

How do you 'kind of' die? What experimental treatment? Clearly, she was hiding something. Visions of Dr.

Frankenstein and his ill-fated monster filled my imagination. I half expected to see a pair of bolts holding her head on. But there were none visible on her long, smooth neck.

"Why didn't you tell me sooner?" Jack said. His voice cracked, betraying emotion normally kept in check.

"I'm sorry, Jack." Rebecca turned back to him and approached his desk. "I wanted to tell you, I really did. But the procedure was so risky and my recovery took so long. I didn't want to get your hopes up, in case it didn't work. I believed it would be better if you had thought I'd died."

"But all this time?" Jack's eyes searched her face. "A year. Claire never mentioned anything."

"I swore Aunt Claire to secrecy," Rebecca said. "I asked her to look after you and she did, didn't she?"

"Yes, she did." Jack nodded. "But I think she should have mentioned—"

"Wait a minute." I waved my hand and took a step forward. "'Aunt' Claire? Madam Voyant is your aunt?"

"Yes." In the look she gave me, I could finally see a family resemblance. There it was on her pink-painted lips. The poisoned-apple smile.

But now, at least something made sense. Madam Voyant's threats and her interest in Jack were not romantic at all. She would have known that Rebecca was still alive and planning to return to Jack. No wonder she wanted me out of the picture. She was protecting her niece's fiancé. From me.

I shook my head.

"Well, now I'm back." Rebecca sauntered around the desk to Jack's side, eased the ledger out of the way, and perched on the desktop facing him. She crossed her legs and ran her fingers up his sleeve. "Back with you, Jack. Back together just like old times. Now, we can pick up where we left off."

Rebecca back with Jack? My head spun with the revelation. I stared at the young blonde. She was only a year or two older, but we couldn't have been more different. Her form-fitting dress accentuated her trim figure. In my serviceable skirt and work apron, I must have looked frumpy and fat. I tugged on the collar of my blouse which suddenly felt tight. Petite, perky, perfect Rebecca. Why wouldn't he choose her over me?

I couldn't breathe. It was as if someone had sucked all the air out of my lungs. I didn't belong here. I had to get out.

I turned and bolted from the office. The day's receipts, the cash register, and the locking up would have to wait. Instead, my feet beat an urgent path straight toward the exit. The front door to Bedlam Books chimed a foreboding knell as it slammed shut behind me.

Peaceful and quiet, the Sage Library at the Center for Mystic Studies was the perfect place to collect my thoughts. No one would think of looking for me here. It was also the ideal spot to collect information and the only public library open after hours. It operated on the lunar calendar, closed during new and full moons.

I strolled among the archives housed in the basement of the Victorian structure. Shelves arranged in narrow rows surrounded me. Instead of books, these stacks were filled with crystal globes, each ball on a stand with a brass plate underneath. My eyes scanned the names of periodicals and dates etched on the plates. Where should I begin my search on Rebecca Burgin?

When digging for details, it seemed prudent to start with the clues I already had. I glanced toward the reference desk at the end of the aisle. A woman sat behind the desk, her head down, intent on her work. Her dark hair was plaited in a myriad of thin braids, each ending in a colorful bead. She jerked her head up, as if she'd sensed my unspoken request. Her face emerged through the curtain of braids.

"May I help you?" she said.

"Yes." I approached, coming close enough to read the nametag pinned to her blouse. Tamara Parks. "I'm looking for an obituary from about a year ago."

"Local newspaper?" Tamara said.

"Yes."

"*Tribune* or *Post*?"

"*Post*, I think." If Jack had been engaged to Rebecca, it seemed logical that she had magical abilities too. Therefore, her family would have chosen a magus publication for the obit. *The Witching Post* was far more likely than the *Oakland Tribune*.

I followed the reference librarian down a row of shelves. Her colorful print skirt swished down the narrow aisle, brushing against glass globes on one side. She stopped alongside a row of crystal orbs the size of bowling balls. Tamara seized a pair of horn-rimmed glasses dangling from a chain around her neck and propped them on her nose. She inspected brass plates through her tortoise-shell specs. I followed her gaze, reading the labels. *The Witching Post*, followed by a range of dates in increments of ten years.

Tamara selected a crystal ball from the shelf and led me to an empty carrel. She placed the ball in a circular depression carved into the desktop, presumably to keep the orb from rolling off the desk.

"Sit down." She motioned to the nearest desk chair. Then she pulled up another and sat next to me. "Name of the deceased?"

"Rebecca Burgin," I said.

Tamara leaned over the crystal and stroked its surface. She gazed into its cloudy interior. Inside the orb, words scrolled past in a blur of black ink like a ream of newsprint feeding through a printing press. The rolling slowed, then stopped. I blinked. Individual words came into focus. An index of some sort.

"I see three entries," Tamara said. "All about a year old. Which do you want?"

"All three, please."

Tamara tapped the orb. The scrolling began again. When the motion stopped, a news article floated into focus. Tamara leaned back in her chair to allow me a better view. I gazed into the sphere and read the article. An obituary dated just over a year ago.

Rebecca Anabelle Burgin, beloved daughter of Lois and Arthur Burgin, her young life cut far too short. Services to be held at Evergreen Mortuary . . .

No account of her life or reason for her death was given. Just a short announcement for the funeral. The dates on the obituary notice would have made her about nineteen years old at the time of death.

Oh, the name of the funeral home. *Evergreen Mortuary*. The same establishment in which my Uncle Horace's memorial had been held. My heart seized. No wonder Jack had been horrified at my uncle's funeral. Imagine mourning your fiancée and having to do the same with your business partner less than a year later. Then my aunts disrupted the service with their disgraceful row. Poor Jack.

If there had been a funeral, wouldn't there have been a body? I imagined Rebecca laid out in a casket like Uncle Horace had been. Or was this a memorial service, and not a funeral at all? But if there was no body, why hold a remembrance at a funeral parlor?

"And the other articles?" I said to the librarian, hoping they would answer my questions.

Tamara hunched over the crystal once more. More articles spun past, cycling backward through time. Seconds later, they stopped on another article. This one was an accident report.

A female passenger killed Sunday morning when the car she rode in crashed into Devil's Ditch has been identified by the Alameda County coroner's office as 19-year-old Rebecca Burgin.

Burgin, who lived in Berkeley, was riding in a white Mercedes-Benz that crashed about 1:24 a.m. The female driver and a second passenger were hospitalized with critical injuries. Burgin was pronounced dead at the scene ...

Despite the coroner's pronouncement, had Rebecca really died? The woman I'd seen less than an hour ago didn't look dead to me. What had really happened?

"Next article, please," I said.

With a few more spins, the third article appeared, a few months older than the previous one.

"An engagement announcement," Tamara said, sliding aside so I could look.

Mr. and Mrs. Arthur L. Burgin are pleased to announce the engagement of their daughter, Rebecca Anabelle, to Jonathan Wickham. The groom-to-be is the son of the late Robert M. Wickham and Mary Goodwill ...

Jonathan Wickham is currently attending Diablo University, studying business administration and English literature. He is an associate at Bedlam Books, an independent bookseller, Robert Wickham and Horace Knightly, props. A June wedding is planned.

I stared at the black and white photograph of the happy couple which accompanied the article. Dressed in a light-colored gown, Rebecca beamed at me from the photograph. Jack, his arms around his fiancée, was smiling, too. Not the sardonic half-smile I'd witnessed in the store, or a controlled twitch of his lip. This was a genuine, joyful grin of the kind I'd not seen on him since we were little.

Pain squeezed my chest as if something very black had stomped on my heart. Aunt Elspeth had been right about many things. Jack had loved, had been engaged, and had been happy.

If he'd had any feelings for me, that would all change now that Rebecca was back. Jack would never smile like that at me.

"Your boyfriend?" Tamara said.

"What?" I straightened in my seat.

"Jack?" Tamara studied my face as if reading from her archives. "Is he your boyfriend?"

"No." I shook my head. "Sweet Merlin, no."

I hadn't mentioned Jack's name. How could she know about him? I stared at Tamara's round face, peering back at me. She blinked and focused again on the globe, but I could feel her probing stare as if her eyes were still locked on mine. Hell's bells, she was a telepath.

"Your secret's safe with me." Tamara didn't say the words aloud. This time, I heard them in my head. "I get a lot of people checking up on their dates. New acquaintances, blind dates, even exes."

"Jack is not my boyfriend." I glared at her, but kept my voice even and low. "He's my business partner."

"Uh huh."

Her smile told me that she didn't believe a word I said. I bristled. How dare she read my mind.

"Anything else you'd like to see?" Still grinning, Tamara pointed a finger at the archives.

"No." I huffed. I didn't want to think about Jack anymore. Oh, but what about "Aunt" Claire?

"No wait! As long as you're looking." I prodded the crystal ball. "Are there any references to a woman named Voyant? V-O-Y-A-N-T."

The image in the crystal blurred once more. Articles scrolled past, accelerating into a gray slurry. The orb began to vibrate and hum. After a minute, the crystal went dark.

"No." Tamara looked up from the globe. "Nothing under that name."

"What about a business listing?" I said.

"Is it a magi-owned business?"

"You're the mind reader," I said, unable to control my annoyance. "You tell me."

"Hmmph." The self-satisfied look disappeared from Tamara's face. She snatched the crystal ball off the desk. "For that, you'll want the Better Broomstick Bureau. Second row. Third shelf."

"Thank you."

Tamara turned and swept down the aisle, carrying the *Witching Post* crystal. I sighed. On my own. At least I didn't have a nosy librarian peering over my shoulder. Or into my head.

Minutes later, I had retrieved the globe containing the records of the Better Broomstick Bureau and was seated back at my carrel. I gazed into the crystal sphere. Its interior remained dark. What had Tamara done to get this blasted thing to work?

I ran my fingers over the smooth, cool surface of the sphere. The glass warmed under my touch. A faint light glowed in the sphere's core, brightening with each stroke. Still no images.

Now what? Ah, I had to make a request. I glanced around, looking for Tamara. How close did she have to be to read my mind? I leaned forward until my lips almost touched the orb.

"Madam Voyant's Psychic Boutique." I whispered the name. A ridiculous precaution. Oh, well.

I stared into the depths of the crystal ball. An official-looking paper fluttered into focus. A business license. I'd done it.

Madam Voyant's Psychic Boutique, Claire Rumplethorpe, sole proprietress.

Rumplethorpe? I stifled a snort. I'd always known that Voyant was a stage name. But Rumplethorpe? No wonder she used an alias. I giggled.

My laughter evaporated the second I remembered that black and white engagement photograph of Jack with Rebecca. Oh, Jack. How could I have been so blind?

My fingers fumbled in my pocket and pulled out Rod's business card. Hmmm. I tapped my lip.

"Mahoney and Tyler," I whispered into the orb.

Voyant's license disappeared, replaced moments later by another. A contractor's license for Mahoney and Tyler. How odd. Why would Rod's business be listed with the Better Broomstick Bureau? There was no address listed on either the business card or the license, but the phone numbers matched. The license listed Michael Tyler and

Moll Flanagan Mahoney as co-owners. Tyler, same last name as Rod's. Could be a relative or something.

"Moll Flanagan Mahoney," I repeated. Flanagan, the name sounded familiar, but I couldn't quite place it. I knew I'd heard it somewhere before. I leaned back in my chair, waiting for the connection to surface.

Chapter Fifteen

I Told You So

Aunt Elspeth, Mother, and I signed a contract with Rod. Two days later, I stood outside the roped-off mystery section and watched as he ripped out the beautiful built-in bookcases to make way for our tea shop. Hardwood creaked and groaned, resisting Rod's prying crowbar and brute force. Sparks sputtered from the warping boards. Uncle Horace had used magic to put up these shelves. Rod couldn't see those shimmering ties, but I could. Charms that had tethered the bookcases to the wall flexed in opposition to Rod's muscle.

Magic snapped like brittle rubber bands. Spells, like everything else in the world, weaken over time. The bookcase cracked and splintered, breaking free from its anchored place on the wall. Something splintered in my heart, too. As if a piece of Uncle Horace had broken away with that bookcase.

I sniffed and blotted my damp cheek with my sleeve. Uncle Horace was Bedlam Books. Every inch of this bookshop contained some memory of him. Every change reminded me that he was no longer here. I blinked and turned away.

Jack had been standing right behind me. How long had he been there? Was he staring at me? Couldn't a girl have a private moment without him intruding?

"Change is hard," I murmured to Jack. I stepped away from the construction zone, so that Rod couldn't overhear us. Not that he could anyway over the noise he was making or the earbuds in his ears.

Jack's hand inched forward as if he intended to comfort me. He must have reconsidered, because halfway to my arm he yanked his hand back to his side. His fingers clenched.

"Change is inevitable," he said.

What a jerk. Why had I expected him to understand? Dirt hadn't even covered my uncle's grave, when Jack started making his "improvements" to the shop. I gritted my teeth.

Then the memory popped into my head of Rebecca perched on his desk and running her fingers up his sleeve. The account of her accident from last year's *Post* had read: *"19-year-old Rebecca Burgin . . . pronounced dead at the scene."* But the young woman who had waltzed into his office and back into his life was very much alive.

"Speaking of changes, how is Rebecca?" I said, affecting a casual tone.

"Fine." His stormy eyes darted away to focus on something on a nearby shelf.

Clearly, it wasn't fine. Curiosity got the better of me. I edged closer to him.

"It must have been quite a shock for you," I said, "having her come back like that without any notice."

"Yes." He nodded.

"I don't mean to pry, but . . ." I softened my voice to a whisper. "Was she really dead?"

"For a time."

"But then, how?" My eyes bored into him, searching for answers.

"Reanimation," he said, finally meeting my gaze.

"What?" I drew back. "But that's dark magic. Strictly forbidden."

"Oh, come on." He didn't even bother to hide his eye-roll.

You'd think I was the old-fashioned one. I bristled.

"But you're the one who's always talking about magic going wrong." I jabbed a finger at him, then gestured at the surrounding shelves. "No using magic in the shop and all that. Besides, reanimation has never worked." I thought of Dr. Victor Frankenstein and his ill-fated experiments.

"Yes, it has." Now, it was Jack's turn to bristle. He straightened and cast me a steely glare. "Your uncle did it."

"What?" My eyes widened. "When?"

"To his familiar."

My jaw couldn't have dropped any lower. How could Jack have known about MacTeague? Mother said that Uncle Horace told only a precious few about his dog. He'd even kept MacTeague a secret from me. Me, his favorite niece.

"Y–you know about MacTeague?"

"Of course." Jack huffed. "I was Horace's business partner."

I didn't know which was more shocking—that Uncle Horace had used forbidden magic on his pet or that he'd confided his secrets in Jack? Either way I could not accept that my uncle would deliberately do something bad.

"B-but that's different," I said, shaking my head. "Mac-Teague is a dog. Not a person."

"Person. Pet. What difference does it make? When you've lost something you ..." Jack swallowed his words with a gulp. I watched his Adam's apple bob over the crisp white collar as he looked away.

"Even so, reanimation is too risky. What if it went wrong?" I thought about my uncle's poor pooch, now mine. MacTeague been reduced to a jumble of white bones. No skin or fur. "It didn't really work with MacTeague. Not completely."

"Well, it worked this time." His reply was curt. Angry even. I knew I'd struck a nerve. Then he stalked off through the stacks.

Maybe Jack was right. I remembered Rebecca twirling in his office in her form-flattering dress. She certainly looked healthy. Despite appearances, I couldn't shake my niggling doubt. For his sake, I hoped I was wrong.

I retraced my steps to the mystery section and stared at the wall where the bookcases used to be. The beautiful old shelves had been transformed into a stark space marred with gouges and peeling paint. Instead of the comforting scent of paper and leather bindings, the smell of plaster dust made my nose wrinkle. The bookcases themselves had been reduced to a pile of lumber at Rod's feet. Broken. My fingers fumbled for the romance novel in my apron pocket and gripped it like a talisman.

These last months had been filled with so many changes. Like waves washing over me, one after the other. First, Daddy leaving us, then Uncle Horace's death, then having to leave school, then Jack's alterations to the bookstore, and now Rebecca. My fingers trembled. Here I was, making changes too.

I stared at the pile of splintered boards that had once been bookcases and shook my head. The damage was already done. Too late to turn back now. We had signed a contract. I thought of my plan to sell tea, romance novels, and mysteries. I imagined cupboards filled with tea canisters where the barren wall now stood. My changes were nothing like Jack's. I had to do this for Mother and me. I wasn't destroying Uncle Horace's legacy. I was keeping his bookstore and his memory alive.

Two weeks had passed since Rod had torn out the bookcases and hauled them away. I stared at the naked wall in the roped-off mystery section. A rectangular hole had been cut in the drywall about a foot above the floor. For the rough plumbing, Rod had explained. In the gap, I could see wooden framing, but nothing else. No pipes anyway. Two weeks ago, he'd cut that hole in the wall. I'd seen neither hide nor hair of Rod since.

But I'd seen too much of Rebecca Burgin. She'd flit into the shop every day to see Jack on some pretense or another. Yesterday when she "popped in", she was sporting a diamond engagement ring on her finger. Not that I could miss it, the way she waved it around. I should have anticipated that she and Jack would renew their engagement. Nonetheless, the sight of her ring made me queasy, as if I'd swallowed a plate of slimy eels.

Jack's reaction was harder to take. Whenever he passed the mystery section, he'd look at the hole and shake his head. Then he'd give me a sort of pitying look as if to say "I told you so." I didn't need his pity. What I needed was my tea shop, and for that, I needed Rod. What the devil was keeping him?

I fished Rod's business card from my pocket. *Rod Tyler, Mahoney & Tyler Construction.* It listed a phone number. Fat lot of good that was. Magi didn't own phones. We communicated through mirrors. A simple incantation was all we needed to connect any magic mirror to the Prism Communication Network. Who didn't own a mirror? My ex-boyfriend Gil had dozens of them, as if he needed an excuse to stare at his reflection. I shuddered. If only I could summon Rod with a spell.

Instead, I would have to find a telephone. You'd think the store would have one. But as many times as I'd been in the office, I'd never seen a phone in there. I slipped the card back in my apron pocket and marched toward the front of the shop. Jack was at his usual post there. His hands held a newspaper, neatly folded to expose only the page he was reading. I squeezed past him to get change from the till. The register dinged as the cash drawer popped open. At the sound, Jack shot me a sideways glance.

"What are you doing?"

"I need change." I scooped out several quarters. "I'm going to find a telephone."

Jack's head jerked up. His brow creased. Inquisitive eyes trained on my face.

"Whatever for?"

"To contact Rod and find out what's been keeping him."

"Why don't you summon him on the Prism?" A wry smile twisted his lips. "Oh, right, I forgot. He's not one of us."

"Very funny." I shoved the change in my pocket and slammed the cash drawer shut.

"No need to get angry. Use the shop phone in my office."

"You have a telephone?" My eyes refocused on my irksome business partner. Jack was so conventional. He was the last one I'd expect to own plebeian technology. Was this some sort of joke?

"It's required for business." His mouth puckered with disdain.

"Where is it then?" I glared at him and planted my hands on my hips. "I've been in your office. I've never seen a phone."

"Cabinet under the Bavarian clock."

I whisked past Jack and headed straight for his office. Once inside, I sought the carved, wooden cuckoo clock that hung on the wall behind his desk. Beneath the time-piece was a simple oaken cabinet. No telephone. The top of the cupboard was bare, except for that stupid picture of Jack with Rebecca. He was probably snickering behind his newspaper, having a good laugh at my expense.

Memories of the store's ledgers loomed in my head. Red ink on the page and the swinging pendulum of the old Bavarian clock. Maybe this tea shop wasn't such a good idea after all. Time and money were two commodities that Mother and I didn't have.

I yanked open the cupboard door. Inside, Jack stored his papers in orderly piles. Beside them rested an old-fashioned rotary telephone. Not even one of those plebian cellphones or something with buttons. This contraption had a circular dial with ten finger-sized holes around its periphery, each labeled with a digit and several letters.

I pulled Rod's business card from my pocket and stared at the strange phone. I plucked the handset from its cradle and heard a dial tone. At least, that was a good sign. After a little experimentation, I figured out how to dial. *Zip, tick, tick, tick.* The phone clicked, counting off each digit of the number as I dialed. Ringing on the other end of the line, then click.

"Hello," I said into the receiver.

"You have reached Mahoney and Tyler Construction," a raspy female voice replied. "We cannot take your call, but please press '1' to leave a message—"

Press '1'? This phone had no buttons. Hastily, I dialed. *Zip, tick.*

"I'm sorry," the woman replied. "I did not understand your response. Please press '1' to leave a message . . ." Her menu of options repeated, while I panicked.

"Hello," I said again, this time talking into the rotary dial. "May I please speak to Rod?"

The phone responded with an infernal "Beeeeeeep" and disconnected. Blast it all. I yanked the handset from my ear and slammed down the receiver. How annoying not to be able to even see the woman on the other end.

I eyed the old-fashioned telephone with its pock-holed dial. Perhaps Jack's phone was broken. I would have to find another. I hustled from the office and headed toward the front door.

Jack looked up from his paper as I passed. "Did you reach him?"

"No." I scowled.

"I could have predicted that." His gaze returned to his paper, but his smirk remained. "How long has it been? Two weeks?"

I twisted to confront Jack. "You don't think he's coming back, do you?"

"No, Cory, I don't."

The infuriating prat didn't even look at me. His words

were spoken with such detachment as if he were reciting a fact he'd just read in the paper. But it wasn't fact. Jack Wickham was wrong.

"He'll be back, you'll see." I stabbed the air with my finger. "We have a contract. Rod's just been busy, that's all."

"For the sake of that gaping hole in the wall, I hope you're right."

Jack snapped the newspaper open, turned the page, then refolded it into a compact bundle. My hands clenched into fists. I wanted to snatch that blasted paper out of his hands and whack him with it. But I couldn't very well do that, now could I?

Instead, I turned for the exit. My fingers grasped the dragon-snout handle and yanked the door open. Shop bells jangled.

"I'm going out," I called over my shoulder.

I stepped onto the pavement of Chanting Way and stormed down the street. A trash lid clanged shut in the alley alongside our shop as the ghoul who inhabited our dumpster scurried from view. Crystal orbs suspended in the display window of the shop next door swayed and chattered like wind chimes caught in the grip of an angry gust. Even the homeless man who usually panhandled in front of the boarded-up shop two doors down didn't ask for change, but huddled in the doorway, pretending to sleep. I caught him peeking at me through matted hair.

My steps slowed. Where would I find a telephone around here? I patted my skirt, feeling the coins in the pocket of my apron. I glanced at the row of magical shops that lined this street. Certainly not on Chanting Way. Even on plebeian streets, public phones were becoming rarer than a three-eyed frog.

I fished Rod's business card from my pocket. No address. Even if I'd had the address, it wouldn't do any good. If Rod hadn't bothered to answer his phone, he probably wasn't there anyway. My shoulders slumped in defeat. I turned and retraced my steps.

As I approached the entrance to Bedlam Books, who should emerge from Madam Voyant's Psychic Boutique but Rebecca Burgin. The very last person I wanted to see. Well, not the very last. That would have been Madam Voyant herself.

"Hi, Cory." Rebecca beamed a smile. She tottered up the sidewalk toward me in high heels and a short, tight skirt. When she got closer, she waved. The light caught the diamond on her finger. "Did Jack tell you the news? We're going to be neighbors."

"Of course, we're going to be neighbors," I said. I didn't need her engagement ring to remind me. My lips pulled back into a tight grin around my clenched teeth. "You are marrying Jack."

"No, I mean sooner than that. I'm moving in with him."

"Really?"

"Yes, this weekend." She grabbed my arm and squeezed it as if we were best friends. "Won't that be fun?"

"Oh, goodie," I said, trying and failing to keep the sarcasm out of my voice. But I did manage to maintain the fake smile.

Rebecca didn't seem to notice. She waved goodbye and disappeared into our shop looking for Jack. My shoulders sunk another notch. Could this day get any worse?

Then a large, white pickup pulled up to the curb beside me. The passenger-side window rolled down.

"Hey, Cory." Rod's voice called through the open window. Finally!

I approached the truck and peered inside. Rod sat behind the steering wheel. Mussed hair, scruffy beard, and rumpled shirt—his usual disheveled charm. Beside him, the passenger seat held a clipboard stuffed with papers. Contracts and work orders from the looks of them. A metal toolbox rested on the floor. My knight in a white pickup had arrived just in time.

"I was just going to summon . . . er, call you," I said.

"Yeah, I know." He smiled a sheepish grin. "Got held up. Couldn't call, 'cause I didn't have your number."

"Number?" I gazed into his penitent puppy eyes, feeling my annoyance melt into puddles of goo. He had my number, all right.

"Your phone number." He pointed at the clip board and our contract on the top of the pile. "You left that blank." His finger tapped an empty line labeled "phone."

"Oh, I don't own a phone."

"No phone? First time I've ever heard that one." He chuckled as if he thought I was playing hard to get. "Anyway, I've brought copper pipe for the plumbing." He jerked his thumb toward the rear. "Back of the truck."

"So you're going to install the plumbing today?" Visions of a working sink filled my imagination. Finally, some progress on my tea shop.

I waited for him to park his truck and escorted him into the shop. At the sound of the door chimes, Jack looked up from his post at the cash register, his conversation with Rebecca suspended. As Rod and I filed past, Jack's face took on the most curiously pained expression as if he had swallowed poisonous mushrooms. I smiled my cheekiest grin as if to say "I told you so."

Rebecca's news that she was moving in with Jack troubled me. Why should I care what she and Jack had decided to do? After all, they were engaged. If they wanted to live together that was their business. Not mine. But nonetheless, I did care.

So while Rod set to work on the plumbing, and Jack was occupied at the front of the store with Rebecca, I made a bee-line for my secret enclave in the back. I pulled the mysterious leather tome from its place on the shelf and carried it to the Children's Corner. I didn't dare stay in my secret hiding place, in case Rod should need me for something. And if Jack caught me, I planned to stuff the book into a nearby shelf and claim it was just an odd collection of fairy tales.

Was that what this really was? Fairy tales? I didn't want to believe that. When I'd asked for guidance, it showed me my tea shop. There was definitely something more to this book.

Once in the children's section, I pulled a cushion from the pile in the corner and plunked down on it. I placed the heavy volume on the floor in front of me. Again it toppled open right to the page with the embracing couple. My dark-haired prince. I stared at the stained-glass-like image of the tall, mysterious stranger. Was Rod my dark-haired prince?

I envisioned him a couple of aisles over working on renovations. The spark in his brown eyes, his lopsided grin, and easy laugh. It's true that he wasn't a magus, like me. But he worked his own kind of magic. My lips hitched in a wistful smile. Magic of a different sort.

I sighed. Maybe this was just a book of fairy tales after all. I turned back to the beginning and began thumbing through its onion-skin pages. I examined the vibrant illustrations colored with brilliant blues, reds, and golds. A boy riding a dragon, two knights jousting, and of course my page with the tea cups.

"That's it for today." Rod's voice startled me. I'd been so engrossed in the book that I'd lost track of the time.

My gaze flicked up to see Rod standing at the entrance to the children's section with his toolbox in hand. His broad shoulders clothed in flannel filled the entrance. On the shelf next to him, three princesses sighed and swooned on the covers of their picture books. The rest of the figures had frozen in their poses, so intent in hiding their enchantments from Rod that they hadn't even bothered to catch the fainting princesses. My own heart fluttered like dragon wings.

"Done so soon?" I said, rising from my cushion. I checked my wristwatch. Rod hadn't been working very long.

"For today." Rod nodded. "I'm missing a part for the plumbing, and I'm still waiting on your cabinets. I did locate your lights though."

Ah, the light fixtures. I glanced up at the old-fashioned fluorescent tubes that spanned the ceiling in regimented rows. What were the exact words that Rod had used to describe them?

"The baffling dig roots?" I ventured. I knew I'd failed, when Rod erupted in a great barking laugh. Warmth crept over my cheeks like a rash.

"Yeah, Degroot's with a 36-inch baffle," he said, nodding up at a burnt-out fixture overhead. "I'll pick up a couple of transformers and that missing part. Be back tomorrow. Same time?"

"Fine," I said.

Rod grinned and winked. Then he headed for the door.

I went straight to the mystery section. Did our tea shop now have a sink? I approached the roped-off area and looked. Nothing appeared to have changed. I imagined Jack's pitying glance—his "I told you so" look. Perhaps he had been right about Rod all along.

Then I glimpsed two thin copper pipes through the opening in the wall. A little progress. I sighed. These renovations were going to take a lot longer than I'd thought.

Chapter Sixteen

The Nameless Book

I stared at the hole in the wall and the exposed copper pipes. Two weeks for a couple of pipes. How long would it take Rod to install counters, sink, and shelves? Would he be back tomorrow as promised? Beside me, the comic books cackled. My earlier gloating had been premature.

I returned to the children's books to straighten up. But when I turned the corner, Jack's presence in the children's section surprised me. I sucked in a breath and ducked behind the bookshelf out of sight. What the devil was he doing here? This was my territory. And where was Rebecca? I glanced behind me. No sign of her. She must have left when I wasn't looking.

About halfway down the aisle, the warped bookcases created a small gap between them, just wide enough to afford a view of Jack. I tiptoed closer and pressed my eye to the slot.

Jack crouched, his eyes fixed on a book spread out on the floor in front of him. The mysterious volume with no name. How careless I'd been to leave it in the open. In my haste to check on Rod's progress, I'd forgotten all about it. Too late now. I fought the urge to barge in and yank it away from Jack. I chewed on my lip and watched.

Onionskin crinkled as he flipped page after page. His eyes remained riveted on the images. His jaw slackened and his face paled, color seeping away with each successive picture.

What was on those pages? I'd seen a prince flying on a dragon, two medieval lovers locked in an embrace, kings and queens and battling knights—the stuff of fairy tales. What would Jack find so engrossing in that? Perhaps the book showed him something different.

I shifted positions, trying for a better view. Rats. Not close enough to see what he saw. I retraced my steps up the aisle and tiptoed into the children's section. Jack remained so absorbed in the book that he didn't turn around. I crept up behind him and glanced over his shoulder.

Bang! The book slammed shut. I jumped backward. Jack's head whipped around. His stormy, gray eyes locked on my face.

"What are you doing here?" His gaze remained unflinching, but his right hand trembled on the cover of the book.

"I was about to ask you the same thing. I didn't expect to find you browsing through picture books."

"Ah, well . . . curious book, this." He tapped its leather cover. "I don't recall ever seeing it before. Where did you find it?"

My secret hiding place. But I wasn't about to tell him that.

"In the back of the shop." I waved over my shoulder. "When I was dusting. Do you like it?"

"Well, I . . ."

He stared down at the book cover. His shaking fingers clenched. I'd never seen Jack tongue-tied. Obviously, he knew more about this book than he let on.

"What do you think of it?" he said. His gaze flicked back up.

Well, I certainly wasn't about to divulge my romantic theories on the embracing couple. So I stuck to the facts.

"It is a bit unusual," I said. "A picture book of kings and queens and princes rendered as if made of stained glass."

"Of course, fairy tales." Jack's hand stilled. His shoulders relaxed. "I'm taking it up front."

"No. Why?" I said, my curiosity piqued.

"I'm going to check it against inventory. No title, you see."

Jack hoisted the heavy book into his arms and stood. I followed him to the front desk. He placed the volume on the counter, then pulled the inventory log and scanning wand from the cupboard underneath. He opened the log to a blank page, then whisked the wand over the cover of the mysterious book.

Nothing happened. No new writing appeared in the log book. Neither did the pages turn to highlight an existing entry.

"That's odd." Jack studied the inventory. His brow knitted. "There appears to be no record of this book."

"Maybe the wand malfunctioned," I said.

"Hmmm. Yes."

Jack gave the wand a vigorous shake. He grabbed a random book from the nearest shelf and swiped it with the wand. Log pages fluttered, flipping to the middle of the inventory. Writing on the page flashed, the corresponding entry highlighted in yellow.

He passed the wand over the nameless book again. Still nothing. Hell's bells. This was no ordinary magical book. Jack knew it, too. He grunted. Dark eyebrows shot up his forehead, then settled in a questioning arch.

"Strange," he said. "I think I should keep this."

He picked up the mysterious tome and headed toward his office. Oh, no. I couldn't let him take my book away. I had to stop him or at least coax him into revealing what he knew.

"On second thought," I blurted. "I don't think that is a simple book of fairy tales."

"Oh?"

Jack's steps slowed. He stopped with his back to me, still clutching the book. Hiding his face from me? My statement had struck a nerve.

What had I seen in that book? Lovers embracing and a teacup. Why, of course. These were symbols of impending romance and my tea shop. Exactly what I'd wanted.

"I think it tells you your heart's desire," I said.

That would explain Jack's flustered reaction when I caught him looking at the book and his reticence to tell me what he saw. It all made sense. His body stiffened. He still wouldn't look at me.

"Why do you say that?" His voice quavered.

"It showed me my tea shop," I said. "What did it show you?"

"Nothing." He shook his head.

The liar. Jack sped off toward his office with the nameless book clasped in his arms. He took it inside and shut the door behind him. While I lamented the loss of my book, I could not suppress a certain smug satisfaction. I had unlocked its secret.

To my amazement, Rod did show up the next afternoon and every weekday thereafter for the next month. He'd only work for an hour or so each day, then he'd disappear again until the next time. But little by little, I watched the transformation he wrought on the dark, empty space that used to house the mysteries. The hole in the wall disappeared, covered behind a bank of oak cabinets. Then a faux marble countertop appeared and a porcelain sink. Shelves materialized on the wall. Fluorescent lights multiplied on the ceiling. Oh, I knew these changes did not appear by magic, but were products of Rod's muscle and sweat. Still, I could not deny that there was a certain magic in his hands, those wonderful, strong, calloused hands.

While he worked, curious women congregated outside the roped-off area, browsing the nearby aisles for books. Their surreptitious glances at Rod did not escape my notice and confirmed that he was built like a hunky romance hero. Sales of romance novels would have skyrocketed, but for the periodic presence of Rebecca Burgin. She'd pop into the bookstore at the most inopportune times. While she was around, I could not conduct my covert transactions. After my encounter with Madam Voyant, I made sure that Rebecca did not witness me peddling romances. Her eyes seemed to track me wherever I went, but her perky smile seemed to droop a bit on one side. Or perhaps that was just my overactive imagination.

The only person in Bedlam Books who did not seem pleased with Rod's presence was Jack. Whenever Rod showed up, Jack glowered at him and retreated to his office until Rod finished for the day an hour or so later. The rest of the time, I had to endure his brooding glances.

At last, the renovations were complete. While Rod moved in tables and chairs, I arranged clean china cups and decorative tin canisters of loose tea on the shelves above the sink. I inhaled, as aromas of bergamot, lemon, chamomile, and chai filled the air. Several teapots, ready for service, lined another shelf. I had my own cash register. No need to bother Jack at the front desk. Mother had even baked a batch of her still warm nutmeg and cinnamon cauldron cakes for the grand opening of our tea shop.

My fingers tapped the romance novel in my apron pocket. Time to put my secret plan into motion. I'd hidden mystery novels in the cupboards under the sink in order to have them handy for sale. "Tea and a cozy" would be my pitch. Excitement wriggled in me like a swarm of tadpoles.

I leaned against the counter and surveyed my new tea corner. Four café tables now filled the former mystery section. Rod carried the last of the wrought-iron chairs past the enchanted velvet rope that cordoned off my café from the rest of the bookstore. He set the chairs around one of the tables, then stretched to limber his muscles. I surveyed the spiral of ironwork on the backs of the chairs. It reminded me of a scroll. Mother had selected these chairs, a fortuitous flea market find. I smiled. What a perfect design for a bookstore café.

"Why the big smile?" Rod said. Amusement sparked in his eyes.

"Enjoying the view," I said.

Rod broke into a huge grin. His barking laugh filled the café. Oh, toadstools, I'd done it again. Another pick-up line.

Heat rocketed through my neck and ears. What was it about Rod? Every time I opened my mouth around that man, I stuck my foot in it.

"I meant the tea shop, of course." A wan smile twisted my lips. "You did a wonderful job."

"Thanks."

Rod ambled over. He stuffed his hands in his pockets, looked down at his work boots, and shuffled his feet. That charming lopsided grin remained. What could he want? Work on the tea shop was finished. Arrangements for payment had been made. I had nothing else for him to do.

He braced his arm on the counter beside me and leaned in, striking a casual pose. I had never been this close to him. The woodsy scent of his aftershave swirled around me. His fitted t-shirt accentuated muscular biceps and pecs. My gaze flitted up to stare into his brown puppy-dog eyes. Those tadpoles sprouted legs and leapt around in my chest.

When had it become so warm in here? My fingers toyed with the scooped neck of my blouse. Had I been the demure Catherine of *Tainted Love*, I'd have swooned in his arms. As it was, the joints in my knees had turned to wax. I gripped the counter at my side to prop myself up.

"I'm going to miss coming here," he said.

"You're always welcome to stop by for books or tea."

He chuckled. "I meant working here."

"Oh, right," I said. How could I be such an idiot? "I don't suppose books and tea are really your ... uh ..." I was going to say "cup of tea," but that seemed trite.

"... thing." He finished for me. He shook his head. "No."

"Oh, well, so that's it then. Thank you."

I held out my hand for a handshake. He took it in his calloused palm. A tingle of electricity surged through my fingers. My mind flashed back to the day of Uncle Horace's funeral and my return to this shop. That day the warm hand cradling mine belonged to ...

Jack Wickham. I blinked and withdrew my hand. I refocused my gaze on Rod's chiseled jaw and stubble beard. His lips moved.

"Would you like to go out for drinks?"

"Now?" I croaked. My gaze flicked up.

"After work, I mean." His eyes sparkled with laughter, creases shooting from the corners. "What time do you get off?"

"We close at six. I could be ready at, say, seven?"

"Great." He grinned and nodded. "I'll pick you up at seven. Where?"

"I'll be waiting for you right in front of the store." I pointed toward the front door.

"Great." Rod winked at me. "See you later."

I waved as he sauntered off. The frogs had risen to my throat, choking off any further reply. Sweet Merlin. I had a date with Rod.

Chapter Seventeen

The Dating Game

Mother was out when I returned to our apartment after work that evening. The note she'd left on the kitchen counter provided no explanation. *Fix yourself dinner, Cory. I'll be back late. Mother.* Although I had no idea where she'd gone, I couldn't deny my relief. Mother would never have given me permission for what I was about to do. And now, she didn't have to know. And what she didn't know wouldn't hurt her. Right?

Without bothering with dinner, I raced to the bedroom. Thirty minutes until my date with Rod and I wasn't even close to being ready. Why had I told him that I'd meet him at seven?

I slipped out of my work clothes and shimmied into my best black skirt, then pulled two of Mother's blouses from her closet. Pumpkin or turquoise? Which would make me look older? I held each blouse under my chin and gazed at my reflection in the half mirror Uncle Horace had affixed to the closet door. Only a man would own an apartment without a single full-length mirror. Even on tiptoe, I could see myself only from the waist up. I huffed. Neither blouse helped me appear more mature or look older than seventeen.

MacTeague gamboled around my feet, his bony toes clicking on the hardwood. The skeletal pup jumped and pawed at my leg, his nails snagging my skirt. I surveyed the puckered fabric. Oh, bat poo.

"Bad dog, M.T." I wagged a finger at my familiar and shot him a look that would have singed the fur off his back, if he'd had any. "Now look what you've done."

The pup hung his head and slunk under the bed with his tail tucked between his leg bones. A tinge of regret at being so harsh gnawed at my gut. But I needed help, not another hindrance. I needed . . .

Aunt Elspeth. But I couldn't call her. As crazy as she was about Rod, I wasn't sure that even she would be too thrilled that I had a date with him, especially when that date involved drinking. Besides, she was the family gossip and I couldn't trust that she wouldn't tell Mother.

Nonetheless, I needed her help. I imagined her with a stylish silk turban wrapping her auburn hair and a matching violet frock draping her lithe frame. If anyone knew fashion it was Aunt Elspeth. So what would Aunt Elspeth advise?

"What do you think, Auntie?" I held up both blouses again. "Pumpkin or turquoise?"

"Pumpkin, of course," imaginary Aunt Elspeth said. "With your pale complexion, turquoise won't do." Had she really been here her nose would have wrinkled as if she'd sniffed a curdled potion.

"But it's summer." I eyed the greenish-blue blouse. "I thought the turquoise was more, you know, seasonal."

"Hmmmm." She arched a tweezed eyebrow. Her manicured finger tapped her lip. "It's drinks, so nothing formal. Still you want to make a lasting impression."

I glanced at my watch. Twenty minutes to seven. I would make a lasting impression all right, especially if I stood Rod up.

"I haven't got time for this," I blurted. "The turquoise or the pumpkin?"

"How about that sundress I picked out for you in Tattings? The moss green one that matches your eyes."

"Of course," I said, thinking of the classic sleeveless frock with fitted bodice and full, flouncy skirt. "Brilliant. Thank you, Aunt Elspeth. You're a love."

As Aunt Elspeth's image faded from my imagination, I flung open the closet door and riffled through its contents, extracting the golden-green sundress. Minutes later, I was dressed, with my hair combed and makeup on, except that I had only one shoe. Its mate had gone missing.

I searched through piles of loafers, flats, and slippers in the bottom of my closet. Not a dressy heel in the lot. Where could that other shoe have gone? I dropped to my hands and knees and peered under my bed. There, I found a sulking MacTeague, chewing on the mate to my shoe.

"M.T., you found it." I snatched the shoe, still serviceable, apart from a few teeth marks on the heel.

"What a good dog," I said, to make amends for my earlier anger. I patted MacTeague's skull, feeling the cold, wet lick of a phantom tongue on my fingers. I smiled. Dog kisses.

The clock on the living room mantel chimed seven. Oh, toadstools. If I didn't get downstairs fast, MacTeague's would be the only kisses I would receive tonight.

I slipped my foot into the shoe, then grabbed my

handbag and sweater. I sprinted down the back stairs, my skirt billowing around my legs like the cap on a plump mushroom.

As I reached the second floor landing, Jack trudged up the stairs holding the mysterious black book. His brooding stare remained fixed on the open book in his hands. My footsteps slowed. Jack looked up. Starting at the kitten heels, his gaze traveled up my torso, taking in the sleeveless sundress before stopping at my face.

"Cory?" His eyes widened. His jaw dropped.

"Evening, Jack."

No reply. He just stared, so distracted that he hadn't even bothered to close the book in his hands. On the open page, the prince and his lady embraced. My dark-haired prince. Had the mysterious book revealed my secrets to Jack? I looked away, but not fast enough. Jack caught my furtive glance. He knew I'd seen.

The onionskin pages rustled like a whisper. Jack closed the book. Not a snap, but as gentle as a tender caress.

"You look lovely." His stare seared my cheeks.

Now it was my turn to be speechless. A blush warmed my face. My fingers itched for my paperback romance, needing its calming reassurance. But that novel remained one floor up in my apartment. Instead, my fingers clutched a sweater and handbag.

"I have to go." I squeezed past Jack and raced down the staircase.

When I reached the front of Bedlam Books, I looked up and down Chanting Way. No sign of Rod or his white pickup anywhere. I checked my watch. Quarter past seven. Had Rod already come and gone? Had he left, thinking that I'd stood him up?

"Hey, Cory," Rod's voice called from behind me.

I turned. Rod sauntered up in a black leather jacket and jeans. Where had he been hiding? I peered around him to the alleyway that ran between our shop and Madam Voyant's Psychic Boutique. He couldn't have been waiting for me in the alley. Perhaps he'd come from Voyant's shop, but the sign in her front window read "Closed." In fact, all the shops on Chanting Way closed at six.

My gaze flitted to his face, taking in his stubble beard, easy smile, and laughing eyes. Those eyes slid over my dress. The smile widened on his face.

"Pretty," he said. His thumb brushed my cheek.

"Thanks." My cheek tingled where he'd touched me.

He chuckled.

"Ready to go?" He jerked his head toward the street.

I glanced in the direction he'd indicated. "I don't see your truck."

"I rode the bike." He hitched his thumb toward a huge black and chrome motorcycle parked at the curb in front of Bedlam Books. Whoa.

He strode to the motorcycle, donned a helmet, and straddled the massive machine. Then he held out a second helmet for me. I hesitated. Such heavy headgear would plaster my brunette curls to my head. I imagined the alternative—a witchy, wind-blown froth of tangles. That wasn't much better. Why had I bothered to do my hair? I sighed and put on the helmet, feeling as if I were wearing a crystal ball.

"Hop on." He motioned behind him.

I pulled on my sweater and looped my handbag over my arm. I eyeballed the section of black leather seat behind Rod. At waist height, there was no way I could simply "hop on." Not in heels anyway.

"How?" I looked at Rod.

"See that peg?" Rod pointed toward a small post jutting from the motorbike's frame behind his leg. "Put your foot on it and swing your other leg around."

Swing your leg around? And here I was in a dress. Oh well. I gathered my skirt and hooked a heel on the post. With a very unladylike hop, I landed on the back of the bike. I tucked my skirt around my legs so that it wouldn't puff out or ride up my thigh.

"Hang on," Rod said.

"To what?" I looked for a handle.

Rod had lowered his visor. Apparently, he couldn't hear me. He turned the key in the ignition and kicked the starter. The engine roared to life. The motorcycle jerked forward. My fingers grasped the only solid hold I could find. Rod.

What a ride it had been! My thighs pressed tight against Rod. My arms clasped about his chest, my body flattened against the smooth leather jacket on his back. My breath quickened. My head reeled from the intimacy of it all. Too close for a man I hardly knew. And delightfully dangerous. When I strolled into the bar on his arm, adrenaline still raced through my veins from the thrill.

We slid into a corner booth. I had barely settled in my seat, when the waitress approached to take our drink order. My first taste of alcohol. Nothing is as alluring as the forbidden, and my skin tingled with the possibilities. Above the bar, neon lights flashed advertisements for popular brands of beer. Bottles of hard liquor lined the shelves. Which should I choose? Rod ordered a beer, but I wanted to appear sophisticated, older. I thought of Aunt Elspeth on the plane and asked for a glass of red wine.

Wouldn't you know it? The waitress carded me.

That should have been the first sign that tonight would not go as planned. But caught up in the excitement of the moment, I couldn't have read the omens even if they had been tattooed on Rod's arm. Fortunately, I remembered the correct spell. As my fingers fished my ID from my handbag, my lips whispered an incantation. In the blink of an eye, I'd added four years to my age. Twenty-one.

I grinned as I handed the ID to the waitress. She eyed my birthdate and handed it back.

Dark wood paneling covered the walls of the tavern and our booth in a dimly-lit corner. A plebeian bar. The place reeked of stale beer. Not a whiff of magic. Except for the spell that my companion had cast over me.

I gazed at Rod, sitting across from me. He propped his elbow on the table and leaned toward me, resting his unshaven cheek on knuckles. The waitress reappeared with our drinks. Rod turned his beer bottle in his free hand. His fingers traveled over the long-neck of the bottle, fingers that had stroked my cheek a short while ago. My fingers retraced the path that his had taken over my skin.

Rod's lips hitched in a charming, lopsided grin. Had he read my thoughts? I seized the stem of my glass and sipped the wine. Stalling, while my mind searched for a topic of conversation.

The fruity libation washed over my tongue, then its tannic aftertaste and the burn of alcohol hit my throat. I stifled my reflex to cough and tried to appear nonchalant. I couldn't let on that this was my first real drink.

"You want something to eat?" he said.

I shook my head and set my glass down on the table between us. The wine glass made a ringing sound, not unlike laughter. Had I grimaced? Had Rod noticed?

"How'd you like the ride?" Rod peered at me through a fringe of straight, black hair. The enchanting, crooked smile spread on his face. All I could think about was how my body had been pressed against his on top of that powerful machine. My neck felt flush. When did it get so stuffy in here?

"It was hot." My fingers plucked at the neckline of my dress. "Rod."

Rod's gaze dropped to my neckline, then darted back up to my face. His laugh only made me more flustered. What had I said?

Hot. Rod. Oh, great. Another pickup line.

"C–cool, I mean." My gaze cut away from him. "You know, the motorcycle and all."

"There you go again," Rod said. His howling laugh filled the bar. "That's what I like about you. Your sense of humor. And the way you flirt."

The unexpected compliment sent a blush creeping up my cheeks. Could Rod have feelings for me? The notion made me giddier than the thrilling motorcycle ride. More light-headed than the wine. Without thinking, I drained a quarter of my glass.

My gaze flitted away, now studying the wine as if I could divine the future in my drink. Tea leaves and mysterious black books, now they could be read. The black book had shown me my tea shop, hadn't it? It had shown me my dark-haired prince this evening, when I was on my way to meet Rod. Surely, that had been a good sign.

"Cory?" Rod's voice.

Rod's caramel eyes searched my face. His stare warmed my cheeks. Or perhaps the sweet intoxication of the wine had gone to my head.

"Sorry," I said. "You were saying?"

"I asked about your bookstore."

"My uncle left me Bedlam Books." I took another gulp, letting the liquor loosen my tongue. "Part of it anyway. Jack and I are business partners. But Jack, he acts like he owns the whole place."

"Yeah." Rod chortled. "I know the feeling."

My eyes tracked Rod's hand as it left the beer bottle and came to rest on the tabletop mere inches from my own. Those strong hands had lifted me down from the motorbike and built my tea corner. How wonderful those calloused fingers would feel in mine.

"You still haven't told me about your business." My fingers traced gouges carved in the tabletop, inching their way toward Rod's hand.

"Not much to tell." He shrugged. His hand nudged mine, sending tingles racing over my skin. But a twitch of his lip and the sardonic smile that followed belied the casual indifference of his words.

"You do own it, don't you?" My hand stilled. I studied his face. "Mahoney and Tyler?"

"No." Rod shook his head. "My brother owns it. Mike Tyler. I work for him."

"So who's Mahoney?"

"Moll."

Rod smirked and withdrew his hand. He leaned back against the vinyl seat and drained the rest of his bottle in one go. His reaction told me more than words ever could. Rod must not have a good relationship with his brother's business partner. Just like Jack and me and our bumpy beginnings.

"Difficult is he, this Moll?" I raised my glass to take another sip.

"She," Rod said. "You have no idea." He signaled the waitress for another beer.

She? Wine sloshed. I set my glass down and stared at Rod.

"Moll?" I said. "As in Molly?"

Rod nodded. The waitress returned with his beer. The interruption gave me a moment to process this new revelation. And I imagined Rod in some sort of romantic entanglement with this Molly. An entanglement that had gone wrong, just like the plot in Wanda Witherspoon's *Poisoned Passion*. That would explain why they no longer got along. I'd have to coax Rod into telling me more.

"I've never met a woman in construction," I probed, after the waitress left. "But I suppose—"

"She's not in the construction business." Rod gulped his beer. He swallowed and waved the bottle. "More the money side."

A cryptic statement. I waited. Rod didn't elaborate. I thought of my aunt and mother. They were my partners in the tea shop and had taken out a loan for the renovations. Perhaps this Molly had financed Rod and his brother?

"Is she a silent partner then?"

Rod guffawed. "Oh, she's not silent ..."

Nearby something jangled. Rod's head jerked up. His mouth snapped shut. He turned in the direction of the sound and stared. No quick glance, a definite lingering look. My eyes tracked his gaze.

A woman wearing a head scarf and sunglasses slipped into the booth across from ours. Her tight-fitting jacket and trousers did not camouflage her shapely figure. She pursed pouty lips and toyed with a charm bracelet on her wrist. Again, I heard the jangling sound.

Rod averted his eyes, now staring down at the table.

Muscles in his arm rippled. His fist tightened on the neck of the beer bottle. No doubt about it. He knew this woman.

"Is she a friend of yours?" I said, keeping my tone conversational and light.

"Who?" Rod's head tipped up, fixing me with innocent, puppy-dog eyes.

"The lady in that booth." My head nodded toward the newcomer.

"Nah." Rod didn't turn to look. Didn't even blink. "Never seen her before."

He chugged his beer, then signaled the waitress for another. The vinyl cushion under me felt hot, gluing the light fabric of my skirt to my thighs. I took a gulp from my wineglass, swirling the cooling liquid over my tongue. It was just a meaningless look, I told myself.

"Now where were we?" I forced a smile and resumed tracing patterns on the tabletop, hoping to entice Rod into taking my hand. "You were telling me about Moll."

"There's nothing more to say." Rod shrugged. I wiggled my fingers, but he didn't take the bait. His playful grin had vanished.

The waitress arrived with Rod's third beer. He took a swig from his bottle, then picked at the label. My stomach rumbled. I wished I'd eaten. The pleasant buzz I'd felt from the wine now made my head spin. I groped for a thread of conversation like a lifeline.

Rod smiled at me. "Tell me something about you."

What could I say? I couldn't tell him about the Millhouse Academy for Gifted Individuals or anything else that would clue him in to my magical abilities. Or that I was a high-school student as that would reveal my age. And I didn't want to even think about my father and how he'd abandoned us. What did adults converse about?

"There's not really much to tell." I shrugged. "I live with my mother and work in Bedlam Books."

"C'mon. There's got to be more to your story than that." Once again, he flashed his charming, lopsided smile. "For instance, how long have you owned Bedlam Books?"

"Only a few months, since my uncle died. And I don't really own it. At least not . . . officially . . . yet."

I was blowing it, but I didn't know what else to say. The wine had gone to my head and muddled my thoughts. Even sober, I'd always been a terrible liar. But I couldn't tell Rod the whole truth, which was that I didn't officially come into my share of Bedlam until I turned eighteen. And I wasn't eighteen yet.

Rod's teasing grin let me know that he didn't believe me. He must have thought I was playing some sort of game.

"That's not what it says on your business card," he said.

"What business card?"

He reached into his back pocket, pulled out his wallet, and took a crumpled and dog-eared rectangle from it.

"This one." He slid the card across the wooden table toward me.

It was a business card for Bedlam Books. One of Uncle Horace's with the magical snow still on the shop windows, except that the names along the bottom had been changed to read "Cory Smyth and Jonathan Wickham, proprietors." The same card that Aunt Elspeth had given to me on the plane to London.

The last time I'd seen that card was on the streets of London in front of the boarded-up storefront of Dawkins and Smyth Booksellers, when I'd been accosted by Paul Dawkins. How did it wind up in Rod's possession?

"Where did you get that?" I said.

"Your shop, of course," Rod leaned back in his seat and grinned. "By the front desk."

No, no. He was lying. We didn't have business cards at the front desk. And Jack would never have listed my name first.

Neon advertisements splashed garish colors across the table between me and Rod. Cautionary yellow replaced the green light, and then changed to a warning-siren red. Their vibrant hues blurred together. The wineglass in my hand trembled, chattering against the wooden tabletop. I tightened my grip to stop its shaking. *Crack!* Slivered glass and wine splashed over my hand and across the table. The wineglass had shattered, broken like the spell that Rod held over me.

Rod swore. I couldn't look at him. Instead I stared down at my wine-soaked hand. Neon lights flashed scarlet on my wet skin. A red plume spread over my palm and ran through my fingers. Not pools of light or wine. Blood.

"You all right?" he said.

"Cut myself," I muttered.

Rod stood and yelled for the waitress.

"Don't." I gripped his arm with my uninjured hand. "It's not that bad. I'll go clean up."

I grabbed my handbag and stumbled past him toward the ladies' restroom. Had to get away from him. Away from whatever allure his charm still held over me.

The ladies' loo was a filthy little room with one stall. I locked the door behind me, then picked a shard of glass from my palm. I examined the puncture wound on my skin and studied lines that crisscrossed my palm. Madam Voyant's voice echoed in my head. *Unlucky at love.* How ironic. Her predication had come true. The picture in the mysterious book had been the lie.

I held my hand under the spigot, watching blood-tinged water swirl down the drain. Icy water numbed my hand. If only it could have done the same to the ache in my head or the one in my heart.

What was wrong with me? It wasn't as if I had green skin or warts. I didn't even have multiple chins with four great whiskers like Aunt Gertrude.

But Aunt Gertrude would never hide out in the ladies' room of a bar feeling sorry for herself. I needed to get out of here, far away from Rod and whatever connection he had to that smarmy ferret Paul Dawkins. I needed a way back to Bedlam Books. Back where I belonged.

I wrapped a paper towel around my hand and searched in my handbag for my compact. I opened the small mirror and summoned Aunt Elspeth.

"What's wrong?" Aunt Elspeth said, answering my call.

"I'm on a date, but it's all gone wrong. I don't have time to explain. I need you to come get me."

I gave her directions as best as I could remember. She promised to pick me up straight away. I'd wait for her outside.

As I left the ladies' room, I glanced toward our table in the corner. The empty beer bottles and broken glass had been cleaned up, but Rod was not sitting there waiting for me. I didn't know where he'd gone and didn't want him to see me leaving. My footsteps hastened toward the exit, and out into the night.

Cool evening air hit my face, laced with fog rolling in from the bay. Just what I'd needed to clear my head. I checked my watch, then glanced up the street looking for the midnight blue, luxury sedan that Aunt Elspeth usually drove. How long would it take her to get here?

A couple strolled past arm in arm. I looked the other

way, shielding my face from view with my good hand. I didn't want anyone to recognize me now. The door to the bar opened behind me. I sidled away from the entrance and walked toward the parking lot. Rod's black and chrome motorcycle remained where we'd parked it. He must still be inside the tavern. Along with my business card. Oh, rats.

It had to be the same card that Aunt Elspeth had given me on the plane to London. She had used "Terpsichore," but I had changed the name to "Cory." Only one card read "Cory Smyth." That card had been in my pocket . . . until my frightening encounter with Paul Dawkins.

I glanced up the street, half expecting to see twitchy little Dawkins stalking me from the shadows. I clutched my handbag tighter. The light-fingered thief must have stolen my card from me. And given it to Rod. But why? Whatever the reason, if Dawkins was involved, it couldn't be good.

The breeze blowing off the bay picked up. No longer pleasant. Goosebumps sprouted on my arms, as much from fright as the cold. I pulled my cotton sweater closed over the sundress and paced the curb, hugging my chest.

"Hurry, Aunt Elspeth," I whispered. "Hurry."

Street lights flickered on up and down the street. Cars sped by. Electric cars, sports cars, even an old VW decorated with peace signs, but none that resembled Aunt Elspeth's. I checked my watch. Twenty minutes had passed. What was taking her so long?

Maybe she'd taken a wrong turn. Stray off the main drag and you were bound to find your way blocked by concrete barriers. Berkeley streets were notoriously unfriendly to vehicular traffic, especially large gas-guzzlers like Aunt Elspeth's sedan.

The bar door creaked open behind me. I turned. Rod's sturdy frame filled the doorway. I gasped.

"Cory?" Rod staggered out of the bar and headed toward me. "What are you doing out here? I thought you'd left. I sent the waitress into the ladies' room looking for you."

Where was Aunt Elspeth? I backed away from him and glanced up the street. A compact car pulled up to the curb in front of me. Not my aunt. All I could think about was my last encounter with Paul Dawkins. Every instinct in my body screamed "Run."

"I'm not used to my dates skipping out on me," Rod growled.

"My hand." My voice had reduced to a squeak. "I thought I should go home."

Rod seized my wrist. He held my hand up and surveyed the makeshift bandage. His eyes seemed to struggle to focus. The stench of beer mixed with stronger liquor came at me with his breath. Hell's bells, he was drunk as a lord.

"Why didn't you say so?" Rod's head swiveled toward the parking lot and his motorcycle. "C'mon."

"No. Please."

I tugged at my hand to pull it free, but his grip on my wrist felt like an iron shackle. He strode across the parking toward his waiting motorcycle, pulling me in his wake. All I could do was stumble after him.

Chapter Eighteen

Tilting at Windmills

Rod's fingers tightened on my wrist, cementing his hold. Hairs on my arm bristled as magic prickled over my skin. I could feel it building like a static charge, concentrated on the place where he gripped me. Defensive magic triggered by panic.

"Let go, Rod," I shouted at him. "Let go!"

My kitten heels skidded and clattered across the parking lot, beating an unsteady tattoo on the pavement. Rod continued his dogged march toward the motorcycle, pulling me behind him. I was not getting on that infernal motorbike with him. Rod was in no condition to operate that machine. And I couldn't trust him, most especially now that I knew he was in cahoots with Paul Dawkins.

"Let her go," a familiar male voice shouted. The overhead lights in the parking lot flickered.

"Jack?" I twisted in Rod's grip to see Jack loping across the parking lot toward us. What was he doing here?

"Huh?" Rod stopped short and swung around.

"Take your hands off her." Jack trotted up, his striped tie flapping against his button-down oxford shirt. He fixed his menacing glare on Rod and grabbed for his arm.

"Jack," I gasped. "What are you doing?"

"What the—?" Rod let go of my wrist and shoved Jack away. He surveyed him with a bewildered, inebriated stare. "Are you crazy?"

Pins and needles pricked my hand. Had it gone numb from Rod's tight hold? Or was it from the magic? Tiny golden sparks had accumulated around my wrist like charms on a bracelet. I massaged my chafed skin to disperse the sparks. Damned defensive magic. Once the reaction started, I never could figure out how to stop it.

"Get out of my way." Jack jabbed a finger at Rod's chest. "I'm taking Cory home."

"Like hell, you are." Rod hurled a stream of expletives at Jack. His buff chest thrust out, filling the fitted t-shirt beneath his open, leather jacket. "She's with me."

Jack straightened, matching Rod in height and stance, but his lean frame was no equal for Rod's leather-clad bulk. I was in enough trouble already. When Mother found out, I was going to catch Hell for underage drinking and cutting my hand. The last thing I needed now was two grown men bumping chests over me like a pair of baboons.

"I'm not going with either of you," I said.

Both men swiveled to face me. Rod's curses trailed off. I swallowed and hid my cut hand, sparks and all, behind my back.

"I'm not going with either of you." My eyes bored into Rod's. "You're drunk. You shouldn't be driving."

"I'm not drunk," Rod mumbled.

"And for your information," I turned to Jack, "Aunt Elspeth is coming for me."

"No, she isn't," Jack said in a tone reminiscent of a parent explaining the patently obvious to a small child. "Your aunt summoned me. She said you needed help."

Aunt Elspeth had sent Jack? Why on earth would she do that? My uninjured hand sought the reassurance of the romance novel I usually kept in my pocket, but my fingers found nothing. Only the fabric of my dress and shaking legs underneath.

"It seems I arrived just in time." Jack's head jerked to face Rod. His eyes narrowed. "Rod, is it? From where I stand, you look rather limp."

"That does it." Rod gritted his teeth. He made a fist and aimed a punch at Jack's nose. I gasped and clasped both hands to my mouth.

Jack ducked. The swing sailed over his head. He bobbed back up and raised his guard, prepared to engage Rod. I scrambled out of harm's way. What the devil were they doing? Engaging in a public fight was sheer stupidity.

Both men danced around each other in the parking lot, elbows in, fists up. Or rather Jack danced. Rod shuffled, his reflexes slowed by alcohol. His brow furrowed, eyes tracking Jack as if he were some pesky mosquito about to be squashed.

"Ah ha, you drunken oaf," Jack said, bobbing and weaving. "Can't even land a decent—"

Rod feinted with his right, followed by an uppercut with his left. I heard the sickening smack of flesh against flesh as his fist slammed into Jack's face. Jack's head whipped back. The overhead lights in the parking lot buzzed and sputtered.

"Stop it," I screamed. "Stop it, both of you."

Blood streamed from Jack's nostrils, spattering his shirt and tie. He tossed his head, shaking off the punch. He swiped his bloodied nose with the back of his hand, then resumed his dance, albeit wobblier than before.

"Is that the best you can do?" Jack smirked through blood-smeared lips.

A pair of patrons leaving the bar looked the other way then hustled to their car. A street person in a ragged coat stopped to watch the melee. It was only a matter of time before the fight drew a crowd. Or those two killed each other. I wrung my hands. Idiotic male bravado.

Orange sparks circled my wrist in a frenzied dance. My agitation had accelerated the reaction and multiplied the magic. Oh, no. I blew on the sparks, trying to puff them out like candles on a birthday cake.

I heard the thud of a fist making contact and then a grunt. I looked up, expecting to see Jack more bloodied than before. But Rod was doubled over this time. Sweet Merlin, Jack had landed a punch!

A cocky grin broadened on Jack's face. He backed off, giving Rod time and space to recover. Rod straightened, slow and deliberate. At the sight of Jack's sneer, Rod's face crumpled into a look of loathing. He roared and lunged at Jack. I winced and backed away. Unless Jack resorted to magic, Rod would rip him limb from limb. But Jack wouldn't stoop so low as to hex a plebian, would he? Either way, I had to stop this.

"Enough," I shouted, flailing both arms.

Red sparks unwound from my wrist as defensive magic unleashed. The spell whistled through the air, then landed between the two men, sparking like a lit fuse.

"Run." I waved both hands in a frantic shooing motion.

Jack scrambled to get out of the way of the sparking spell. Rod stared with dull, uncomprehending eyes. *Boom!*

Boom! *Boom!* The chain of magic detonated like firecrackers blowing up at Rod's feet.

Rod's body catapulted backward and landed on a parked sports car. He bounced like a rag doll on the hood, then tumbled over the other side. The car alarm wailed. Headlights flashed. I clasped trembling hands over my mouth. What had I done?

I ran to see what had become of Rod. As I approached, he pushed himself off the ground and staggered to his feet. He surveyed his limbs, appearing to check for injuries. He brushed off his leather jacket. Hell's bells. I'd hexed Rod. I'd actually hexed him.

"I'm sorry," I said. "So sorry. Are you all right?"

Rod regarded me with a baffled expression, the same puzzled look he'd had just moments before the explosion. As I reached for his arm, one small red spark leapt from my finger to his sleeve. A harmless residue of diffused magic.

"What the . . .?" Rod shook off the spark. His expression changed from confusion to wide-eyed terror. "You? You did that?"

He mumbled something unintelligible and backed away from me, then turned and sprinted for his motorcycle. He hopped on the bike and fumbled for his keys. Didn't even bother with his helmet.

"Rod, no." I chased after him. "You shouldn't be driving."

"Stay away from me, you—"

The revving of the motorcycle drowned out the rest of his words. He roared past me on the motorbike and sped down the street. I stood in the parking lot, watching the red taillight fade away like a spark from my errant spell.

Conflicting feelings churned in my gut. I'd never forgive myself if he killed himself on that blasted motorcycle, drunk and without a helmet. I never meant to hurt him, even though he was . . . Actually, I wasn't sure who or what he was.

Hurried footsteps approached, Jack running toward me. Shouts and screams of panic came from inside the bar. I heard the sound of something heavy being thrown against the inside of the door. The bar door shuddered, but did not open. A brief aureole of magic shimmered around its frame. Jammed shut. Jack must have sealed it by magic.

"Let's get out of here." Jack grabbed my elbow and steered me toward a silver coupe parked at the curb.

He didn't have to ask twice. I was already in heaping cauldrons of trouble. Jack opened the passenger-side door and tucked me inside. Another hit thudded the bar door. Magic splintered, giving way a little more.

The driver-side door opened and slammed. *Thud*! Another beat against the bar door. Engine revved. Tires squealed. Our coupe peeled away from the curb just as the spell shattered and people tumbled out of the bar.

I couldn't look. I studied Jack instead. Blood smeared his face and stained his white shirt and tie. Dirt smudged his sleeves and trousers. Yet his cheeks were flushed, his eyes bright. My hands clasped in my lap were clammy and cold, but he looked oddly exhilarated.

"Are you all right?" I said.

"I'm fine." The hint of a smile played at the corners of his mouth. "It takes more than a little nosebleed to stop Jack Wickham."

"Then you weren't hurt by the . . . the explosion?"

"No." Jack didn't glance my way, but kept his eyes focused on the road ahead. "I saw it coming."

Jack's warnings replayed in my head, those he'd uttered on the day I'd first met Rod. *He didn't believe you were really a witch. But what happens when he sees something he can't explain?* Oh, toadstools. Jack had seen it coming.

I crossed my arms and glowered out the front windshield. I didn't know which felt worse—tonight's stunning revelations about Rod or that Jack had been right about him all along. Even so, I would never have hexed Rod if Jack hadn't started that fight.

"What were you thinking?" I said. "Picking a fight with Rod."

"I did not pick a fight." Jack's jaw clenched. His knuckles whitened on the steering wheel. "The drunken Neanderthal had it coming. I saw the way he manhandled you, dragging you off like some primeval prize." Jack took his eyes off the road long enough to glance at me. His gaze dropped to the paper towel wrapping my hand. "What did he do to your hand?"

"This?" I waved my injured hand at him. "Rod didn't do this. I did. I cut myself on a glass."

"You don't have to cover for him." Jack scowled and redirected his glare at the traffic in front of us. "Your aunt told me you were in trouble. And I know what I saw."

"It wasn't like that." I twisted in my seat.

"What was it then?" he said, gazing out the windshield. "And what were you doing with him in a bar?"

"Just talking. My glass broke, and cut me. He got drunk, and I didn't want to ride home with him. That's all." I deliberately left out the part about the business card and Paul Dawkins. Jack didn't need to know that, and I didn't want to be reminded.

"Mmmmm. If you say so." Muscles at the corners of his mouth twitched. An ever-so-slight smirk. He didn't believe me one bit.

I huffed and crossed my arms. I stared out the

passenger-side window to keep from having to look at him. Greek letters hung from the porches in this Berkeley neighborhood. Fraternity houses. We were approaching the university and a more familiar area of town. Not much further to Chanting Way.

"That was a brilliant bit of magic you did back there," Jack said.

Oh, a compliment. So now he was playing nice, was he? Well, I was in no mood for nice.

"No, it wasn't brilliant." I rounded on him. "It was an accident. I didn't mean to. And I never would have if you hadn't come charging in like some kind of demented white knight."

A smug little smile spread over his lips. I didn't recall saying anything funny. There was nothing funny about an out-of-control spell or what I had done to Rod.

"What are you smirking about?"

"You called me a white knight," Jack said. "I like that."

"A demented white knight." I glared at him. "You misinterpreted everything. You were tilting at windmills."

"So I'm Don Quixote, am I?" Jack's grin broadened, as if at some inside joke. He shot me a sly, sideways glance. "That would make you Dulcinea."

"Dulcinea? Wasn't she a peasant girl?"

"Not to Don Quixote."

If this was his idea of a joke, I didn't get it. Clearly, I was missing something.

I redirected my gaze out the window. We had stopped at a traffic light, two streets over from Chanting Way. The turn signal clicked the passing seconds. Jack dabbed the blood from his face with his handkerchief. He pocketed the soiled hankie, then drummed his fingers on the steering wheel.

"He doesn't know the first thing about you." Jack's voice had softened to an almost tender timbre.

"Who?" I said. "Don Quixote?"

"No. Rod."

I jolted upright in my seat. The light changed to green. Jack made the turn and kept his eyes on the road. My eyes were glued on him.

"How do you know?" I said.

"I've watched him in the store. I doubt he owns a single book. Those asinine comic books don't count."

"So?" I shrugged. "Maybe he's not much of a reader."

"But you are." Muscles rippled in Jack's neck. His jaw tightened. "He doesn't know you. He doesn't know the first thing about you."

"And you do?" I choked back a laugh, but could not disguise the sarcasm in my voice.

Jack stared straight ahead and drove. His grip tightened on the steering wheel. He swallowed. His Adam's apple bobbed over his blood-stained collar.

"You drink Lady Grey tea," he said. The tenderness in his voice had returned. "No milk, honey, or lemon. When you're happy, you hum. When you're avoiding me, you hide behind a book."

How could he possibly know all this about me? Had he been spying on me all this time? My fingers groped for my romance novel, but instead twisted my cotton dress.

"When you're nervous," he said, "you tap that foolish romance novel you keep in your pocket."

Foolish? So now my romance novel is foolish? My eyes lowered to the bunched up fabric in my lap. My fingers hastened to smooth my skirt. And how did he know about that?

The car rolled to a stop. I glanced out the passenger side

to see the display window of Bedlam Books. Home. But I wasn't ready to leave just yet. Not until I got to the bottom of this. Jack was certainly not himself tonight. The moon wasn't full, was it?

"What the devil has gotten into you, Jack?" I said. I could think of only one other explanation. My meddlesome aunt. "Has Aunt Elspeth bewitched you?"

"Elspeth hasn't bewitched me." Jack turned toward me. His brooding eyes searched mine. "You have."

Me? My own eyes couldn't open any wider. I hadn't put a spell of any kind on Jack, hex or otherwise.

"No, I haven't."

"But you have." His expression grew earnest, his stare intent. "From the moment you walked back into my life."

If I didn't know better, I'd think that was a declaration of love. But the thought of Jack misty-eyed and moonstruck over me? Impossible. Preposterous.

"I don't believe this," I declared.

"I can hardly believe it myself," he said. The trace of a smile reformed on his lips. He shook his head. "There are a hundred logical reasons why this won't work."

He ticked off his reasons, counting them on his fingers as if he were balancing his books.

"You're impulsive," he said. "Irrational. You oppose every improvement I try to make. Then there's your family, their petty disputes and abominable behavior—"

"I beg your pardon." I straightened in my seat. My hands flews to my hips. I almost speared him with my elbow. "What about you? What about Rebecca? Aren't you engaged?"

"Yes," Jack sighed. He drummed his fingers on the steering wheel again. "The thing is . . . Becca's not the same. It's like she's a different person."

I could not contain my eye roll. "Then why did you ask her to marry you?"

"We were engaged before the accident. And after she returned . . . I don't know." He shook his head. Creases spiked between his eyebrows. "It just sort of happened."

"Well, if you don't want to marry her, break off the engagement."

"It's not that simple . . . I . . ."

Jack's eyes refocused on me. His all-business demeanor dissolved into a longing gaze. The same odd expression I'd seen on his face earlier this evening, when we'd crossed paths on the stairs.

Hell's bells. Jack was in love with me. A gaping look was all I could muster in response. Had all the world gone mad tonight?

I was already in a kettle of brew. I had no intention of adding a love triangle to my list of transgressions. The last thing I needed was Rebecca and her Aunt Claire hexing me. They already disliked me. This would be like jumping from the cauldron into the fire. There was only one possible course of action, so I did the first responsible thing I'd done all evening.

"Sorry, Jack," I said. "But I don't feel the same way about you." I lied. "I'm not going to be responsible for breaking up your engagement. You need to make up your own mind about Rebecca. Without me."

I shoved open the passenger door and leapt out of the car. I couldn't have moved any faster, even if I'd conjured wings.

Chapter Nineteen

Tainted Love

Mother still had not returned when I let myself into our shared apartment. All alone, I didn't wish to dwell on the events of earlier this evening—my disastrous date with Rod, or Jack's confession on the way home. Now that I'd rejected him, would Jack tell my mother what I'd done? I would have dire consequences to face tomorrow. For now, a shower, a hot meal, and a tawdry romance offered the perfect escape. I curled up on the living room sofa in my pajamas with a novel in my freshly bandaged hand and MacTeague nestled in my lap. Tonight's indulgence? Wanda Witherspoon's *Tainted Love*.

Tainted love. How ironic. That described my fiasco of an evening. Hunky Rod turned out to be a drunk with shady connections to Paul Dawkins. And Jack's confusing declaration of love? What would it be like if we were together? I pushed the thought aside, and shook my head. I couldn't date him as long as he was entangled with Rebecca. Men were nothing but trouble.

At least I still had my pet pooch and a good book. My fingers stroked MacTeague's skull. I opened my paperback and thumbed through the steaming pages. A dog-eared page marked my place.

Ah, yes. Heath, our hunky hero, had fallen prey to the machinations of the femme fatale, the voluptuous Lady Gwendolyn Fairbanks. Meanwhile, the demure Catherine, the true heroine of the tale, had been pining away in the wings for our Heath. Although Catherine's affections may have escaped the notice of Heath, Lady Gwendolyn was not so naïve. Nor was it beneath her dignity to dispose of her rivals in as underhanded a manner as she could devise. Thus, Lady Gwendolyn called upon the services of one Mr. Lovelace, a Lothario oilier than the pomade in his hair, with a most indecent proposal.

"I am not here for pleasure, Mr. Lovelace." Lady Gwendolyn smiled her most beguiling smile. "I have a business proposition. The matter of a little wager."

Gwendolyn slid her fingers to her ample bosom, marking how Lovelace's greedy eyes tracked her hand. She retrieved the small silk purse she kept in her bodice. Coins jingled.

"I like the sound of this." Lovelace grinned. A small mole on his left cheek hitched halfway to his eyes. "What's the wager?"

"Your reputation with the ladies precedes you. A seducer of women, I hear."

"You misunderstand me, milady." Lovelace lowered his eyes in false modesty. "Seduction is such a harsh word. I think you will find that all of my paramours were willing participants."

The wound on my palm throbbed, an all-too-present reminder of my mishaps earlier this evening. How could my date have started so well and ended so badly? Rod's behavior had changed abruptly. He had been charming until our conversation about Moll Mahoney, and until the strange lady in the next booth had arrived. In my mind, the woman with the bracelet morphed into the devious Lady Gwendolyn.

"Of course." Gwendolyn swung the silk purse by its strings like a pendulum, watching Lovelace's eyes tick back and forth. "But the woman I have in mind is neither a silly girl whose head is easily swayed nor one of your lonely society ladies. Catherine is what you would call a virtuous maiden and she is very much in love with someone else. But if you are not up to the challenge ..."

Gwendolyn clutched the purse, arresting it in mid-swing. She clasped her hand to her breast, as if to tuck the purse away. Lovelace gasped.

"No." His fingers reached for the prize, stopping just shy of Gwendolyn's breast. An unpleasant smile greased his lips. "I relish a challenge." As he pulled his hand away, his fingertips grazed her bodice. "What would you have me do, milady?"

An unearthly howl filtered up through my living room, but not from my dog. I jumped in my seat. What was that? MacTeague's head bobbed up, bumping the book from my fingers. I fumbled for my paperback. Oh, drat. I'd lost my place. At the best part, too.

MacTeague leapt from my lap. My skeletal familiar pattered to the fireplace, placed his paws on the hearth, and cocked his head to one side as if listening.

"You did what?" A woman's shrill shouts rose up from the apartment below. "All because of this? This filthy pack of lies?" She shrieked again.

Purple plumes of magic spouted from the hearth. The first cloud caught MacTeague squarely on the snout. He backed away, shaking his head. Then bounded toward the fireplace again, tail wagging up a storm. If he'd had any vocal chords, his barking would've been deafening.

Poof! Another plume of magic shot up the flue. This time, a multi-colored paper fluttered out of the fireplace like ash carried up with the smoke. Except it wasn't ash. It was a half-crumpled page from a book.

Poof! A third blast of magic sent reams of paper spewing from the hearth in rapid-fire succession. My living room filled with a flurry of thin pages swirling around me, blowing like oversized snowflakes in a blizzard. I raised my arms to shield my face from the battery of paper projectiles.

Pages shuffled in midair like a deck of cards, assembling into a neat stack. A binding and black leather cover materialized around them, then the packet plummeted to the floor. A large book now lay on my living room carpet. I stared. Hell's bells, the mysterious tome.

Jack had been holding this book when I'd passed him on the back stairs earlier this evening before all the trouble began. The howl I'd heard must have been Rebecca. What had he told her?

I glanced from the book to the hearth. No more magic erupted from the fireplace. But I could still hear remnants of a heated argument filtering up from below. Jack's baritone rumble, Rebecca's high-pitched shriek, breaking glass, a slamming door, then eerie silence.

Despite the dustup below, no damage had been done to my living room. MacTeague nudged the volume with his nose, then looked up at me. His tail bones wagged. The book appeared harmless enough. I toted it back to my seat on the sofa.

I flipped through the massive volume. The early pages depicting the story of a little prince were just as I had remembered, including the illustration of a little boy riding a dragon.

I turned several more pages. I gazed at a picture of a fair-haired lady laid to rest in what appeared to be a glass casket. A grown prince knelt by her side, his head bowed. Although this lady was pretty, the scene reminded me of one of *Mother Grime's Nasty Rhymes,* the one in which a homely woman begged a witch for a spell to make her beautiful. The witch gave her a charm for beauty sleep, but the woman was so unattractive that the transformation took a hundred years. "Dozing Dreadful."

A few pages later, I found the teacup that represented my shop. An illustration of two knights jousting followed. I knew what would come next. My page. The one of the embracing couple.

I gasped. A jagged stub with singed edges was all that remained of my favorite page. What had happened to my dark-haired prince? Someone had set him on fire. Not only that picture, but several more following that one had been destroyed.

Had Jack destroyed these pages? I knew that he disapproved of Rod, but he didn't seem the sort to burn books because of it. Or had Rebecca? And why?

I put the mysterious volume aside. Clearly, it could not foretell the future. I had been wrong about this book. I had read too much into its pages. It contained nothing but fairy tales.

I never saw Mother that evening. She must have returned after I went to bed. And when I left for work the next morning, her bedroom door was closed. I reported to

Bedlam Books early, hoping to arrive before Jack. The minute I entered the back door, I knew that I had not. A chill permeated the atmosphere inside the shop, and Jack waited for me in my tea corner. I found him sitting at the first table, stiff and upright in his seat, fingers drumming on the tabletop. He whipped around to face me, a purple bruise on his face where Rod's fist had found its mark last night. His chair scraped the floor as he bolted to his feet.

"We need to talk," he said.

That didn't bode well. But if I was to be the recipient of more bad news, I would rather have it sooner than later.

"Of course." I nodded.

I walked to the opposite chair and motioned for him to sit down. But Jack remained standing, shifting his weight from one foot to the other.

"I wish to apologize for last night. I meant no offense. I . . . uh . . ." He swallowed and looked down, appearing to stare at the table top. He fingered the small scar on his upper lip. "I said things in the heat of the moment that I now regret. I made a mistake. Believe me, it won't happen again."

Well, bowl me over with a broomstick. Had Jack just apologized? Now, I was even more curious about what had transpired between him and Rebecca last night. The row that I'd overheard and the singed book didn't look good for their relationship. But clearly, they'd settled their differences. And Jack had apparently decided to remain with her.

"Okay," I said. But regret twined around my heart. He had Rebecca, and now I had no one.

I stood up and took half a step toward the counter. I needed to prepare my shop. But Jack lingered as if he expected something more. What more could he want? I tapped the romance novel in my apron pocket.

"I think it best," I forced a congenial smile, "that we put the whole incident behind us. After all, think of Bedlam Books." I gestured at the bookcases surrounding us. "We must work together for the sake of the business."

"Yes, work together. You're quite right. Things between us should remain purely professional."

"Yes," I said. "Purely professional."

"Good. We are agreed." Jack gave me a tight-lipped nod. His eyes had turned a steely blue, as cold and clear as a January sky. "Well, then."

He turned and marched from my teashop. But the chill left in his wake settled like a winter frost on my heart. I hustled to the counter to brew a pot of warming tea, the first of many that day.

The summer sun could not burn through the low fog blanketing Chanting Way that morning. But the damp mist proved a boon for my business. Customers crowded the tea shop, filling my tables and my coffers.

Jack kept his distance. I caught an occasional glimpse of his tall frame passing through the stacks like a shadow. Avoiding me. Not that I minded. His absence provided the perfect opportunity to put the rest of my game plan into action. Hawking the mystery paperbacks.

"May I interest you in a mystery along with your tea?" I said, setting a steaming cuppa in front of a gentleman customer. "We're running a special today on mystery novels."

The silver-haired gent looked up from his newspaper and raised his eyes in polite interest. I pulled a paperback from my apron pocket.

"Today's featured mystery? *50 Ways to Cleave Your*

Lover, a collection of mini-mysteries by Dirk Griswell." I flipped open to the table of contents and reeled off a few chapter titles. "Run her down with a van, Stan. Use a garrote, Dot."

The gentlemen grimaced and shook his head.

"Not your cup of tea?" I slipped the book back in my pocket.

"Too grim." He glanced down at his teacup.

I followed his gaze and noticed the pewter toad on his tie tack. I had an idea. My fingers fetched a different paperback from my pocket.

"Perhaps you would be interested in Holly Specter's latest whodunit, *Croak and Dagger?*" I flipped the book over and read the teaser on the back cover. "Amphibian expert, Dr. Arthur Went, is murdered while on the trail of a rare tree frog with poisonous properties. Did his amphibious quarry do him in? Or is there a more sinister plot afoot?"

The man's head tilted back up. The glint in his eye informed me that I had sparked his interest. I slid the book onto his table.

"I'll leave this here in case you want to browse."

I strolled off to wait on another customer. When I glanced back at my silver-haired gent, he was engrossed in reading. His tea sat untouched. He never did finish his beverage, but he did purchase the book.

At six o'clock, I collapsed into an empty chair and wrapped my fingers around a steaming cup of Lady Grey. I inhaled, allowing the citrusy aroma to fill my nostrils. I sighed, quite pleased with myself. I'd done a fair trade in romances and mysteries today. Uncle Horace would have been proud.

From the front of the shop, deadbolts clicked. Jack closing up for the day. Leaving my hot tea on the counter, I closed out my own cash register and gathered the day's receipts. As I made my way to the office to deposit my proceeds, Jack's footsteps faded toward the back of the store.

His office was empty when I entered. His desktop had been swept clean, all his papers put away. I circumnavigated his large, claw-footed desk to reach the carved Bavarian clock hanging on the wall behind it. Mounted on a hinged panel, the clock could swing away to reveal the store's safe embedded in the wall. Whispering the code, I opened the metal safe and stowed my receipts inside, right on top where Jack couldn't possibly miss them. I gloated, thinking about the surprised look on his face when he entered my earnings into his books tomorrow. Then he would be forced to admit that my tea shop had been an excellent idea.

Humming a little tune, I practically skipped back to my tea corner to finish my waiting tea. But as I neared, a foul odor accosted my nose. Not the spiced pumpkin of Mother's cauldron cakes or the piquant notes of peppermint, lemon, and bergamot from the teas. Instead, the pungent odors of garlic, onions, and something not unlike wet dog. My nose wrinkled. I knew that distinctive stench. I'd smelled it before.

"Madam Voyant?" I sputtered.

My footsteps hastened to my tea corner, where I found a steaming ceramic dish on one of my tables. It had to be one of Madam Voyant's vile concoctions, the kind she used to bring for Jack. But what was it doing on MY table?

I snatched the reeking casserole and looked around for any sign of the scarf-draped gypsy woman. My ears strained for the sound of the bells that jingled under her clothes. Or the many bracelets that jangled on her wrists.

The tinkling sound. The charm bracelet. The woman in the bar with the scarlet lips. Could that have been Madam Voyant?

Thoughts of my romance novel spun in my brain, thoughts of Gwendolyn Fairbanks and her diabolical schemes. Madam Voyant was the jealous sort. She'd made that abundantly clear on the very first day we'd met. Then Rod, a handsome construction worker, just happened to appear in my shop. Coincidence?

My head filled with thoughts of the loathsome Mr. Lovelace and his wager with Lady Gwendolyn. Had Madam Voyant sent Rod to spy on me? Had she hired him to seduce me? Had she set up the whole thing in some misguided plot to keep me away from Jack and save him for her niece Rebecca?

I had been late for our date last night. Rod had appeared in front of Voyant's shop as if he'd just come from visiting her. What if she'd followed us on our date? She must have been that other woman.

I gasped. The casserole slipped from my hands and crashed to the floor. I watched as shards of broken pottery scattered. Stew splattered the floor at my feet and splashed the books on the lower shelves. Pearl onions rolled like sticky marbles among the table legs.

Gales of giggles erupted from the comic books. Jack's hurried footsteps approached. My hands clasped over my mouth. The casserole, our books. What had I done? Jack, who was always so particular about food in the shop, would have a fit. After all that had happened between us, I couldn't face Jack or his stormy glances now. So I ran.

Chapter Twenty

Out of the Cauldron and Into the Fire

I dashed out the back door of the shop and sprinted up the stairs to our flat, too disconcerted to think clearly and too flustered to face Jack. That I'd probably just ruined his dinner and made a mess in the shop was the least of my problems. Had Madam Voyant been spying on me? Had she hired Rod to seduce me? And if so, what would she do next?

"Cory?" Jack's voice called after me, echoing up the stairwell.

I mounted the remaining steps, breathing hard. My fingers fumbled for the key, finally pressing it into the lock. I bolted inside my apartment, slammed the door, and collapsed with my back against it. Hopefully, Jack would take the hint and not follow me. I needed time to think.

Mother and Aunt Elspeth were perched on the living room sofa. Both turned to face me. A steaming teapot and a tray of sandwiches rested on the coffee table in front of them. Tea set for three. Oh, toadstools.

"Aunt Elspeth?" I stumbled into the room. "What are you doing here?" I already knew the answer. She had tattled on me to Mother.

"We've been waiting for you." Mother studied my face. Her brow rumpled. "Elspeth told me about last night, dear. A date with Rod? Without my permission? And at a bar?"

"I . . . uh . . ." I gestured helplessly to the door behind me.

I wanted to make a dash for the exit, but I would probably run into Jack on the stairs. After I'd splashed stew on our precious books, I knew he'd be angry. Either way, I was in big trouble.

"Come sit down." Aunt Elspeth beckoned to me, her hair covered in a violet turban that matched her silk blouse and slacks. She scooted over to the nearest stuffed chair, leaving space for me on the sofa right next to Mother. "Now, tell us what happened."

The breath I'd been holding expelled in a single puff. Resigned to my fate, I meandered to the sofa and plunked down, Mother on one side and Aunt Elspeth in a chair on the other. Me trapped between them.

Mother poured a cup of tea, while Aunt Elspeth offered me sandwiches. Trying to soften the blow? I stared at the pile of dainty tea sandwiches with their crusts sliced off. My stomach flip-flopped. I couldn't have felt any queasier if I'd eaten Madam Voyant's snot-and-eyeball casserole.

I sighed. Time to come clean. Mostly.

"Rod was in the shop yesterday, finishing up," I said, "and he asked me on a date. I couldn't ask for your permission, because you were out when I came home. And I didn't know where we were going."

I related how Rod had taken me to a bar. I told how he had proceeded to get drunk, leaving out the bit about my own drinking . . . and the other woman . . . and the business card. Then I showed Mother the gash on my palm and explained how I had cut myself on a glass.

"So I summoned Aunt Elspeth for a ride home," I said. "You wouldn't have wanted me to ride with Rod in his condition, would you?"

"No, I wouldn't." Mother huffed. "But you shouldn't have been out on a date without telling me in the first place." She wagged her finger at me and her voice became shrill. "And to a bar? With an older man? You have no idea what could have happened."

"But I was fine until I cut my hand. And I called Aunt Elspeth, didn't I? Where were you last night? Why were you out so late?"

I must have hit on something, because my mother's mouth clamped shut. She didn't answer my question. She looked down at her teacup.

"Well," she said, her tone softening, "It was very sensible of you to call for a ride. I suppose I should be glad for that. And that nothing worse happened other than a minor cut. But I'm not happy about this."

Miraculously, my spun tale was working on Mother. Aunt Elspeth eyed me askance and bit her lip. She poured milk into her tea and stirred.

"I spoke with Jack last night," Aunt Elspeth said, pausing for effect. Oh no. What had he told her? Did he snitch on me about the drinking?

"What did he say?" I squeaked.

"It wasn't so much what he said as how he looked." Again, she paused. "He looked as if he'd been in a scuffle."

"While I was waiting outside for you," I said. "Rod followed me and insisted that he drive me home. That's when Jack showed up and provoked a fight."

"Jack fought over you?" Aunt Elspeth gushed. "Oh, how romantic." She stopped stirring her tea and leaned forward in her chair, her eyes now rapturous and wide.

"It wasn't romantic at all," I sniped. "What were you thinking by sending Jack?"

"Rod is rather muscular." Aunt Elspeth looked away, appearing to study the sandwiches on the tray. But her mouth twitched as if holding back a mischievous smirk. "If he made trouble, I wouldn't be much help. It's not as if I could zap him with a hex in public."

No, of course not. Apart from parlor tricks for entertainment, magic wasn't done in public. Respectable magi certainly didn't go around hexing people. Only someone really unsavory would do that. Except that I had.

Heat spread over my cheeks like a rash.

"You didn't?" Mother gasped. Her teacup chinked against the china saucer. She must have read my guilty look.

"I did," I said, my voice small. "Jack and Rod started fighting in the parking lot. I was upset and lost control." My gaze flitted away, now staring down into my lap. "Damned defensive magic."

"You always did have a problem with that, dear," Mother said. "Ever since you were a little girl. I remember the time you—"

"Not now, Millicent." Aunt Elspeth's sharp words cut short Mother's tale. "I want to hear the rest of her story." Her tone practically giddy, she turned back to me. "You zapped Rod?"

"Yes." I nodded. "I hexed Rod. Blew him right off his feet."

"Then what happened?" Aunt Elspeth leaned her scarf-entwined head forward.

"He . . ." I took a deep breath, then blurted out the rest.

"He jumped on his motorcycle and ditched me there and then."

"He didn't!" Aunt Elspeth drew back, clutching her chest as if she'd been dealt a blow. The scandalized look on her face made me feel more wretched.

"I know you don't want to hear this, Cory," Mother said, her look stern. "But I think it turned out for the best. Rod wasn't right for you anyway."

"Obviously," Aunt Elspeth intoned.

"That's what Jack said," I muttered.

Jack's words of last night repeated in my head. *He doesn't know the first thing about you.* I glanced from my mother to Aunt Elspeth.

"Did he?" Aunt Elspeth's lip twitched.

"On the way home," I said, "he rambled on about how Rod wasn't the reading sort and didn't know anything about me. At first, he was kind of sweet. But then he started acting strangely."

Aunt Elspeth sputtered her tea. She set down the teacup and dabbed her lips with a napkin. "Why do you say that?" she said.

My thoughts filled with Jack ticking off my faults on his fingers. *Impulsive. Irrational. Abominable behavior.*

"Because Jack listed all the things that were wrong with me, then told me that he liked me." I could feel the defiance, confusion, and hurt boiling up in me the way it had last night. "But it doesn't matter anyhow, because I told him that I didn't feel the same way about him."

"You did what?" Aunt Elspeth leaned in. She was perched so close to the edge of her seat that I half expected her to slide right off onto the carpet.

"What did you expect me to say? He's engaged to someone else."

Aunt Elspeth did slip off her chair this time. She grabbed for the coffee table to steady herself. China jangled. Tea sloshed in the cups and spilled onto saucers and the table-top.

"He's not married to her yet," she said. "He's obviously confused." She wiggled back onto her seat and smoothed the front of her slacks.

"Of course, he's confused," Mother chimed in, blotting up the spill with her napkin. "First, his fiancée dies and now all of a sudden she's back. Imagine how confused you'd be."

Aunt Elspeth stared at me and squeezed my forearm. "Oh, Cory, please tell me you didn't refuse him."

"I did." My hands knotted into fists. "Now it's too late. Jack must have changed his mind, because this morning he apologized for last night. Clearly, he's chosen . . ." As hard as I tried, I couldn't get her name out. It just stuck there in my throat. Rebecca.

"I wouldn't be so sure about that, dear." Mother said in her gentlest mother-knows-best tone. "I've known Jack since he was a boy. He's been in love with you since you were children."

My mother was right about many things, but I had serious doubts about her theories on Jack. She finished mopping up the spill, but even she couldn't clean up Jack's mess.

"Oh," I gasped. "The casserole."

When I had left, Voyant's toxic stew was spilled all over my lovely tea shop. My nose wrinkled at the memory of the stench. That concoction would send my customers fleeing faster than a spraying skunk.

"What is it, dear?" Mother leaned forward and grasped my arm.

"Madam Voyant was just here." I flapped my arm free and pointed to the shop below. "Downstairs. She brought a casserole for Jack, but I dropped it all over the floor."

"Good for you." A grin widened over Aunt Elspeth's face. She might have been pleased by the unfortunate accident, but I wasn't.

Visions of Voyant rose in my imagination, mingling with those of the strange woman from last night. Voyant with her painted claws and not-so-veiled threats. Her dark eyes raking over me. Her scarlet lips whispering to Rod, plotting my demise.

"What else happened to you?" Mother grabbed my arm again. "What are you keeping from us?"

I glanced over at her. Worry had etched lines in her aging face.

"It's just . . . well." I sighed. "Last night at the bar, there was this woman. Her hair was covered with a scarf and she wore dark glasses, so I can't be certain. Things were going fine until she arrived. That's when Rod really started to drink. He stopped talking and kept watching her."

"That sounds like Voyant all right." Aunt Elspeth's eyes narrowed to cat-like slits.

"That's what I thought," I said. "But why would she ruin my date with Rod?"

"Don't you see, Cory?" Aunt Elspeth hunched over her teacup, as if divining secrets in the floating leaves. Her knuckles whitened on the bone china cup. "She knows that Jack's in love with you and not her niece. Maybe she was keeping tabs on you. She'd do anything to get you out of the way."

"That can't be right, Elspeth." Mother shook her head. "That couldn't have been Claire Voyant. Madam Voyant left on vacation, a cruise of some sort. Her shop's been closed for weeks."

What? Voyant gone? Then who was the mysterious woman in the bar? And if Madam Voyant didn't bring Jack that casserole, then who did?

"I need to go back downstairs." I jumped to my feet and squeezed past Mother. "I have to mop up the shop."

"All right," Mother said. "But we're not finished with this conversation. And you're grounded until further notice. No going anywhere without a chaperone, except the bookshop and this apartment. Is that clear?"

"Yes, Mother."

I raced to the broom cupboard and threw open the door. A pile of bones tumbled out onto the wooden floor. MacTeague, my familiar, had been hiding from Mother again. The skeletal pup pranced around my feet, his back end shimmying like a California earthquake.

Startled, Mother jumped from her seat on the sofa. "Cory, can't you control that dog?"

"Not now, MacTeague." I pushed the pup aside. I didn't have time for play. My fingers grabbed for a bucket and mop.

"Dog? MacTeague?" Aunt Elspeth's head swiveled to look. When she caught sight of M.T., she burst out laughing. "That was the skeleton in Horace's closet?"

"Yes," Mother said. "I see nothing amusing about it." She shot Aunt Elspeth a quelling look, then bustled toward me. "Do you need any help?"

"No, I'll do it myself." I raced past her toward the door. "I won't be long."

My playful pet gamboled about my feet, threatening to trip me up. Aunt Elspeth whistled for him. M.T. paused and cocked his head to one side, listening.

"Come here, MacTeague, you little rapscallion."

Aunt Elspeth clapped her hands on her thighs, inviting him up on her lap. MacTeague scampered across the room, toe bones clicking on the floorboards, and leapt into my aunt's waiting lap.

"It was bad enough that Horace had a dog as a familiar." Mother glared at M.T. and sat back down. "But that monstrosity? Really."

"You know, Millicent," Aunt Elspeth said. "Sometimes you sound just like Gert—"

I never heard the end of their conversation. I'd taken advantage of the distraction to make my escape. I left our apartment and pelted down the two flights of stairs, a mop in one hand and the metal pail in the other.

I could hear Jack's baritone grumble before I reached my tea shop. Some sort of incantation, I assumed. I sniffed. Hopefully, his spell would eradicate the stench. But it was no spell at all. Jack knelt on the floor of my tea shop, scooping up spilled stew with a shard of broken pottery. Muttering under his breath, he emptied his load of viscous goop into a waste basket, then ducked back under a café table to shovel another scoopful.

"Jack?" I said. "What are you doing down there?"

He straightened. His head shot up, slamming hard into the underside of a cast iron table. I winced. That must have hurt. Jack dropped the shard of pottery and groaned. From a rack in the corner, the comic books burst into hoots and guffaws.

"Are you all right?" I set down the mop and bucket and ran to him.

"Do I look all right?" He shot me one of his scorching looks and scowled at the laughing comics.

What did I expect? A warm reception? A gushing word of thanks? Not after I'd ruined his dinner, made a mess in the shop, and startled him into banging his head. I grabbed his arm and helped him into the nearest chair.

"Sorry," I muttered.

He reached for his head, absently smearing stew into his thick hair. Streaks of casserole slicked his tresses like mucus-colored pomade. Eew.

"Ugh." He pulled his hand away.

The comics exploded in giggles again. Jack cursed under his breath and bolted for the counter where I kept my tea supplies. He washed his hands in the small tea shop sink, then ran wet fingers through his hair to wash out the stew. He rinsed his hands again, flicking water from his dripping fingers. Not seeing a towel, he reached for the cupboards under the sink.

Oh, no. Not that cupboard. I'd hidden a stack of mystery novels in those cabinets. I couldn't let Jack find them. He'd confiscate them and ruin my plans.

"Not there." I dashed to the counter and wedged my body between him and the books. "You're . . ."

Breath siphoned from my lungs. From his half-bent position, his eyes were level with mine, wide with surprise and changing color by the minute. Sky blue to stormy gray with flecks of gold flashing in them like lightning. The effect was mesmerizing. My words arrested on my tongue as if he'd cast a charm over me.

A droplet dripped from that errant curl on his forehead and blipped onto my nose. I blinked. Spell broken, my tongue loosened.

"You're dripping all over my things."

"Oh." He shuffled a step backward. His eyes shot away, glancing down at his wet hands and then around the shop as if at a loss for what to do next.

"Sit down and I'll get you a towel," I said.

Using my body to block his view, I snatched a clean towel from the cupboard. When I turned back to him, Jack was seated at the nearest table, watching me with a bewildered stare. So unlike the stuffy, confident man I knew him to be. His lost expression reminded me of the boy he'd once been.

Without speaking, he took the towel from me and dried his hair. How startling to see him with a ruffled mane of unruly curls. His hair had always been neatly combed, except for that one rebellious forelock.

"Am I bleeding?" He bent his head forward, inviting me to look. I ran my fingers through his tousled locks until I found the raised lump on his scalp.

"No blood. Just a good-sized goose egg."

My fingertips brushed the bruise. He jerked his head away, eyeing me with a surly stare. He fingered his scalp and grimaced. The boy Jack was gone. The man Jack had returned.

"You shouldn't go around sneaking up on people like that," he snapped.

Fancy him accusing me of spying. I planted my hands on my hips.

"I wasn't sneaking." I pointed to the mop and pail. "I went to get a mop to clean up the mess. I'm sorry about your head and the casserole, too. It was an accident. Honest."

A sound somewhere between a growl and a harrumph emerged from his throat. He turned away from me, surveying what was left of the spill. Remnants of stew still stained the floor along with a few pearl onions. The shard that Jack had been using to clean up was all that remained of the broken casserole dish.

"I never expected to find you down on the floor," I said. "Wouldn't it be easier to use magic?"

"I told you before." He glared at me. "There is too much magic in this place as it is. One wayward spell and the whole shop could erupt in chaos."

The comic books snickered. Jack glowered at them with a look that could have ignited the lot. I recalled his encounter with a certain custard pie. Those cheeky comics could be trouble. But did Jack really believe that a harmless cleaning spell could bring down the whole shop?

Then again, he had been down on his hands and knees cleaning up a spill. When he'd ordered me to dust by hand, he wasn't just being a jerk. He really believed it.

"Shouldn't you be upstairs having dinner with Rebecca?" I said.

"We ... um ..." Jack looked down and stared at the wet towel in his hands. "We had a fight."

Ah, that explained a lot. Was the snot-and-eyeball casserole his punishment?

I glanced at the mess on my tea shop floor, then back at Jack. From his seat, he eyed the spill too. He massaged his head. Poor Jack.

I wrapped a couple of Mother's pumpkin cauldron cakes in a paper towel and handed them to him. Then I gestured to the back staircase, the route to his apartment.

"Why don't you go put some ice on your head? I'll finish cleaning up here."

Jack nodded. He rose from the chair and trudged toward the back door. I grabbed the pail, filled it with water, then began mopping up the old-fashioned way.

Jack stopped at the border that separated my tea

corner from the rest of Bedlam Books. I looked up from my mopping. He turned his head, staring at me over his shoulder.

"Yes?" I said.

His jaw worked as if he wanted to respond, but he said nothing. He shook his head, an almost imperceptible movement. Oh, but his eyes. I'd seen that look before, that heart-breaking look of longing. Mother's words whispered in my head. *He's been in love with you since you were children*. And in that moment, I could almost believe that Mother was right.

Chapter Twenty-One

Leaping Lizards

On the following Sunday, when Bedlam Books was closed, I knocked on Jack's apartment door. His flat occupied the floor between our street-level bookstore and the apartment above where Mother and I lived. My trembling fingers clutched a cardboard box with air holes punched in the lid. A peace offering for Jack.

This was Aunt Elspeth's idea to thank him for coming to my "rescue." She had accompanied me to the pet store to pick it out, as I was now grounded and needed a chaperone to go anywhere outside the building. I did want to smooth things over between Jack and me, and the gift seemed like a good idea at the time. Now I wasn't so sure. Maybe he wouldn't be home and I could slink back upstairs unseen.

Jack opened the door and stared. His eyes widened and his mouth slackened. He couldn't have looked more astonished if I'd rapped his knuckles with a wand. My knees knocked together under my frayed denim skirt. Scuttling noises sounded from the box. My fingers tightened on the carton. If I squeezed any harder the container would collapse and squish the little fellow inside.

"Hello, Jack." I launched into my rehearsed speech. "I wanted to apologize for spilling your dinner the other night. And I realized that I never did thank you for taking me home from the bar. I wanted to make amends for my earlier behavior. May I come in?"

An eternity seemed to pass while Jack parsed my words. He glanced down at the box and back up at me. I waited. Would he let me in or slam the door in my face?

"Come in." Jack ushered me inside and closed the door behind us.

My eyes roved the room, taking in the details. Floor-to-ceiling, built-in bookcases flanked the fireplace. Upholstered chairs, a settee, end tables, and floor lamps completed the arrangement. Jack's living room was traditionally furnished and orderly.

"Please sit." He motioned toward a high-back chair upholstered in striped chintz. Who had chosen that fabric? It didn't seem like Jack's style.

I balanced on the edge of the chair cushion. Jack sat down across from me on the sofa. I eyed the embroidered floral print on the settee and the beaded shade on one of the lamps. Not the chocolate leather and earthy tweeds in Uncle Horace's bachelor apartment. These feminine details suggested a woman's touch. Rebecca's, no doubt.

Where was she? My gaze flicked toward the doorway to the kitchen, expecting to see her lithe figure and perky blonde curls. But there were no sounds of another person in the apartment.

"What can I do for you?" Jack assumed his polite shopkeeper's voice.

"Oh." I sprang from my seat and held out the box to him. "I bought this for you."

At my rising, Jack jolted to his feet as well. He took the box and lifted the lid. Inside a squishy red salamander nestled in a bed of moist moss.

"A salamander?" Jack's eyebrow quirked up.

"Yes," I said. "To make up for the dinner and all. Not that I meant you should eat him, of course. Because some salamanders secrete a poison and, well, that would be rather nasty, wouldn't it?"

"Yes." He nodded, then shook his head. "I mean, no. I mean . . ."

He glanced down at the salamander and back up at me. His brow knitted. His blue eyes turned pale gray, fog rolling in.

Seeing his baffled expression, I knew I owed him a better explanation. The problem was that I didn't know what prompted me to choose a salamander for Jack. Did I think of him as a slimy lizard, like Gil, or Rod, or Paul Dawkins, or all the other rotten men in my life?

"It's just." I swallowed. My fingers twisted the fraying threads on my skirt. "It's just that I never saw you with a familiar. I thought you might like one. If it doesn't suit you, you can take it back—"

"No." He shook his head. A definite no, not a confused headshake this time. "This is fine. Thank you."

Jack reached into the box and took out the salamander. The creature scrambled up along his shirt sleeve and nuzzled against the button-down collar. From its lookout on Jack's shoulder, its head jerked up and down as it completed a set of lizard push-ups. The little fellow did seem to like Jack.

"As a boy, I used to have a lizard." Jack's mouth

crooked into a hint of a smile like the faintest sliver of a waxing moon. "Named it 'Dragon.' Not very imaginative, I know." He scooped up the salamander and replaced it in the box. "And you?"

"I never had a lizard."

"That's not what I meant." Jack shook his head, and the crescent moon waxed a little fuller. "Do you have a familiar?"

"Oh, yes." I nodded, but what could I say about Mac-Teague? What kind of magus has a dog for a pet? Especially one without flesh. "I . . . uh . . . I inherited Uncle Horace's."

"MacTeague?"

My head nodded, then jerked up. What? How did Jack know about MacTeague? But then snippets of a much earlier conversation bubbled up in my brain. *Reanimation . . . Your uncle did it . . . To his familiar.*

"MacTeague's still around?" Jack said.

"Yes," I muttered. On my face, I could feel the warmth of his curious stare, but I couldn't look at him. I didn't know what else to say. Did Jack know that MacTeague was now a little wagging bundle of bones?

Reanimation. That sort of magic was strictly forbidden. Dark magic. *Venenum.* As attached as I'd become to the little pooch, I still could not believe that my Uncle Horace would have resorted to dark magic. My knees buckled. I sank onto the settee. My fingers twined in the fabric of my skirt like the vines embroidered on the floral upholstery.

Jack hesitated for a moment, then settled down beside me. He sat stiffly with the salamander box on his lap, his knees pointing forward, long legs together.

The small sofa was a cozy fit for two. His thigh bumped mine. A wave of heat radiated up the side of my leg. He shifted, moving away, as did I. My eyes refocused on my lap. His elbow brushed my bare forearm, sending a bolt of electricity tingling over my skin. Jack must have felt it, too.

"Would you like some tea?" he said, leaping to his feet.

"Yes," I said, relieved that there was now some distance between us. "Please."

"I'll be right back."

Jack placed the box on the seat cushion beside me, then strode toward the kitchen. His leaving siphoned some of the tension from the room. But I felt jumpier than a warty toad. Now I knew how Mother felt whenever MacTeague leapt out of the cupboards at her.

I took a quick, silent stroll around the living room, hoping to shake off my jitters. The layout of Jack's apartment appeared identical to Mother's and mine, except that a wall separated his kitchen from the parlor. Now that I really looked, nothing in this room seemed to fit Jack. Not the too-small settee, nor the striped chintz on the chairs, nor the lampshades with their delicate fringe of beads. Nothing except the built-in bookcases on both sides of the fireplace.

My eyes scanned the nearest bookcase with its rows of tightly-packed books bound in leather. Old books mostly. Classics and collector's editions or stuffy, academic titles of the kind one might find on the shelves of the Oxford University library. I smirked. Now these were Jack's.

A cupboard door banged in the kitchen. China clinked, then the sound of running water. I turned back to peruse the bookcase. Mother had given him all of my uncle's books. Were some of Uncle Horace's books here in Jack's collection?

My gaze stopped on one particular volume. What was this? My fingers teased the leather-bound tome from the shelf and caressed the worn cover. I inhaled, breathing in the smell of old leather, glue, and ink. I opened the book, taking care not to crack the binding further, and read the information on the title page. A rare first edition of *Great Hexpectations*.

A teapot shrieked from the kitchen, its whistle like a warning siren. The tea. Jack would be coming back through the kitchen door any second now. I couldn't let him find me snooping through his possessions.

I scanned the crowded shelf, now unable to find a space for the book in my hands. Those accursed charmed books must have slid together to fill in the opening. Jack was the sort of man who would notice if things were out of order. He probably had the days of the week inked on his underwear.

I could hear Jack's footfalls, still in the kitchen, but coming closer. Hell's bells. My fingers fumbled *Great Hexpectations*. I seized the book, but not before a small card slipped from between the pages and fluttered to the floor.

I thrust my hand between two random volumes to create a space on the shelf and slipped the old classic into the gap. Then I bent to snatch the card from the floor. A bookmark with a floral design and a sentimental poem on the front. I was about to stuff the bookmark between the books as well, when I caught sight of the name on it. Rebecca Burgin.

Sweet Merlin. I stared. The bookmark was a keepsake, the kind given out at funerals. Rebecca's name was engraved on the card along with her dates of birth and death. Except that Rebecca wasn't dead. Anymore.

The door between the kitchen and the parlor opened. Jack entered, carrying two mugs. Oh, toadstools. I slipped the bookmark in my pocket, then smoothed my skirt to disguise my actions. Had Jack noticed? Act nonchalant. I strolled to the striped chair and settled on the edge of the cushion.

"Here we are." Jack handed me a steaming mug. "Lady Grey. No cream or sugar." He smiled. Or was that a smirk?

"Thank you." I took the mug in sweaty palms.

"Have you seen my books?" Jack motioned toward the bookcase where I'd been snooping moments ago. "I have some wonderful, rare volumes in my private collection." Had he spied on me from the kitchen?

"I, uh . . ." I choked on my words. A head shake was all I could muster.

"No, of course not." He glanced down at my pocket where I'd stuffed Rebecca's remembrance card. "You prefer genre fiction." Was this his way of telling me that he knew I'd taken the bookmark?

Jack pushed the salamander box aside and took up his former place on the settee. He sat, cupping his mug of tea in both hands, watching me with the most peculiar expression. His gaze held such intensity. Surely, he knew. I sipped my tea, my hand shaking so much that I almost spilled.

"Is everything all right?" Jack set his mug down on an end table and leaned forward.

"Yes." I lied. The purloined card felt hot against my leg as if burning a hole through my skirt.

Then I heard the uneven patter of heels in the stairwell outside the apartment. *Click-clack. Click-clack.* The latch flipped and the door swung open, revealing Rebecca framed in the doorway. Like a woman captured in a cubist painting, her alignment appeared strangely off. Her right arm toted a load of shopping bags, nothing in her left. But it was her left shoulder that drooped. And her left eye. And the left side of her mouth. As if that whole side of her body was slowly melting candle wax.

When she spotted me in the apartment with "her" Jack, her perfectly-penciled right eyebrow shot up and blue eyes widened. Her pink-painted lips turned down into a disapproving pout, the right side now lower than the drooping left.

"Cory?" she said. The right corner of her mouth perked up, but not fast enough to disguise her displeasure. "What are you doing here?"

Before I could reply, Jack popped up from the sofa. "Cory brought me a salamander. Here, let me help you with those." He loped to her side, and proceeded to take her shopping bags. "Can I get you some tea, Becca?"

Jack didn't wait for her answer. He took her left arm and helped her to the remaining chair. Instead of her youthful bounce, she now walked with a limp. I marked the uneven clomp of her high heels across the hardwood floor.

Leaping lizards. I hadn't seen Rebecca down in the shop for weeks. The change in her appearance shocked me. My jaw hinged open. When I caught myself gaping, I willed my mouth shut.

"I'm afraid I can't stay." I set down my mug and rose to my feet. It took all my self-control to keep my legs steady. "Mother's expecting me. I really must go. Thank you for the tea."

"That's too bad," Rebecca said, but the waves of displeasure radiating off her told a different story. She didn't even bother to fake a smile.

Only Jack seemed sorry to see me leave. He took a step toward me. But I wasn't about to let him stop me. I strode to the door, beating an urgent retreat out of the apartment and onto the landing.

"Thanks again," I called over my shoulder as I bounded up the stairs to the safety of my own apartment.

Once inside, I listed against the closed door. My fingers ferreted the stolen remembrance card from my pocket. What had happened to Rebecca?

Hearing me enter, MacTeague scampered from my bedroom and pawed at my legs. His hind end shimmied, tail bones wagging like a conductor's baton. And I knew. Dark magic had given him life again, but reduced him to a pile of bones. Clearly, something had gone wrong with Rebecca, too.

Chapter Twenty-Two

No Sleep

I tossed and turned in my bed all night. In my restless dreams, Jack rode on dragons, delivering bouquets of squishy, red salamanders to Rebecca. Some other piece would fall off of her body with each delivery, until there was nothing left of her but her pink lips and painted-on smile. When I awoke, my thoughts were as tangled as the sheets binding my legs.

What time was it? I glanced at the clock through bleary eyes. 8:15? Sweet Merlin. I was late for work. No time for breakfast. I'd have to settle for tea down in the shop.

I hurriedly dressed and rushed downstairs then through the back door into Bedlam Books. Around the first bookcase, I found myself face to face with Jack.

"Oh," I gasped.

I stood for a moment, gulping air like a fish out of water. I stared up into his stormy gray eyes. His stance stiffened, business-like and proper.

"In my office, please," Jack said.

An unmistakable urgency punctuated his words. His

clipped gait spoke volumes. More trouble brewing. Was he angry at me for bolting out of his apartment yesterday? Had he noticed that I'd pilfered his bookmark? Or was he just irritated with me for being late this morning?

"I'm so sorry," I blurted. I followed him across the store, my mouth running as fast as my feet. "I couldn't sleep a wink last night. My alarm didn't go off this morning. I don't blame you for being angry with me."

I finished the last sentence as I crossed the threshold into his office. Jack closed the door behind us. He turned to face me.

"What makes you think I'm angry with you?"

In my confusion, my fingers fumbled for the romance novel in my apron pocket, but instead found Rebecca's memorial bookmark. Guilt flamed my cheeks.

My eyes tilted up to stare at Jack. A sliver-moon smile tugged at the corners of his mouth. He looked more amused than angry. What was going on?

"Isn't that why you've called me in here?" I said.

"No." Jack shook his head. His eyes darted away. "I didn't sleep well last night either. I've been working." He strode to his desk and pointed to a ledger lying open on the blotter. "I have something to show you. See. Here."

I crossed to the massive hickory desk. A small, antique terrarium now rested alongside Jack's blotter. The style of the glass enclosure reminded me of Uncle Horace's bric-a-brac in the basement, but this was cobweb-free, its panes clean and metal polished. Inside, I could see the outline of the little red salamander peering up at me from under a layer of mud. Apart from a framed photograph of Rebecca, Jack didn't usually display personal items in the office. But given Rebecca's attitude toward me yesterday, I surmised that she didn't want my gift in their apartment.

I forced my gaze away from the salamander to where Jack pointed—his ledger on the desk. I leaned in to scan rows and columns of numbers. Account numbers and figures divided into debits and credits.

"Our accounts?" I said.

"Yes. Look at the bottom line." Jack prodded the page with his ink-stained index finger. "Our second quarter results."

My gaze tracked his finger to the monetary total at the bottom of the page. A modest sum scribbled in black ink. My eyes widened.

"Black ink," I whispered.

"Yes, we're in the black again." Jack grinned, not a reserved half-smile, but one full of joy like the grin he'd had in his engagement photo. "For the first time in two years, Bedlam Books has had a profitable quarter."

"Sweet Merlin," I whispered. We turned a profit, a modest one, but a profit nonetheless.

"Yes." Jack chuckled. "Don't you see what this means? My business plan is working."

His business plan? What about my contributions? My tea shop and the romance novels I'd sold. Of course, Jack didn't know about the romances or the mystery novels either. I'd recorded the proceeds from my clandestine sales as income from my tea corner, and surreptitiously updated the inventory log.

"I'd tried for years to get Horace to do things my way," Jack said, pacing the floor. "But as junior partner, I couldn't put my ideas into play."

He paced with a nervous energy, an agitation I'd never seen in him. In his excitement, he didn't appear to notice my irritation. He might as well have been lecturing to the salamander.

"Now look." Jack strode back to the desk and tapped the ledger again.

His chest puffed under the buttoned-down shirt and tie. So proud of his accomplishments. Clearly, he thought his plan to sell only classics and literary works had saved Bedlam Books. I knew better.

Jack placed his hands on my shoulders. Through my blouse, my skin warmed where he touched me. Although his touch was gentle, my shoulders sank as if a great weight had landed on them. What would he say when he found out that his plan had not been implemented at all?

"We did it," Jack said. His smoldering gaze held me captive. "I, with my plan. And you."

"Me?" My head jerked.

"Yes, you." His voice had softened to a tender caress. "You with your tea shop."

His eyes had turned a smoky gray, a tempest swirling in those irises. Gazing into them was like looking into the clouded interior of a crystal ball.

Crystal ball. Madam Voyant. How would he react if she told him that all along I'd been selling genre fiction behind his back? Finally, he was treating me like a partner, but I had deceived him.

Shame scorched my face. I averted my eyes and pulled away. That Jack had acknowledged my contribution only increased my resolve. He must never, ever find out about the romance novels.

"That's great," I mumbled. I pointed over Jack's shoulder toward my tea corner. "I have to prepare my tea shop, and I'm running late. Please excuse me."

For the next week, business in my tea shop was brisk. I hadn't time to contemplate Rod Tyler or the mysterious woman at the bar. As for Madam Voyant, it appeared that Mother was right. Her Psychic Boutique next door remained shuttered. No sign of her with her many scarves and jangling bangles. Rebecca did not venture down into our bookstore either, although I was still haunted by the memory of her deteriorating appearance. But I did seem to run into Jack every time I left the confines of my tea corner. Had Bedlam Books shrunk overnight?

Over the course of the week, Jack's appearance had changed as well. His meticulously-pressed dress shirts developed uncharacteristic rumples and creases. Dark circles appeared under his eyes. Had Rebecca's transformation rubbed off on him? He must have been working late and up early, because the lights were always on in his office when I arrived in the morning and left in the evening.

That Friday, at the end of the day, I closed out my register, gathered my receipts, and headed to his office to lock them in the safe. Jack was not there. From the sound of his footfalls, he was headed toward the front door, presumably to lock up. I circumnavigated the large, claw-footed desk to the Bavarian clock mounted on the wall behind it. I stowed my receipts in the office safe, hidden behind the clock. As I closed the safe, my gaze dropped to the cupboard under the clock, where Jack stored his papers in orderly piles. Something fluffy poked from the half-closed cupboard.

I nudged the door open for a peek. A pillow and blanket had been stashed in the cupboard on top of the ledgers. What were they doing here? Jack's comment from Monday morning percolated up in my brain. *I didn't sleep well last night either.* Could this explain all those early mornings and late nights in the office?

I didn't hear Jack's approach, until he shuffled into the office behind me.

"Jack," I turned to him and pointed at the pillow. "Have you been sleeping in the office?"

"I, um . . ." Jack's eyes flicked to the pillow then darted away. "Becca and I, we, um . . ." He swallowed. His collar askew, his Adam's apple bobbed over the top. "We had a fight." He pointed to the salamander in the terrarium on his desk. "Shortly after your visit."

But that was on Sunday. I ticked off the days on my fingers.

"So you've been sleeping in your office for a week? But it's your apartment." I jabbed my finger in the air, pointing in the direction of the flat above us. "If anyone should leave, it should be her."

"You don't understand." He rounded the desk and sank into his old wooden office chair, which groaned. Propping both elbows on the desk top, he dropped his head into his hands, letting his fingers worry his scalp through his thick, dark hair. "I can't. She's not well."

"That's not your fault." I shrugged.

"But in a way, it is." His gaze flicked up to face me, a gale brewing in his eyes. Blue turning gray then obsidian. "She came back for me. I can't desert her when she's . . ." His jaw stiffened. "I made her a promise. A Wickham always keeps a promise."

Oh, his eyes. I could not look away. In the depths of those stormy irises, I read desperation, hurt, loss. And under them, the circles of exhaustion pooled deeper. Poor Jack.

"Well, you can't keep trying to sleep here. Look at you. You're exhausted." My eyes pleaded with him. My fingers tugged on his rumpled sleeve. "Come with me."

"Where are we going?" He did not resist, but rose from the chair and let me lead him.

"Upstairs to get you something proper to eat and to see Mother. She'll know what to do."

Together, we walked out the back door and up the rear stairs to my apartment. When we passed the landing to his flat, Jack hesitated. He stared at the door for just a moment. I imagined him banished to their sofa, his lanky frame folded up on that too-small, floral settee. That wouldn't be much more comfortable than the office chair. A barely audible sigh slipped from his lips. Then we trudged up the remaining flight to the apartment I shared with my mother.

I ushered him inside. Jack surveyed his surroundings. Through his sleeve, I could feel his tension melt away. Mac-Teague, who usually greeted me at the door, must have been hiding. No bother. He would jump out sooner or later.

"Mother?" I scanned the living room and kitchen, expecting to see her graying curls. No sign of her either.

The cryptic note she'd left on the butcher-block kitchen counter provided no clues. *There's soup in the fridge for your dinner, Cory. I'll be back late. Mother.* Out again? For the third time this week. What was going on? Oh, bat poo. Just when I needed her too.

I knew I couldn't ask Aunt Elspeth for advice about Jack. I knew just what she'd say. She didn't like Madam Voyant at all and wasn't too keen on Rebecca. She didn't need an invitation for more match-making and meddling. And my Aunt Gertrude? No, thank you. Mercifully, I hadn't seen her since Mother and I moved out following my aunts' row at Uncle Horace's funeral. I'd have to solve this one on my own.

I looked at Jack. He slid onto the bar stool across from me at the kitchen counter. He eyed Mother's note.

"Would you like some soup?" I offered.

After a week with little sleep, exhaustion seemed to be taking over. Jack didn't say a word. Just nodded.

I found a kettle of Mother's mushroom and wild rice soup in the refrigerator. While Jack watched, I heated our dinner on the stove and popped four of Mother's home-made rosemary breadsticks into the oven, the kitchen filling with the earthy aromas of mushrooms and herbs. I pulled one of Uncle Horace's huge ceramic soup bowls from the cupboard and ladled the steaming broth into it for Jack.

"Mmm, this is good," Jack said after the first taste. He tucked into his dinner with relish.

"So?" I blew on my hot soup to cool it, before taking a sip of the comforting brew. "Who does the cooking at your place?"

"Becca," Jack said. "She never used to cook, but when she moved in, Claire gave her some recipes."

My nose wrinkled at the memory of Voyant's snot-and-eyeball casserole. Ewww. The poor man. I pushed one of my two breadsticks across the table. Jack didn't refuse.

After we'd eaten, he helped me with the dishes. Still Mother hadn't returned. I even tried summoning her using the large mirror over the living room fireplace. Oddly, she didn't pick up. Her image didn't materialized in the looking glass. Where could she be?

I glanced at Jack, listing against the kitchen counter. He wouldn't last until she came home. He'd run out of conver-sation, his eyelids leaden.

"I could take the couch." He gestured toward Uncle Horace's chocolate leather, three-seated sofa.

"After spending a week sleeping in an office chair?" I shook my head. "No, you need a bed. Besides Mother's note said she would be home late. Imagine how shocked she'd be to find you on the couch." I motioned toward my bedroom door. "You should take my bed. I'll take the couch."

Jack started to protest. Crossing my arms, I channeled my best imitation of bossy Aunt Gertrude. The look I gave him would have siphoned the mists from the moors.

"I can see that I don't have a choice," he said, as a small smile tugged at the corners of his mouth.

"No. You don't." I steered him toward my room. "This used to be Uncle Horace's study, but Mother completely redecorated it."

Jack's eyes travelled over the built-in bookcases on the wall filled with my books, the cozy little reading nook that Mother created by the window with the spider-spun curtains, and, where Uncle Horace's huge desk used to rest, the full-size bed with puffy comforter and pillows.

"This is wonderful," he said, stepping inside. "Are you sure?"

"Absolutely." I nudged him toward the bed. Then I grabbed a spare pillow and blanket from the closet, before either of us could change our minds. "Good night."

I closed the door to the bedroom behind me and settled on the couch. The soft leather crackled, as I punched the pillow to fluff it up and arranged the blankets around me. MacTeague's bony nose poked out from under the sofa. He jumped up and wriggled under the covers beside me.

"There you are, you little rascal." I wrapped him in the blanket and hugged him close. "I wondered where you'd gone."

As I drifted off to sleep, his phantom tongue licked my cheek. I imagined Jack asleep on my pillow in the next room. In my dreams, I brushed that errant curl from his face and kissed his forehead. Good night, Jack.

Chapter Twenty-Three

Aunt Gertrude's Ultimatum

The two a.m. toll of the grandfather clock dimly registered in my dreams, followed by the tumble of the skeleton key in the lock as Mother entered. She tiptoed past MacTeague and me on the couch, but I didn't fully wake until the clock chimed seven early the next morning. Through sleepy eyes I saw that Mother's bedroom door was closed and MacTeague had gone back into hiding.

I freshened up in the bathroom, then softly tapped on my bedroom door to rouse Jack. When he opened the door, he looked much more rested than he had last night. The dark circles under his eyes had faded. How delightful to see his dark hair, usually so neatly combed, now a tousled mop.

"Did you sleep well?" I whispered, unable to contain my smile.

"Yes, thank you." He nodded. Then apparently tracking my gaze, he attempted to finger comb his hair into place.

"You can use the bathroom, while I change." I pointed

down the hall. "My mother came home very late. We'll have to be quiet to not wake her."

He nodded again, then ambled toward the hall bathroom. Once he was out of sight, I closed the door to my bedroom and shimmied into a fresh skirt and blouse for the day. I grabbed my work apron off the couch and donned it, heading to the kitchen to fix us a quick breakfast of instant oatmeal, tea, and juice.

Minutes later we were both out the door. Jack stood beside me, while I turned to lock the apartment door behind us. My fingers fiddled to fit the key into the lock, but the old skeleton key wouldn't cooperate this morning. What was wrong with this blasted thing?

"Don't wait for me." I nodded toward our bookstore two floors below. "You should go on down."

As he turned to go, a sensation like icy water trickled over my fingers gripping the key. The hairs on my arms bristled. Someone or something gasped.

"Did you hear that?" I whispered to Jack.

My eyes searched the dimly-lit landing and back stair. Nothing there.

"No." He turned back toward me. His eyebrows quirked up. "Hear what?"

Just as suddenly, the cold sensation vanished. The bolt tumbled, and the lock clicked shut.

"Must have been my imagination," I muttered, pocketing the key. Yet I tiptoed down the back stairs, staying as close to Jack as I dared.

After a busy Saturday in the shop, I had almost forgotten about the weird sensation on the back stairs this morning.

That is, until late that afternoon. Passing Jack's office to fetch a book for a customer, I overhead a shrill female voice through the closed office door. Rebecca's.

"I saw you, Jack," the woman said. "How could you?"

"Nothing happened," Jack's baritone rumble replied. "I slept. That's all. We weren't even in the same room."

My footsteps slowed. My ears perked, listening. I knew I shouldn't be snooping, especially not on a lover's quarrel, but this one involved . . . Me.

"Then where was she?" Rebecca said, her voice piercing like the high-pitched whistle of a tea kettle.

"That's not relevant. Nothing happened."

"How could you do this to me? I'm your fiancée." Loud sobs interrupted her words now. "You don't love me. You think I'm ugly."

"No, Becca. Please stop."

"I came back for us, Jack. You promised you wouldn't leave me. No matter what. You promised."

I couldn't listen anymore. My fingers clutched the romance novel in my grip. I'd read enough romances to recognize a manipulative ploy when I heard one.

I sped away from the doorway as quickly and silently as my flats could carry me and headed back toward my tea corner. Three aisles over, Rebecca's words bubbled up in my brain as if chasing after me. *I saw you, Jack.* Saw us? How? Where? No one was in the stairwell last night, when I took Jack upstairs. Or this morning?

If overhearing Jack and Rebecca's conversation wasn't vexing enough, a most unexpected visitor showed up at the shop. A half hour before closing, my Aunt Gertrude stormed into Bedlam Books. Despite her short stature, customers scuttled to get out of her way. Her gray-haired head parted our patrons like a silver bullet through a pack of werewolves.

"Aunt Gertrude?" I wiped my hands on my apron and hurried over to greet her. "What brings you here?"

Aunt Gertrude presented her cheek for a kiss. I gave her an obligatory peck. She didn't return the greeting. Unlike Aunt Elspeth or Mother, Aunt Gertrude was as prickly as the hairs on her chin.

"I just came from tea with Elspeth and your mother," she said. "I thought I'd come and see what you've done to the store."

Tea with Elspeth and Mother? Knock me flat with a feather. The last time I'd seen my Aunt Gertrude, she was feuding with Aunt Elspeth over my uncle's casket. Since then relations between them hadn't exactly been cordial.

"Oh," I said. "So you and Aunt Elspeth are on speaking terms?"

"You might say that." Aunt Gertrude pursed her lips but offered no more. Her avoidance suggested the opposite. Had my aunts had another row? I didn't dare ask.

Aunt Gertrude surveyed my tea shop. She strode to the nearest empty table, ran her index finger across the table top, and examined it. Checking for crumbs? Apparently satisfied, she settled into the chair and looked up at me with an expectant air.

"Well," she said. "Aren't you going to offer me tea?"

"But you just said—"

Aunt Gertrude quelled my protest with a glare. I swallowed my words and forced my lips into a shopkeeper's smile.

"Of course, what can I get you?"

"Darjeeling and a cauldron cake. Sugar. Two lumps. No milk. And be quick about it."

I hustled to the counter to fill my aunt's order. On the way, another customer signaled to me from his table in the corner. I nodded to acknowledge him and held up my index finger in the "just a minute" sign. Aunt Gertrude did not like to be kept waiting.

I set a cup of steaming brew in front of her, two lumps of sugar, along with a cauldron cake on a separate plate. I turned toward my waiting customer. Aunt Gertrude's voice summoned me back.

"How can it be this chilly in July?"

"Is it?" I glanced toward the door, wishing that Aunt Gertrude was on her way out.

"Odd weather we're having." She plopped the sugar cubes in her beverage and gave her tea a leisurely stir. "Haven't you been outside?"

"No, we've been busy today."

I snuck a peek over my shoulder at the waiting gent. My now unhappy customer frowned and checked his watch. I shifted my weight from foot to foot, inching away from my aunt. Aunt Gertrude either did not or would not take the hint.

"Don't just stand there." She nodded her head toward the empty seat beside her. "Sit down."

"I'm sorry, Aunt Gertrude. I can't." I gestured toward the waiting man. "I have other customers."

"Harrumph." Aunt Gertrude scowled. "It's not every day your aunt comes for a visit."

She cleared her throat making a sound like a cat coughing up a hairball. Her hacking drew horrified stares. Aunt Gertrude glared back. My remaining customers gulped down their tea and scattered like cockroaches from a spotlight. My waiting gent departed in a huff along with them. There's one customer who wouldn't be back.

"There," Aunt Gertrude said, when my tea shop had cleared. "Now sit."

Dutifully, I sank into my seat. But my hands clenched, wanting to throttle her for chasing away all my business. My eyes focused on her neck. Folds of skin billowed over her high-necked collar. Did Aunt Gertrude even have a throat?

"Your mother and Elspeth did a fine job with this place." Aunt Gertrude sipped her tea and nibbled at her sweet treat.

Mother and Aunt Elspeth. No mention of me? Her intentional omission irked me.

"This shop was my idea too," I said. My eyes narrowed, zeroing in on her round face. "You didn't come here to admire my tea corner. Why did you come, Aunt Gertrude?"

Aunt Gertrude sputtered, spewing crumbs from her mouth. She took a hasty sip of tea, swallowed, and dabbed her wrinkled lips with her napkin. She cleared her throat, no hairball antics this time.

"I can see there's no use filling a cracked cauldron," she said. "I'll be blunt. Are you seeing Jack Wickham?"

"What?" My jaw dropped, then clamped shut.

I glanced toward the surrounding bookshelves for any sign of Jack's tall frame. Thankfully, he must still be holed up in his office out of earshot. The last thing I needed was him overhearing this conversation. Not that I would tell my busybody aunt anything about my personal life.

"I don't see how that's any of your business," I said to my aunt.

"As matriarch of this family, I'm making it my business." Aunt Gertrude puffed herself up. "I was against this partnership from the start. But Horace wouldn't listen. He insisted on leaving Bedlam Books to you against my better judgment. My brother never did have a lick of sense."

I gasped. I knew Aunt Gertrude had not wanted me here. She'd made that clear at the funeral. Yet how could she heap insults on Uncle Horace and in his own establishment no less?

"How can you say that about Uncle Horace?" I bristled.

"Because it's true. I'm not afraid of the truth." Aunt Gertrude affixed me with her self-righteous glare. "My brother was a fool, full of fanciful ideas. He was a terrible businessman. And you." She prodded the air with a stubby finger. "You're just like him."

"I beg your pardon."

"You want proof?" She slapped her palm on my tabletop. Teacup chattered against china saucer. "A good businesswoman would have taken Jack's offer. You're still a child. You should be in school."

"I am not. I'm seventeen." I rose from my chair and pointed toward Uncle Horace's office, imagining his imposing frame behind the massive desk. "Uncle Horace left me his business. He wanted me to carry on for him. He believed in me."

"Horace?" Aunt Gertrude guffawed. She shook her head. Loose skin jiggled from her jowls like a turkey's waddle. "Bedlam Books was losing money. He'd signed over the building to us to keep from losing that, too."

Aunt Gertrude's criticism rushed over me, washing the foundation out from under my feet. My knees buckled. I sank back into my chair.

"Now, Jack, there's a businessman." Aunt Gertrude nodded her approval. "The Wickhams have always been the sensible ones in this venture. They are the only reason this business is still afloat."

I shook my head. Aunt Gertrude continued her lecture,

but I no longer heard her voice. Instead, Jack's words from a much earlier conversation reverberated in my head. *I have money from my mother's estate. I've been shoring up the business from my inheritance.* Jack's business plan hadn't saved Bedlam Books. His money had.

Aunt Gertrude prattled on. "I can only imagine what foolish notions your mother and Elspeth put in your silly head about Jack ..."

I recalled my odd conversation with Jack earlier this week, when he'd showed me the ledgers. His agitation, the rare smile, his words of praise. My fingers reached for my shoulder where he'd touched me. I thought of the salamander I'd given him, now prominently displayed on his desk.

"Listen to me." Aunt Gertrude's strident tone pulled me back to her conversation. "Promise me that you will not jeopardize the future of this business by initiating a romance with Jack Wickham."

Hairs bristled, rising like hackles on the back of my neck. I had not initiated the romance. Jack had.

My aunt's words rankled. Her insinuation of incompetence was not lost on me. Quick to praise Jack, but she had not given me an ounce of credit, when everything I had done was for Bedlam Books. And now she wanted to butt into my personal life, too? Enough. I would not capitulate to her bullying.

"NO."

"What?" Aunt Gertrude slammed her fist down on the tabletop. Her empty teacup shattered. "You would defy me?"

"You're not my mother. You can't tell me what to do." I jumped from my seat. Both hands balled into fists. "What Jack and I do is our business and ours alone."

"Insolent girl." Aunt Gertrude sprang to her feet,

surprisingly agile for an old dame. Her jaws snapped like an enraged crocodile. "I forbid you."

"Get out of my shop," I shouted, jabbing my finger toward the door.

Aunt Gertrude harrumphed. Her nostrils flared. She straightened, inflating her chest so that all four feet eleven inches of her seemed like much more.

"You've not heard the last of this," she hissed, jutting her chins in the air.

She turned and marched toward the door. I followed close behind, chasing her and her bullying ways out of my shop. She would not win. I would have the last word.

"Yes, I have," I shouted at her retreating form. "And if I wish to date Jack Wickham, I will."

From behind me, someone gasped. Just like the sound I'd heard in the stairwell this morning. But this time, the exclamation of surprise was so loud that even the slamming shop door and the jangling bells did not drown it out. Aunt Gertrude and I had not been alone. I whipped around to see who had witnessed my fight with my aunt.

Rebecca and Jack stood together by the front register. Their eyes stared, wide with shock and amazement.

Heat rocketed over my face. How could I have been so stupid? I'd been so engrossed in the argument I'd forgotten I was within earshot of Jack and Rebecca. My own foolish words repeated in my head. *If I wish to date Jack Wickham, I will.* Oh, dragon dung. I'd stepped in it with both feet this time.

I couldn't even look at Jack. Rebecca's face grew dark. While the left side of her mouth remained shut as if locked in rigor mortis, the right side twisted in murderous, jealous hate.

Chapter Twenty-Four

No More Secrets

"Jack?" Rebecca glanced from Jack to me and back again. Blood drained from her already pale complexion. Her pink-painted lips quivered on the right side. Not a muscle moved on the frozen left side of her face.

And Jack? He was not looking at her at all. His gaze fixed on me, his eyes as stormy as ever but with a spark I'd never seen. The small sliver of a smile that I'd witnessed in his apartment the other day reformed on his lips. His veneer of self-control fractured as his grin broadened. Through the cracks, I glimpsed the boy I once knew.

He loved me. Mother was right. He really did love me. My heart fluttered like bat wings.

Rebecca gasped. Her face now turned a splotchy red. She too had noted Jack's expression, discerning its meaning as clearly as her psychic Aunt Claire reading the lines on a palm.

"Jack," she said, venom in her voice. "There's something

you should know about Cory. She's been keeping secrets from you."

"No." I shook my head. Of course, I had secrets, but not any that Rebecca knew.

"What?" Jack snapped to attention, his eyes riveted on Rebecca. "What are you talking about?"

Rebecca's right eye slotted toward me, then narrowed until it was almost as closed as her frozen left eye. "You should ask Cory what happened to all those missing romance novels."

Hell's bells. How did Rebecca know about those? Madam Voyant had witnessed my clandestine dealings, but she was gone. Her shop next door remained closed.

"What?" Jack turned to face me. His eyebrows jumped up his forehead, hovering underneath the errant curl.

Voyant must have ratted me out to her niece. How dare she? I straightened, thrusting out my chest. My hands balled into fists. If Rebecca wanted a fight, I would give her one.

"Just what are you implying?" I stepped forward and wagged a finger in her face. "You're trying to make trouble for me. You've been against me since the first day we met. Both you and your aunt." I turned to Jack. "Did you know that Madam Voyant even threatened me?"

Rebecca guffawed, a forced fake laugh from her crooked lips. Her gaze flitted away to Jack.

"You don't honestly believe that, do you?" She traced her nails up and down Jack's sleeve. She batted the eyelashes of the one working eye. "Only a desperate girl would fabricate such a lie."

My mouth dropped open, gobsmacked. She was the desperate one. Hers was the lie. She wouldn't even look at me. The way her fingers walked up Jack's sleeve reminded me of Voyant with her painted claws. It made my skin crawl. My hand itched to swat Rebecca away as if she were a poisonous spider making her way up his arm.

"It isn't a lie," I shouted.

"Smoke and mirrors to distract you from the real issue." Rebecca pursed pouty lips and tutted. "Jack, I didn't want to be the one to tell you this about your own partner, but all this time Cory has been selling romance novels behind your back."

Jack stared at Rebecca with a glazed look as if under her spell. Then his head swiveled to face me. His brooding eyes held me captive.

"Cory, is this true?"

"Well, I—" I could not lie to him. Yet I could not tell him the truth.

"Of course, it's true," Rebecca said. "I witnessed a transaction myself."

What? Rebecca had never seen me selling the romances. She couldn't have. Rebecca's lips curled. There it was. That poisoned-apple grin.

"Cory?" Jack said. In his pleading eyes, I saw the boy with the broken-hearted look. Then he turned to Rebecca. "Please leave us, Becca. It seems Cory and I have business to discuss."

"But Jack?" She squeezed his bicep in a possessive maneuver. I felt as if she had dug her vicious claws into my own arm and drawn blood. I winced and hugged my chest.

Jack's jaw stiffened. He brushed her hand from his arm and pointed her toward the exit. Rebecca huffed, but the gloating look she shot me in parting made it clear that she knew she'd won.

"I'll be upstairs, if you need me, Jack." Her voice seemed to come from miles away.

A charm bracelet on her wrist jingled as she limped

toward the back stair to the apartment she shared with Jack. How could I answer him? Damned if I told the truth. Damned if I lied.

The back door to the shop clicked shut with the finality of a death knell. Rebecca was gone, but her damage had been done. I had no choice but to come clean and hope Jack would understand.

"I'm sorry." I looked him in the eyes when I said it. My turn to plead. "I didn't do it to hurt you. I did it for Uncle Horace and Bedlam Books."

"You told me you hadn't seen those books. And all this time, you've been lying to me? How? Why?"

The spark went out of Jack's eyes. I read disbelief and disappointment in his searching stare. Pangs of guilt twisted my gut as if a boa constrictor had wrapped me in its coils. I had deceived him. I was the snake.

"Come with me and I'll show you." I beckoned for him to follow.

I led him toward my secret enclave at the back of the shop. At my heels, Jack's wingtips pounded the floorboards, his clipped gait the countdown to my downfall. With each footstep, I heard echoes of Uncle Horace's booming voice. *Five. Four. Three. Two. One. Ready or not, here I come.* Like a child in a game of Hide and Seek, I wanted to run. Wanted to hide. But I was no longer a child, and the game was over.

At the back wall of the shop, I turned left thrice and then once more. I was inside the cozy enclave of bookcases where I had hidden my secrets. Secrets I was about to reveal.

"Nooooooo," Jack's voice shouted. "Cory, come back."

I spun around, expecting to see Jack right behind me. He had stopped outside the entrance to my hidden corner.

He held both hands up, palms forward as if pushing on something solid. There was nothing between us but air.

"I haven't gone anywhere," I said. "I'm right here."

I waved my hand. His eyes did not track my movement. The tempest in them grew wilder by the second.

"Gods, Cory, let me in," he shouted, chest heaving underneath the button-down shirt.

What the devil? I marched toward him, grabbed hold of his tie and yanked him toward me. His chest and head jerked forward, arms splayed. His face pancaked against something solid. A shimmer of purple exploded across my vision.

What had I done? I let go of Jack's tie and clamped both hands over my mouth.

The violet glow widened like a ripple, momentarily revealing a magical barrier stretching between the bookcases at the entrance to my hiding place. The flash disappeared as quickly as it came, rendering the obstruction invisible once more.

Jack staggered back from the barrier. He groaned, clasped a hand over his mouth, and dabbed his nose. A muffled curse word spilled from his lips.

"I'm sorry, Jack," I said. "So sorry."

He bent forward with his hands propped on his knees. He drew and expelled a long slow breath. When he looked up again, his composure appeared restored. Only the thunder in his eyes betrayed his agitation.

"Okay, I know you're in there," he said, his voice measured and even. "If you can hear me, please don't help me this time."

"I wouldn't dream of it." I backed away from the entrance, hands raised.

Jack approached the barrier and felt it with outstretched

hands. "Fake bookcase," he muttered. "A door of some sort. There must be a knob or a lever here someplace."

A fake bookcase? That's what he saw? A fake bookcase with shelves and boxes done up to look like leather-bound books? Like the one on the back wall of Daddy's bankrupt bookstore?

I stared at the empty air between us. This door was nothing like that one. Jack would find no knob or lever here. I could pass through as though no barrier existed. Why would it allow me through but not him?

Jack pushed against the unseen wall, now resorting to brute strength to force it open. He backed up a few steps and rammed the barrier, leading with his shoulder. Magic shimmered and flexed, but would not yield.

Jack backed up further. He was going to try again, this time with a running start. Even I could see the poor man was going to hurt himself. Jack rushed the barrier.

"For Merlin's sake," I shouted at the portal. "Let him in."

Magic shattered, making a sound like breaking glass. I flattened my body against an adjacent bookcase to get out of the way and peered through parted fingers. Jack hurtled past me and crash landed in the pile of empty cardboard boxes that had once held my romance novels.

"Oh, bat poo," I whispered under my breath. Had I done that? "Are you all right?"

I ran to him and grabbed his arm to help him up. Even through his shirt sleeves, his skin felt hot to my touch. Was that his anger burning against me?

"I asked you not to help," he said, shooting me a surly glare. He jerked his arm away as if he were the one who'd been scalded.

"Sorry," I muttered, backing off. "For the life of me, I

don't know what created that barrier or why it obeyed me but not you."

Jack looked down. His shirt and trousers were wrinkled, his striped tie askew. He stood and brushed himself off. He mumbled something under his breath that sounded like an apology. But I'm sure it couldn't have been.

He surveyed his surroundings, taking in the small cubicle formed by bookcases. Paperback books and old leather-bound volumes crammed the shelves. Empty cardboard cartons, several crushed by his fall, took up much of the floor space.

"I thought I knew every inch of this bookstore," he said. "What is this place?"

"My secret room," I said. "I found it when I was a kid, looking for a place to hide."

"Why would it let you enter?" He jabbed a finger toward the now transparent barrier. "And not me?"

"Believe me, I haven't a clue." I shrugged. "You know as well as I do that in Bedlam Books, things have minds of their own."

Jack stared as if puzzling over a discrepancy in his ledgers. Then his gaze flicked away to the crushed cartons at his feet. He picked up one of the damaged cartons and proceeded to flatten it. A canary-colored paper fluttered onto the floor. Jack plucked it up.

"A packing slip," he said, his eyes widening as he read. "These are my boxes."

I nodded. "I found them in the basement. I couldn't let you return those books only to have them destroyed. So I moved them here."

Jack dropped the packing slip and the flattened box. He riffled through the rest of the boxes, tossing aside empty containers as he dug through the pile. In the bottom of the last carton, he found a dozen paperback romances—all that remained of my purloined inventory.

"Where are all the books?" Jack's head jerked to face me, eyes searching mine. "These cartons were full. I packed them myself."

"I sold them," I said.

"You sold them?" Jack's eyes couldn't have opened any wider. "Every one?"

"Why does everyone seem so surprised that I can sell books?" I bristled. "Yes, I sold them." I pointed to the partially-filled box. "What you see is all that's left."

Jack glanced down at the few paperbacks in the carton. His gaze flicked away to stare at the bookcases. Slowly, his jaw melted open. I tracked his gaze to the titles on the shelf. Oh, toadstools. He had discovered the paperback mysteries.

"Gods, Cory," he growled. "Not the mysteries, too?"

"I didn't take them." I raised my hands in a gesture of surrender. "Honest. They found their own way here."

Jack's eyes grew grayer. Overcast. Accusation and hurt swirled in his irises.

"But you've been selling them behind my back."

"Yes." I nodded. "In the tea shop. Tea and a 'cozy.' I know I should have been honest with you from the start. I never meant to hurt you. I did it for Uncle Horace. I did it for Bedlam Books."

Jack's mouth closed, his lips pressed in a tense line. He swallowed. His Adam's apple bobbed over the crisp collar. I could not fathom what he was thinking. He kept his thoughts to himself, his feelings as buttoned-up as his shirts.

"Jack, I'm so sorry."

But he did not reply. His eyes had turned an icy blue. No sign of the boy underneath. Only cool, distant self-control.

His expression hardened, the granite exterior locked back in place as if a magical wall had been erected between us. Only this time, I was the one locked out.

"Jack?" I reached for his arm.

He averted his eyes and shrugged free of me. He left without a word or backward glance. Just like my father had. I listened for the sound of his wingtips retreating across the floorboards. I wanted to chase after him, but my feet wouldn't move. The door creaked open and shut to the jangle of shop bells. Those chimes that once sounded so cheery now played a melancholy tune.

Where was he going? I could guess. My confession had driven him back into Rebecca's arms.

My fingers groped for the romance novel in my apron pocket. I pulled out the book and stared. *Tainted Love*. Oh, the irony. Unlike my novel, truth had not saved the day, the heroine did not get her Heath, and the villainous Lady Gwendolyn Fairbanks with all her underhanded dealings had won.

I choked back my tears. No happy endings for me.

Chapter Twenty-Five

Dark Knightly of the Soul

My terrible day didn't end when Jack walked out on me. I climbed the stairs to my apartment after work and found Aunt Gertrude and Mother waiting for me in the living room. My overbearing aunt had wasted no time making good on her threats.

Aunt Gertrude sat frowning across from my mother, poised in one of Uncle Horace's tweed armchairs. Dressed in black from head to toe and crowned with her lacquered gray hair, she reminded me of a judge on the bench. And I was on trial.

"Come here, Cory." Mother patted the cushion of the chocolate-colored leather sofa beside her.

I sighed and sank onto the couch beside my mother. Unlike the last time, no tea or sandwiches had been set on the coffee table to soften the blow. Could this day get any worse?

"I've filled in your mother about your impertinent behavior this afternoon." Aunt Gertrude cleared her throat.

"You should also know that Rebecca Burgin summoned me. She tells me that Jack Wickham slept here last night."

"Is that true, Cory?" Mother's eyes fixed on me. Worry etched lines on her forehead.

"Yes, but . . ." For a moment, I didn't know where to begin. But then indignation at Rebecca for tattling on me burbled up in my chest. How dare she? My defenses rose like bile into my throat.

"She didn't tell you the whole story. They had a fight last week. She kicked him out. He'd been sleeping in the office in Bedlam Books for days."

"That's not your affair." Aunt Gertrude leaned forward and slapped her hand on the coffee table as if pounding a gavel to restore order.

But I would not be deterred. If Aunt Gertrude would not listen, surely Mother would. I swiveled to face her.

"Mother, you should have seen how tired he looked." My words tumbled over each other to get out. "That's why I brought him here. I wanted your advice. But you weren't home and didn't answer my calls. Where were—"

"Am I to understand that you were alone in this apartment with Jack Wickham?" Aunt Gertrude bellowed, cutting off my justification in mid-sentence. "And he spent the night?"

My eyes widened in horror at her implication. My mouth gaped open, words arrested on my tongue. My innocent intentions had been mistaken for . . . Oh, toadstools.

"We didn't sleep together, if that's what you're implying." I planted my hands on my hips, nearly spearing my mother with an elbow. I scowled at my aunt. "I slept on the sofa."

"That is true, Gertie," Mother piped up. "When I came

home, Cory was asleep on this couch. I assumed that she had tried to wait up for me."

Aunt Gertrude harrumphed. She leaned back in her chair and planted her elbows on the arm rests, stubby fingers tented in front of her double chin. Contemplating? I held my breath.

"That is some consolation," she said. Then she shook her finger at me. "But appearances suggested otherwise. This is not proper behavior for a young lady. Clearly, you need better judgment and . . ." She cast her withering glare at my mother. "More supervision."

Mother's turn in the boiling cauldron.

"Now, Gert, you know that's not fair." Mother stiffened and returned her older sister's steely gaze. Only then did I see Mother's eyes were puffy and red. She had been crying. I'd been too caught up in my own drama to notice. What had happened to her?

Before I could ask, Aunt Gertrude's laser stare cut back to me. She didn't have to pound the table this time for me to know that she was about to announce her verdict. My fingers dug into the edge of the couch cushion. I braced myself for impending doom.

"Cory, you leave me no choice but to contest the entire will—"

"You can't do that." I leapt to my feet. My fingers balled into fists.

"Oh, yes, I can. And I will."

"But Mother and I need the income. How will we—"

"It's not your job to take care of your mother." She leaned forward again and pounded the wooden coffee table with her fist, punctuating her words with each strike. "You are a child." *Bam.* "It's your parents' job to take care of you." *Bam.* "Your job is to finish your education." *Bam. Bam.*

"BUT—"

"Sit down and let me finish," Aunt Gertrude's voice thundered over my protests.

She sprang from her chair, raising herself to her full height. Although she was several inches shorter than I, the look she cast me would have quelled the caw from a crow. My words evaporated on my tongue. Mother tugged on my arm, gently pulling me back down onto the sofa. Still hovering over me, Aunt Gertrude cleared her throat.

"I will contest the will, unless..." She paused for effect, letting the hiss of the final 's' hang in the air. Then she counted off her conditions on stumpy fingers. "One. You go back to school and leave the running of Bedlam Books wholly and entirely to Jack Wickham. Two. You are not to date him or in any way entangle your business with romance."

The memory of Jack storming out on me spun up in my brain. The disappointment on his face and the coldness in his gray-blue eyes haunted me. My book-selling, tea shop deception had ruined any chance of a romance with him.

"You don't have to worry about that anymore, Aunt." I muttered under my breath, but not quietly enough.

"Whatever happened, dear?" Mother grasped my hand and squeezed.

"Don't encourage her, Millie." Aunt Gertrude pursed her wrinkled lips. Her chins quivered over her high-necked collar. "I am not finished." Her index finger stabbed the air. "Furthermore, you are to quit working at Bedlam Books immediately."

"Quit?" Muscles in my legs twitched. I wanted to jump up again, but my mother held me firmly in my seat. My eyes looked up, now beseeching my aunt. "But who will run my tea shop?"

"Your mother can take over at the tea shop," Aunt Gertrude said, settling back in the tweed armchair. Her matter-of-fact tone suggested that the issue had already been discussed and decided. Without me.

"Mother?" I twisted in my seat to face her. Surely, she would take my side. Surely, she had some counter argument to dissuade my aunt. I could not give up Bedlam Books. That was too much to ask.

"Dear, I'm afraid I must agree with your aunt on this one point." Mother squeezed my hand again and patted my sleeve. "After everything you've been through, I think you need to get away from Bedlam Books for a while."

"Away? But where?" I couldn't go back to my old school in London. We didn't have money for the tuition. And as it was July, school wasn't in session here either.

"Your father is in town, and he wants to see you."

Mother's words washed over me like a tidal wave. If I hadn't been sitting already, I would have fallen to the floor. The last time I saw my father was just after the dissolution of his London bookstore. Without a word or goodbye, he walked out and didn't come back. That was months ago and I hadn't seen nor heard from him since.

"Daddy's here?" My voice squeaked as if I was five years old again, instead of seventeen.

"Yes, his boat is docked in the marina," Mother said.

Connections clicked together in my brain like the pieces of a puzzle. Mother's mysterious absences. Her late nights. Her red eyes. She'd been meeting with my father. A million questions burst from my lips.

"How long has he been here? Is that where you were last night? Is he back? Why didn't you tell me?"

"It's not that simple. Cory, please." Mother raised both hands, palms forward to slow me down. That she didn't raise her voice like Aunt Gertrude, but spoke calmly, only increased my alarm.

She had more news to share. And from the deepening creases on her forehead, it wasn't good news either. My fingers worried in my lap, picking at the coarse fabric of my work apron.

"Your father and I are divorcing," she said. "He doesn't want to stay. He wants to travel again. On his boat. And that's no life for me."

"So that's where you've been all week? Talking with Daddy?" I searched her eyes, looking for answers.

"Not just your father." She paused and took a breath. "I've also been meeting with Elspeth's lawyer. He's handling the divorce. Drawing up the papers. We've little left after the bankruptcy, so there isn't much to divide." She placed her hand over mine again and squeezed. "I'm sorry, dear."

"Oh." I stared down at her hand, resting on mine.

This was a lot to process. My father's leaving was one thing. That could be reversed, and we could be a family once again. But a divorce? That sounded so ... final. The revelation swept all my foundations out from under me as if washed out to sea.

My lower lip trembled. Moisture pooled at the corners of my eyes. But I wouldn't cry in front of Aunt Gertrude. I wouldn't give her the satisfaction. I bit my lip and blinked back any tears.

"Your father wants to see you." Mother coaxed me back to the conversation. "He's invited you to spend the rest of the summer with him on his boat. He's sailing to Cabo San Lucifer tomorrow. He's promised to have you back here in time for school."

Imagine being trapped on a little sailboat for a month. With my father. Who walked out on us. No Mother. No Bedlam Books. No Jack. No MacTeague either.

"And if I don't want to go?" My eyes flicked from my mother to my aunt, searching for any sign. Any hint. Any hope. There must be some way out of this.

Aunt Gertrude's pinched mouth and resolute gaze telegraphed otherwise. She was as immovable as a mountain with the empathy of a rock.

"Well, then, as I said . . ." She leaned back in her chair, tenting her fingers as before. "You leave me no choice but to contest the will."

After the bankruptcy of my father's shop, I had some idea of what that could mean. Lots of legal wrangling. Looking at my stern Aunt Gertrude, I could imagine what a judge would say. The list of my transgressions ticked off in my head: underage drinking, caused a brawl at a bar, hexed a plebian. I cringed. And if we lost the lawsuit, Mother and I would lose Uncle Horace's bookstore. For good.

I'd already ruined things with Jack. If I were gone, there would be no one to stand in his way. He could implement his business plan as he'd wanted all along. Surely, he would not be sorry to see me go.

"And if I agree to leave with my father, then you'll drop the suit." My eyes bored into Aunt Gertrude's. I wasn't about to agree to anything without confirmation. Too much was at stake.

"Yes." She met my gaze with equal intensity and nodded.

"And the trust will remain intact?" I said.

"Yes," Aunt Gertrude nodded again. "You and your mother will share in any profits to be had."

"And I will take care of the shop and keep an eye on

Jack for you." Mother patted my arm, her hand warm and comforting on my skin.

I swallowed hard. While Aunt Gertrude had many qualities that I did not like, she was unfailingly truthful. She would do just as she had promised. Either way, I could not win.

If I took her devil's bargain, at least Mother and I would still have a stake in Bedlam Books, although I would be banished. I looked from my aunt to my mother. Her half-smile, while meant to be encouraging, only accentuated the wrinkles accumulating on her brow. After all my mistakes, did I have another choice?

"Agreed." I could barely choke out the word. Every impulse in my being fought against it.

As soon as the word left my lips, something monstrous and bleak stomped all over my heart. I reflexively reached for the romance novel in my pocket. But nothing could offer me solace today.

Chapter Twenty-Six

Dirty Gertie

Armed with a small suitcase and a book bag filled with my favorite romance novels, I resigned myself to my fate of a month aboard my father's sailboat. After tearful good-byes from Mother, Aunt Elspeth drove me to the Berkeley Marina that Sunday. The marine layer should have burned back to the coast well before noon, but it clung to the bay, the sky overcast like my mood.

I'd had no opportunity to speak with Jack, as Bedlam Books was closed today. After he had learned that I'd been selling genre fiction behind his back, I wasn't sure he would talk to me anyway, and I wouldn't dare risk an encounter with Rebecca by knocking on his apartment door. On Monday morning, he would learn of the deal I'd brokered with Aunt Gertrude and that I would not be in his way any longer. While he might forget me, I could not forget the disillusioned look on his face when we'd parted yesterday afternoon.

My father stood waiting for me in the parking lot by

a chain link fence and gate that cordoned off the docks. His graying hair, partially hidden under a captain's hat, was nearly shoulder-length now, much longer than when I last saw him months ago. His face and arms were bronzed. Wearing a colorful Hawaiian shirt and casual slacks, he looked more relaxed than I'd seen him in years. As our eyes met, a smile spread over his trimmed salt-and-pepper beard.

"There's my girl," he said, as I stepped from Aunt Elspeth's sedan. He spread his arms wide, inviting me into a hug.

Conflicting feelings churned in my gut. Part of me wanted to be his little girl again, wanted everything to be just like before. But another part of me knew that wasn't possible. When he left, a rift had torn between us. One that could not be so easily mended.

"Daddy." I hugged him nonetheless, for a moment basking in the warmth of his embrace. But perhaps he felt my tension too. He released me, ending with an awkward pat on my back.

"Hello Elspeth." He peered into the car at my aunt still sitting behind the wheel with the engine idling.

"Ulysses." Aunt Elspeth smiled back, her lips pressed tightly into a tense line. I didn't need a crystal ball to know that, like me, she was not at all happy with this arrangement.

As I grabbed my luggage from her car, she twisted in the driver's seat to face me. "Summon me if you need anything, Cory. Anything at all."

"Thank you, Auntie." I nodded. "I will."

I waved goodbye, watching as her sedan pulled from the parking lot. Gravel crunched under the tires, crushed like my heart. A spark snuffed out within me as her taillights disappeared in the distance.

"What have you got in here?" Daddy's voice pulled me

back to the moment. With a teasing grin, he hoisted my backpack on his shoulder. "As if I didn't know."

"Books, of course."

"We'll have so many adventures, I'm not sure you'll have much time for reading." His hazel eyes sparkled, enticing me. "Come see."

He hefted my suitcase and led me down a wooden gangway toward the boat slips. The docks jutted out into the harbor in orderly rows like the bookshelves in our store. But instead of books, boats of every description and size filled the berths on each side. There were sailboats, motor boats, and yachts. If Daddy had not been leading the way, I would have never found his boat.

We stopped in front of a modest white sailboat, a Beneteau tethered to the docks. Its bare masts pierced the gray sky, sails still buried under their blue canvas covers. The name Rhapsody had been painted in blue script on the back. Except for a faint aura of magic that glowed purple around the hull, it appeared much like any normal sailboat.

He spritely hopped on board, despite my heavy luggage and a smidgen of middle-aged girth. He plunked my suitcase and backpack on one of the benches.

"Welcome aboard the Rhapsody, m'lady." He bowed from the waist and extended his hand to me with a flourish.

I giggled in spite of myself and took his hand, as he helped me onto the boat. Then he unlocked a wooden door to the cabin below and motioned for me to enter.

Down a short ladder were our living quarters, a galley kitchenette on my left and a modest bathroom on the right. Straight ahead was a built-in wooden table with cushioned benches along each side, which doubled as couches for sleeping. Above the benches, cubbies and little round portholes lined the sides of the cabin. Beyond the table, another opening lead to an alcove at the front of the boat used for additional sleeping quarters. These cramped confines would be my new home for the rest of the summer?

"You can sleep in the front berth," Daddy pointed toward the alcove. "You'll have more privacy there. I'll be fine on one of these benches."

My father tucked my backpack and suitcase into a cubby, and lifted a bench cushion to show off the storage space hidden underneath where he'd stashed a spare sleeping bag and pillows. What I wouldn't give to see MacTeague hiding in one of those, but my precious pup was back home with Mother. Daddy grinned as he showed off his prized vessel. I pasted a smile on the outside, but inside I cringed. I hoped the weather would be nice and I could be out on deck most of the time.

The table had been set for lunch. Lobster rolls and iced tea for two. I slid onto the bench across the table from my father. He doffed the captain's cap and tossed it on the bench beside him.

"Eat up." Daddy gestured toward my plate. "And tell me what you've been up to."

"Um," I took a sip of my iced tea, stalling. So much had happened. Where could I begin? And did I really want to tell my father? I decided to go with the obvious.

"I've been working at Bedlam Books," I said. "You know, like old times."

"How's Jack?" Daddy said. "I hear he's just like his old man, Robert. Couldn't call him Bob. You'd catch hell for that." He chuckled. "Robert Wickham always was a stuffy, buttoned-down, stick-in-the-mud."

How could I answer that? Yes, Jack could be uptight at times. But then again, he could be kind and noble, like when he rescued me at the bar. And oh, those mesmerizing eyes.

"Yes . . . well, no . . . Not exactly . . . Look, I don't want to talk about Jack."

"What happened? You two have a fight?"

My father took a bite of his sandwich, washed it down with a swig of iced tea, then studied my face. He was fishing, trawling for gossip, just like Aunt Elspeth. I averted my eyes, staring down at my lunch. I could feel the heat coloring my cheeks, pink like the lobster on my plate.

"I said I don't want to talk about it."

"Ah, I knew it." My father slapped the table top. "But don't you worry. You can do better than boring, old Jack." He beamed at me. "You're my girl. You're just like me. We're fun and carefree."

Jack might be a bit boring, but he was faithful. He kept his promise to Rebecca, even though the magic that brought her back was breaking down. I was sure that he would never walk out on his family, like my father had. What HAD my father been doing these past months?

"I'm more interested in what you've been doing, Daddy."

"Travelling again." He gestured, sweeping his arms wide as he spoke like a circus barker. "Sailing the Caribbean. Basking in tropical paradise. Having adventures." Then he placed his big paw over my small hand. His voice softened. "I know this is hard for you, Cory. But the bookstore . . . being tied to one place . . . wasn't right for me. And when it failed, that was my wake-up call. I needed to find myself again."

"But what about Mother and me?" I pulled my hand back. My eyes probed his. "What about your family?"

"After twenty odd years, your mother is tired of moving around. We've grown apart." His shoulders shrugged the Hawaiian shirt. "But you . . ." He pointed at me. The twinkle reappeared in his hazel eyes. "You're young, full of adventure. Think of the fun we'll have together."

His enthusiasm was contagious. Despite my misgivings, I felt my resolve fade. Perhaps I could give him another chance.

"Where will we travel?" I said. "What would we be doing?"

"Just what I've been doing these past months." He gestured wildly, the circus barker back again. "Sailing to exotic ports. Eating the local fare. Living off the odd job here and there. Experiencing the world."

As I was beginning to fall under his spell, other thoughts punctured the charm. Even when I was a child, I sent postcards to my uncle. Mother and I communicated with Uncle Horace regularly. But while my father had been busy living his new life, he had not contacted me. Not once.

"Why didn't you call me? Why didn't you write?"

Daddy pointed over his shoulder at a cracked mirror mounted on the side of the cabin next to the bathroom. The glass had fractured, jagged shards still clinging to the surface of the mirror.

"I had a little accident. It got broken in a storm. Haven't had time to get it fixed yet."

That explained a lot. Magi didn't use phones. We summoned one another on the Prism Communication Network using magic mirrors. If his was broken, then . . .

Panic twisted in my gut. If we had no mirror, I couldn't summon Aunt Elspeth. I couldn't talk to Mother to find out what was happening at Bedlam Books. Or with Jack.

"So how did Mother . . .?" I stared at my distorted reflection in the fractured glass. "How can anyone reach you?"

"When in port, you can usually find one. Besides, I find that being difficult to locate isn't always a bad thing . . ."

I didn't hear the rest of what he said. I pulled my backpack from the cubby. My fingers fished inside. My eyes searched its contents, frantically looking for my compact mirror. Did I remember to pack it?

As my fingers closed on the compact, contents spilled on the table next to my plate. My favorite romance novel, the one I'd carried with me all these months, tumbled out and skidded across the table toward my father. Its title, *Tainted Love*, blinked in Valentine red along with the author's name underneath, Wanda Witherspoon.

My father picked up the book and let out a hearty guffaw.

"What's so funny?" I said.

"You and your romances." A playful sparkle lit his hazel eyes. "What do you know about Wanda Witherspoon?"

"She's my favorite writer. Author of the acclaimed *Poisoned Passion* series and famed recluse. She's never appeared in public. No one knows much about her."

"Ah, but you do." He burst out laughing again.

Clearly, I was missing something. I'd told him everything I knew about Wanda Witherspoon. Even *Wicked-pedia* had little information on her, apart from a list of her romance titles. And I should know. I'd checked often, looking for the release dates of each new novel.

"What do you mean?" I said.

"Because Wanda Witherspoon is a pen name." He leaned back in his seat. The smile broadened across his face. He teased out the moment. The suspense was killing me. What did he know? Finally, he said, "The real Wanda is your Aunt Gertrude."

"NO! You can't be serious." My eyes widened. My mouth gaped.

Aunt Gertrude? Prim and proper Aunt Gertrude a romance writer? Wanda Witherspoon her *nom de plume*? What could my bossy maiden aunt know about romance?

"How do you know this?" I practically leapt from my seat.

But Daddy leaned back in his. His broad grin telegraphed that he was relishing every moment of this.

"I bumped into Harlan Quinn in Cabo San Lucifer. He's retired now and cruising on his yacht."

Harlan Quinn was the former publisher and editor for Pentacle Publishing's "Blushing Heat" romance line. This promised to be juicy news. I scooted forward on the bench seat and leaned over the table.

"While drinking and talking about the book business, he found out that I knew Gertrude Knightly." Laugh lines shot from the corners of Daddy's eyes. "So he starts asking about 'Dirty Gertie' and boasting about their secret affair."

"No," I feigned scandal, clutching my hand to my chest like the ingénue in one of my romances. Then I burst out in girlish giggles.

"The relationship went south, and she broke it off, claiming that it almost ruined her writing career. Afterward, she assumed the pen name of Wanda Witherspoon. And there you have it." His robust laugh filled the little cabin again.

Aha! Now I understood why Aunt Gertrude was so against mixing business with romance, and so opposed to my relationship with Jack. But maybe I could use this new knowledge to my advantage.

"And no one else knows this?" I leaned forward and asked in a conspiratorial whisper.

"I don't think so." Daddy shook his head. "I think your mother would have mentioned that."

"Good, let this be our secret."

I stared at the cover of my book, suddenly seeing new possibilities. Aunt Gertrude had managed to keep her youthful indiscretions and her *nom de plume* a secret from both her younger sisters. This was family gossip that even Aunt Elspeth did not know. Armed with this new information, I now had a powerful card to play. One word to Aunt Elspeth, and this would be secret no more.

My smile widened. I scooped my spilled belongings back into my pack, leaving the folding compact mirror within easy reach on the table. I was about to stuff a small white business card in with the rest, when I paused. Rod's business card. What was Rod's connection with Dawkins?

"Daddy?" My eyes shot up to look at my father. "What do you know about Paul Dawkins and his embezzling?"

"Why do you ask?" With the change in subject, creases spiked between my father's eyebrows. His mirth faded.

"You weren't the only one bumping into people." I averted my gaze, now staring down at the business card. "When Aunt Elspeth and I went back to London to pack up my things, I ran into Paul Dawkins outside your old bookshop."

"What were you doing there?" Concern punctuated his words.

I sighed. "Looking for you."

"Oh, Cory." My father's big hand reached across the table toward me, then retracted and fisted. His voice rose. "What did that thieving weasel Dawkins want with you?"

"He was looking for you. Said something about owing someone lots of money."

"Yes," he paused as if thinking. "Some loan shark named Flanagan."

"Flanagan?" My gaze flicked up. There it was, that name again.

My fingers folded on Rod's business card. Mahoney and Tyler Construction. Rod's brother, Mike Tyler, was co-owner of the business, and his partner was a woman. Moll Flanagan Mahoney. She and the loan shark couldn't be related, could they? I shook my head. Just an odd coincidence.

"Yes," Daddy said. "That's what I heard. While we still had our business, Dawkins embezzled from our store to make regular payments to this Flanagan fellow."

My mind flashed back to my father's London bookstore and the day we found Dawkins' checkbook and the mysterious payments drawn on our accounts. I pictured the checkbook and the notes Dawkins had scribbled on the stub. "MT" followed by a string of numbers. A bank account.

"MT," I whispered. "The notation in the checkbook."

"That's right."

I replayed the day that Mother and Aunt Elspeth had hired Rod Tyler. I recalled his devil-may-care grin and his words as he handed me this business card now gripped in my trembling fingers. *My company offers financing. Nothing down and no payments for the first sixty days.* Could MT be Mahoney and Tyler?

"Cory, what's wrong?" My father's voice seemed to come from miles away as if he were still out at sea.

I stared down at the cabin's varnished wooden table, seeing a different table before me—the rough bar table with neon lights splashing colors across its scarred surface. Then Rod sat across from me. Not my father.

What was it that Rod had said about Moll? *She's not in the construction business. More the money side.* Moll Mahoney and that ruffian Flanagan were more than related. They were the loan sharks.

"Oh, Daddy." I slid the business card toward him on the table. "MT. Don't you see? Mahoney and Tyler."

"Where did you get this?" He picked up and studied the card. His brow furrowed.

"Mahoney and Tyler were the contractors that did the renovations for our tea café." I stabbed my finger back toward town. My words rose in pitch along with my panic. "If not for Aunt Elspeth, Mother and I would have taken their financing as well. Hell's bells. We almost borrowed from the same loan shark."

"Now calm down." Daddy motioned with both hands palms forward. He shook his head. "They can't be the same. Dawkins' loan shark was in London. How would they have found you in Berkeley?"

"Aunt Elspeth made a sample business card for Bedlam Books," I said, my voice shrill and breathless. "It had my name on it and our address. After I ran into Dawkins, it was gone. He must have stolen it. But then Rod had it."

"Who's Rod?" Daddy leaned forward. His hand fisted. Sinew rippled on his tanned arm.

"Rod Tyler." I jabbed at the card. "The contractor. Mahoney and Tyler. Daddy, there was only one card. And he had it."

"Are you absolutely sure?" My father scowled.

"Yes, Daddy." My head bobbed up and down. I jumped from my seat. "The loan sharks were in my bookstore. I need to go back home now. I need to warn Mother. I need to warn Jack."

Chapter Twenty-Seven

Tainted Trinkets

The same thugs who were after Paul Dawkins had been inside my shop. After all the renovations he'd done, Rod knew every inch of our bookstore. I cringed remembering how I'd accidently hexed him at the bar. What revenge would he plot for me in retaliation? There was no telling what those hoodlums would do. If Dawkins, a grown man, was terrified of them, what would they do to Mother?

I seized my compact mirror from the cabin table and tried to summon Mother then Jack to warn them about Mahoney and Tyler. Hello? Hello? But only my anxious reflection stared back from the magic mirror. No one answered at either apartment. Neither Mother nor Jack was home.

But as promised, Aunt Elspeth did answer my summons. We decided that she would come for me at the marina and take me back to Bedlam Books. Then we would split up. She would find Mother, while I went to find Jack.

My father and I waited for Aunt Elspeth by the gangway

gate. True to her word, she pulled into the marina parking lot to pick me up minutes later.

"I should come with you," Daddy said. His stance stiffened in stark contrast to his relaxed attire and bright Hawaiian shirt.

But after my bitter parting with Jack, I wanted to meet with him alone. The last thing I needed was my father eavesdropping on that conversation. I repressed a grimace.

"No, Daddy." I pasted on my most reassuring smile and shook my head. "Someone should stay behind, just in case Jack or Mother comes looking for me here."

"Are you sure?" Worry creased his brow.

"Yes, I'll be fine. Really." I patted his arm. Then my fingers reached into my backpack, pulled out my compact mirror, and pressed it into his big palm. "Here, I want you to keep this. Now I'll always have a way to contact you."

His hand closed around the mirror. Moisture leaked from the corners of his eyes.

"I love you, Cory girl. Be safe out there."

I hugged Daddy goodbye. Not a half-hearted embrace, like the one we'd exchanged when I first arrived, but a full-on bear hug this time. This goodbye was not forever. As long as he had my mirror, I knew I would see him again.

I pulled from his embrace, threw my backpack and suitcase into Aunt Elspeth's car, and hopped in after them. As Aunt Elspeth's sedan peeled away from the Berkeley Marina, I turned to wave. Although Daddy smiled and waved back, I didn't need to be a mind-reader to know that he wanted me to stay. But this time, I was the one leaving. I had to. I had to warn the others.

Aunt Elspeth's car screeched to a halt in front of Bedlam Books. I leapt from her vehicle, slung my backpack over my shoulder, and raced toward the front door. Although it was mid-afternoon, the marine mist had crept inland, shrouding Chanting Way in a haze of gray. Through the leaded panes, I could see lights on inside the closed shop. Jack must have been inside working today.

My fingers jammed the key into the lock and tugged on the dragon-snout handle. In my haste, I almost forgot to lock it again behind me. Then my feet beat a path through the maze of bookcases to Jack's office.

"Jack?" I rapped my knuckles on his office door, then pushed it open. But the office was dark. Jack was not sitting at the claw-footed, hickory desk.

I wove a path toward the back of the shop and my tea corner. Here, cheery lights illuminated the clusters of wrought iron café tables and chairs. The aromas of cinnamon and nutmeg from Mother's freshly baked cauldron cakes filled the air. My eyes spied a batch on the counter, wrapped in floral paper, ready for tomorrow's customers. Mother had been here not long ago.

"Mother?" I said.

Scuffling noises sounded from under the cupboard. The door creaked open a crack. A little bony snout poked from the space and sniffed. MacTeague. My precious pooch must have followed Mother down here. He always did love a game of Hide and Seek.

"Hi, MacTeague." I crouched down in front of the cupboard. I snaked my hand inside to scratch his skull. He rewarded me with a lick from his phantom tongue.

"Where's Mother?" I asked him, although he had no vocal chords and could not bark.

But as if in reply, florescent lights flickered. *Bzzt! Pop!*

Section by section across Bedlam Books, banks of ceiling lights went out. Darkness enveloped the shop. Far from the front of the store, I could not even see the feeble afternoon light through the display window.

"Mother?"

My ears pricked, listening. I blinked, willing my eyes to adjust. Even without electricity, the store remained dimly lit in eerie light, illumination that did not come from outside, but from within Bedlam Books itself. Each book, each enchanted object, emitted a faint, silvery glow—an aura of magical energy. I never realized just how much magic was here until I knelt in the middle of an unlit shop filled with glowing merchandise.

Click-scrape. Click-scrape. Click-scrape. The slow progress of labored footsteps echoed, coming from the rear of the store.

Startled, I jolted to my feet. My backpack slipped from my shoulder and landed with a thud on the floor beside me. Oh, toadstools. That noise betrayed my presence.

"Jack?" I said, my voice now as shaky as my knocking knees. My ears tracked the measured sound of the footfalls. Coming closer. "Rebecca? Is that you?"

I eased the cupboard door closed with my leg, shutting my pooch safely inside. My eyes locked on an approaching figure. Its black silhouette, backlit by the glow of the books, lurched down the aisle toward me. I took a single step backward.

An arm encircled me from behind. Another hand clamped over my mouth, stifling my scream. I grasped the leather-clad arm that held me, trying to pry it loose. I squirmed and kicked to wrest myself free.

"Easy, Cory." Hot breath panted against my ear. A stubble beard scratched.

I gasped. I knew that man's voice. My ears had once ached to hear the sound of it. Rod Tyler.

The revelation hit me like a stunning hex. I could not move. My arms and legs would no longer cooperate. Rod's sinewy arm pinned me from behind, my back pressed against his chest.

The shadowy figure clomped into the tea corner, leading with the right foot, dragging the left behind. The woman's slim frame, robed in a youthful pink sundress, was contorted and stiff as if with age. Her distorted face, framed in golden curls, floated into view. Rebecca.

"You can uncover her mouth," she said. Her lips twisted into a sneer. "No one will hear her scream."

Hell's bells. What was going on here? What was she planning to do to me? Make me like her? Over my dead body. Or maybe that was the plan.

The hand over my mouth loosened its grip.

"Heeeeelp. Mother." I shot a glance toward the back door, praying she was still around here somewhere.

"Not here," Rebecca said, tittering. "She left a half hour ago with your Aunt Gertrude."

"Jaaaaaack," I screamed. I craned my neck toward the front door, hoping against hope to see his tall frame weaving through the stacks toward me.

"He's not here to help you this time, sweetheart." Rod's taunting words hissed in my ear, his stubble beard against my neck as abrasive as his words.

I struggled against him, but was no match for his brawn. Both Rod's arms now encased me tighter than an Iron Maidenform corset.

"Where's Jack?" My eyes bored into Rebecca's.

"He's gone." She hobbled another step closer. The crooked smile on her pink lips widened.

"Gone? Where?" My voice squeaked.

"To the marina to find you," she said. "But he won't. Not until it's too late."

Rod guffawed, his mocking at my expense. His laughter rumbled in his chest and vibrated against my back, but he might as well have punched me in the gut. My breath gushed from my lungs. He'd never been interested in me. My dark-haired prince was nothing more than a hired thug. And Jack was too far away to help me now.

Rebecca took another step toward me. "You should have stayed away." She jabbed a warped finger. "I warned you. But your kind never learns."

"You warned me? When?" I nearly spat the words at her. "Your aunt did that. She threatened me. And you told Jack that was a lie."

Rebecca arched her penciled right eyebrow. A smirk contorted her lips further.

"I'll let you in on a little secret," she said. "I have a lot in common with my aunt. You see, we're both clairvoyant."

She giggled again. Clearly, she thought this was some sort of joke. But it didn't make sense. That reanimation spell must have done more than mangle her body. It must have addled her brain.

I squirmed and kicked against Rod, but his cast-iron grip only tightened around me, pinning my arms to my sides. Panic flittered in my chest. I could feel the defensive magic prickling over my skin. Maybe if I could keep Rebecca talking long enough, help would come.

"Have you gone mad?" I said. "What are you talking about?"

"Allow me to tell your fortune." Rebecca waggled her right eyebrow and snickered. "You see, you're going to die.

The unfortunate casualty of a burglary. Committed by the same group of crooks that ruined your father's bookstore."

What? I was so surprised that the fight went out of me. My body went limp in Rod's arm like the swooning maidens in one of my romances. Rod must have told her about Mahoney and Tyler. Did she know about Paul Dawkins, too? How much did she know about my father's bookstore?

"You don't know anything about my father or his business."

Rebecca grinned. Well, half of her mouth grinned, displaying two rows of perfect, white teeth. The left side remained closed as if sewn shut.

"That's what you think," she said. "A banshee from the U.K. came into my aunt's shop asking questions about you. She left her calling card."

"Moll Mahoney." The name slipped out of my mouth in a hushed whisper.

Rod flinched. His arm around my chest cinched tighter, causing me to gulp for air.

Oh, she's not silent, Rod's words, spoken in the bar about Moll. Their truth struck home. Moll Mahoney was the banshee, and her wail a harbinger of death and destruction.

"Yes, that's the one." Rebecca nodded. Her blonde curls bobbed in the eerie light. "Too bad she didn't get rid of you herself. But she proved useful in other ways."

I scowled at her. "Liar!"

Rebecca's eyes narrowed, regarding me through slotted lids. She reached her right hand toward me. A bracelet circling her wrist rattled. I stared at the single silver pendant swinging like a pendulum from her outstretched arm. A charm in the shape of a human skull, the wristlet made of human teeth.

My eyes tracked Rebecca's hand and that cursed bracelet coming closer. I recoiled, slamming the back of my head against Rod. Whatever hex that bangle contained, I wasn't about to let it touch me. I knew a dangerous talisman when I saw one. This was *Venenum*, black magic of the worst sort.

"Get that thing away from me," Rod said as he jumped backward. Even he knew that charm was bad news.

He let go, shoving me hard toward the café counter. My right arm bashed against its edge. A bolt of electric pain jolted down my arm. I bounced off and landed on the floor next to my backpack. I winced, gripped my throbbing limb, and looked up.

"Grab the money from the office safe," Rebecca said to Rod, but she kept her eyes on me. "There should be plenty in there to repay you handsomely. And ransack the office. Make it look like a random burglary."

Rod nodded, but his eyes remained locked on her bracelet. He backed out of my tea corner, then he turned and pelted down the aisle toward Jack's office.

"You'll never get away with this," I said. "Jack will identify Rod. He'll know. My aunt will tell him."

"Maybe." She lurched toward me. "Or maybe he'll believe his sweet Becca instead."

She extended her arm and pointed at me, her pink, painted nails like talons. The tainted charm dangled, swinging closer to my face.

I scuttled away on all fours like a crab. My shoulder hit the cupboard behind me, then my back. Oh, bat poo. My eyes shot to either side. Trapped against the cupboards. Nowhere else to go. Amulet coming closer.

"No." I swatted at her arm.

Sparks discharged from my fingertips. Rebecca winced and yanked her hand away as if she had received a nasty shock. She shuffled two steps backward.

I stared at my own right hand. A chain of golden sparks wrapped my arm whirling around my wrist like the lights on a Ferris wheel. Well, I'll be a mummy's uncle. It seemed I had my own talisman, a beautiful bracelet of defensive magic.

"So you want to play, do you?" Rebecca regarded me with the wary stare of a cobra eyeing a mongoose.

"No." I shook my head. My chest tightened. Bile burbled up my throat. Defensive magic was no match for the evil she had. There must be some way out of this. Think.

A scuffling noise sounded from the cupboard near me. MacTeague. I'd shut him inside those cabinets. I held my breath. But Rebecca heard him too.

"What are you hiding in there?" she said.

Before I could stop her, she bent down and threw open the cupboard door. My skeletal pup bounded out and lunged at Rebecca. His bony jaw hinged open, revealing a mouthful of sharp canines.

"Aaaiiiii," Rebecca shrieked. She scrabbled to get away, raising her arm to shield her face.

The bracelet made of human teeth dangled in front of MacTeague's snout. His jaw clamped down on Rebecca's wrist and the cursed talisman. *Poof!* A cloud of acid green magic puffed into the air and engulfed my pet.

"MacTeague," I shouted. I covered my mouth and nose with my sleeve and leaned away from the toxic cloud.

My dog yelped. Impossible. MacTeague didn't have vocal chords.

When the smoke cleared, my familiar was gone.

MacTeague had disappeared without a trace. I stared at the open cupboard door, half expecting to see my petite pup. No ivory snout poked from under the sink. No bony tail shimmied to greet me. The cupboard was bare.

"Noooooo," I screamed. "What have you done to my dog?"

Rebecca straightened to her full height. She shook the magic dust from her pink skirt. No jangle from her wrist. The bracelet had disappeared, too.

"That vile creature got what it deserved. You've no idea what you've done." Rebecca shook her naked fist at me and bellowed. "My bracelet destroyed by that . . . that beast."

"Gone," I whispered, as the realization sunk in. MacTeague was gone.

Rebecca's nostrils flared as she drew in a deep breath. Her body lifted off the ground, her pink dress and golden hair billowing about her.

"No. No," she rasped.

Her face paled, now appearing like the skull on the amulet. Her eyes rolled back into her head. Her whole mouth opened in a keening shriek. A piercing howl filled the shop and tore through my bones and flesh like a sharpened blade.

I clamped both hands over my ears, stumbled from my tea corner, and careened into a nearby bookcase. Her penetrating cry stabbed into my brain. The sparks encircling my wrist multiplied, their color deepening from gold to amber.

An undercurrent of expletives rumbled beneath Rebecca's shriek. Rod's voice. He staggered into view with his hands over his ears, swearing up a storm.

This was the banshee's talisman. Her magic unleashed when it was destroyed, its wail a herald of death. Who would die? Me? I deserved it. Bedlam Books was in danger all because of me. I had brought disaster here.

The agony in my head grew. The room began to swirl and spin like the sparks whirling around my wrist. The chain of defensive magic lengthened, exacerbated by my distress.

The room pitched. I slid to the floor, the banshee's keening wail ringing in my ears. I curled up in a ball and buried my head in my hands. The defensive magic was still visible as a coppery glow on the inside of my closed lids.

"Cory," a deep voice rumbled. At the sound of the beckoning voice, the banshee's cry faded.

"Uncle Horace, is that you?" I opened my eyes and looked up.

My dear Uncle Horace stood over me, gazing down over his portly girth. His cheeks were rosy above the full beard. His eyes shone with mischief under eyebrows bushy and wild. He looked just as I had remembered him. But something wasn't quite right. There was a thinness about him.

"What are you doing down there, child?" he said. "Still hiding?"

A dog barked, the high-pitched yip of a small breed. A black, furry head poked from Uncle Horace's arms. A tiny terrier from the looks of him, a pooch about the size of my MacTeague but with hide and hair. Could it be?

"MacTeague?" I whispered.

"Yes." A chuckle shook Uncle Horace's rotund frame. He patted the furry little head. "He's a good dog. Protected you as I knew he would."

"The banshee's talisman didn't kill him?"

"Don't fret, child. You can't kill something that's already dead. Her curse merely returned him to me."

Dead. Of course, both MacTeague and Uncle Horace were dead. Was this his ghost? I shook my head. Uncle Horace wasn't the sort to hang around moaning and groaning.

"Am I dead?" I said.

"No." Uncle Horace chuckled again. "You must get up. You must go back. Jack needs you. Bedlam Books needs you."

"But I lied to Jack and ruined our partnership. I led those hoodlums to our store. Because of me, Mother and Aunt Elspeth hired Rod. I let him in. I've made a mess of everything."

Uncle Horace shook his head. His whole body appeared to ripple with the motion, becoming translucent. I could see the outline of the bookcase behind him through his body. Uncle Horace was fading away, leaving me again.

"No." I reached for him. "Don't go."

Uncle Horace vanished in a shimmer of silvery dust. My fist closed on empty air. I should have known. He'd had an ethereal quality about him as if he were nothing more than a magical pop-up in one of my children's books.

The banshee's siren wail rose again in my ears as if someone had turned up the volume. I grimaced and cradled my head in my hands. I squinted through half-closed eyes. Orange sparks of magic now spiraled up and down my arm.

As abruptly as it had started, the piercing shriek silenced. I opened my eyes and blinked. Familiar bookcases towered over me. I patted my arms and legs, feeling for skin and muscle and flesh. Not dead. Alive.

Rod's grunts, crashes, and the sounds of furniture splintering echoed from the other side of the store. Reminders of when he had demolished my uncle's bookshelves to construct my tea corner. Only now Rod was ransacking Jack's office. But where was Rebecca?

I eased myself to my feet and peered around the bookcase into my tea corner. At first, I saw nothing in the silvery gloom. But then I spotted her body, heaped on the café floor next to the counter. She moaned and stirred. Was she hurt? Should I help her?

I should have run, but curiosity got the better of me. I crept closer. The pink fabric of her sundress pooled around her legs. Her hand with its pink nails grasped at her chest. But instead of golden tresses, her hair now appeared raven black. A trick of the light perhaps?

She groaned and pushed herself off the floor. Her head tilted up to face me. I gasped. Not Rebecca.

"Madam Voyant?"

Chapter Twenty-Eight
Word Play

Confusion flashed across Voyant's face. She glanced down at her pink dress and her gnarled left hand with its pink-painted nails. Mesmerized, I stared at her so stunned you could have knocked me flat with a feather. I grabbed the back of the nearest café chair for support.

"You're mistaken." She shook her head. "I'm Becca." But the voice was not Rebecca's. Instead she had answered in Madam Voyant's sibilant purr. And she knew it too. She clutched a clawed hand at her throat.

Her right eye opened wide. She grabbed her hair and examined the long, dark tresses. Not Rebecca's perky blonde curls.

"No," she rasped.

What devil's deception was this? Her body remained disfigured, the left side locked as in rigor mortis, just as Rebecca's had been. But her features were Madam Voyant's. Had she and Rebecca traded places? The only thing I knew for sure was that the banshee's bracelet was somehow involved.

Voyant pulled herself up to the café counter. In one swift move, she swept all of Mother's freshly-baked caldron cakes onto the floor. Then she hoisted up the serving tray that held them and stared at her reflection in the silver salver.

"Hey," I leapt from my post at the edge of the tea corner. "What do you think you're doing?"

I scrambled on the floor behind her to collect the scattered cakes. But Voyant ignored me as if I wasn't there. She dabbed at her left cheek and droopy left eye.

"Nooooo." She sobbed. "Ruined. I'm ruined."

She turned the tray checking her image from different angles then froze. The mirrored surface caught the coppery glow of defensive magic still swirling around me. Her eyes narrowed to slits. Her lips twisted in murderous hate.

"YOU," she hissed. "You did this."

She slammed the tray back on the counter and grabbed something from the shelf. *Shwiiiing!* I heard a metallic ringing sound, but didn't know what it was. She spun to face me, hiding the object in her right hand behind her back. Oh, bat poo.

"I didn't do anything," I said, leaving the remaining cakes on the floor. I raised both hands and slowly backed away, palms forward in a gesture of surrender.

"You and your beast destroyed my bracelet." She lurched toward me. "You did this to me."

"Wait a minute." I jabbed my finger back at her. "Your bracelet? Not Rebecca's?"

Words from Rebecca's earlier joke resurfaced. *I'll let you in on a little secret. I have a lot in common with my aunt. You see, we're both clairvoyant.* Oh no. Not clairvoyant. Claire Voyant.

"Rebecca was never reanimated, was she?" I squared my shoulders to face her. My stare lasered in on her, daring her to deny it. "It was you. It was you all along."

Voyant's eyes cut away. She wouldn't answer. My guess had hit the mark. That wasn't Rebecca with Jack. All this time, it had been creepy Madam Voyant. Ewww. The realization soured my stomach quicker than her snot-and-eyeball casserole had.

"If only you had listened and stayed away," she said, her voice now menacing and soft. Her head jerked to face me again. Her right eye twitched. "I would never have needed that bracelet. I would still be young. I would still be beautiful."

Warning sirens went off in my head. She whispered an incantation. Her body levitated, her dragging left foot now hovering inches above the wooden floorboards. She pulled her arm from behind her back. In her right hand, a large knife glinted in the eerie light. She smiled. The poisoned-apple grin.

Great galloping ghouls! I turned and ducked into the stacks, sprinting through the maze of bookcases toward the front of the shop. The defensive magic around my arm lit my way. Damned sparks would serve as a beacon, leading her or Rod right to me. I glanced behind me. While I might be able to outrun her, I could not hide. I needed a spell. The reference aisle.

I switched direction and wove my way toward the reference books. Around the next turn, I glimpsed a man's tall silhouette striding down the aisle toward me. Rod? I skidded to a stop, but not fast enough. He saw me.

"Cory?" Jack's baritone voice carried down the aisle.

"Jack," I gasped. My heart flittered like bat wings. He'd come back.

But before I could reach him, a swish of leather sounded from the next aisle over. Rod, cloaked in black, swept from the shadows behind him.

"Jack, look out," I yelled.

Too late. Rod clamped a hand on Jack's shoulder and swung him around. Jack's arms rose to protect himself, but not fast enough. Rod landed a solid punch to Jack's stomach. Jack groaned and doubled over.

"That's payback for the bar," Rod said with a sneer. Then he countered with an uppercut to Jack's jaw.

Jack's head snapped back from the force of the blow. He staggered a pace or two. Rod closed in, fists raised for another punishing blow.

"Noooo," I screamed.

I needed to summon help. But how? I'd given Daddy my mirror.

"Going somewhere?" Voyant's voice hissed from behind me.

I twisted to look. Voyant swooped down the aisle toward me, seeming to glide rather than walk. The blade flashed in her fist.

I whipped around a tall bookcase and down the corridor into the reference section. I scrambled past bookcases stuffed with dictionaries, encyclopedias, and volume after volume of magic. Damn Jack's prohibition against using magic in the shop. I needed a spell, and I needed one fast. Think, Cory, think. Here I was in the reference aisle, and I couldn't come up with a single curse.

"Ooof!" A man grunted from the other side of the bookcase. Rod? Jack? I couldn't tell which.

Boom! Something heavy careened against the bookcase

next to me. A cabinet-shaking thud and a tangle of obscenities followed. Beside me, the wooden shelves creaked and shuddered.

Rod's meaty fist smashed through the back of the case, sending books toppling to the floor at my feet. His eyeball peered at me through the newly-created hole in the shelves, then his fingers like grappling hooks reached through to clutch at me. I squealed and sprinted to the far end of the reference aisle. My head swiveled, checking around the bookcases in each direction.

I needed a spell. Now. But what? I'd never done anything but domestic spells. I'd never hexed anyone. At least, not on purpose. The thought of Rod in the parking lot of the bar popped into my head.

The rope of magical sparks whirling around my shoulders accelerated, glowing hot against my cheeks. I'd never had so much defensive magic accumulate on me. If I unleashed any spell, even one as harmless as a cleaning charm, I wasn't sure what would happen. What if Jack was right when he forbade me to dust by magic? Would I blow up our bookstore if used that spell now?

Madam Voyant emerged from the shadows at the other end of the reference aisle. She glided down the corridor toward me, but I rooted myself to the floor. Perhaps the defensive magic whistling around me made me reckless. Or perhaps it was because she no longer possessed the banshee's dark charm. Or perhaps it was the thought of her talon nails tracing up Jack's sleeve. Indignation burned within me. My hands balled into fists. If Jack could fight, so could I. If that scheming Harpy wanted a battle, I would give her one.

"You've really gone round the twist, you old bat." I shouted down the aisle at her. "What did you expect from a cursed bauble purchased from a banshee? She's a loan shark, you know. What did she charge you? An arm and a leg?"

From across the shop, the comic books burst into fits of hilarity, but Voyant didn't laugh. Her lips pursed into a thin, tense line.

"Very funny," she said. "Too bad you won't live much longer."

I swallowed hard. The dusting spell was all I had, so this had better work. I hoped that it wouldn't destroy the whole building in the process, but there wasn't time to worry. I had to save myself. And Jack. I angled my body toward the left bank of shelves and raised my arms as if conducting an orchestra.

"*Pulvis,*" I spoke the incantation. Then turned to the right side.

"*Pulvis?*" I repeated, more out of desperation than conviction. A dusting spell. This was insane.

Sparks sprang from my fingertips and leapt to the nearest shelves. Dust lifted from the books and swirled into miniature tornadoes, sweeping along a column of dictionaries.

Voyant traversed a third of the corridor, closing in fast. I scrambled back a step or two. Panic pattered in my chest. More defensive magic accumulated on my skin. My fingers twisted helplessly in my twill skirt like those whirlwinds spinning on the shelves.

The tiny twisters wound down both sides of the aisle, kicking up clouds of enchanted dust as they spun. Magic crackled like static. Heavy tomes on the shelves shimmied, jittering from their slots. Voyant's progress slowed, as her eyes now tracked the movement of the cyclones.

BANG! BANG! BANG! One by one down the row,

books flew off the shelves, flung into the aisle by the passing tornadoes. Huge reference tomes catapulted into the corridor from both sides. Caught in the middle, Voyant yelped, then retreated. Her hurled obscenities were no match for a barrage of books. Whoever said "Stick and stones may break my bones, but words will never hurt me," had never been hit by the *Unabridged Web-ster's Dictionary* or all twenty-six volumes of *Wicked-pedia.*

The dust settled. Heavy reference volumes littered the corridor, along with Voyant's half-buried body. Disarmed and bruised, she lay still. Defeated.

I blinked. Too stunned to move from my spot. A dusting spell had done all that? Sweet Merlin. I stared at my fingers. Sizzling red magic now wrapped my shoulders like a garland of crimson sparklers on the Fourth of July.

Rod staggered into view. At the sight of me, his eyes grew wide. He jabbed a finger toward me. A stream of disjointed words tumbled from his lips.

"Fireworks. Explosion. Parking lot. You."

"Bravo, Rod." A disheveled Jack hauled himself around the bookcase. "I see you still have a few brain cells left."

Jack's body listed against the bookshelf. He paused to catch his breath, chest heaving beneath his torn dress shirt. He unbuttoned his collar and tugged the mangled tie from around his neck.

"When she unleashes that magic," Jack said, letting the tie drop, "she'll blow you and this whole establishment sky high."

I gulped and glanced from Jack's rumpled tie on the floor to the coil of defensive magic around my shoulders. I imagined it exploding like a string of fireworks. Rod's burly body would be tossed as if he were a rag doll.

Rod backed away, muttering. "What do you mean?"

"That's right." Jack smiled as if he'd gone mad.

What was he doing? Of course, this was an act. Or was it?

"That bit with the tornadoes and the dictionaries." Jack hitched his thumb toward the destruction in the reference aisle. "That was a simple cleaning spell. Compared to that, what she's got is like a room full of dynamite."

Rod's face paled. The swagger vanished from his stance. He glanced at Voyant's body buried under the books, then back over his shoulder toward the front door. He turned and bolted toward the exit.

The lock on the front door chattered. Rod cursed again. Then the tinkle of chimes rang through the shop and the door slammed shut. I flinched. Leaded panes rattled as if shaken by a blast.

Behind me in the reference aisle, Voyant moaned. Jack's gaze flicked to the woman batting books off her crumpled body, slowly rising from the heap. Flashes of pink fabric reflected in the silvery aura of magical tomes scattered on the floor around her.

"Becca?" Jack picked his way through the littered floor toward her.

"Not Rebecca," I said, unable to contain my contempt. I stabbed my finger at her. "That's Madam Voyant."

"Oh, Jack," she purred when she saw him. She batted her eyelashes and reached for him. "Help me."

He started to kneel beside her, but at the sound of her voice, he wavered. Down on one knee, he stopped. His eyes fixed on her distorted face and raven hair.

"Claire? Why are you in Becca's clothes? Where's Becca?"

As she had done with me, Voyant averted her gaze and would not answer him. If she would not tell him the truth, then I would. I wouldn't let that schemer deceive him any longer.

"Rebecca was never here, Jack," I said as gently as I could. "It was Voyant all along. She purchased a cursed talisman. Her bracelet."

"She's lying," Voyant said, venom in each word. "You don't believe her, do you?"

Jack looked back at me then at Voyant. His gaze snapped to her now empty wrist. She tried to hide her right hand behind her back.

"Why?" He searched Voyant's face. Confusion swirled in his eyes. "Why would you do this?"

"Jack, please." Her talon fingers grasped at his sleeve. Her mouth turned down into a pout. But Jack's jaw went rigid.

He shrugged free and stood up. He paused, still staring at her. I could only imagine what was he was thinking. The banshee's talisman had been so potent, and Madam Voyant's transformation so complete, that it had fooled even him. His fist clenched and unclenched. His face hardened into a mask of granite, but a tempest whirled in his eyes.

"Becca . . . Claire . . . whoever you are," he said through gritted teeth. That he didn't raise his voice, didn't shout, made his words sound all the more menacing. "Get out of here. I never want to see you again."

"But you promised," she said, the cajoling purr back in her voice. She pawed at his sleeve. "The engagement."

"There is no engagement," he shouted, jerking his hand away. "Rebecca is dead."

He regarded her now with the same look of loathing that he had reserved for Rod. Voyant's face soured like curdled cream. Her eyes raked over Jack as if dismembering him limb from limb.

"You should have loved my niece to your grave, Jack."

What? My jaw dropped open, then snapped shut. Did she really think he should pine after Rebecca for the rest of his life? That woman was a few twigs short of a full broomstick.

Voyant's right hand delved into the books. Then she lifted it high, the knife clenched in her fingers. The deadly blade glinted.

"Look out!" I shouted. "She has a knife."

Jack grabbed her wrist. The knife fell to the floor with a clatter. Voyant whimpered.

"Rod," she called out for her goon.

"He's gone." Jack's head jerked toward the door. He hoisted her to her feet. "If I were you, I'd join him before this whole place blows up. Cory, show her."

He seized Voyant by the arm and steered her down the aisle toward me. No longer levitating, her feet skidded on the books, resisting.

"You're lying," Voyant said. "This is a trick."

"Am I?" Jack stared back, his brooding gaze trained on Voyant. He pushed her toward me. "Cory, touch her and we'll all see what happens."

Goosebumps sprouted on my flesh. Magical sparks swirled around me faster. Slowly, I approached. I'd never had so much defensive magic accumulate on me. It had always discharged before this. Even I didn't know what would happen. Did Jack really mean for me to touch her?

I looked at Jack, my eyes pleading with him to give me a sign. His face betrayed nothing. Only a slight twitch of his lip. Jack and his darned unflappability.

I felt the blood drain from my face. My shaking right hand extended toward Voyant. The chain of magic snaked from my shoulders and wound down my arm, until it accumulated in a tight coil around my wrist. Crimson sparks migrated over the back of my hand and danced on my fingertips, burning bright in the dim light.

Voyant recoiled. Her gaze remained glued on my hand. Red sparks reflected in her wide stare. She rubbed her arm, the same spot where I had shocked her earlier. But that shock had contained only a fraction of the magical energy that now surged over my skin. I gulped and inched closer. A single spark arced into the air toward her.

"Aaaiiiii," Voyant shrieked and dodged out of the way.

She blew past me in a whoosh of pink fabric. The sparks on my arm flickered in the breeze but did not extinguish. The errant spark whirled in the disturbed air, then settled back on my skin with the others. Seconds later, chimes clanged as the shop door slammed once more.

"Ha!" A wide grin broke over Jack's face as his mask of self-control shattered. A bloodied, but jubilant Jack strutted the floor of Bedlam books, kicking aside dictionaries as if booting the miscreants from our shop. "They're gone. We did it. Cory, you were brilliant."

I didn't feel brilliant. I stared down at my hand, covered in sparks like a fiery glove. I had no idea how to stop it. I could disperse a little spark without causing too much damage. But so much defensive magic?

"You can turn it off now," Jack said. His voice seemed to come from miles away. "Cory?"

My mind replayed the explosion in the parking lot, seeing it all in slow motion. Rod's body had been tossed into the air and onto the hood of that car like a dried leaf in a whirlwind. Another image superimposed itself over that one. Tornadoes of dust. Books flying from shelves. Sweet Merlin.

"The dusting," I said, my voice quavering. "You weren't

kidding about that, were you? All that talk about too much magic in the shop and spells going awry wasn't just a ruse." I swallowed. "The whole shop? Kaboom?"

I looked at Jack, hoping against hope that I was wrong. But I already knew the answer. The smile faded from his face. His gaze refocused on my hand. Muscles in his jaw worked.

"Cory, you can turn it off, can't you?"

I shook my head.

Chapter Twenty-Nine

My Dark-Haired Prince

Sparks covering my right arm sizzled like a lit fuse. Time was running out. I needed to find some way to snuff them out, before I blew all of Bedlam Books to smithereens. But what could I do?

"It's defensive magic," I said, casting Jack a pleading look. "Completely involuntary. I can't control it. The more anxious I become, the worse it gets." Right now I was jumpier than a cauldron full of bullfrogs.

Jack fingered the scar on his upper lip. His gaze remained riveted on my arm, his brow furrowed as if puzzling over a discrepancy in his ledgers. But the grimace on his face indicated this was a far more serious matter than the balance on our books.

"Isn't there a counter-spell?" he said. "An antidote?"

I shook my head. "None that I know of."

"Then how have you dealt with this in the past?"

"The spell has only ever discharged in self-defense and it hurts whoever I touch."

Jack flinched. It was just a step, but the echo of his wingtips on the wooden floor reminded me of how he'd stormed out in anger yesterday afternoon. I couldn't bear it if he walked out on me again.

"Please, don't leave," I said.

My right hand reached for him, sparks dancing on my outstretched fingertips. I jerked my hand back and hugged my trembling arm to my chest.

Jack swallowed. His Adam's apple bobbed in his throat.

"What about a talisman? You always tap that..." His eyes dropped to my twill skirt. "Where is your romance novel? The one you always keep in your apron pocket."

I glanced down at the pleats of my skirt. I wasn't wearing my apron today. No pocket for my romance novel. Where had I left it? In Daddy's boat? In Aunt Elspeth's car? In all this confusion, I couldn't remember.

"I don't know," I said. "I seem to have lost it. Anyway, I don't see how that will help." My romance had offered me no solace after my argument with Jack or after Aunt Gertrude's ultimatum. If it couldn't ease my pain in those circumstances, how could it disperse such a powerful spell? My shoulders sank. "You were right. They're nothing more than frivolous fun."

"No." His denial was sharp, almost vehement. So unlike the temperate Jack I knew. My head snapped up to face him, but his eyes had drifted away to stare at something on the floor between us.

"I was wrong," he said, his tone softening. He turned back to me. "You must use whatever power it has for you."

"There might be a few left in my secret corner."

"Then we'll go there and find one."

Jack's brooding gaze settled on my face. I nodded, stepped aside, and motioned for him to lead the way.

The glow of protective magic on my arm lit our surroundings. Toppled books littered the most direct route to the back of the shop. Rather than pick a path through the debris, Jack led us on a more circuitous route. I wove through the stacks behind him, choosing my steps carefully lest I trigger another disaster. At the back wall of the shop, Jack stopped, stepped up to the wall, and waved me ahead. I turned left thrice and then once more.

Crackle! Pop! Sparks splintered from the defensive chain and shot from my fingertips. Oh, no. A frisson of electricity sizzled over the invisible barrier that separated my secret enclave from the rest of the shop. Veins of static spread like a spider web across the entrance.

I gasped and stumbled inside. The barrier went dark. I held out my right hand, still ringed in crimson magic. This time I could not see outside the entrance, blackness obscuring the bookshelves beyond it.

"Jack?" I shouted. My words reverberated as if bouncing off the walls of a deserted stairwell. My agitated fingers twisted the fabric of my skirt.

"I'm here," he said, his voice muffled.

Jack's head poked through the portal first. My hand jerked toward him, wanting to pull the rest of him through, but I knew I couldn't touch him. I clasped both hands over my mouth.

The curtain parted. For a brief moment, I glimpsed the bookshelves outside as Jack passed into my secret enclave. Then the barrier grew dark once more.

"You made it through." I sighed in relief. One obstacle overcome.

I turned, walked further in, and waved my arm to illuminate the darkness. The floor was bare. What had happened to the boxes? The cartons that had held my romances were no longer here.

"The romance novels," I said. "They're gone."

Again my voice echoed, mocking me. My gaze flicked to the bookshelves. No aura emanated from charmed merchandise. Instead I saw row upon row of empty shelves. The dusty tomes and paperback mysteries that had packed the bookcases were missing as well. Hell's bells.

"ALL the books are gone," I said. "What now?" Panic choked off further words.

"Over here."

I spun around. Jack remained near the entrance, leaning over something. I crept closer, careful not to touch him. Sparks around my arm hissed like a rattlesnake.

A large, leather-bound book lay by itself on the shelf. The object gave off silvery light. Sweet Merlin. The mysterious tome.

"How did that get here?" I said.

"I was going to ask you the same thing." Jack didn't look at me, but stared down at the enchanted volume. "I thought it had been destroyed."

I'd last seen that book upstairs in my apartment, when it had reassembled itself on my living room carpet. A whirlwind of pages swirled through my thoughts. I recalled the burnt and torn-out pages. The howls of rage I'd heard that evening had come from Rebecca . . . No, from Madam Voyant. Had she tried to incinerate the whole thing?

"Why?" I said.

"She said it was a pack of lies." His teeth gritted. His fists clenched.

"How would she know?"

"Because it's about me." He jabbed a finger at the book. "The story of my life."

"Your life?" I shook my head. That couldn't be.

A gust of wind blew through my enclave. Or was it a spell? The sparks on my arm flickered in the breeze. The cover of the book flew open, images flitting into view. The little prince. The boy with the dragon. Jack's words percolated to the surface of my consciousness. *I used to have a lizard as a boy. Named it Dragon.*

"This was you?" I sputtered, pointing a shaky finger at the page.

Jack nodded.

Onionskin pages fluttered. Stained-glass illustrations lit in charmed light like the windows of a church. I watched as the boy in the story grew into the young man grieving over the maiden's death. Jack's gaze lingered on the image of the deceased beauty.

"Becca." He uttered her name in a gravelly whisper that seemed to catch in his throat. Pain flickered in his eyes.

I could only imagine the anguish he was feeling. What would it be like to lose your girlfriend so tragically, only to have her reappear months later, and then discover it was all a ruse? How cruel. And I felt ashamed that I had been jealous of her.

"I-I'm so sorry," my voice guttered like a flame in the wind.

Jack's gaze intensified on my face, the blustery look in his eyes more discomforting than the breeze stirring the air around us. I turned away. My eyes sought the distraction of the mysterious book.

Pages flipped once more, burying Rebecca under a sheaf of onionskin. More recent images from Jack's life appeared. The teacup representing my tea corner. The dueling knights. Ah, Jack's fistfight with Rod outside the bar. The pages settled, resting open on a charred stub. I knew what that page had contained. It had been my favorite image, the one of the embracing couple. Was that about Jack, too?

My eyes flicked up to stare at Jack as if seeing him for the first time. Gone was the buttoned-down, bottled-up, neatly-pressed Jack that I knew. A mop of unruly curls framed his face. With half the buttons missing, his dress shirt gaped open, revealing a lean, muscled chest. My breath siphoned away at the sight of him. Tall and handsome, Jack looked every bit the hero, as if he had stepped off the cover of one of my paperback romances.

"You?" I muttered. "My dark-haired prince?"

"Dulcinea," Jack whispered. He regarded me with the same haunted look of yearning that I'd seen in him as a boy.

A wild tempest swirled in his eyes. Sky blue morphed to smoky gray. The sparks on my skin shone in his irises like miniature flames. Smoke. Fire. Could it be that his smoldering glances were not anger at all? Or was it my own awakened desire that I saw reflected in his eyes?

The heat of his stare was too intense. I averted my gaze, choosing instead to watch his mouth. I chewed my lip.

"That page," he said. "You know what it means. What we must do."

"Embrace?" I could scarcely utter the word.

My skin tingled at the thought of his touch. Under different circumstances, I would have welcomed it. But what would happen if I touched him now? Would the curse accumulating on my skin fling him from me? My eyes flitted to the welt rising on his cheekbone and the blood stains on his shirt. Hadn't I caused him enough pain already?

"No." I shook my head. "I could hurt you."

"I'm willing to take that chance." Jack stepped closer and held out his hand.

He was willing, but I wasn't. What additional scars

would I leave if I touched him? Would I destroy us both and take all of Bedlam Books with us? Defensive magic prickled my skin. Sparks cast a ruddy glow over his face.

"Don't. Please." I put my hands up to ward him off. "It's too dangerous."

Jack ignored my protest. He seized my right hand, sparks and all, and pulled me toward him. Breath gushed from my lungs. Magic wound down my wrist and up his arm, linking us both. Not blown apart. Quite the reverse. My body jerked forward, drawn by more than the strength of his tug.

My hand landed against Jack's sturdy chest. His warmth surged through my palm, heat counteracting the fire on my fingertips. Resistance evaporated, and I melted into his embrace. Sparks swirled around both of us now. His cheek rested against my head. His whispered breath blew on my hair.

My head tipped back. His mouth hovered above mine, close enough to taste. I closed my eyes and inhaled, willing his lips to mine. His kiss pressed my lips, softly at first, then with more urgency. And I kissed him back.

My ears rang with the crackle of detonating spells. Fireworks boomed inside my head. Bursts of pink and purple, more beautiful than the enchanted pyrotechnics that used to go off over the children's section, streaked the insides of my eyelids.

The kiss ended far too soon. My eyes blinked open. Darkness blanketed my secret enclave. No magic swirled around us. No deadly sparks circled my wrist. What had happened? I already knew. My defenses had been disarmed by his kiss.

Still clinging to Jack, I glanced toward the shelf where the enchanted tome had lain open. No aura glowed there either. The mysterious book had disappeared once more. I could see through the barrier to the bookcases beyond my hiding place. Charmed merchandise glimmered from the shelves. Everything outside my secret enclave appeared just as we had left it. Had the explosions been all in my head?

"Is it over?" I whispered to Jack.

"That depends," he said. His eyes searched mine with another of his smoldering looks. "Do you want it to be?"

"No." I smiled and shook my head.

I twined my arms around him and nestled my head under his chin. His hold on me tightened. It had been so long since anyone had held me like that, and I didn't want him to let go.

"Does this mean that you're not angry with me anymore?" I said.

"I'm furious with you for lying to me," he growled in my ear. "But I'm angrier with myself. I should have been the one to save Bedlam Books."

Jack stared down at the empty corner where the cartons of romances novels had been. He wasn't thinking about his fistfight with Rod. He was thinking about his business plan, the one that I had foiled.

"You know," I said, "if you hadn't removed the romances and mystery novels, I never would have sold so many."

"How so?" Jack's eyes searched mine.

"By removing those books, you created demand for them," I said. "Don't you see?"

But from Jack's puzzled look, I knew he didn't.

"Well," I said. "The surest way to convince someone that she needs something is to tell her that she can't have it. No one knows that better than I do."

The memory of my public dispute with Aunt Gertrude

sent heat rocketing over my cheeks. A self-conscious grin crept over my face.

"Your Aunt Gertrude." Jack laughed, then his smile faded. "When she told me about your bargain with her, I thought I'd lost you for good." He caught my hand, clasping it in both of his as he had on that first fateful day at Uncle Horace's funeral. His hands felt warm on mine. "What made you come back?"

"When I realized who Rod was, I had to warn you." My head tipped up to gaze into his mesmerizing eyes. "You were right about him all along. Not just him. You were right about many other things. And I..." I swallowed, then my confession spilled from my lips. "I didn't want to leave...you."

"But your agreement," he said. "What are we going to do about your aunt?"

"I have an idea." A teasing smile spread across my face. I felt the mischief dancing in my hazel eyes. Just like it had in Uncle Horace's. "But I'll need your help."

Chapter Thirty

The Family Business

I fidgeted in a new swivel office chair behind Uncle Horace's large, claw-footed desk. As I mentally rehearsed my proposal, my fingers traced a deep gouge in its surface, a scar left behind in the attack on our bookstore. Tucked safely in my apron pocket was my copy of Wanda Witherspoon's *Tainted Love*. Aunt Gertrude would be here any minute, and I needed to practice my pitch to her until it was perfect. It still wasn't quite right.

By my side at the massive desk, Jack sat in a matching office chair and sorted his papers, still straightening the mess left behind. Mother positioned a potted snake plant with thin, strappy leaves on top of the cupboard behind us and stepped back to assess her handiwork. A glass bowl, filled with moist moss and mud, sat beside it. Inside, I could make out the outline of the salamander half-buried in the mud. Miraculously, the little fellow had survived, although his terrarium had been smashed to bits when Rod ransacked our office.

The salamander's home was not the only casualty of Rod's vandalism. Neither the Bavarian clock nor Jack's office chair survived. Now two portraits hung on the wall above the cupboard and hid the office safe. In one, Uncle Horace smiled down at us, holding what appeared to be a little furry black slipper. MacTeague. The other was a portrait of Jack's parents. In it, Old Man Wickham was actually smiling, instead of the grim scowl I remembered from my childhood. This version of him was much younger when he still had hair. He gazed at us through aviator-framed glasses, not the little wire pince-nez that I had seen balanced on the end of his nose. His arm encircled a beautiful, young woman. Jack's mother. I never knew her. She died before I was born, when Jack was just three years old. But in her face, I could see his features. And she had dark curly hair that tumbled to her shoulders with the same errant lock as his that dipped over her forehead.

"What do you think?" Mother said.

"Marvelous," I said, beaming up at my Uncle Horace. How fitting that he would be watching over us. "What do you think, Jack?"

He straightened the blotter on the desk, positioning it to cover the gouge. Then he turned to look.

"That looks great." He smiled and nodded. "Mrs. Smyth, do you think you might help me with my apartment? It could use some redecorating. I have a sofa and a couple of lamps I'd like to replace."

"Of course, my dear boy." Mother patted his shoulder in her affectionate way. "I'd be delighted. You've always been like family to us."

Family. Brilliant. Just the thing that was missing from my proposal.

No time to contemplate further. A loud knock that

rattled the bookstore's display window panes announced my aunt's arrival. Mother hastened from the office, and opened the shop door to usher Aunt Gertrude in.

"Afternoon, Gertie," Mother's voice carried across the quiet shop. "They're waiting for you in the office. I'll leave you all to discuss your business."

"Here we go," I whispered.

Jack winked at me and squeezed my hand. Then he squared his shoulders in a crisp white shirt, straightened his striped tie, and folded his hands in front of him on the desk, prepared for my aunt's arrival. My nerves wriggled like tadpoles in my gut. I took a deep breath and tried to still them. My fingers smoothed the apron in my lap and patted my romance novel for luck.

Seconds later, Aunt Gertrude burst into the office, dressed in her signature black as if she was on her way to a funeral. I swallowed and hoped it wasn't mine.

She shut the office door behind her and settled in a wing-backed chair across the desk from us. Jack and I together on one side, Aunt Gertrude on the other. She didn't even waste time with pleasantries.

"I'll get right to the point," she said. "You should know that I've already consulted with my lawyer. But I will hear what you have to say."

She leaned back in the chair. Her elbows rested on the chair's arms, her fingers tented in front of her chin.

"Thank you, Ms. Knightly," Jack said, his polite shop-keeper's voice on full display. "As senior partner of Bedlam Books, I appreciate the trust you've placed in my father and now me. But . . ." He cleared his throat. "I think you under-estimate your niece's contributions. Her café and book sales have boosted our profits. And I value her new ideas. I find that I can't run the business without her."

She wagged a stubby finger at Jack. "But her education—"

"I've already looked into that, Aunt." I had anticipated that argument and didn't give her time to finish. I rattled off my rebuttal before she could counter. "I'm only missing a few high school credits. I've enrolled in evening classes at Diablo Adult Ed to prepare for my GED. And I plan to apply to Serpentine Valley Community College starting in the winter term. Aunt Elspeth has offered to help with my tuition."

"How will you juggle your studies with your work?" Aunt Gertrude's steely gaze zeroed in on me.

"Mother will run the café as planned," I said. "I can work part-time. Jack and I can come up with a schedule. And if it ever becomes too much for me, I'm sure we can work something out."

My eyes cut over to Jack, telegraphing that it was his turn. My fingers worried in my lap, picking at a fraying seam in my apron.

"Yes, of course." Jack nodded, now meeting my gaze.

Flecks of gold sparkled in his blue eyes. He spotted my fidgeting. For a brief moment, he unclasped his fingers as if he would reach for my hand. Then just as quickly, he clasped them again. His gaze darted away, but a smile lingered on his lips.

"Hmmm." Aunt Gertrude studied us both, her stare as unsettling as an owl eyeing a tasty mouse. "Clearly, you two are besotted with each other. Mixing business with romance is a bad idea. Nothing good will come of this."

The time had come for my play. I reached into my pocket and extracted my romance novel. I slid the dog-eared paperback across the desk toward her. The title,

Tainted Love, blinked in Valentine's red. The author's name flashed. Wanda Witherspoon.

"Aunt, have I ever told you that Wanda Witherspoon is my favorite author?"

"I can vouch for that." Jack chuckled. "She has been carrying that fo', er, particular romance in her pocket since she started here. It's her lucky charm."

Aunt Gertrude looked askance at my romance novel. Her mouth pursed. For a moment, she stared without comment or comeback.

"Yes, but ..." She paused. "What does that have to do with—"

"According to Daddy, quite a lot," I said. The mischievous grin spread over my face. "He bumped into Harlan Quinn down in Cabo."

Aunt Gertrude's eyes widened. Her thin eyebrows shot up. Her mouth opened, then snapped shut. The hairs on her chin quivered. Her dress rustled as she shifted in the high-backed chair.

"That man never could keep his big mouth shut," she muttered under her breath. Then her owl stare focused back on me, only the tasty mouse had morphed into a more worthy adversary. "All right, I'm listening."

"You see ..." I motioned over my shoulder at the portrait of my dear uncle on the wall behind me. "I think Uncle Horace knew exactly what he was doing when he put my shares in trust with you, Aunt Elspeth, and Mother. Ink runs in our veins. Books are our family business. And I think he meant it to be our WHOLE family. ALL of us."

"I see." Aunt Gertrude leaned back in her chair and stared over my head at my uncle's portrait. She drummed her fingers together, tapping as she contemplated. Then she stopped and focused on Jack.

"And you're okay with this arrangement, Jack?"

Although I'd told him of my plan and he'd agreed, I wasn't entirely sure what he would say now. Would he reconsider when face to face with my domineering Aunt Gertrude? He'd finally come to accept me as his business partner. But what about the rest of my family? Especially my aunts with "their petty disputes and abominable behavior." His former words.

But like it or not, they were already involved. And inviting them to participate seemed like the only way I could keep my share of Bedlam Books . . . and my place with Jack. I shot him my most pleading look.

"Well . . ." He swallowed and fingered the silvery scar above his lip. "Naturally as senior partner, I would have final say on any decisions. But if that's what it takes to stop this lawsuit . . ." He locked eyes with me, warmth swirling in his irises. "Then yes. I agree."

"What do you say, Aunt?" I smiled my best imitation of Daddy's beguiling grin. I reached my right hand across the table toward her. "Do we have a deal?"

Three months later on October 31st, Bedlam Books hosted an exclusive book launch event. The reclusive Wanda Witherspoon appeared in person at midnight to sign *Moonstruck Madness*, her latest book in her acclaimed *Poisoned Passion* series. Ours was the only bookstore in the country to host her. A line of women arriving for the event stretched down Chanting Way and around the block.

Mother had set up a high-backed upholstered chair like a throne in the center of Bedlam Books. In front of the chair rested a table for the book signing, piled high with copies of

Wanda's latest romance. A red carpet led down the center aisle between the bookcases toward it.

Seated on the throne was Aunt Gertrude. Only no one would recognize my matronly aunt in the woman who graced the seat of honor. Aunt Elspeth had given her a complete romance makeover. Instead of her usual black, she wore a dress of emerald green velvet with a raven-feather collar. The dress had a modest décolletage, not her usual high stiff neckline. Her silver hair framed her face in a froth of soft, gray curls, and her hat sported three raven's quills. Aunt Elspeth had even given her a beauty mark just above her lip. The transformation was remarkable. My Aunt Gertrude looked like Romance Royalty.

Mother staffed our tea corner, serving up hot mulled cider, brewed teas, and her freshly-baked spiced pumpkin cauldron cakes. Scents of cinnamon and nutmeg wafted throughout our shop and took the chill off the night air. Aunt Elspeth walked the line, taking book orders and chatting up the waiting customers. Jack and I worked together at the front counter, ringing up purchases. The constant cha-ching of the old fashioned cash register suggested that tonight's receipts would set a record for Bedlam Books.

I had long since abandoned Mother's pencil skirts and business attire for my own. Tonight I wore my favorite flirty tartan wool miniskirt, black tights, and my softest sweater. We were so busy that I had no time for idle chat with Jack. But I felt a jolt of pure electricity every time I brushed against his fingers while handing off books or other merchandise. And the tight quarters behind the register meant that sometimes I had to squeeze behind him to wait on a customer. Not that he seemed to mind. In fact, I don't think I've ever seen him look happier. His smile was not the polite shopkeeper's version, but a wide grin that reached to his eyes.

At our 2 a.m. closing, as the last customers ambled toward the door, a tall, distinguished man entered the shop, carrying a bouquet of red roses so dark they almost looked black. He strode up the red carpet dressed in a gray suit with a lavender tie and matching handkerchief in his breast pocket. And he had a mustache, a thin gray mustache waxed to rapier points. I knew it was rude to stare, but I watched the gentleman pass us and head up the aisle toward my Aunt Gertrude.

"Could that be—?" I whispered, spearing Jack with my elbow.

I crept to the corner and peeked around the bookcase at my aunt and the gent. He stopped in front of her signing table and presented his gift of flowers. Then he bent and spoke to her in words too soft to hear. But my aunt's eyes lit up and her cheeks blushed.

"It must be him." I ducked back behind the bookcase and stifled my giggles.

"Who?" Jack said.

"Harlan Quinn, of course." I grinned. My stuffy aunt had an admirer. And since she was occupied, this was the perfect opportunity for a stolen moment with Jack.

I took his hand and led him around to the other side of the bookcase, where we would not be seen. A quick glance to either side ensured that we were finally alone. I crooked my finger and beckoned him closer.

"But your mother and aunts?" he said. Despite his protest, the husky timber in his voice betrayed that he was a willing accomplice.

"Mother will be cleaning up in the tea corner. Aunt

Elspeth would approve." I nodded toward the signing table. "And Aunt Gertrude seems to be occupied."

A smile widened on Jack's face. His head swiveled to double check that my family was not nearby. He dabbed at the silvery mark above his lip. He was always fingering that old scar. What accident had caused that? He didn't have it when we were younger.

"Jack?" I said.

"Hmmmm?" His mumbled reply.

"How did you get that scar over your lip?"

He hesitated. His eyes darted to the glowing merchandise on the bookshelves around us. He had that faraway look in his eyes that Mother gets when she's reminiscing.

"Well?" I said, curiosity aroused.

He stared at the bookcases, still not looking at me. Was that a tinge of color rising on his cheeks? His lip twitched.

"Early in my apprenticeship to Father and your uncle," he said. "I, um, I blew up the comic books."

"You did what?" I gasped. My eyes couldn't open any wider. Jack was always so precise, so controlled. I couldn't imagine him blowing up anything.

"How?" I said.

"Dusting." He rubbed a finger over his scar. "I learned firsthand that custard pies aren't the only practical joke in their arsenal and a punch line isn't just an expression."

The twitch of Jack's lip exploded into a sheepish grin, then a chuckle. I giggled. Jack had a streak of mischief after all. It seemed I had a lot to learn about my new partner. I couldn't wait to for the lessons to begin.

I waggled an eyebrow and flashed him my sauciest come-hither smile, a grin that would have turned Lady Gwendolyn Fairbanks purple with envy.

Jack chuckled and scooped me into his arms. I took his

face in my hands and pulled him into a kiss. The taste of him sizzled on my tongue. Bursts of violet and pink detonated once more behind my eyelids.

Out of the corner of my eye, I glimpsed the leafy likeness of my Uncle Horace, hanging from its place at the end of the aisle. The carved visage winked at me and flashed a jovial grin.

Acknowledgments

Bringing this book to fruition was truly a journey filled with many challenges, unplanned detours, and unexpected twists. So many people encouraged me along the way to keep writing and moving forward. I'd like to thank a few of them here. Special thanks to Elisabeth Tuck for her expert editing and critical eye for detail. Also this novel wouldn't exist without the valuable input of my critique group partners: Fran Cain, Susan Berman, David George, Elisabeth Tuck, Jill Hedgecock, and Melanie Denman. Never shy about sharing their opinions, these talented writers greatly improved this novel with their insights and suggestions. Having blazed the publishing trail ahead of me, they were also generous in sharing their experiences and advice. I couldn't have done this without them, nor would it have been nearly as fun.

I would like to express my appreciation to Charlotte Cook, my original writing instructor, for her professional guidance and lessons in craft. The first draft of this novel was started more than a decade and a half ago, while I attended her Wednesday evening writing class. I also need to thank Annette Genova for reading an early version of this novel. Her contagious enthusiasm motivated me to keep believing in this project, despite the numerous queries, rejections, and revisions required. A special shout-out to Melissa Worcester, who ignited my love of fantasy by introducing me to *The Hobbit* way back in the sixth grade, and who offered words of encouragement decades later when I penned my first attempts at fantasy fiction.

I need to thank my now-grown children, John and Mary, for reigniting in me a love of story. Reading books together with them reintroduced me to some fabulous children's literature and sparked my writing adventure. Their imagination and creativity continues to amaze and inspire me.

And finally, to my dear readers, I sincerely thank you for travelling this road with me.

About the Author

CHERYL SPANOS writes short stories and fantasy novels for teens and adults. A former software engineer, she earned a Ph.D. in Computer Science and worked in computer-aided design and full-stack web development. In between, her life path veered into literary and artistic pursuits.

Her children's fiction has been published in *Hunger Mountain, Beyond Centauri,* and *Stories for Children* magazine. Her short stories have won several awards, including Honorable Mention for Mainstream/Literary fiction in the Writer's Digest Annual Writing Competition. *Bedlam Bewitched* is her debut novel. She lives in California with her two adorable guinea pigs.

Dear reader, if you loved *Bedlam Bewitched,* please visit my website (www.cherylspanos.com) and sign up for news on my upcoming novels. Also please consider leaving a review on www.amazon.com.

Many thanks!